DARK AS PITCH

AVA CORTES: CRIME THRILLER SERIES
BOOK 2

RAQUEL BYRNES

AVA CORTES: CRIME THRILLER SERIES

Deep Dark Lies

Dark as Pitch

Fade to Dark

JOIN WITHOUT WARRANT'S MAILING LIST

Follow the link to stay up to date with Without Warrant!

https://BookHip.com/QKWGDKS

You'll receive a **free** copy of

Girl Awakened: A Dana Gray Prequel.

"Moon dust in your lungs, stars in your eyes. You are the child of the cosmos and ruler of the skies." Author Unknown

ONE

Shards of sunlight sliced through the rusted metal roof of the warehouse, catching the fine dirt disturbed by Sky's feet. She hummed as she stood in the shaft of light and tilted her face toward the warmth before spinning lazily again. Her dress flared out, creating a gossamer shadow that showed the shape of her legs. She caught sight of it and giggled. A light, tinkling laugh she knew others loved, especially men. The woven crown of dandelions atop her head slipped, and she grabbed it, squishing the flowers to her nose to crowd out the smell of pee and trash.

A moan behind her drew her attention, and she rolled her eyes, turning to face the bound man on the filthy floor. Beaten and semi-conscious, he struggled against his bonds. She frowned, kicked dirt into the man's face, and sighed.

"Babe, he's waking up!"

"Just hang on. This is *really* hard to do with my stitches." Hunter grunted from the shadows. "My hand still hurts, you know."

He dragged the barrel closer to the light, fighting with its shifting contents as he sucked down air. Sky grinned as she watched him. She liked the way the sweat glistened on his forehead.

The man on the floor twitched. Likely the drugs wearing off. "You better hurry. If he wakes up, he might scream or do something annoying."

Hunter let go of the barrel with a grunt and dropped it on its side, sending murky fluid onto the ground. Growling, he kicked the container, his sweaty hair spiked up around his head. He glared at Sky, panting.

"I don't know what we're even doing anymore!"

"What we're doing?" Sky tilted her head and gazed up at him. Broad shoulders. Great hair. Big. Like a TV show football player. She liked how delicate she felt next to him. And how well he listened. She stepped closer to him, sliding her hand across his heaving chest. His heart thundered under her palm. She smiled. "We're surviving, baby. We're fighting back, doing what's necessary."

He made a face, but Sky couldn't tell if he was puzzled or if the scar on his cheek just made it look that way. Either way, the scar was hot. It made him look like a badass instead of the golden retriever he was.

Gesturing around them, he looked at her with wide eyes. "Doesn't this feel like too much? I mean—"

"Nothing is too much to protect what we have!" Sky said. She took a breath. "Look, I'll do it, okay? I just need help after."

He shook his head. "Why can't we just leave him here?"

"He'll start to smell and someone will find him. We need him to disappear. He did that a lot anyway, from what I hear. Why do you think I had you bring out a barrel?"

"I guess I was just hoping..."

"What? What is it?" She didn't mean to shout, but he was starting to irritate her. Hunter didn't do well with yelling. His eyes got all shifty, like he wanted to run. She drew a slow breath. Cleansing. Centering. "I'm sorry, babe. I shouldn't have taken your voice. What's the matter?"

"It's just that sometimes they don't fit and I have to..." He lifted his knee and made a stick-breaking motion with his hands.

"They don't feel it, if that's what you're worried about."

"But it's still gross." He looked down at her, eyes pleading. "Do we have to do this?"

"He threatened us, Hunter. He said he had evidence and everything!" She pointed at the man still groaning on the floor next to them. "This is the only way to keep us safe. You *know* that."

"Yeah, but—"

"Hey, I've been passing by that area for years. For literally years. It's abandoned and all covered in weeds. There's trash everywhere. People use it as a dump. No one is going to go sniffing around out there."

"Are you s—"

Their prisoner's head lolled toward them as he tried to push himself up.

"Time's up, Hunter," Sky whispered as she turned and picked up a small revolver from the chair in the corner.

Hunter saw it, and tried to step back, but she caught his T-shirt and pulled him close. She kissed him until his breath hitched. Then she turned Hunter's face with her palm, kissing his neck as she slipped the gun into his hand.

He pulled back, eyes swimming. "Y-You said you would do it."

"We will. Together." Sky wrapped her hand around his. Aiming the gun at the bound man, she slipped her finger over Hunter's on the trigger. "As always."

"As always," Hunter whispered as he closed his eyes, turning his face away.

Sky kept her gaze steady. She wanted to be sure this man who'd threatened to hurt them died. She waited until his eyes fluttered open, until the moment his gaze refocused and landed on her before she pulled the trigger.

TWO

The lights of the patrol cars slashed red and blue down Mission Avenue, capturing the dried weeds and trash-filled gutters in bright snapshots against the night. The flashing property once housed a multiple-screen drive-in theater but now sat razed and partially leveled for a giant 'California Playground' scheduled to open in a couple of years. The developers promised a state-of-the-art wave pool, green energy luxury housing, and upscale shops.

At least, until a body had been found in one of the many trenches that scarred the property. Special Agent Ava Cortes strode in her running shoes across the soft dirt toward the construction site, cordoned off and guarded by a patrol officer.

She didn't get it. Why would people need a wave pool when the Oceanside Pier and an actual beach were only three miles down the road? Still, she'd read that it would revitalize an older neighborhood filled with retirees and sixties-style homes. Wondering what such a grisly discovery would do to the optics of the project, she flashed her California Bureau of Investigation badge at the young Oceanside Police Department officer. He nodded and lifted the crime scene tape for her to duck under.

A forensic tent in the distance shrouded the scene, and the late June mugginess made her T-shirt cling to her skin as she approached. She'd just finished a run and sweat poured out of her like she had dengue fever. It didn't help that the temperature lingered at an unusual seventy-five degrees despite the nine o'clock hour.

During her run, she'd received a call from Detective Manaia, an old colleague, who'd asked her to meet him at the crime scene in the older part of Oceanside. She tightened the band holding her long black ponytail in place and smoothed down the wispy bits. A car sped by on the street behind her, music blasting, the neighborhood still humming.

Laughter and loud voices floated to her from a group of people gathered across the street, watching the police activity. They called out questions about what was going on, but she ignored them.

A mercifully cool breeze kicked up and fluttered the green, tattered construction material still clinging to the chain-link. She made her way toward the tent, passing night crew workers leaning on their shovels or sitting on drink coolers watching the forensic techs in white protective suits working in the distance.

A medical examiner's van blocked most of the tent from view. She walked through the rusty chain-link gate. The smell of dirt hung in the air. Earthmovers, used to grade the property, sat silent. All construction had been shut down for who knew how long this time. Another length of crime scene tape, strung between a debris pile and two stacks of wooden pallets, cordoned off the inner area. She ducked under, holding up a hand against the glare of the halogen lamps. They stood on tripods like alien sentinels, lighting up the scene. Moths circled, bumping and fluttering around their warmth, casting flickering shadows on the ground.

She spotted Detective Tony Manaia talking to an officer. She and Manaia had worked together two years before on her first case after getting punted to White Collar Crimes. The joint Oceanside Police Department and CBI task force investigation turned out to be a wild case. Manaia, talking with a field evidence tech, saw her and waved.

The wind shifted. Ava braced herself when the smell hit her. The unmistakable stench of decay.

"Ava!" He hurried to meet her, his smile just as charming as it had been two years ago. He wore a Hawaiian button-down shirt underneath a black blazer and trousers. His Samoan heritage gave him thick, dark wavy hair and deep brown eyes, but he lacked the bulk of his brothers. His mother gave him both his dimples and the nickname Runt, which Ava had learned one night at a family BBQ. Though compared to her own five-foot-five height, being *only* six feet didn't strike her as a disadvantage. "Thank you so much for coming."

"No worries." She looked around. "Where's your partner?"

"Oh, his daughters have this big dance competition in Las Vegas," Manaia said with a shrug. He tended to speak with a staccato delivery that made him sound like he was always in a hurry. "You met them. The twins."

"Vegas? Aren't they nine?"

"That's what I said." He nodded toward the scene. "Lemme show you why I called you."

Manaia led her toward the forensic tent. "I wasn't sure at first, because of the state of the body, but it's him. It's Brent Cutler."

Ava's gut dropped. "You're sure?"

"I'm positive. I stared at his face for hours at a time when I debriefed him." Manaia put his hand up. "We'll run his prints and dental to be sure, but I'd bet money it's him."

The screech of tires floated over from another street as Ava counted at least six Field Evidence Techs wandering in and out of the tent. That much staff meant word had already spread about who the victim likely was.

"How'd they find him?"

"This site, it's been stop and start for the last few months. They pass one hurdle. You know, with the city or EPA or whatever and ten days later, they have to stop again. Some other environmental agency files another court order." He pulled a jar of menthol rub out of his jacket pocket, unscrewed the lid, and applied some beneath his nose.

Ava gestured for him to hand it over and then did the same. "Anyways, with work starting and stopping so much, we get a lot of vandalism. Also, theft, and trash dumps in between construction. It's a nightmare for the crews, to be honest." He showed her a photo on his phone of a padlock that had been cut on the gate. "I talked to the construction manager on the phone an hour ago. He's at the hospital with his kid. I'm meeting with him tomorrow. He said the gate gets locked when they have to shut down operations. No one really checks on the place. Except maybe an additional pass by local patrol. So no one walks the site while it's shut down."

They stepped around a pile of heavy-duty bins filled with trash.

"So, the morning crew starts up the job again after months, everything is normal, no signs of vandalism, nothing," Ava said. "Then they have a shift change, and the night crew starts over there." She nodded toward the tent next to them. "Is that right?"

"Yeah. They were excavating dirt and whatever else they do for grading."

"But since the company didn't pay for security and the site had been shut down for months... the body could've been buried there at any point."

Manaia shook his head. "The body isn't in the best shape. Lemme show you."

An excavator sat next to the tent, its two boom arms and front-mounted bucket nearly tucked underneath the structure.

Ava and Manaia pushed through bug netting that blocked the pulled-back entry flaps, and, despite the strong menthol smell, the stench of the body hit her like a cloud bank. Inside, lit by more garish light, a fifty-five-gallon blue plastic drum lay on its side in the dirt. Black sludge pooled around it and had drifted underneath a body sheet. The cracked lid sat next to it. A couple more techs worked at a portable table with samples. One looked over, her eyes catching Ava's, and she nodded.

"Dr. Alicia Cooms," Manaia said in introduction. "This is Agent Cortes, the one I told you about."

"Agent Cortes." An older woman, soft sixties with short hair and thick black glasses, Cooms looked smart and serious, with the sinewy arms of a runner or swimmer. Given the greenish cast to her gray hair, Ava guessed the latter. She nodded to Ava and moved closer. "San Diego County Medical Examiner."

As head of the entire office, Dr. Cooms wouldn't normally be the one to come out after hours. Ava greeted her as Manaia squatted next to the body.

He looked up at her. "You ready?"

She nodded, and he lifted the plastic sheet. Covered in dirt and the oily black sludge, she barely recognized him. Filthy and flopped over, he lay chest down, his face turned toward her, lip split, eyes swollen shut and slick with muck. His arms and legs were bent at odd angles like a discarded toy. A single bullet hole marred his smooth forehead. A recent death, given the state of decay. A sliver of guilt moved through Ava. Something had been going on with Brent during their case, but she'd never found out what. Now she wondered how things would have played out if she'd pushed.

She scanned the ground around the body. "No casings in the barrel?"

"Dr. Cooms is guessing it was a revolver," Manaia said. "We'll confirm with ballistics."

Ava eyed the tractor boom. Affixed straps dangled from the bucket. "Tell me what happened."

He stood, fanning away the smell. "So, the night crew out there got the go ahead to start grading in a new location. They noticed disturbed ground and thought it might be buried trash again." He gestured at the excavator as he spoke. "They used the straps to hoist it out, but it slipped. Apparently, the barrel was already leaking. It fell from a good height and popped open. They said he spilled out with the oil or whatever's covering him. Not a lot, like a gallon or two maybe."

Ava walked a circle around the body. Brent had been a handsome man. Tall, athletic, strong. He ran marathons and hit the gym often if her memory of surveilling him served. When he wasn't face-down in powder or enjoying the company of a paid date. He'd also turned against some of the most powerful people in Southern California. Rich and ruthless friends often made the worst enemies.

He still wore his wedding ring despite Ava having heard his marriage had broken up. She pointed to his discolored wrist. "His watch is missing. He wore that big square one, remember? A vintage piece I think."

Manaia nodded. "We'll send out a bulletin to all of the pawn shops."

"I think it was an heirloom. You should ask his father if he had an insurance policy on it. They'd have excellent photos of the piece." She took in the rest of the details. For his testimony, Brent had worn an expensive couture belt to court. He wore it now. Titanium buckle, textured black calf leather, classic quiet luxury. Subtly expensive. "Did you find a wallet?"

"We haven't gone through his pockets," Dr. Cooms said, turning around. "But I patted him down. Nothing. Not even keys."

"He had a driver. His license was suspended."

Ava pointed at the victim's hand. "They took the means of identifying him but didn't recognize the big-ticket accessories. His wedding ring looks platinum, and his belt is couture, if I recall."

"Meaning?" Manaia asked.

"I don't think this was a robbery gone bad." Ava turned to the ME. "Am I right in thinking the time of death was a few days at most?"

Dr. Cooms nodded, glancing at her digital tablet. "We estimate the victim was in the oil for at least two days, possibly three, due to skin slippage and other decay. I believe he died shortly before going into the barrel"

Ava ground her jaw. "If I asked you to guess at the caliber?"

"I'd say a twenty-two-caliber round to the head caused him to expire, but we'll put a pin in that until we get back ballistics, toxicology, and the autopsy."

"I'm assuming he was killed elsewhere?" Ava glanced at the loose dirt. "Anyone find a shovel?"

Dr. Cooms shook her head. "And the crew's equipment was locked up and accounted for. The killer must've brought their own."

"So, he just picked a spot and started digging?"

Manaia shrugged. "I mean, yeah. The crew told me they filled up the holes a few months ago when they had to pause operations. Some kind of safety thing."

"Also, there doesn't seem to be a significant amount of blood near the victim or in the barrel, but again, we'll have to test the fluid inside."

Ava took in the site once more but agreed with Dr. Cooms. They needed more data.

Manaia thanked the ME, who went back to her table of evidence. He nodded for Ava to walk to his side of the body, then, "What do you think?"

She glanced down at the body in front of them. "Whoever dumped Brent didn't know about the construction starting up again. Which is usually announced in papers and radio, even community email blasts. The person who did this isn't really plugged into the city."

"He knew about this place," Manaia argued.

"Yeah, but... that's a different level of assimilation." Ava scanned the area around the property. Nothing but a field to the west, the San Luis Rey River and trail to the north, and Highway 76 to the south. With the piles of dirt and debris, you couldn't see the dump site from the main road, but it wasn't really that far *from* the road. A field length away. The killer would have had to scope it out on foot to know about the covered up holes and loose ground. It wasn't a huge leap of logic. People would know construction disturbed the earth. It just seemed like an odd choice to dump a body right by a busy street. She glanced at Manaia. "But you're right, whoever it was knew the area, that's for sure."

"How do you think Brent's connected?"

"I have no idea. The guy came into our orbit via a money laundering scam and a madam. He seemed to have turned his life around over the past few years, so I have absolutely no idea *what* Brent got himself into this time." She shook her head and sighed. "Unfortunately, the fact that I knew the victim from another case doesn't make it CBI jurisdiction. It's not, uh—"

"Complicated enough?" Manaia asked. "What if I told you we pulled two other bodies out of blue barrels a couple of months ago over at the Oceanside Pier, near the jetty."

Ava frowned. Her job with the CBI took her out of town often to consult on other cases that didn't hit their desks. Had she missed something? "I remember hearing about bodies washing up on shore. The paper said they were likely swimmers from up the coast. It didn't mention anything about barrels."

Manaia nodded. "Two victims did wash up on shore, a young guy and a girl. That part is true. But they were also in blue barrels. A fisherman out on the jetty at dawn saw them and called it in so we were able to get a tent up pretty quick. Good thing. The surf camp was starting up around there. Those kids didn't need to see that. But the victims hadn't drowned. They were shot. With a twenty-two."

"You guys lied?" Ava tilted her head as she looked up at him. "That's refreshingly sketchy of you, Detective Manaia."

He put his hand to his chest, shaking his head. "Not my doing. Someone spread a rumor before we could release anything. Probably a rookie or staff at the station. The news ran with it, and we just didn't correct anyone. And when they realized the victims were homeless nobodies, they lost interest."

"Were they?" Ava asked. "Homeless?"

"Neither had a current address. We know the female victim was arrested for solicitation, but the charges were dropped. The ME's office sent out some queries on the second victim, but that's about all we've got on them. You know how slow things run out here," Manaia muttered, glancing over at Dr. Cooms.

"So, aside from the blue oil drums and the caliber, did anything else connect the victims to each other?"

"I mean, Brent and the female victim both have a connection to the sex industry."

"Did he still? Wasn't he on probation?"

"Right." Manaia raised his brows. "That always stops them."

Ava smiled. "Did the other male victim have tracks on his arms or signs of drug abuse?"

"No." He shuffled on his feet. "Still not enough?"

"Two of the victims came in from the sea, their origin could've been miles north of here, making the barrels a coincidence. Those blue drums are at every garage, mechanic shop, and industrial facility around here."

Manaia nodded. "I get that but hear me out. I agree that the barrels are a bit of a stretch. And while they *were* shot with the same caliber, a twenty-two is a common target and recreational weapon. But if you add in the markings, the cases have to be connected."

"Add in the what?"

"They were on the first two victims' torsos. Brent's body has the same markings, just on his hands." Manaia slipped a flashlight from the inside pocket of his suit jacket. To Dr. Cooms, he said, "Alicia, hit the floodlights, would you?"

She did, and the tent went dark. His flashlight lit up with the blue of UV light. The tiny parrots on his shirt glowed. His teeth, white as the moon, disappeared as he lifted the sheet once again. He shone the light on the back of Brent's hands. A pattern etched into the skin glowed to life. Strange and glyph-like, it reminded Ava of intersecting fractal shapes and geometric lines, almost mathematical.

"Well, that's interesting." She took out her phone and snapped a few pictures. "Any idea what the substance on top of the wounds is?"

He shrugged. "Some kind of pumice?"

"Poultice," Ava murmured, thinking. Flashes of things she'd read about homeopathic medicine and ritualistic symbols flickered behind her eyes. Nothing she'd come across in that field matched the ones on the body. "What did the mixture contain?"

"For the first two victims we found traces of salt, ink, some oil. We'll have to wait for the tests to come back to confirm the same mixture is found here," Dr. Coombs voice floated in the darkness.

"Huh. What's the glowy part made out of?"

"It's some kind of UV reactive binder," Dr. Cooms said from further away in the darkness. "I'll have to verify the one on this victim is the same substance, but it appears to be at first glance."

"Ava," Manaia began, his face glowing like a specter in the dark tent. "I now have three bodies and when the press puts that together all hell will break loose. Some wacko is carving glowing symbols on victims, dumping them in public spaces, and we've gotten nowhere. We sent the symbols off to the FBI as soon as the first two bodies were found. Who knows when we'll hear back from them. Add in Brent's past with OPD and the CBI? Just wait til his dad gets involved."

She nodded. "What *is* Dane Cutler doing lately? I heard he's on the chamber of commerce or something now."

"He's a city councilman and old friend of the mayor. The Chief of Police was asked to personally notify him about his son. He's probably there now."

Her gaze snapped to his eerie purple one. "Your ME didn't even make a positive identification yet."

"It's just a matter of time before the media vultures screech up to the curb." He switched off his flashlight. "Can we get the lamps back on?"

Dr. Cooms lit up the tent again.

"The markings got my attention, I'll give you that," Ava said, blinking in the bright halogen light.

"Is that a yes or no?" Manaia looked over his shoulder at the Field Evidence Techs swabbing the bucket, then at Ava. "Given Brent Cutler's history with our madam and now he ends up killed in the exact same way as a sex worker was two months ago, I mean..."

She took one more look at the barrel next to Brent's body. A sweetheart deal had kept him out of prison, one she'd helped broker. Only to have him wind up in an oil drum like two other bodies.

"I'll bring it up to my team lead, but I can't promise anything. I'm not in charge of PIT."

"I didn't ask for the Priority Investigation Team or whatever you call yourselves. I want you, Ava. I've seen what you do out there." He looked at her with that earnest, good guy face.

She gave him a slight nod and walked away, looking up a contact and hitting dial. As she paced, she spotted a coin in the rubble. Old and caked with dirt, she picked it up to examine it under the halogen lamps. A shooting star carved on the surface brought back memories of arcade games on hot summer nights. Her lost days.

August picked up after a few rings, the sounds of a restaurant behind him. "Everything ok?"

Ava closed her fist around the game token. "I need a favor."

THREE

Ava woke the next morning still thinking about Brent and the strange, glowing shapes carved into his skin. She'd tossed and turned all night. Now the aches and pains of staying too long in bed when she should have given up on sleep needed to be dealt with. She got up, ate a couple of dry waffles, and decided to go for a run to clear her head.

Ava donned her swimsuit, a tank top, and a pair of athletic shorts, then wandered the house looking for her running shoes, checking all the nooks and crannies of the old home. A pretty blue and white cottage a block from the beach, Ava had moved into it with her grandmother after her family had been killed. Sofia Cortes had lived in the cottage with Ava's grandfather, raised Ava's father there, and stayed through widowhood with her walking buddies and conservation efforts, finally passing away at home after a long battle with cancer.

The home, paid off, had remained in a trust with a rental company managing the property until Ava had aged out of the foster system. The practical choice would have been to sell it and move to a smaller, cheaper apartment closer to the airport. A place easier to leave when she got a new case. But she had no intention of selling. She loved it here.

After locating her missing shoes under a chair, Ava slipped them on and strode onto her porch, squinting in the bright morning sun. She did some stretches, glancing down the sloping street straight toward a strip of sparkling blue ocean, then set off on an easy jog toward her favorite spot a mile down the coast.

The smell of the sea hit her as she took the sidewalk path overlooking the shore below, passing stairways every quarter mile that led down to the sand and ocean waves. She'd never forget her first time seeing the ocean. That had been a time filled with uncertainty and fear. After moving in with her grandmother, she'd learned to love the ocean. She walked and walked the beaches in her grief, letting the forlorn calls of the birds be her voice. One place where she always found solace was a small section of beach carved out by a rocky outcropping that jutted out over the sand.

She called it Alcove Beach, though it had no real name. Ava bounded down the steel stairway leading to the shore and found a spot near the wall of stones next to the railing. The beach was rocky, not great for sunbathing or for kids to make sandcastles, so it usually remained empty. Joggers and roller skaters used the street-level sidewalk above. Other than that, Ava had the small section of beach to herself.

Perched on a large boulder, she listened to the waves crash and let her heart rate slow. Her mind still circled around the image of Brent, slick with muck, staring up at her from the dirty asphalt. After she'd left the scene the night before, Detective Manaia sent her an invitation to the secure network, and she'd taken a peek at the case, looking for a different angle to try. He was right. They had nothing. Despite all her time digging into Brent's life, she still had no idea what he'd gotten himself mixed up in this time.

She thought back to that time right after getting kicked off the PIT team, not taking anyone's calls, still under investigation. She hadn't been in a great headspace. She'd been convinced there was something Brent had been hiding, but his father was too connected. Thrown off after her very public lashing, she'd backed off, intending to pursue it after more evidence surfaced, but that never happened. The brass wanted the case closed. So they shut her out. Brent got a deal, and Cartwright went to prison. She should have pushed to keep the case open.

Movement down the beach caught her eye, and she spotted her former partner turned boss, Agent August Blake, walking on the sand toward her, looking like a rugged movie star. August couldn't hide that he was from money if he tried. He wore a white button-down shirt, his cuffs rolled to the elbows, charcoal chino pants, and perfectly styled dark espresso hair that fell slightly over his light brown eyes.

"Hey!" Surprised, Ava rose from the boulder. "What are you doing here?"

"You sounded off on the phone last night." He leaned against the rock retaining wall. "You always come here when something's bothering you. And while you hate morning workouts, you hate standing still when you're grappling with something more." He crossed his arms. "What's going on?"

"Nothing." She adjusted the messy bun atop her head, shaken loose by her run. "Really. You didn't have to drive almost two hours to check on me."

"You asked for time off." He shook his head. "You don't do that."

"Maybe I do now."

He slipped off his sunglasses. "We've consulted on at least five outside cases since you've been back on the team, and since Black Oak, you're ready for the next official PIT one. Practically champing at the bit. You wouldn't take time off and risk missing it."

Ava crossed her arms over her chest. "You mean chomping?"

"Horses champ at the bit. It's an equestrian term."

"How many ponies did you have as a child?"

He narrowed his amber gaze at her. "What are you doing? Is it PIT? I know we've been waiting awhile for our next case, but I thought you were finding your footing with the team."

"No, it's nothing to do with you or the team. I just need some time off to work an old case."

"You don't have any old cases. You're physically incapable of moving on from a case until it's solved." He tucked his sunglasses into his shirt pocket. "And you don't close a case unless you know you completely tied everything off." His dark brows furrowed. "In fact, I've never seen you look back. Not once."

She smiled. He never missed a thing. "Okay, technically it's a new case, but with some old players. I didn't want to get you involved."

He shook his head. "That's not how we do things anymore. No secrets, remember?"

"Okay, you first. How was dinner last night?" Ava covered up the pit in her stomach with a grin.

He blinked at her. "That is personal. This is work."

"So, a girlfriend, then," Ava teased.

He cocked his head, scrutinizing her face. "Quit stalling."

Ava chewed on the inside of her cheek. "Look, I don't want to pull you into something that could blow up. I think I may have missed something before, and someone might be dead because of it."

"Walk me through it, Ava."

The sound of the waves rumbled through her, and she let out a breath before looking up at him. "I worked on a case with the Oceanside Police Department two years ago. We were investigating sex trafficking, prostitution, and money laundering. My partner at the time was Detective Tony Manaia, with the OPD's Crimes of Violence Unit."

"This was when you had just started with White Collar Crimes? You cleared that case if I recall."

"Yeah, I helped solve it, but looking back, I was messed up, August. *Angry.* I couldn't shake what had happened with the Ghost Town Killer." Ava paced along the wall, then stopped in front of him, her eyes on the sea. "I think I should've pursued something at the time. I should've listened to my gut and I just... I didn't."

August pulled a piece of gum from his pocket and shoved it into his mouth. "Tell me about the new case."

She shook her head. "You need to see it."

———

On the way back to her house, Ava brought him up to date on her conversation with Detective Manaia the night before. The previous two bodies, the one they'd found at the drive in, the markings, everything. She ran into the house to grab the tablet while still talking. He followed her inside, leaning against her counter, his hands shoved in his pants pockets, as he watched her move around the kitchen. Ava found the tablet, pulled up the file for him, and handed it over. "I couldn't shake the feeling that Brent was hiding something. He was acting strangely nervous for someone with an immunity deal."

August's gaze slid across the screen, his jaw working as he read. She paced in front of him, chewing on the inside of her cheek, thinking about those strange markings.

"I can't concentrate when you're circling me like a vulture," August said.

Ava put her hands up and wandered over to the couch.

After a few minutes, he said, "And this Detective Manaia asked you specifically for a CBI consult last night?"

"He asked me as a friend, I think. We'd both worked with Brent when we took down Eliza Cartwright. He made detective first-grade off the case."

"I remember. The Sea Sirens Escorts madam." August nodded, handing the tablet back. "What's your connection to the other victims?"

"I only know the latest one. Brent Cutler." She explained that Cutler had found himself involved in some kind of escort situation and brokered a deal with the CBI to bring down Eliza Cartwright in a sting targeting her escort service. "Eliza, real name Lisa Carter, is currently serving ten years in the Metropolitan Correctional Center,

San Diego. She could've gotten less time, but she wouldn't give up her black book names."

"So, Detective Manaia thinks the victims are connected and part of a series. Do you think he's onto something?"

"He's spooked, and that's saying something. He's a solid investigator. One of the best I've worked with."

"Do you know him well?" August didn't look at her when he asked.

"Enough. We kept Brent steady when he was spinning out. I guess you could call that a bonding moment."

"Now he's dead in your backyard."

"We all live relatively near the coast, but I don't think where he was found had anything to do with me. Not yet, anyway."

August rattled the keys in his pocket, chewing his gum. "And you think you have to make it right."

"I have to figure out what I missed back then."

He nodded, pushing up from the counter. "I figured. Come on. We have a meeting."

"A meeting?" Ava followed him into her house. "Is that why you're in town?"

"I told you why I was in town." August took his phone from his back pocket and handed it to her. Then he went to the kitchen, pulled out a mug from the cabinet, and poured the dregs from her coffee pot. Just like he used to. No one would ever suspect it'd been over two years since he'd been in this house. Ava forced her attention to the news website on the phone screen while he sipped his coffee. A headline across the top read: *Political Scion Found Murdered and Stuffed in an Oil Drum...*

"Oh, crap," Ava said.

"The Brent Cutler case isn't a solo quest anymore. It's an official CBI case, thanks to the mayor's call last night. Apparently, the Chief of Police is pissed Detective Manaia went over his head."

"You'd think the Chief would welcome our help."

"Yes, well, he remembers you."

She chuckled. "That's fair."

"Vincent told me about the investigation first thing this morning when I was already on my way and wouldn't you know, you're already up to speed."

Ava grabbed his mug, took a sip, and smiled. "I guess you should work on keeping up then."

———

She took a quick shower, dried her hair, then dressed quickly. Dark slacks and a cotton, sky-blue blouse she wore when it was hot. Tailored to both hide her weapon and to allow an unobstructed pull when she needed one, the outfit met the CBI's business casual regulations. Ava kept her long hair loose because research showed it made people appear more approachable. She grabbed her personal phone, a burner not connected with the day-to-day of her work cell, and dropped it into her purse. Finally, she slipped on the Doc Marten boots she wore in the field, and they headed out in his SUV.

They hit the I-5 freeway south. August slipped them into the carpool lane as they hit traffic. The ride offered ocean views and the occasional peek at the Pacific Surfliner commuter train. Oceanside Police Department used the San Diego Medical Examiner's Office for forensic needs their in-house team couldn't handle. Forty minutes away in Kearny Mesa, the office provided lab work, autopsies, and other specialized forensic services for the County of San Diego, in which the City of Oceanside was located.

Ava sat in the passenger seat, reading the rest of the newspaper article. The press already seemed to know everything the police did.

Well, that's not ideal.

"At least they didn't mention the bodies being carved with markings," Ava muttered. "That would definitely freak people out."

They talked about what Manaia had shown her, with Ava holding up photos on her secure tablet for August to see as they sat in traffic.

"You're the queen of obscure knowledge," he said. "What do you think?"

"I am sort of amazing."

August rolled his eyes. "What do the carvings mean?"

She looked out the window, thinking about the gunshot, the broken bones, the darkness of the barrel. It meant a brutal, broken mind. Shaking her head, she said, "I'm not sure yet."

Ava switched to perusing the case file, reading out the notes on Brent Cutler to August. After the Sea Siren case two years ago, Brent had done a stint in rehab. According to Manaia's notes, he'd gotten into working out. He'd also opened a wine tasting room with backing from his father, called Bramble Wood Cellars. Though why anyone with a substance abuse problem would open up and work at a place that sold alcohol was beyond Ava's comprehension.

"It's apparently pretty good, from what I hear," she said. "My friend, Christy, went there for her mother-in-law's sixtieth birthday and said they had great farm-to-table dishes."

"Is that the one with the fairy hair??"

Ava chuckled. "The pixie cut, yeah,"

"Tell me about Detective Manaia. It's not every day you throw out compliments like, 'Best detective I've ever worked with'"

"He's a good guy. A family guy. He was the youngest homicide detective in the county back when he started. So, when they wanted a liaison to work with the White-Collar team, he came highly recommended. Manaia knows this town. He helped me get Brent Cutler to crack."

"Brent didn't have a lawyer?"

"He had a team. The Cutler family is loaded. They own land and a few mid-tier hotels in the area. His father rubs elbows with the other rich mucky mucks in San Diego County. But Brent wasn't exactly a stellar decision maker. His father kept a tight grip on the finances, especially after his legal trouble. He didn't want his father to know all of his dirty deeds, so he talked with us instead of his lawyers." Ava jotted down a note in her leather notebook. "Which reminds me, is Rondeau in town yet? I need to ask him to check on life insurance for Brent. He's not married anymore so who gets his millions?"

"He and Talia are driving down this morning. They'll set up at the police station." August took the offramp toward Overland Ave. "Who brokered the deal?"

"I did. Working with his attorney and the Department of Justice, the three of us put together a solid case. Brent, our confidential informant, agreed to wear a wire during multiple meetings with Eliza Cartwright. He did, and we got what we needed, so he got a pass on his soliciting prostitution charges."

"But you think you messed up."

"Eliza said some things to him during their conversations. She kept alluding to how everyone has their dark secrets. Something like that."

"And you think this might have something to do with his death?" He pulled into the parking lot of the Medical Examiner's Building.

Ava grabbed her messenger bag and slung it over her shoulder. "It was enough to get my attention last time and I ignored it. I'm not going to make that mistake again."

FOUR

The boxy white and yellow Medical Examiner and Forensic Center building looked ironically cheerful, given its function. Vast windows and liberal use of skylights gave the space a light, almost welcoming aesthetic. The Forensic Center was, in fact, the pride and joy of San Diego. The massively expensive, state-of-the-art and sustainability-enhanced facility housed over eighty thousand square feet of diagnostic and research space, forensic laboratories, and administrative offices.

Forensic staff processed evidence for a county of nearly three and a half million citizens. Built to grow, the facility fostered a relationship with the University of California at San Diego, Ava's alma mater. The center provided training and education for UCSD students in pathology, tissue harvesting, and organ donor operations, all while promoting low water usage for its sprawling landscape. California fan palms and live oak trees rounded out the coastal feel.

They gave their names at the reception counter, and the attendant directed them to the autopsy suites. The department didn't take long to find, and they entered the glossy, white-tiled room. A middle-aged man in scrubs was standing at a hanging scale, adjusting a basin next to the metal autopsy table when he saw them.

"You're the CBI agents?"

"We are," August said. "We're here to see Dr. Cooms."

"Ah, yes." The man snapped off his nitrile gloves and dropped them in a bin before striding over with a smile. Bushy ginger hair, green eyes, tufts of gray at his temples. "I'm the Assistant ME, Dr. Ryan Tavers."

"Agents Cortes and Blake," August said as they shook hands. "We're here about the Brent Cutler case."

"The ME is performing the autopsy on him as we speak. She asked not to be disturbed, but she left the files for the other victims for you."

"You did those autopsies, right? The first and second victim's?" Ava asked. "I read them. Very thorough."

"I did, yes." Tavers looked between them and then said, "So, shall I give you the run down?"

"Drop it on us," Ava said, smiling at his bluntness. She took out her leather notebook and pen.

Tavers walked over and grabbed some files from a built-in desk in the corner. He explained that victim one was a male, twenty years old, shot once behind the ear with a twenty-two-caliber round, placed in a blue oil drum and tossed into the sea. The second victim, a female, also twenty, had been shot by the same gun and deposited in a similar oil barrel, though tests hadn't come back on the oil to see if it matched.

"I don't think the containers leaked until the waves tossed them against the jagged rocks of the jetty." Tavers handed August the file. "One of them opened a crack and the smell alerted a fisherman that something wasn't right."

"Any idea where the barrels went into the water?" August asked. "Did anyone run current modeling?"

"We did, yes." Tavers nodded. "The bodies were found in a standard fifty-five-gallon barrel, sealed, made of HDPE plastic. The amount of fluid in the barrel coupled with the fact that it was oil, which is less dense than water, slightly increased buoyancy. The gases created by decomposition further increased buoyancy over time as well."

August nodded. "So, they could float or bob semi-submerged for weeks if the seals held."

"Which they would have if it weren't for the jetty rocks cracking the first one. But the second was still sealed."

"But where did they come from?" Ava asked. "It couldn't have been a passing ship. These kids were local."

August checked the sailing app he kept on his phone, and Ava squinted at the graph. "Southern California currents often run north to south. They shift seasonally, but given the buoyancy of the barrel, the near shore currents, and onshore winds this time of year, we could be looking at a short excursion. Maybe even a smaller vessel."

"So it's safe to assume the killer didn't know about currents. Unless you think they dumped them close enough to wash ashore on purpose."

August shook his head. "I don't see why they'd do that purposefully but could be a possibility."

She turned to Tavers, who'd been watching their conversation, "Your report said they died sometime in March?"

"Uh, yes. They were found two months ago, in April but I'd put the time of death for both of them closer to early March. The breakdown of the tissue was a real issue in establishing identity. Dental still hasn't come back."

"But you did figure out who they were. Detective Manaia mentioned a collar for prostitution on the female," Ava said.

"We did, yes. Though the bodies were found clothed, no wallets or other identification were present. We did establish the identity of the female relatively quickly. I managed to get a thumb print from her via a degloving procedure. Her print was in the system from an arrest during a sweep at a nightclub last year. A driver's license associated with the print gave her name as Cindy

Aquino. The prostitution charges were dropped from what I'm told."

Ava furrowed her brows. "Why?"

Tavers shrugged. "I didn't ask. But I do remember her legal name popped up in a missing person's search from three months ago."

"Who filed it?" Ava leaned over to peer at the file in August's hand. Cindy Aquino had worn lash extensions and pinned her hair in an updo for her driver's license photo. She looked young and beautiful in a party-girl kind of way. "The missing person's report."

"A friend."

"Not a parent?"

"No. She was listed as a runaway by her grandmother two years ago. After the autopsy, the office attempted to contact her via the number she left but were told she was in Florida in a nursing home. Dementia. We searched for other living relatives, but the mother is suspected of being homeless, location unknown. No father to speak of. Cindy Aquino is one of our frozen storage residents for now."

"Is there any way to find out who filed the missing person's report?" Ava said.

"The form provides the option for the reporting party to leave contact information so, maybe," Tavers said. "Detective Manaia might have an easier time finding that for you."

"And the male?" August asked, handing the file to Ava. "Same background?"

She studied the victim's DMV photo. Blond hair, blue eyes, freckles on his red and peeling nose. He must've surfed.

"I must admit, I don't know much. His identity was a mystery until today. During the autopsy, we found a surgical screw in his humerus from a severe break a few years ago." Tavers reached into the file Ava had in her hands and held up an x-ray of a broken arm. "The hospital in Ventura that performed the surgery five years ago dragged its feet getting back to us, but after the third victim's name dropped last night, we suddenly have our answers this morning. His name is James Wright." Tavers pointed to the file. "Detective Manaia pulled the public and personal records as soon as we heard back. Other than a bust for holding Oxy, he was clean."

"This says he was reported as missing as well." Ava leafed through the report. "But only a month ago?"

"Yes, by his parents. They said they waited because he had the habit of traveling on a whim but always kept in touch. He stopped and they got worried."

"He led a nomadic life," Ava said mostly to herself. "Were there any other similarities between the victims? Did Cindy Aquino have any surgeries or severe breaks like James Wright?"

"Nothing came up during her autopsy. As far as other similarities, we'll have to wait for the results to come back. We sent them in weeks ago, but I have a feeling we'll hear back soon." He pointed toward the door behind them. "The male did sustain injuries to his face and torso that Ms. Aquino lacked, but it is unclear if they were a result of his manner of death. He's in our cold room next door if you want to take a look."

———

Ava preferred the focused photos and detailed reports of an autopsy rather than standing over victims' brutalized bodies. Still, the curious markings seemed significant, and she wanted to check if the ones on Brent differed from the first two victims.

She and August followed Dr. Tavers as he led them into the autopsy suite where James Wright lay on a table in a smaller viewing room, still partially wrapped in the plastic and sheeting of long-term storage. Bright lights overhead made his remaining skin appear almost marble in its pale stillness. The smell of formaldehyde and antiseptic cleaner burned her nostrils as she stood next to the victim.

"The skin of the male victim is less degraded on the chest. We should start there." Tavers donned a paper surgical smock and gloves. He peeled back the coverings to reveal deeply discolored lower limbs. "The oil was hard to remove. It took a few of us some time. We collected it and filtered out particles. They're going through tests right now."

"How much in each barrel?" Ava asked.

"About seven and a half liters, so two gallons give or take. We disposed of the barrels after documenting them extensively." Armed with a pointer, Tavers directed their attention to the carved lines on the victim's chest.

"As you can see, this is deeper than a scratch. I've seen this kind of cut used in ritual scarification, in the tribes of New Guinea for instance. Deep etching that would have certainly drawn substantial blood but didn't." He pointed to the pink tissue peeking through the slits made by the knife. "The cuts were fairly deep."

Several death rituals came to mind, none of them even close to what happened to James. "He was dead already?"

Tavers nodded. "They both were. The symbols on the female victim match his."

"So do the ones on Brent Cutler." Every detail from the night before flashed through her mind. "And someone carved the symbols on him after he died? Like the first two victims?"

"Yes. I took a look when he first came in."

"Any idea what they mean?" August asked.

"No, and the instrument is interesting too." Tavers pointed to another section of the carving on the chest. "Whoever did this used a *very* sharp, thin-bladed carving tool. Like one might use to fillet fish."

Ava jotted that down in her notebook. "How did you find out the symbols glowed?" "We check every victim with UV to see if there are any substances or residue that might have been missed by the human eye. You'd be surprised how much we find just by changing the lighting. I will say, I've seen UV reactive tattoo ink, but this is something else entirely. We had to send it out for specialized analysis. They're a private company, not a city lab, which is why we have results already." Tavers went to the laptop on the desk, tapped a few keys, and a wall-mounted screen lit up with the test results. "We've got sea salt, coconut oil, India ink, which is made with carbon black, water, and a binding agent. That's usually something like gum arabic or shellac, but a different material was used here instead. These are the results on that substance." He pointed to a document on the screen with multiple bars on a graph. "The luminescent quality is from a UV reactive binding powder."

"Are any of the ingredients hard to get or tracked in any way?" August asked, his temple flexing subtly as he clenched his jaw.

"No, they're all readily available to the public. The UV binder is often used for festivals like raves or Burning Man. You can get both the sea salt and the coconut oil at any grocery store, the ink from an art studio or online." He shrugged. "As the report states, I sent the photos of the symbols to the FBI at the time of the autopsies. Nothing yet. Maybe now that the third victim is getting some press, we'll get a call back."

Ava looked up from her notebook. "Was there anything else out of the ordinary with the victims?"

"I don't know if you saw it in the report, but both their stomachs were empty. As if they hadn't eaten in at least forty-eight hours. They were dehydrated as well."

"Possible exposure?" August asked.

"I observed no discernible sun or wind damage. No notable increase in liver or muscle enzymes to indicate heat stroke or otherwise."

"So, they were inside, but unable to eat or drink?" Ava clarified.

"They could have been fasting. Forty-eight hours isn't that long, but I thought it was significant."

"It is," Ava said, drawing the last of the symbols in her notebook. "It stretches out the timeline. The killer had to have both time and privacy to do all this to them. That brought extra risk of discovery or escape by the victims. A huge risk given he wanted to do it again with Brent." She nodded at the markings on James Wright's chest. "The carved symbols, the applied poultice, the glowing ingredients." She glanced at August.

"It means the killer isn't finished yet."

FIVE

On their way out, Manaia called Ava asking if the team could meet up to review updates before they spoke with Brent Cutler's family. He gave her the address of a diner roughly halfway between the police department and the Cutler residence and asked to meet there in an hour.

On the drive back to Oceanside, Ava accessed the full autopsy reports and the rest of Dr. Tavers's findings. She read it as August listened to seventies Irish punk music while heckling bad drivers. The familiarity didn't escape her. August beeped at an insistent big rig, commenting about blinkers being a thing, breaking her out of her reverie.

With a shake of her head, Ava went back to her notes. Despite all the other data and evidence, she kept returning to the symbols. They were a peculiar, violent note. She'd studied death rituals at university, body modification as well. Something felt wrong with the way the killer went about it, but she couldn't put her finger on what. She didn't know enough to know what she didn't know. She needed to talk to someone who did.

A little before noon, they met up at the Day Break Diner, a breakfast and lunch place housed in a silver train car style restaurant. The return trip had taken more time than anticipated and Ava's stomach growled as they walked in. A mural of a goofy sea lion leaping past a happy sunrise decorated the wall behind the counter. Inexplicably, the sea lion wore a cropped T-shirt with the name "Sandy" across the front. In Ava's experience, this kind of attention to detail promised great food.

A familiar voice called her name, and she spotted her fellow PIT coworkers, Dr. Talia Clay and Agent Martin Rondeau, sitting with Detective Manaia in a booth near the window. As she and August worked their way over, Ava thought about the few times she'd eaten there. With friends. On happy occasions. It had been years since she'd been here. She shook off the memories as she approached the table.

Talia sat next to Rondeau in the center of the booth, her impeccable suit unrumpled as always, long thin braids twisted into a bun atop her head, makeup impervious to the summer heat. Poached from the FBI, Talia's papers on evidence collection techniques pushed to new levels law enforcement's ability to recover previously unusable samples. The forensic and science backbone of the team, Ava had grown to deeply respect her professional opinion and had followed her research since last seeing her at Black Oak.

Talia smiled when she saw them. "You two have been busy. It's been what, five hours since we were officially handed the case and I already have a list of results to review."

"Sorry, that's on me," Ava said as she and August sat at one end of the booth with Manaia taking up the opposite seat. "I have a prior connection to the victim. One of them at least."

Detective Manaia greeted August with a handshake across the table, thanking him for the CBI's help. August, with all the graciousness his boarding school attendance instilled, acted as if Manaia hadn't ruffled feathers all along the ranks of both the OPD and CBI brass.

As soon as they sat down, a server dropped off extra menus. He wore a teal T-shirt with the saying, 'O'side Vibes' emblazoned across his chest.

Rondeau, a tall, sinewy man with a faint West Virginia accent, wore his blond hair in a short, slightly shaggy cut despite his background of working security for high-value targets with the military. He wore an avocado-green polo and black slacks, his begrudging nod to regulation attire. The fact that he was the best digital and technical wizard in the CBI meant August didn't really care what he wore.

"We're set up at the OPD station in one of their meeting rooms," Rondeau said, nodding at Talia. "They've got a pretty sweet audio and video lab too. We'll be ready for incoming camera feeds from the canvass."

Manaia stirred his coffee. "Dr. Tavers called and said you guys had a lot of questions. Did you get your answers?"

"We got more questions." Ava didn't need to see the menu's offerings. She knew all the usual beach favorites. Burgers, deli sandwiches, fish tacos. Instead, she folded the paper placemat into an origami fox. A habit she'd had since college. Keeping her hands busy helped her concentrate. "Did you get a call from the FBI yet on the symbols?"

"We did. They said it's in the queue." Manaia shook his head. "Dr. Clay here said I should shoot them over to the CBI's Behavioral Sciences Unit."

"You should," Ava said. "They traffic in weird crap like that."

"Also," Manaia continued, "We finished the canvass from last night. A few patrol officers went out this morning to hit the stores and gas stations in the area to check for any cameras, but there's not much out there. We had better luck where the first two bodies washed up." He looked at Ava. "Where should I send those results? Are we using the OPD network or what?"

"Send everything my way. I work the information hub, coms and phones, any network packages," Rondeau said to Manaia. "It'll get to the right person. I guarantee."

Ava nodded at the server who dropped off ice water before taking their orders. Ava, Rondeau, and Manaia got the Sandy Burger special —a plain cheeseburger with ground fried onions on the bun — and fries. August ordered a turkey sandwich on wheat, no mayo. Fruit on the side instead of fries. Ava shook her head at his order. He played rugby at university and hadn't lost the athletic build since he still insisted on eating like a heart doctor. Talia chose a grilled chicken burger with fries, splitting the difference.

Ava caught Rondeau's attention. "Can you look into the night-club sweep that caught Cindy up with charges? I want to know who ordered it, why, who was arrested, and their outcome."

"Do you see something there?" he asked, his eyes lighting up with interest.

"I sure hope not. Tony, I think there's a coffee place near the jetty, by the RV parking. They have a camera on the outside of the little building. I've seen it."

Manaia nodded, typing on his note-taking app. "We'll extend the area we check."

While Manaia talked with August and Rondeau, Ava described the skin and salt markings to Talia.

"They don't fit for some reason. The symbols don't make sense," Ava said, as pages of books slipped through her mind. "I need to talk to somebody."

"Why do you feel there's something 'off' about the carvings?" Talia sipped her iced tea. "Can't they just be the delusion of a killer? Maybe they *have* no meaning."

"Maybe." Ava glanced out the window at the swaying palms towering over the parking lot. "The entire case is off though. The victims, how they were killed, the empty stomachs. It's not just the unknown markings."

They chit-chatted, touching on how unusually hot it was, the never-ending construction on the freeway, Manaia complaining about the upcoming Fourth of July celebrations.

"Oceanside does the fireworks show early," he explained to

August. "Usually on the thirtieth. There's already a party atmosphere, especially at the beaches."

Their food arrived, and Ava shook a ton of salt over her fries to August's poorly concealed horror.

Swallowing a bite of her burger, she said, "We need to figure out how he finds his victims. Lots of people will be out and about for the festivities, so he'll have plenty to choose from. All on the streets with a killer who likes to ritualistically carve up his victims." She sipped her tea, glancing around the diner at the sunburnt patrons. "It's gonna be a mess."

Manaia nodded, pointing a fry at her. "We have to take down this killer fast. Dane Cutler is already lighting multiple fires under my butt as of this morning."

"Dane can wait. We need to notify James Wright's family first."

"Yeah, uh, the police chief wants to hold off on that for twenty-four hours, maybe forty-eight. The press is already whipping themselves into a frenzy over Brent Cutler's body and they haven't connected the other two victims yet. That gives us room to investigate before they start stalking our every move."

"We can ask the family to not speak with the press," Ava said.

"He wants a lid on things until he can meet with the mayor and Cutler."

"You can't be serious. James Wright's parents deserve to know as soon as possible."

Manaia shrugged. "It's what the Brass wants. I heard Cutler wants everything released like, now. The other names of the victims, their past, the gory details of the case, all of it. So it'll probably happen sooner rather than later, but the Chief wants us to take advantage of this time as much as possible."

"Why would Brent's father want the press involved?" Talia asked.

"Cover," Ava said with a frown. "Right now, Brent is the only victim they know about. So, all they have for content is his story. The sordid details of Brent's past with the Sea Siren Madam and all the dirty laundry they just spent two years burying. The horror of a serial killer on the other hand and they'd no longer be focusing on Brent's indiscretions."

"All I know is we need to speak with Cutler as soon as we finish here," Manaia said.

"Haven't the Wrights been calling every week?" Ava asked, her cheeks flushing hot.

Manaia hesitated, then, "Come on Ava, you know all hell will break loose when the first two victims get connected with Brent"

"Maybe you guys shouldn't have hidden that the first two victims were murdered," Ava said.

"Wasn't my choice. Look, if it gets released that we have three bodies and no suspects, all bets are off. We need the time to get ahead of this killer. Right now, he might not even know we *have* the first two bodies." Manaia put his palms out. "I get that it sucks, but it's only a day or two."

"Do you know what a day or two feels like when you don't know what happened to your loved one? Or why?" Ava caught August's eye twitch. She sat back in her seat. "We should do it soon."

Manaia nodded. "We will."

August touched her elbow with the back of his finger, and she looked at him. He knew why this was so important to her.

He said, "Vincent called while we were leaving the ME's office. She arranged for us to speak with Cutler this afternoon. I'll talk to her about the notification for James Wright's parents. She'll talk to the Chief and get more information."

Ava sighed. "Okay, let's go talk to Cutler."

"Didn't he file a complaint against you?" Rondeau asked, a smile tugging at his lips.

She smirked. "Yeah, he did. He wanted my badge."

"I heard he almost got it," Rondeau said.

"Well, he didn't." Ava dipped one of her fries into the little paper container of ketchup on her plate. "He's gonna *love* seeing me again."

SIX

The Cutler Mansion, as the local paper called it, sat atop a rise overlooking The Strand, a paved path that ran parallel to the beach. A favorite spot to exercise and its proximity to the Oceanside Pier made it a popular place no matter the time of day.

The family's property occupied a quarter of an acre with six-foot high wood fences, privacy bushes, and a towering metal gate to keep out the riffraff. A large chunk of land on the coast where even mansions sit uncomfortably close to each other. The Spanish colonial architecture mirrored a lot of large houses in the area. Suited to the climate and modeled after the old missions dotting the coast, the whitewashed walls, terracotta details, and ironwork bars blended nicely with the landscape.

A group of smartly dressed reporters stood next to news vans parked across the street, and a large crowd of at least fifty people milled around outside the wrought-iron gate with cell phone cameras out, recording themselves live at the scene. A few security guards stood near the entrance, looking bored.

As August and Ava pulled up in their CBI suburban and Manaia in his unmarked car, the crowd of citizen journalists moved, looking into the windows as they drove onto the property. Reporters material-ized, pushing through the crowd, their mini-microphones tapping on the glass. Security pushed them back as the gate closed, but they stayed at the bars, shouting questions and taking photos.

Ava slipped out of the passenger seat and walked around a large stone fountain dribbling in the center of the circular driveway. Done in mosaics of blue, red, orange, and yellow, the fountain comple-mented the architecture. Manaia adjusted his suit jacket, and Ava realized he wore another nature-inspired button-up, only this time the pattern contained different kinds of palm trees against a pale blue background.

He cleared his throat. "So. Cutler doesn't know you're coming."

"Say again?" Ava asked, walking with him and August to the large double doors. Carved with depictions of palm trees and falling coconuts, they looked enormously heavy.

"He specifically requested you *didn't* come, actually," Manaia continued.

She noticed August clench his jaw before he slowly let out a breath.

"Well, thanks for the five second heads up," Ava said.

"Of the two of us, you knew Brent the best. I figured you can use that when talking to Cutler. And honestly, would you have really stayed behind if I'd asked you?"

Ava opened her mouth to say something, but the door opened without anyone knocking, and a man in a Brooks Brothers suit, silver fox hair, and a stern expression stared down his patrician nose at Ava. They introduced themselves and asked to speak with Dane Cutler about his son.

"Gavin Ford. I'm the Cutler family attorney," he said as they climbed the lushly carpeted steps in near silence. "Mr. Cutler is in the study."

They followed him down a wood-paneled hallway, past portraits of faces vaguely similar to Cutler's, to a door standing ajar. Ford knocked once, then pushed through without waiting for an answer. Ava followed, spotting a figure near the window. He stood with his arms crossed over his chest, legs apart, staring through the drapes at the ocean. Ava wondered if he staged his pose to present himself as a titan of industry. A portrait of him in his younger days hung over the fireplace mantel depicting him in the same pose, confirming her theory.

Dane Cutler spent a great deal of his time hobnobbing with other rich guys on the golf course or at the country club and had the skin to prove it. Liver spots and sun damage dotted his arms. He wore a cream linen shirt and trousers appropriate for an ice cream social. Though they made considerable noise walking in, he didn't turn around.

Instead, the lawyer walked up to him and whispered. Both men looked over their shoulders with grim faces. Cutler's gaze froze on Ava, and he frowned.

Manaia stepped forward. "Mr. Cutler, thank you for speaking with us."

Cutler ignored him, turning to point at Ava. "What is she doing here?"

Manaia tried again. "Sir, we'd like to speak—"

"*She's* here trying to figure out what happened to your son," Ava said. "Not exactly my choice either."

He blinked at her and shouted, "I'll tell you what happened to him. You were the deal maker, and he got killed."

August shook his head. "Let's stay on topic, Mr. Cutler—"

"That's bullshit and you know it," Ava said. "He came to *us* with information, not the other way around. He wanted immunity for what he knew, and though he didn't deserve it, he got it."

"I refuse to speak to any of you if she's here," Cutler spat, the vein at his temple throbbing. "Either she goes, or I don't talk."

"Then we don't talk," August said, gaze going hard. "You can get your information from OPD, though I hear they're backed up for a few weeks. Your choice."

Ford leaned in again, and Cutler nodded, then said, "Whatever. But she keeps her mouth shut."

August turned to her, "Agent Cortes?"

Ava put her hands up in surrender.

She wandered around the large study as August and Manaia asked him questions about Brent's state of mind, his friends, if he had enemies. Cutler answered sharply, resentful. Brent was fine. Everyone loved him. No, his son didn't have any problems with anyone. That was all in the past.

Cutler's shelves contained photos of him and nearly every famous person who had ever passed through Oceanside over the past forty years. Singers, celebrities, athletes, politicians, even a president. But the majority of them were of his son. Brent golfing, riding horses, sailing. She'd seen similar photos at August's family home in Los Angeles. He too had a complicated relationship with his wealthy father.

Cutler refused to give solid answers, instead complaining that Ava and Manaia pushed Brent into admitting to things he didn't do to build their case against the Sea Siren Madam, Eliza Cartwright. Detective Manaia redirected with questions about any threats, even old ones. Cutler claimed there'd been none before Brent's disappearance.

Ava watched him from the bookcase. The way his gaze slid from August's when he answered, the constant movement of his hands. In his pocket, wiping his bottom lip, pulling on his buttons. She couldn't help herself.

She spoke now, something else she couldn't help. "Mr. Cutler, the autopsy report for your son says his stomach was empty and that he was dehydrated." A bluff based on the other bodies. "Indicating he'd been kept for at least forty-eight hours before he was killed. He'd been buried at least two or three more days until he was found. Any reason why you didn't notice he was missing for all that time?"

Cutler scoffed, his eyes bulging. "Because he was a grown ass man, and I didn't keep tabs on him! He was doing well, despite what you did to him!"

"We are going to end this interview if she continues harassing my client," Ford said.

August shot her a look and then took Cutler through the two years after the trial. How he'd funded the wine tasting room for Brent.

"He lives... lived in the apartment over the venue," Cutler said. "He was rebuilding his life."

She could feel his gaze on her as she perused his books. He had good taste. She pulled a volume from his shelf that matched one she owned herself. Turning, she said, "So he had money trouble?"

"I didn't say that."

"You had to buy him a job and a place to live. I thought I heard his inheritance was in question?"

"It was not. He just needed to get back on his feet before dealing with finances," Cutler snapped. "In the meanwhile, I invested in my son. Is that a crime?"

"What else did you invest in him?" Ava asked, moving closer, his first edition of Henry Scott-Holland's poems in her hand. "We both know Brent had expensive tastes."

"I don't know who you think you—"

She dropped the heavy book on his desk with a thud. "Was money disappearing yet?"

Cutler froze. His face lost color. He consulted with Ford for a moment in terse whispers before he said, "He and I had an argument over his emergency credit card."

"What about the card?" August asked, writing on his tablet.

"Brent's card was maxed out. There were several large cash withdrawals. When I confronted him, he said he'd taken the money for a friend that was in trouble."

Manaia took a step forward. "Did he give you a name?"

"No."

"Mr. Cutler, did Brent even have friends?" Ava asked. "When I knew him, he'd just busted up his own marriage by sleeping with his childhood friend's wife. They divorced as well, from what I hear. I know he had been rebuilding his life, but he burned a lot of bridges before the trial."

"What the hell are you getting at?" Cutler asked. "He had a few hard years, he struggled with addiction."

"I mean to say, sir, that he lost all his old friends. Did you know any of his current ones?"

Cutler hesitated. "I... no, I did not."

"So, you have no idea who this troubled friend might be?" Ava asked.

"He said he had a friend in need, and he was trying to help. I didn't give him the third degree."

Ava tilted her head. His eyes were puffy, rimmed with red from crying. "Was he in trouble, Mr. Cutler? Do you think he might have relapsed and fallen into bad habits?" He turned back to August and Manaia without answering. "Regardless of what happened two years ago, I really am here to help find who did this to your son."

Cutler remained silent for another moment, then glanced back at Ava. "He'd been sober for eighteen months. He still went to meetings. He had those coins they earn. The meetings were court ordered at first, but he kept going. He said they helped, and he drove in every morning."

"Drove in? Which meetings was he going to?"

"The ones by the donut place. Over on Foussat Road. Why?"

Ava refused to look at August. "And the women?"

"He was done with all that," Cutler said, crossing his arms.

Ava nodded, picking up the book again. She listened to August push for more information, asking about the ex-wife and life insurance. Cutler didn't know much about either. Ford said he'd look into it. As far as they knew, the ex-wife lived in London. She'd moved after the affair and trial. With no grandkids to speak of, Cutler had lost contact with her.

"He still wore his wedding ring," Manaia noted. "Was there a chance at reconciliation?"

"No," Cutler muttered, shaking his head. "Brent had a fatal kind of hope. Even if all things pointed to something going under, he wouldn't give up on it."

Ava thought that was the saddest thing she'd heard in a while. From her experience, Brent had two vices: women and drugs. When she'd arrested him two years prior, he was high as a kite on cocaine and disembarking a party boat filled with ladies of the hasty date variety and midnight ballerinas.

"The watch," Ava said suddenly. Cutler turned to glare at her. "His watch was missing. That big square one. It was yours, correct? Or your father's?"

Cutler's face fell. "He wasn't wearing it?"

"Had you seen it recently?" Ava asked. "He had a tan line."

"A tan line." Cutler rubbed his own wrist. "He was wearing it a few days before he disappeared. I saw it when we met for dinner."

"He was working on his relationship with you," Ava murmured. She leaned on the corner of his desk, making herself smaller, less confrontational. "He *was* trying."

Cutler simply nodded. "He was. Things were looking up for him and then..." he shook his head, blinking rapidly as he turned. "He had a good heart."

"Whoever he was, your son, that he is still," Ava summarized the poem, handing Cutler his book open to Holland's haunting piece about lost loved ones. "Help me find who did this to him."

Cutler stared at it for a moment, lips pressed together. "What do you need from me?"

They told him they needed him to get the information about the credit card in question, the watch's insurance photos and file, and the life insurance papers to them as soon as possible. As they left the study, he asked to speak with Manaia alone. Ford escorted Ava and August back to the front door. They wandered past the fountain to the property's fence, staying in the shade as they waited.

August refused to look at her, which usually meant something bothered him. She waited him out, noticing a bright blue mosaic tile in the dirt near the fountain. She picked it up, dropping it into her pocket. Finally, he asked. "Why did you go after him so hard? It's like you wanted to fight."

"He was pissed when we got there. He needed to get that out before he was going to say anything useful." She glanced at the door. "And you saw him. He wouldn't stop moving his hands, wiping his face, those were clear signs of deception."

"Or stress. Did it ever occur to you not to burn bridges you may need later?"

"I can swim." She turned to face him. "What are you really upset about?"

"You cross so many lines, Ava." He looked away, his brows furrowed, jaw set. "You know I had a problem with drinking at UPenn"

"And you quit so that you didn't become an abusive drunk like your father," Ava said. She never drank around him. "What's the matter?"

"Yes, I quit. With help. The university allowed sobriety meetings on campus, and they saved my life."

"I'm not knocking the program, August, what—"

He gestured toward her face. "I know that look you get."

"What look?"

"The one you had when Cutler mentioned Brent's meetings."

"Listen—"

"No, *you* listen." August held her gaze. "That sanctity, the anonymity at those meetings. You're thinking of invading a privacy that might be the only thing holding those people together."

Ava shook her head. "Is there another way you can think of to find out what was going on with Brent? He pushed everyone else away."

"There's the Bramble Wood Cellars employees."

"I doubt the wine room staff know about their boss's dirty secrets," Ava said.

Burying his hands in his pockets, August held her gaze, a stubborn set to his lips. "They won't tell you anything. Discretion is a safety net for everyone involved in those meetings. If anything, questioning them might spook someone who needs to be there."

"I'll think of something."

"What does that mean?" August raised a brow. "Ava—" His phone rang, and he growled, answering as he strode away.

Manaia came back out, and Ava walked with him to his car. He glanced over at August. "What was that about?"

"It's hard to work with me sometimes," Ava muttered. "What did Cutler want?"

"He said he didn't want you talking to the press," Manaia said with a smile as he climbed into the driver's seat. "He doesn't trust what you'll say."

"Smart man," she said. By the SUV, August spoke on his phone, his body tense, head nodding. He ended it, then walked over to Manaia's car.

"That was Vincent," August said to him. "You're going to get a call from your Chief."

"About?"

"James Wright's family. We're making the notification now. The mayor approved it."

"Great. I'm sure that'll be a fun—" Manaia's phone rang. He answered it, and they walked away.

"You talked to Agent Vincent about the notification?" Ava asked, feeling a tug of guilt in her stomach about upsetting him as she climbed into her seat.

"I told you I would. Funny thing, she said you'd already called her to discuss it before I even brought it up."

"The family deserves to know, August." When he didn't answer, she looked over, catching his gaze. "I didn't go around you. I went around the chief—"

"I told her you were right. Which I would have told you, had you asked me again." His gaze traveled over her face. "They've waited long enough."

As they left, the opening gate disturbed birds nesting in the tree overhead, and their pale fluttering pulled Ava's gaze to the group of onlookers just outside the fence. A young woman in a billowy linen sundress stood in the crowd. Thin and tanned, with braided hair bleached nearly white by the sun, she stared at Ava like she knew her. Then, in one smooth motion, Ava watched as the young girl dragged her index finger across her throat.

SEVEN

At nearly three in the afternoon, they hit commuter traffic as the people working near the coast flooded back to the more affordable Vista, a similar-sized city that shared a border with Oceanside. A mere seven miles from the ocean, the Mediterranean climate and rolling hills gave the area a pleasant rural feel. Ava stared out the window, her thoughts on the young woman and the threatening gesture. She could relate to her distrust of law enforcement, especially at that age. The police who'd rescued her from the man who'd taken her family were burned into her mind. But so were her encounters with patrols during her wild years. Ava's relationship with authority was a mixed bag.

They parked in front of a two-story retail building. A mural depicting crabs and starfish tanning on the shore with tropical birds flying against puffy clouds overhead decorated the front wall. Both of James's parents worked inside. She and August were waiting for Manaia to show up—he'd been right behind them—when he called Ava. She put him on speaker.

"Got called to a domestic situation," Manaia said. "It's bad. Go ahead and make the notification. I'll get the details later."

"Are you sure?" Ava asked. August raised his brow, and she shook her head.

"Yeah, just make sure the parents know to keep things to themselves for now. The press, you know." Manaia said.

Ava promised and ended the call.

"Doesn't want to go against his Chief with this notification?" August asked.

"That's what I'm thinking." Slinging her messenger bag across her body, she walked with August to the antique store. The laminated sign taped to the front window offered to buy estate collections and hand-crafted goods. James's mother, Carol, owned the antique consignment shop, and her store logo, Carol's Collectibles, clung to the glass of the entrance door.

August pulled it open. "This is it."

Once inside, Ava realized it was a two-story antique mall. Much larger than she first thought. The sheer number of things felt dizzying. Every type of trinket and knick-knack cluttered the shop's surfaces and stuffed display cases. Piles of vintage magazines sat on shelves next to crystal candy dishes. Chandeliers overhead held dozens of dangling Christmas ornaments that reminded Ava of her grandmother's tree. She caught the scent of dust and old lady perfume and books. Ava loved the smell of books. She'd spent her childhood nestled in their comforting pages.

They passed a couple of customers on their way to the checkout counter. Two older women dug through a wooden box filled with ironstone pottery. A woman in a work apron stood at the register. Blonde hair, freckles, same eyes as her son. She chatted happily with a man of similar age as they unwrapped plates from old newspaper, setting them on the glass counter. The woman giggled at something he said as they approached, and Ava thought it would be a long time before she'd do that again after they left.

"Can I help you?" Her nametag read Carol. August and Ava flashed their badges discreetly. The woman's hand flew to her chest, eyes going wide. "Is this about... are you here about Jimmy?"

"Is there somewhere we can talk privately?" August asked, nodding to the man who'd put his arm around Carol. He had a ring of hair around his bald crown, dark eyes, and a gruffness about him.

"You can say what you gotta say here," he said, extending his hand to August. "Stan Ulbreck, Carol's husband."

Ava regarded him. Lips pressed tight. Tense shoulders. He didn't want them there.

"But not Jimmy's father?" Ava used the mother's preferred name for the son.

He narrowed his gaze. "He's my stepson."

"Jimmy's father died ten years ago. What is this about?" Carol spoke up. "Have you, uh, located him?"

"Ma'am, we should really be somewhere you can sit down." August motioned toward a corner of the store with a rocking chair.

"I need a cigarette," Carol said and reached under the counter, grabbed a leather pouch, and made a beeline for the back of the store. "Can you... can we talk outside?"

Ava and August glanced at Stan who shrugged and exited from behind the counter to follow his wife. Ava hurried ahead, catching up with Carol. The door led to a rear parking lot with one car, an orange Camaro. Only cracked asphalt and a full dumpster shared the space. Carol sat against the hood while she tried to light a menthol in the wind. Her hands shook, and Ava took the lighter, cupping the flame for her. Carol puffed a couple of times and pulled back.

"You alright?" Ava murmured. "You know why we're here?"

Carol nodded as she exhaled, her eyes filling. "They don't send agents to tell you your kid is fine."

"What happened?" Stan asked as he walked up.

August stood upwind of the smoke. "Before we speak, I have to ask you to keep what you learn to yourselves for a couple of days."

"Why?" Stan asked.

Ava ignored him, tilting her head to catch Carol's gaze. "Mrs. Ulbreck, I'm so sorry to inform you that we recovered your son's body. James is dead, ma'am."

Carol crumbled, her head falling forward as she let out a soft, sorrowful, "Nooo."

The mournful sound twisted Ava's gut.

Stan shook his head, looking almost angry. "How?"

"Do you want me to go on?" Ava whispered to Carol.

Carol nodded, wiping her eyes with shaking fingers, smoke trailing up into the sky. "Tell me everything."

Ava told her that the ME believed her son died three months ago and that while police located his body near the jetty two months ago, there had been difficulty identifying him due to the state of the remains.

"What state? I don't understand," Stan cut in. "Did he drown? Was he one of the people the news said drowned?"

August nodded. "Yes. He was one of those two people. But he didn't drown. He was shot. His death was ruled a homicide by the medical examiner."

"What? Who would... who would murder Jimmy?" Carol's voice rose. "He was just a kid!"

"That's what we were hoping to talk with you about," Ava said, glancing at Stan. "Is there anything you can tell us that might help us figure out why this happened? Do you know if he'd been having trouble with anyone?"

"No, he didn't fight with people." Carol fought to answer their questions between sobs and taking drags on her cigarette. She shivered despite the heat.

August asked about enemies, fights at school, in the neighborhood. Anything that might indicate how he met such a violent end. Stan looked up when his wife got quiet and cleared his throat.

"Jimmy dropped out of school to live what you call, 'the van life.' You know about that?"

"Yeah," Ava said. "People live in a converted van or RV, they usually work a remote job, travel."

"Yeah, that," Stan said. "Anyways, he was a surfer. And he wanted to get on the competition circuit. He had a VW camper van that I restored for him. It had all the bells and whistles. He lived in it."

"You reported him missing only a month ago," Ava began. "I understand that he led a nomadic lifestyle. Was he often out of touch?"

"Yes. Jimmy traveled up and down the coast meeting up with buddies, surfing, hanging out. He didn't always keep in touch. I say that because that's the reason we didn't think he was missing. But then he missed Mother's Day." Stan nodded at Carol. "He'd never do that. He might've been a little flaky, but he wouldn't have done that."

"And then his work called us," Carol said. "He did data entry or something online for a medical company. I was his emergency contact. They said his laptop went offline and he hadn't been answering his phone for weeks. That's when we panicked."

They talked with them both about friends. Jimmy didn't make them easily. He was sensitive, prone to melancholy.

"Was he a loner?" Ava asked.

"Not really. He did like people. He was just quiet." Carol shrugged. "But then his friends from school fell away when he dropped out. And he was doing his own thing."

Ava nodded. "So he was just traveling up and down the coast meeting up with people he knew along the way?"

"Essentially."

"Did he stay anywhere long enough to make new friends?" August asked.

"Not really. He didn't like to stay anywhere too long," Stan said.

"Did he ever mention anyone named Cindy Aquino?" Ava asked.

Carol and Stan both shook their heads.

"What about kids in your neighborhood? Any friends there?" Ava tried. "Did he ever mention the name of a coworker? Or maybe someone gave him a ride, and you saw a car?"

"No, he wasn't home much," Stan said.

"What about legal trouble?" August cleared his throat. "He has prior arrests for having narcotic pain medication on his person without a proper prescription."

"That was," Carol shook her head, looking at Stan. "That wasn't his fault."

Stan sighed, his eyes closing for a moment. Then he said, "Jimmy was in a dirt bike accident a while back. He broke his arm really bad and needed surgery. They gave him pain meds after and things just got away from him. He went to rehab, court ordered, and he got better."

Carol nodded. "He was better."

"I'm more interested in what was going on in his life recently. Any girlfriends? Did he date?"

"There was that one girl," Stan said. "The one with the scooter."

Carol nodded, dropping her cigarette butt on the asphalt and exhaling while she stepped on it with her flip-flop. "Jimmy brought a young lady home for dinner one night unannounced."

"He'd never brought a girl home before," Stan added.

"We didn't even know he was back in town, much less dating anyone. And they just showed up on our doorstep all spic and span."

"What do you mean?" Ava asked.

"They had like, matching outfits or something. Summery. He'd grown out his hair." Carol crossed her arms. "I don't think she liked us very much."

"Why is that?" August asked.

"Like I said, we didn't know they were coming so I had to scramble. I made spaghetti with jarred sauce. We did some garlic bread with a loaf we already had. It wasn't bad." Carol looked to Stan, who nodded his agreement. "Jimmy only ate a little. And the girl, what was her name?"

"Meadow." Stan rolled his eyes.

Ava perked up. "Meadow?"

"That's right. She didn't eat a single bite. Just moved the food around her plate with her fork. They didn't really talk either, so we weren't quite sure why he'd brought her. Honestly, she was a bit odd."

"Odd how?" Ava asked.

"I don't know. She said that she and Jimmy were vegetarian now and the sauce was filled with death and chemicals."

"I offered to make her a PB&J sandwich," Carol said with a shrug. "She said no thanks."

"That's it? She's a food snob?" Ava prompted.

Stan shook his head. "No, not just that. She had this conservative bohemian way about her. Polite, well spoken. Modestly dressed, but a little dreamy, if you know what I mean. I thought she might've been a little high or something."

"Was Jimmy into that?" August asked. "Maybe a little pot? It's legal here in California. People sometimes use it for pain management."

"No. I mean, he used to be a pot smoker I think," Carol admitted. "I smelled it once in a while but never found anything. And not since rehab. He certainly wouldn't show up to dinner on drugs or bring someone who was high to the house. I think she was just nervous or something."

"She talked about yoga," Stan said. "I think she either took classes or taught them. Something like that."

"Stan's right, though. It was an odd dinner," Carol said. "Jimmy seemed off. I originally thought it was nerves. You know bringing a girlfriend home to meet the parents is big. But now that he's..." she shook her head. "I don't know. Something was going on."

Ava leaned forward. "What made you feel that way?"

"Well, the girl, Meadow, she kept talking about getting healthy. How she couldn't get Jimmy to admit that something called a "gut shot" was what he needed for his stomach. That his body was a temple and should be treated as such. She said she knew we were close and that he'd do it if I asked. I just thought that was a strange thing to say when first meeting your boyfriend's mom."

"Did she say what it was?" August asked.

"Some kind of concentrated juice. Ginger, I think," Stan said. "Anyway, I asked Jimmy about it while we were all talking, and he looked over at me suddenly, like he'd just snapped out of a daydream or something and said he hadn't been listening. He did that a few times during dinner, right Carol?"

She nodded, biting her fingernail. "I thought it was anxiety. The girlfriend."

"Anyway, she ended up leaving some of that juice stuff for us on the table when they left. She had it in her purse." Stan shrugged. "After dinner, they said goodbye, got on a rental scooter, and drove off."

"How did you know it wasn't her scooter?" Ava asked.

"It had a city logo. That big letter O surfing a squiggly wave."

Ava nodded, making a note of that.

"That's the last time we saw him," Carol said.

"What did she look like?" Ava asked.

"I told you, she had this vibe—"

Ava put her hand up. "Hair color, eye color, like that."

"Oh, uh," Carol looked at Stan. "Long brown hair, tan. I think she might be part Asian or mixed, if that makes sense."

Ava pulled the secure tablet from her bag, navigated the forensic reports, and pulled up the DMV photo of Cindy Aquino.

They both nodded. "That's Meadow."

August's gaze snapped to hers. "Jimmy brought this girl to dinner?"

Stan took a step back. "Oh shit. She's the other body in the news?"

Carol stared at the tablet, going white. "They're both gone?"

"Do you still have the gut shot juice?" Ava asked.

Stan furrowed his brows. "I threw that shit away as soon as they left. I didn't want any of that Cali-weird stuff in my house."

Ava caught a look from Carol but let it go. They talked a little more, but other than the dinner, they'd had no other interaction with

Cindy Aquino. They walked them through their questions one more time before going back in through the shop's back door. August accompanied Stan to the front. Ava hung back and slipped Carol her card.

"If you think of anything, call. Doesn't matter how small, doesn't matter what time."

Carol nodded, her eyes filling again as she took the card. She pushed it into her bra, hiding it. Interesting.

"Here," Carol said and reached onto a shelf, taking a cellophane bag with a cookie the size of a playing card from a basket. She glanced up at August and Stan before handing it over. "I give these to new customers. It's a business card but, you know in cookie form. The sticker on the back has the store information."

Ava thanked her, dropped the cookie in her messenger bag, and followed her back to the cash register. They thanked Stan and Carol before leaving the store. Out in the parking lot, August leaned in.

"Did you get anything from Carol?"

"Not yet." Ava crinkled the cellophane bag between her fingers. "But we might."

"The first two victims weren't just killed together, they knew each other," August said, beeping the fob at the SUV. "What are the odds they knew Brent?"

"Given his proclivities and Cindy's prostitution arrest, I'd say the odds are good."

"We should take another run at Cutler."

Ava shook her head. "Brent hid his bad habits from his father. But someone else might know about Cindy Aquino's secrets."

August's brows furrowed, "Who?"

"The guy who dropped her charges." She showed him the message from Rondeau about the nightclub sweep where Cindy had been arrested. He'd checked court documents, police records, and witness reports. "Seven arrests. Six charges. The mug shot is missing too."

"Someone pulled Cindy out of it." August shook his head. "That smacks of a special arrangement."

"Deputy District Attorney Jared Iverson." Ava read the name off the file. "I wanna talk to him next."

EIGHT

Located just a few miles from the drive-in crime scene, the Oceanside Police Department headquarters sat in a shopping center surrounded by a credit union, a chiropractic office, a Gas and Go, a nail place, and fast-food restaurants. The fifty-thousand-square-foot law enforcement building housed various divisions, as well as the local library branch at the end of the strip mall. Its Spanish Colonial Revival architecture was a favorite for municipal and civic buildings in Southern California. The red-tiled roof, sand-colored stucco walls, arched entryways, and potted palm trees lent modern echoes to the historic architecture of the area.

They pulled in front of the station a little after five p.m. and Ava's stomach growled, the hamburger from Sandy's a distant dream. A cool breeze washed over the asphalt as the worst of the heat melted into early evening. Manaia met them in the lobby and escorted them through the locked entrance. Inside, the station resembled a political office with an open-plan layout and dozens of desks in the bullpen. A series of workrooms at the end of a long hall housed whiteboards, tables, networked computers, and other supplies needed for casework.

"I set everyone up in the war room," Manaia said. "It's the biggest area we have available."

"What happened with the domestic call?" Ava asked as they walked.

"It's messy. A couple of our illustrious firefighters, who just happen to be brothers, got into it," Manaia shook his head. "It spilled onto the street outside the station. I know one of the guys and offered to help mediate."

"They're in the same house?" August asked, hanging his shades on his collar.

"Not anymore," Manaia said.

They stopped in front of a faux-wood door with an embedded screen window in the center. Inside, Ava saw both Talia and Rondeau working at the large conference table. Manaia swiped his ID fob at the door lock, and it opened with a click. When they entered, the scent of popcorn made Ava's stomach growl.

"Hey!" Talia said, looking up from a file. She'd been working in the field evidence lab and had changed into burgundy scrubs since lunch. "I got something you guys need to see."

Manaia checked his phone. "Sorry, just a sec. OPD detectives are interviewing the staff at Brent's wine room, and we've got a few people left to talk to who worked near the drive-in crime scene. We're pulling any security feeds they have."

"I'm getting them," Rondeau said. "A few guys from Crimes of Violence are going through everything as we speak."

Manaia nodded. "Great. I have to go and help with the interviews, but I'll be back soon." He looked at Ava. "We have an appointment. The construction site manager, the guy whose kid was sick last night? He's coming in to speak with us in forty-five minutes. Earliest he could get here."

"That's perfect." Ava sidled next to Talia and stole a handful of popcorn from her bag.

Manaia pointed at Ava. "You want to do it, right?"

"Is that a serious question?" she asked, stuffing popcorn in her mouth.

"Had to ask. You wanna use the place with the thing in back?"

Ava nodded, and he hurried off, calling, "Forty-five minutes," over his shoulder.

August grabbed a bottle of water and sat down at the table opposite her. "What place is he talking about?"

Ava explained that the powerful and connected witnesses from the madam case negotiated an out-of-the-way place for interviews and meetings. They didn't want to be seen entering and leaving a police station. The DA's office accommodated the request so Ava found a location that offered convenience and cover—a bookstore a few streets over with a café in back that offered privacy.

While they settled in, Ava rattled off a text to Rondeau about the Deputy District Attorney for Cindy's case. His phone dinged. He glanced at it, then looked over at her with a thumbs up. "Already on it."

"Let's get started," August said, taking out his smart pen and tablet. "Martin, let's hear what you have."

Rondeau stood and used a small remote control to light up the display screen hanging on the wall.

"Okay," Rondeau began in his slight West Virginia lilt, "I've been wading through the swamp of social media, phone records, and bank statements for Brent. His social media is a bust. Only has two accounts, and he posts the same thing on both maybe once or twice a year. Generic Christmas graphics and the like. No messages. We'll see what his phone texts have when we get access. He pays someone to run the social media page for the wine tasting room. Nothing personal there. His phone records are forthcoming. His carrier wanted a subpoena and Vincent expedited that. We should get those tomorrow." He clicked the remote to show a screenshot. "Finally, there's a glitch with the bank records, some kind of authorization code I've never seen. I called Vincent on that too. She said we might have to get the lawyers involved."

"I wonder if that isn't the father with second thoughts about allowing access," August asked.

Ava thought August was probably right. Dane's money was mixed up with his son's, which might prove embarrassing if that information got out. She relayed to the group what happened during the visit with Cutler and their meeting with James Wright's parents, Carol and Stan.

Rondeau frowned. "The two vics were dating? Huh. And why would she use a fake name with Wright's parents?"

"Maybe she wanted to hide her identity from them," Ava said. "Question is why?"

"You said we needed to see something?" August asked Talia.

She nodded, wiping her mouth. Standing, she used her secure tablet to cast files and documents onto the wall display screen.

"I noted some preliminary observations during Dr. Cooms autopsy of Brent Cutler. She's writing her report, but there are a few items of interest. First, according to a quick test, he had none of the usual street drugs or alcohol in his system. I asked her to run more extensive tests for synthetic drugs just in case. Also, he sustained multiple contusions to the face prior to death, though not severe enough for COD. Second, he was shot in the forehead, not behind the ear like the first two victims. I leave it to you, my dear, to determine the significance of that, if any."

"I saw that at the scene. Brutal." Ava continued to stuff popcorn in her mouth, glad that Cutler had been right about his son. "And the oil?"

"That's interesting," Talia said, and a series of graphs and printed reports scrolled across the screen as she spoke. "We filtered out the particulates and examined them. They appear to be metal, solvents, and random grit that might be sawdust. I'll have a clearer picture after analysis comes back, but the oil is consistent with a metal shop or mechanic's garage given the grade and additives."

"Let's run a query on local businesses that would have the blue barrels and the oil," August said to Rondeau, who nodded, typing on his keyboard. "I'll ask Detective Manaia to send out someone from Crimes of Violence Unit to ask some questions."

"It's going to be an extensive list," Rondeau said. "This city has a lot of industrial businesses."

"I figured," August said. "I know someone at the California Department of Toxic Substances. They track compliance for hazardous waste like used oil. Maybe they can narrow down the number of businesses for us by compliance issues, type of oil, etc. It will only cover people who actively report on the barrels, but it's a start."

"During the autopsy, we also discovered that Brent Cutler, like the first two victims, exhibited signs of dehydration and shrinking of the stomach. He hadn't eaten in a couple of days."

"So, he was kept like the others before he was killed?" Ava asked.

"All I can tell you is that he was denied food and water in the days before he died," Talia said. "Either by himself or others. But this is also odd." She tapped her tablet. A close-up photo of a decayed female hand appeared, followed by a close-up of the tissue via microscope. "Dr. Tavers mentioned a yellowish discoloration on Cindy Aquino's fingers. Her right hand, thumb, forefinger, and middle finger. He noted the similar but fainter stains on James Wright's fingers as well, but Dr. Cooms and I did not find any staining on Brent Cutler's hands. No ID on the stains yet, but I'll keep you posted."

Ava nodded and turned to August. "I want to know where the barrels came from."

Rondeau swiveled back and forth in his chair, catching popcorn in his mouth. "I mean, I appreciate the confidence in my technical prowess, don't get me wrong. But he asked me for that list, like, two minutes ago."

She shook her head. "I mean the location from which they drifted ashore. Manaia's files mentioned that he talked with Harbor Police when the first two bodies were found."

"You want to speak with them again?"

"I do, yes." Ava checked her watch and stood, grabbing another handful of popcorn. She nodded. "But first, we've got a date with a construction manager."

NINE

The bookstore café fostered an intellectual, university library kind of vibe despite it being sandwiched between a pet supply store and a barber shop. Its logo, a crow standing on a pile of books with a mug of coffee in an outstretched claw, said it all.

Ava nodded to the barista as they strode past hanging plants in copper containers that crowded out the harshest light from the angled sun. They arrived early, so Ava ordered a fudge brownie and an iced mocha, while August asked for tea. While waiting for their order, she sifted through the free flyers and cards on the counter. A bookmark with the café's logo caught her eye. A schedule on the back offered author readings, poetry nights, and a book club. She pocketed it.

When they got their order, they made their way to a gorgeous burlwood desk by the window holding a variety of milks, coffee stirrers, and a broad choice of sweeteners. August fought with the imprecise honey bear dispenser while Ava perused the piles of well-loved paperbacks atop stools and on the ends of the counters. He took a call and peeled away, whispering in the corner before he ended it. The momentary smile afterward told Ava all she needed to know. It wasn't a work call.

They strode to the rear of the bookstore café to a small alcove. Comfy chairs, a settee, and a coffee table filled the space. Like a parlor in an old Victorian home, it set them apart and offered privacy. Ava sank into a wing chair in a chintz pattern, and August took up the end of the settee closest to her. He rubbed his eyelids, stifling a yawn. He never slept well in the field. Manaia texted saying he met the site manager in the parking lot and they were walking over.

"The name thing is strange," August said, stirring his tea. "Why did Cindy Aquino give a false name at dinner? I can see a client if she's a sex worker, but your boyfriend's parents?"

"You know what bugs me more? Let's say she was a yoga instructor like she mentioned. How did she end up getting arrested for prostitution in a sweep, then?" Ava snagged a local art show flyer from a stack on the coffee table and folded it into a paper lily.

"Maybe she turned her life around." August looked at her for a moment. "You and I both know that's possible."

She'd told him about those hard days in her teens. Strawberry-blonde hair, ice-blue eyes, and laughter in the sun flickered up from the depths of the past. She shook her head, banishing the memories.

He opened his mouth to say more, but Manaia and an older man in jeans and a polo walked back. The construction manager introduced himself as Horatio Jones and shook their hands with calloused ones. Natural gray hair cut close to the scalp, laugh lines at the corner of his eyes, he smiled with genuine warmth.

"Sorry I couldn't meet you at the crime scene last night. My kid had an appendicitis attack during a sleepover. She was dancing with her friends in the living room and then just collapsed. The parents called us saying she was already on her way to the hospital." Jones sat down in a chair. A barista brought glasses of water for them, and he drank it, absently rubbing his watch.

"Is she okay?" Ava asked.

He nodded. "Yes, ma'am. They got her into surgery in time. It didn't rupture which was the worry."

"I'm sure you're anxious to get back to your daughter, so I'll just jump into things," Ava said. "Are you catching heat for what happened at the site?"

He blinked, startled. "Yeah, a little."

"What's going on?"

"We kept the site secure with a chain and lock at the front and back gates. The fencing is still solid, and we made repairs. I checked the equipment shed. No vandalism. Nothing stolen."

Manaia slid over a copy of the photo of the destroyed lock he'd shown Ava the night before. "Freshly cut."

"And nothing looked out of place during your walk through?" August asked.

Jones shrugged. "Not really, but it's a construction zone. Nothing stays anywhere for very long."

"So, you closed up," Ava said, drawing in her leather notebook. She sketched out the area in rough blocks. The dump site, the street that ran behind it, the main road, the river walk. She handed Jones her pen. "Show me where you walk when you open up and close down the site."

As he did, something occurred to Ava. The weight. "Mr. Jones, the killer brought a bolt cutter, a shovel, and a blue barrel weighing approximately two hundred pounds. He'd have to deal with a lot of equipment without being seen. You know the site better than anyone. What would be his best approach?"

August produced his tablet with an aerial map of the area. Jones ran his finger along Foussat, a road that ran along the western edge of the property and either cut left into a huge housing development or continued toward the groundwater treatment facility.

"That's a maintenance road?" Ava asked.

"No," Jones said and pointed to a section of the map. "But it branches off into a maintenance road *here*."

"No cameras out there. No houses. No retail or industrial buildings. You could drive a bus through there and no one would notice."

"Wait... no... okay, hold on." Jones raised his index finger, stared into the distance as he thought. "I don't know about a bus, but what about a van?"

She stilled. "What do you mean?"

"I saw one, a couple of days before."

"Tell me," Ava said.

Jones did a security patrol every night before the night crew started. He'd gone to check for vandalism on the portable bathroom and some sheeting at the back of the site. That took him parallel to a maintenance path not accessible from the main road.

"I saw a white van just idling out there. I thought maybe it was the electric guys because it was paneled, you know, not a passenger van."

"Could you see who was driving?" August asked.

Jones shook his head. "It was too dark."

"Can you think of anything else about the van or that night that might help?" August asked.

"Not off the top of my head." He stood. "Look, I'm sorry to cut this short, but I need to get back to my daughter."

Ava rose with him and handed him her card. "If you think of anything, give me a call."

They walked Jones out and then August drove her back to her house, dropping her off at nearly seven in the evening.

Starving, Ava sank into her favorite living room chair, sipping on her mocha, lost in thought as she perused food delivery options, thinking about the white van Jones mentioned. She texted Rondeau about it.

RONDEAU

Do you text Talia this much?

I feel like you brought this on yourself by being a Cyber Samurai.

> This is my burden to bear. I'll give the
> Crimes of Violence team scanning the
> security videos the heads up.

Ava smiled as she put down her phone. She tried to focus on the delivery menu for her favorite Thai place, but images of symbols carved on dead skin floated behind her eyes. She shifted their angles in her memory, contorting the lines, trying to make them fit symbols that she knew, but to no avail. She needed help.

Still, the designs on the bodies reminded her of markings she'd come across in a class she took in junior college before transferring to UCSD. She looked up the OCC website on her phone, navigating the class list, and verified her old professor still taught a 6:30 to 9:30 Humanities class. That meant the professor's class should go on break around eight. Ava checked her watch and raced out the door.

Walking out to her SUV, her phone buzzed. A keyword alert, the kind she would set during a press-heavy case.

The notification read #*Oceanside Police Chief.*

Ava climbed into her car as she clicked a video link. A bright blue chyron reading "Breaking News!" scrolled across the screen. The image switched to a female anchor in a blood-red blouse. She wore a solemn expression, her perfect hair glossy under the studio's lights. She reported that the Oceanside Police Chief, Matt Brower, had released a statement only moments before regarding what online sources were calling The Blue Drum Killer.

The video cut to the police chief in full uniform standing at a podium inside the OPD headquarters talking to the press. Muscles bunched at his jaw as he spoke in clipped sentences, anger smoldering in his eyes. She and August had just left the station, and no one had mentioned anything about a press conference.

Brower's jaw worked and his mouth formed a straight hard line as he answered questions. She watched the video, groaning when the DMV photos of all three victims appeared on screen. He spoke each of their names slowly, solemnly, and then reported that OPD believed they were killed by the same person.

The anchor spoke over the chief's muted video as she stared at the camera with barely concealed triumph.

"CNB News 7 has also received exclusive video from an anonymous source a few minutes ago. This is never-before-seen footage of the moment the body was discovered. We must warn you, what you're about to see may be disturbing."

The screen now showed a grainy, low-light video of a blue barrel dangling from straps attached to a lift bucket. Several construction workers shouted, but the sound of the video was too low. They waved their arms and pointed before one of the straps snapped and the oil drum tumbled onto the ground. The video cut away as the lid popped off, a blur covering Cutler's body before going black.

"What the hell." Ava whispered. "No one said anything about a video."

The anchor, back on screen, shook her head. "This newly released video shows the moment the third victim was discovered. Sources say he was badly beaten and may have been robbed as well."

"Are we just giving them our files now or what?" Ava snapped at the anchor on the screen.

The news reporter revealed that Cindy Aquino had a prior arrest for prostitution and that her mother was a mentally ill homeless person wandering the tunnels of Las Vegas. She disclosed that James Wright never finished high school, lived in an old van, and had a record for dealing narcotics. What the anchor didn't do was bring up the salacious details of Brent's arrest for solicitation or his involvement with a madam. They referred to him as a local business owner with a troubled past. The anchor continued.

"Despite repeated questions by reporters, Chief Brower did not say what many citizens of Oceanside and the surrounding area are thinking. That given the macabre method of disposal and that the cause of death is an execution style bullet behind the victim's ear, all evidence indicates that a serial murderer is stalking the beach cities.

Many are asking what the police are doing to stop The Blue Drum Killer?"

They've already named him. Ava stared out the windshield. Warm light from the setting sun cast the puffy clouds in cotton candy pink against a cobalt sky.

"Dammit, Cutler."

TEN

A blue velvet sky sprinkled with glittering grains of light hovered over the campus as the warm evening sunset dissolved into night. Giant palm trees angled high above the buildings, swaying slightly with the warm breeze as Ava walked onto campus. Soft landscape lights lined the paths leading into the quad. The night class vibe felt like she was walking through a memory, except she didn't fit the timeline anymore. When she started at Oceanside Community College, she'd been twenty and trying to claw her way out of a life spinning out of control. The soaring white sandstone facades, quiet alcoves, and rolling lawns had been her sanctuary. A place of peace and order where she had none.

She strolled through the cool evening toward the Humanities buildings, passing the student store. Tall sidewalk lamps loomed over the pathways, lighting up the campus against the deepening night. The traffic hadn't slowed her down, so she had time to kill. The scent of the food court on the second story pulled her in. She hadn't eaten an actual meal since lunch and decided to grab a quick bite.

In the buffet-style eatery, she ordered a spicy grilled chicken sandwich and a side salad, so the specter of August didn't make her feel like total garbage. She almost snapped a photo of her plate to send as evidence of her healthy choice before remembering his smile at the end of that mystery phone call.

The cafeteria overlooked a grassy knoll currently displaying modern art in the shape of topiary bushes. They depicted marine animals. A dolphin arching mid-flight, an octopus with vine tendrils dangling like arms, and a giant, open clam carved out of a light green bush. Soft lighting installed beneath the topiaries created a sense of movement. Or maybe it was the wind. She found the cookie Carol had given her and dialed the number on the wrapper. It went to voicemail. Ava left a message.

"Hello, Mrs. Ulbreck. This is Agent Cortes from the CBI. We spoke earlier. I just wanted to check in. See how you're doing. I know the news broke about Jimmy's death. Sometimes the press says things that can be tough to take so give me a call if you need anything."

She finished her meal, keeping an eye on the wall clock, making origami frogs out of pages from her notebook until it was time to find Professor Katsaros. When she'd been a student, Katsaros had taken breaks near her classroom door, talking with students, maybe bumming a cigarette because she didn't officially smoke anymore. Ava had liked her from the first class. Katsaros hadn't grown tired of Ava's endless questions or arguments. She'd welcomed the challenge. A celebrated teacher during her university tenure, Katsaros held published works in the field of human culture, particularly societal practices surrounding marriage, birth, and death. After early retirement, she'd taken the adjunct professor job at OCC to stay active in the field. The junior college was lucky to have her.

Just like she had years before, Dr. Katsaros stood with a group of students by her door. She said something, and they all laughed. Ava strode closer, lifting a hand in greeting, wondering if she'd be remembered.

Katsaros stilled, squinted in the overhead light, pulled her glasses down over her eyes and said, "Ava Cortes, as I live and breathe. What are you doing back here?"

"I was hoping for a consult." Ava flashed her badge. The students all looked at the professor, who waved them away and crossed to meet Ava. "I'm surprised you remember me."

"Well, your name does come across my news feed every now and again," she said with a smirk. "You're a little notorious, aren't you?"

Ava chuckled. "Not sure my boss would phrase it as nicely."

Dr. Katsaros still wore her hair in a shaggy, rock and roll kind of cut, only now, a swath of silver-gray hair fell over her intelligent eyes. A Bauhaus band T-shirt tied at the waist, an ankle-length black skirt, and combat boots gave her a soft Gen X vibe. She smiled and offered Ava a clove cigarette, which she took. The school banned smoking, so they walked off a bit, away from people.

"A friend brings these when she visits from Vegas," Dr. Katsaros said, patting her pockets. "I can't get them around here anymore."

"That's probably because they're illegal in California." Ava pulled a lighter from her messenger bag. She lit the professor's first, and then her own.

Dr. Katsaros grinned. "I won't tell on you then."

"This is probably the least of my boss's concerns, Professor."

"Please, Ava, I think we're more colleagues now than student and teacher, don't you think? Call me Helena." She leaned against the building. "I heard you went on to UCSD. What's it been, a decade?"

"Give or take. I transferred right after your class," Ava said, relishing the candy taste of the clove.

"Someone said you studied chaos?"

Ava nodded. "Amongst criminology and complex systems. One of the systems I covered extensively during my studies was social behavior. Particularly criminal culture."

Helena took a drag, considering Ava as she let smoke escape from the corner of her mouth in a lazy rivulet. "Your Constellation of Crime Theory?"

The reason behind the theory, the face that haunted her dreams, flashed into Ava's mind. She gritted her teeth and nodded. "That's the one."

"I've mentioned your paper to my classes, you know. We discussed your theory about crime organizations and how their interconnectedness is both their strength and their weakness."

"They didn't buy it, huh?"

"Oh, many did," Helena nodded, gazing into the distance. "It was a lively discussion. However, many also questioned your assertion that you could follow those connections to finding a particular person."

"Unfortunately for the bad guys, the criminal world is both small and incestuous in its ties. A microcosm that small breeds too many connections to hide from someone who knows how to find them. Trust me, I'll show them it's possible."

"Pretty cool that this theory, born right here, is helping you all the way up in the CBI," Helena said, shaking her head slowly.

"That's actually why I'm here. I'm working a case and need your expertise."

"I'm intrigued."

Ava reached into her messenger bag, pulling out her tablet. "You taught a section on ancient symbolism in the new world. I think I've come across something in a case the CBI is investigating. I was wondering if you could give me your opinion on some symbols?"

"Of course. What kind of case?"

Ava weighed her words. "Symbols were found on victims of a homicide, carved into the skin. The images I'm about to show you are a little graphic."

"I'm even more intrigued." Helena took the tablet Ava handed her and slipped on her glasses. "Oh wow! These are atrocious."

Swiping through them slowly, Ava explained the basics of the case. She went over the victimology and the autopsy findings of the etched skin postmortem. She also brought up the ingredients in the poultice.

"Sea salt, India ink, and coconut oil are natural," Ava said. "The UV binder seems to be the only outlier ingredient."

"Alright, first of all, these may not be symbols. Not in the sense that I think you mean. When they're carved into the skin like this, on the hands and the forehead, the chest, that's where we commonly see the placement of sigils."

"What's the difference?"

"Symbols are solely a visual representation of a concept, like the dollar sign. But a sigil has intent. They're often used during a ritual to evoke outcomes or manifest something like protection." Helena tilted the tablet, peering at it like a piece of art. "Though I haven't encountered these sigils before, they usually represent elements like fire, or even concepts like the spirit realm. Sometimes even belief systems, like a cross or a pentacle." She continued to zoom in and out of the pictures before continuing, "If I had to guess, I'd say these fall closer to the latter."

"Are you saying these symbols are religious?" Ava asked.

"I wouldn't go so far as to say they're religious, but based on the design, order, and use of symbolic patterns, I'd wager they're part of someone's belief system, though I don't know how organized that system is. This is highly esoteric, not at all mainstream. This appears to be more of a potpourri situation."

Ava narrowed her gaze. "You think the killer mixed ideas?"

Helena nodded. "It's a good bet, actually," she pointed to a symbol in the group. "See this one? I haven't seen anything like this before. It has all of these elongated ovals with pointed ends, do you see?"

Ava nodded. "Do you think it's the unsub's design?"

"Possibly." She put her hands up. "I could be wrong. I don't know every symbol out there, but it's odd. Like a shape you'd see designed, not necessarily rendered by mathematics or nature."

"Can you give me any direction where to start looking? A name of a group?"

Helena slipped her glasses off and chewed on the end of the arm. "Moon worship can be either feminine or masculine. But the Mother Night symbol used in these is evoked mostly when the moon disappears."

"Like an eclipse?"

"Absolutely. Also, the lunar cycle has three days of darkness. In some belief systems, particularly agricultural ones, moonlight, dying to darkness as it wanes, and then reappearing can represent renewal. Rebirth."

"Cycles," Ava mused. "Patterns in the ether."

Helena handed back Ava's tablet. "It is a very unique mix of ideas. But the sea salt and the ash, the coconut oil are all associated with the beach, aren't they? Given our proximity to the ocean, I'd start there."

"Ash?"

"India ink is made with carbon black, essentially soot from burning wood. Something we see often in bonfires, on the beach, for instance."

"Regardless of their different origins. When you look at the symbols the killer chose, do they tell a story somehow? Could the killer be sending a message?"

"That's an interesting question." Helena took another drag, her gaze on the photos as she mused. "I think the answer lies in the construction of the message rather than the message itself."

Ava shook her head. "I don't understand."

Helena flicked the ash off her clove. "This all feels very ritualistic. The preparation and application of a substance to the body after death is personal. Intimate. However, the manner of death, it strikes a wrong note, no?"

"The execution-style shot behind the ear." Ava nodded. "It's discordant. Brutality followed with care and preparation of the body. Do you think it could be remorse on the killer's part?"

"If it was, I doubt they would've shot all three victims," Helena said. "This treatment of the victim is discordant in a way I don't even think the killer realizes. The skin isn't just decorated, it's carved with ideas, beliefs the killer used their bodies to display."

"He sees them as possessions."

"Well definitely his in some way. Add to the mix the act of

stuffing a fellow human into an oil barrel and then discarding them like trash, and you get a portrait of a person who is unspeakably callous. And yet, there is the burial care. It's as if the relationship with the victim is almost..."

"Dysfunctional," Ava finished.

Helena nodded. "We have to consider, given the taking of life, that the scarification done to the bodies afterward was not likely a ceremonial rite the victims consented to."

"You think the killer was establishing ownership?"

Helena shrugged. "Now we're getting into the criminal mind. That type of psychopathy is more your field of expertise, I would imagine."

Ava shut off her tablet, aware of the time. "What do you think about the glowing element to the sigils?"

"Sticking with the natural materials and beach theme, perhaps the UV is meant to mimic the bioluminescent power of sea creatures like jellyfish and krill."

Ava stubbed out the half-finished clove cigarette with her boot, then picked up the butt, slipping the rest of it into the front pocket of her bag.

"Let me ask you this," she said. "Could these ideas actually be part of a cohesive organization or does this feel like something out of a psychopath's twisted mind?"

"Why not both?"

"Professor—"

Helena chuckled. "I'll tell you what I've seen here with my students. Unless deeply tied to a prior religious family culture, and sometimes because they *are* bound to an inherited belief system, modern young adults seem drawn to an à la carte version of their parent's beliefs. They tend to graze. To take what they need from different systems and use them as a self-help salad. At least for a time."

"So, this could be a personal belief system?"

"Sure." Helena smiled. "The best way to find out who practices a system of belief is to find out who it's supposed to serve."

"Supposed to?" Ava asked.

"Yes. Often with these kinds of groups, we find it isn't always who we think." She looked over at the students shuffling toward the classroom. "Let me know how this goes, if you can. Hopefully I'll see you again before another ten years go by." She winked and walked around the corner to her classroom.

As Ava made her way back to the parking lot, she passed a student store employee handing out study session snacks from a basket. He tossed her a free snack bar, and she caught it, smiling her thanks. Shoving it into her messenger bag, she chuckled when she saw a seagull walk from underneath a patio table and pass her nonchalantly with a fry in its beak. Ava dug around the bottom of her bag for her keys but stilled when she spotted a young woman staring at her from across the quad.

Long, flowy gauzy dress, hair braided in a crown atop her head, yellow flowers tucked in. Like she just finished walking through a meadow in a shampoo commercial. Though she stood partially in shadow, Ava could swear she was the same young woman who'd threatened death at the Cutler mansion.

Ava took a step toward her. "Hey, do I know you?"

The young woman stared at her, then turned and rushed into the student store a few feet away. Ava hurried after her, slipping past a group of laughing students. She moved quickly through the store, peering down each aisle of books, toiletries, and snacks until she spotted the young woman near the PE equipment. She stood with her back turned, facing the tubes of tennis balls.

"Excuse me," Ava said, reaching for her. "Miss—"

The young woman whirled, fury on her face as she swung a tennis racket at Ava's head.

Years of practicing katas and muscle memory kicked in. Ava blocked most of the blow, but the odd shape of the racket slammed into her forehead. Pain exploded at her brow. Her body went on autopilot, slamming her palm into the girl's solar plexus. The girl flew backward, landing on her back as the racket went clattering away.

The young woman screamed, her face turning red. Ava's hand went to the holster under her blouse as the girl scrambled to her feet. She backed up a few steps, then turned and sprinted for the front door. Ava chased after her, blood obscuring her vision from the cut to her brow. She chased the girl until they hit a crowd of students. Ava spotted papers and coffee on the ground surrounding a shocked middle-aged man who staggered to his feet.

She scanned the crowd. Her gaze jumped from student to student, searching for fair hair, the dress. Nothing.

Her fingers swiped at the cut above her eye as she looked down, wincing at what she saw.

A ring of dandelions lay trampled on the sidewalk.

ELEVEN

Face hot, breath ragged, fury blazed through Sky as she walked stiffly through the music building. She shouldn't run. That would make people look. She stopped herself from glancing back to see if the agent had figured out where she'd gone. Taking a deep breath, she tried to stop the shaking of her hands, the pounding of her heart, the rush of adrenaline that made her want to both laugh hysterically and scream.

"That bitch," Sky whispered. Again and again, as shame washed over her. The agent had stopped her like she was nothing. And she wasn't even taller than Sky!

Sky had seen the customers' faces in the student store when Ava threw her. Their smirks and whispers. She balled her hands into fists, gasping for cleansing breaths while stabbing her fingernails into the flesh of her palm as she strode out the back of the building to the overflow parking lot. There, she unlocked her electric scooter from the rack, climbed on, and took off like a shot.

When Sky had seen the agent outside the Cutler mansion, it felt like a cold stone in her gut, the idea of them closing in on them. Then she'd gone and threatened one of them. She shouldn't have done that, the throat slicing gesture. The threat had drawn attention to herself, to them.

Stomach squirming, she took the side roads, running through the situation in her head, working on the right kind of answers before he found out what happened. Figuring out what to say and what she hoped to keep secret. It all started with the construction crew the other night.

Sky worked evenings until midnight at the Coffee Corner, a small hut at the edge of a parking lot a mile down the road from the beach. A throughway for people heading inland for clubs or restaurants, cars pulled into the lot, drove up to the one-window stall, ordered a drink, and idled while Sky made it. Hot summer nights were good for business, and the frosty drinks coming out of the blender kept them coming.

Cramped, with nothing but a clip-on fan to keep cool, she liked not having to work with anyone. They always ended up starting shit with her. During her shift, she made the drinks, worked the small register, and ran to the grocery store across the lot for more supplies when the mini fridge ran low on all the different milks and syrups. The customers usually chatted with whoever was in their car or listened to the radio while they waited with their windows open. Some tried to talk with her, but she pretended not to hear them over the engine and blender until they gave up. Mostly, they acted like she wasn't even there, but her sparkling smile kept the tip jar full, so she didn't care.

One night, a couple of days after she and Hunter had dealt with their Brent problem, she'd been daydreaming at work, thinking about making out with Hunter, worried he was getting shaky in his resolve, wondering what she could do about it. She thought maybe she should take him to a class when she caught a snippet of conversation.

An older couple ordered a few drinks and a heated muffin to share. She threw the pastry in the microwave and started on the first mocha while they chatted about something going on at the old drive-in property. Police activity. Sky froze, her scoop of ice hovering over the blender as she listened.

"Oh yeah, there are all kinds of cop cars over there, and one of those coroner vans," the older woman said to the man behind the wheel. "I'd never actually seen a coroner van before! I heard the crew found a body in a barrel."

Sky cobbled the drinks together as fast as she could, and as the couple pulled away, she pulled in the tip jar from the shelf outside the window, put out the closed sign, and shut the hut down. Texting her boss, she claimed food poisoning and then shut off her phone. She didn't want to hear his complaints.

She unchained her electric scooter, climbed aboard, and headed back out to the drive-in construction site. There, she hiked toward the crime scene the back way. A group of giant old pepper trees swayed in the night wind, and she used them for cover. Creeping as close as she could to the yellow crime scene tape, she watched the forensic people in paper overalls take samples while a man spoke with a woman just inside the crime scene tent. Police lights lit her face in red, then blue, then red again as she talked with the guy in a Hawaiian shirt.

Sky couldn't hear them, but saw the man point to the bulldozer with straps hanging from it. The construction workers had tried to lift the blue barrel, the straps broke, and Brent's body had tumbled out like some kind of slimy octopus's baby. Sky saw Brent's leg bent all weird when they lifted the sheet and had to stifle an errant giggle. Hunter had really messed the guy up to get him into the container. Brent's bones had sounded like branches snapping when he'd done it.

More cops came and started walking with flashlights along the back of the property. Too close for comfort. But she'd seen enough. She drove back to her apartment, her grip on the handles so tight her knuckles ached as she thought about him.

"He won't find out," she whispered to the trees. "He won't."

News of the murder had hit the following morning. Reporters said that the CBI was now in charge of Cutler's murder. She didn't know what that was, so she looked it up. They were state agents with federal powers. A few videos mentioned past cases, and articles reported on an Agent Ava Cortes who had been investigated for violence. In one of the videos, a news creator named Ricki Rogers had called Agent Cortes a huntress. That had set Sky off, and she'd wrecked her room as she raged about the unfairness of it.

Afterward, she'd gotten dressed and headed to the Cutler Mansion, where she figured the reporters were hanging out. She saw Ava Cortes there again, pulling past the crowd at the gate, flashing her badge like she owned the place. She'd argued with a big, handsome agent then they left together.

The woman's energy felt like trouble. Hostile, even. As their SUV pulled away, Agent Cortes scanned the crowd as if looking for her, and when they locked eyes, Sky couldn't help herself. She wanted to prove she was a huntress too, so she made the throat-slit gesture. She shouldn't have done it.

She'd expected a scared or shocked look on the agent's face.

She got something else.

Cold fascination, a kind of zeroing-in that Sky sometimes saw in the hawks that hunted in the marsh behind her apartment building.

After Cutler's house, she told Hunter about Agent Cortes. After she got him to stop hyperventilating, she told him they were going to keep everything to themselves. The body, the CBI, all of it for now. They vowed to steer clear of any place that could be associated with Brent. In fact, that night, the only reason Sky found herself at the community college was because her boss had made her drop off coupons on the campus offering a buy-one-get-one-free iced mocha deal if they showed their student ID when ordering.

Sky shook her head, angry tears whipping past her temples as she drove the scooter at breakneck speed through the night. That construction site was supposed to be abandoned. It had been for literally months when they buried Brent there. She'd watched it for weeks before.

"Why do things *always* go wrong for me!" she shouted at the night.

At her apartment, she parked and went inside. In her room, she slipped her dress off and stared at her bare breasts in the cheap mirror hanging on the back of her bedroom door. An angry red mark covered the area just beneath her chest bone. Probing the spot with her fingers, she winced, and a wave of nausea moved through her. No one hit her anymore. *No one.*

Sky screamed. Ripped the mirror off the back of the door. Stomped on it, shattered it. People always tried to ruin things for her, but not this time. Not again. The CBI didn't know who they were dealing with. She had power, *real power*, and he wouldn't allow anything to happen to her.

TWELVE

After her tussle with the hippie chick in the student store, Ava went home, cleaned the cut above her eye and used some tension tape to hold it together under a bandage. With the coverage of Brent's death, Ava wanted to make sure she didn't miss anything, especially from those who knew him best. She decided to crash the last two AA meetings offered that night. Both of them were duds. Exhausted, Ava went home and fell asleep with an ice pack on her face.

The following morning, she woke up with a purple bruise under her left eye and thought it might work in her favor at the AA meeting that morning. Hurrying to get ready, she replaced the bandage she'd put on the night before and called it good enough. Light traffic had her sliding into the strip mall's parking lot with a few minutes to spare.

With a headache brewing behind her brow, she joined a group of people making their way into a storefront. The space had an open arrangement. A coffee and cookie table in back, and rows of chairs facing a podium up front. Ava looked around, happy to see a larger crowd than she had seen at the previous night's meetings.

The crowd milled around inside, getting coffee, talking, and snacking on cookies. She joined them, grabbing a coffee and nodding to the woman next to her. The older woman took one look at Ava's bruised face and gave her a sympathetic smile.

Ava's phone buzzed. The heartbeat pattern of a call. When she spotted August's number, she moved toward a quiet corner to answer.

"What's up?"

"The team is meeting at OPD in a half an hour—" A group of guys near her laughed at a joke, and August paused. "Where are you?"

She looked at the Styrofoam cup in her hand and said, "I'm getting coffee."

"Why do you sound weird?"

"I don't sound weird. You sound weird." A man walked up to the podium and smiled at the crowd. The conversations quieted, and people headed for the chairs. "I'll see you at the meeting," she said and hung up.

Taking a seat, Ava sipped the bitter drink, a flutter of guilt in her gut. August wasn't being reasonable. She was just observing, really. Ava thought the very public death of a regular attendee might get mentioned, but the meeting seemed to progress as normal. They talked about what they could control and what they couldn't. About thankfulness and the determination to work the program. Ava ignored the time, unwilling to leave early in case someone said something useful. They didn't.

Once the meeting broke, she loitered for a few minutes outside the storefront with the ones who smoked. She stood off to the side, checking traffic and alternate routes to the police station. She was definitely going to be late and dug in her bag for her keys when she heard a man talking with a woman a few feet away say Brent Cutler's name.

Trucker cap, movie poster T-shirt, and jeans. He wore his scraggly hair long, which paired nicely with the handlebar mustache that captured all the smoke drifting out of his lips. He shook his head.

"I didn't know that Brent was in that much trouble. I mean he just said he was trying to help a friend."

"That's terrible," said the woman in an expensive business suit. "I heard him speak once. He seemed like a pretty good guy."

Mustache guy nodded. "Yeah, and he was just trying to do something good, to make things right, you know?"

Ava pulled the unfinished clove cigarette from her bag's front pocket, put it to her lips and walked up. "Can I bother you for a light?"

He nodded, reaching over. "You're new?"

"I guess you could say that. I'm uh, having a hard time. I lost someone I've known for years," she said and looked away. "I just found out last night he was murdered. It's horrible. The news is victim blaming. Again."

Out of the corner of her eye, she caught the man and woman glance at each other, a tacit agreement.

Mustache guy said, "Are you talking about the victim they found at the drive-in?"

Ava nodded, wiping her watering eye. It stung with smoke. "Did you know him?"

"Just that his name was Brent." The woman sipped her coffee. "The rest we found out how anyone finds anything out anymore. The media." She was younger than the man, maybe early thirties. Muted makeup and nails said business professional, maybe a lawyer.

"I didn't realize he was in so deep," Ava said, trying to start up the conversation they'd been having before.

Mustache guy looked at her for a beat and then nodded slowly. "Yeah, rescuing a friend in trouble shouldn't cost you your life."

"Maybe we should go to the police or something," the woman said. "An anonymous letter, maybe?"

Not a lawyer.

"And say what?" Mustache guy's eyes held a defeated look. "I got no name and no actual understanding of the situation. Just that a guy

I know was trying to do something good, to make things right, and then ended up dead."

"I wonder if they're okay," Ava muttered. "The friend."

"Do you think maybe it's someone he met from the Sea Sirens?" the woman asked.

Ava shrugged.

Mustache guy cut her a look. "How well did you know him?"

"More than most, probably," Ava said. "He seemed to be rebuilding his life."

"Yeah, well, it's all getting dredged up now," Mustache guy said. "Seems like your mistakes follow you, even into death."

Ava thought about that on her way to the police station. About Brent and his troubled, mysterious friend. He'd spoken about them both to his father and his fellow addicts. There had to be something there. She called the Medical Examiner's office, got passed around until they connected her with Dr. Tavers.

"Hey there," she began. "I know we have them identified, but I wanted to also run the victims' DNA through CODIS and GenBank. See what pops."

"What are you looking for?" Tavers sounded intrigued.

"Not sure yet. I'll know it when I see it."

THIRTEEN

Ava walked into the war room at the Oceanside Police Department twenty minutes late, head pounding. August and Talia sat at the conference table talking to Rondeau, who stood with his tablet in hand while some kind of graphic played on the display screen. Ava slipped into the empty seat next to August, apologized for her tardiness, and pulled out her leather notebook and fountain pen. She looked up to find everyone staring at her.

"What?" Ava asked.

August's gaze lingered on the bandage over her brow. "What happened to your eye?"

"Oh, that," she said, waving his comment away. "Nothing."

"Nothing?" Talia piped up. "You look like you've been jumped."

"I do not. It's just a purple spot by my nose, I'm fine. I promise."

August leaned back, rubbing one eye with the palm of his hand. "Tell me I'm not going to get a call about this."

"I would, but my slightly uptight new boss has repeatedly asked that I not withhold the truth." August narrowed his eyes, but she didn't miss the twitch in the right one. "Wow, ok. For your information, a *teeny* incident occurred at the junior college last night." She fished a bottle of aspirin from the depths of her messenger bag, reached over and washed down four with the water bottle next to August.

"Tell me what happened." August took in a long breath through his nose. "All of it."

"All of it. Okay" Ava leaned back to stare at the ceiling. "When we were leaving the Cutler mansion, we drove past a crowd by the gate, remember?"

August nodded.

"Well, some little manic hippie chick made a throat cutting gesture at me as we were passing."

The minuscule nerve at the corner of August's eye was getting a workout. "I only understood half of that."

"Why are you just mentioning this now?" Talia's brow creased.

"Because it wasn't a real threat."

"Clearly," August said, gesturing at her face.

Ava rolled her eyes. "I ran into her again last night at the junior college and she whacked me with a tennis racket in the student store. It wasn't a big deal."

"Did she sneak up on you or something?" Rondeau asked. "Aren't you, like, a ninja?"

"No. I walked right up to her," Ava muttered. "And then I lost her."

"Why were you there in the first place?" Talia asked.

"I needed a consult—"

Detective Manaia walked into the war room. His eyes grew wide when he saw her.

Ava pointed at him. "Don't even start."

The team shuffled to start the meeting. Manaia went first, as he had another meeting after. While he handed out papers, August leaned in close, his breath at her ear.

"Do I smell cloves?"

She fought a grin. "I was talking to someone this morning who was smoking."

He raised a brow. "He must have been standing awfully close."

Ava turned her attention back to the case files as Manaia updated them on the canvass done by the Crimes of Violence Unit by the drive-in crime scene. After the Chief of Police announced a serial killer, the tip line was getting more calls than they could handle and they were pulling in help from Vista PD.

"We're getting sightings of blue oil drums everywhere," Manaia said. "The cameras surrounding the drive-in crime scene are another story. There's nothing out there, really, as I'm sure you've all seen. We hit businesses up and down Mission Avenue, going both ways, checking for footage. There might be something on a few gas station security feeds. We're looking now. And I'm checking the license plate readers for a few days before and after the body dump to see if we catch any vehicles casing the area. Maybe we'll get lucky."

"And the watch?" Ava asked, checking her notes.

"I just received the insurance photos and descriptions from the vic's father." Manaia slid printed copies across the table to each of them. "Insurance puts the watch's value at a little over fifty thousand dollars. It's also engraved," he said and held up his copy of the back of the watch face. It read: *To my son, from a proud father.* "I pushed out a bulletin on the piece and have a couple detectives from the unit going to pawn shops and making calls."

When he finished, Rondeau stood. "Speaking of insurance, we heard back about Brent's life insurance policy. He never removed his wife Cassandra as the beneficiary." A series of official-looking forms slid onto the display screen. "Since Cassandra lives in London now, we have someone from the International Crime Coordination Center speaking to the Metro Police out there to get a statement. She's not a suspect, but the policy amount warrants a conversation. It's three million dollars."

"Any sign of the white panel van Horatio Jones described?" Ava asked, flipping to her notes on the interview. "He mentioned it had been in the area two days before the body was discovered. I'll bet the killer was casing the area before the body dump. They would have no way of knowing from the locked down site that construction would start up again days later."

Rondeau pointed at Ava. "Thanks for mentioning that, Rocky. I saw your report on the network. We're looking for it as well." The display screen darkened, and he brought up a photo of the construction site map with red dots on the surrounding building roofs. "This is a map of the CCTV and surveillance cameras. We've been processing whatever Detective Manaia sends our way. So far, we've eliminated most of the businesses nearby along Mission Avenue leading to and away from the drive-in site. We're still waiting on parking lot cameras from a shooting range, an HVAC place, and the nearby skate park."

"And the water treatment facility?" Ava pointed at a large structure.

"They should have cameras on the maintenance road going in. I'm not sure how far down their surveillance spans. Add to that how overgrown it is out there and we're looking at low visibility. I pulled the security feed anyway. You never know. I once found a target's face in the reflection of a garden gazing ball."

Ava chuckled. "Did we get into Brent's financials yet? Or his phone?"

Rondeau spun the pen in his fingers and looked at August. "I'll leave that for the head honcho to answer."

August wore the ghost of a smile. Always so damn serious. "I spoke with OPD's Financial Crimes Unit. It turns out the code Rondeau found earlier banning access to the bank account was some kind of DOJ hold that shouldn't be there. I kicked the situation up to Vincent and the lawyers. She'll get us what we need." August tapped his smart pen on the tablet in his hand. "Brent's personal and business phone records should release today. Voicemail, texts, emails, browser history. I know you're juggling a lot, but dive in as soon as you can." Rondeau gave a salute before looking back at his tablet. August turned to Talia. "Dr. Clay?"

She motioned to Rondeau, who laced his fingers together,

cracked his knuckles, and then tapped on his laptop. A few seconds later, a computer model appeared on the display screen. A rendering of the body and the barrel played, illustrating how the killer positioned various limbs and the subsequent breaks to the victim's legs and spine. The model also indicated the height of the fluid inside the barrel. She walked them through the newly completed autopsy report, elaborating on questions and clarifying answers.

"Dr. Cooms ran the bullet retrieved from the victim's skull through the ballistic database. Only hits in the system were for the bullets from the first two victims. The .22 short cartridge is commonly used in pocket pistols and mini revolvers. Mainly used as self-defense weapons or by recreational shooters as quiet rounds."

Ava wrote herself a note. "I'll start a query on deaths with that caliber in the area, focusing on young adults."

Rondeau reached into his bag and pulled out a stack of papers. "Done. You're welcome to take a second look, but we're not seeing anything close within the past three years."

Ava glanced at the pile of incident reports. "Did I ever mention that you're the coolest computer guru I've ever met?"

"Can you make that my name in your phone?" he said with a grin.

Talia flipped through her report. "Next one, Martin."

"On it, ma'am." He tapped, and several images of Brent Cutler's autopsy appeared on the display screen. Draped with blue sterile towels, his bruised skin looked pale as marble. Rondeau zoomed in on a close-up photo of Brent's face and neck.

Talia used her pointer. "The barrel in which the victim was entombed was not full and the report noted a strange substance in the nasal cavity and under the eyelids. Dr. Cooms inspected the substance with a scope. We're waiting on the results of the samples she took."

"Do you have a guess on what the substance could be?" Ava asked.

"I'd really need the labs back before I can provide an opinion, but it doesn't appear to be metal shavings or sawdust like the particulates pulled from the oil," Talia said, sitting down. "It appears organic."

"Any idea how it got there?" August asked.

"It looks like someone blew it in his face." Talia shrugged. "I'll have to wait for the data before I can say more."

"Can I show them the eyeball?" Rondeau asked Talia, who nodded. A shot of Brent's eye flashed onto the screen.

"This is interesting. I ran tests on the vitreous humor—that's the gel-like substance of the eye. Standard tests like an electrolyte analysis, ketone and glucose levels, metabolites, drugs, and so forth. I found that his sodium concentration was way off, which is a marker for dehydration."

"He'd been in captivity for a day or two without water. Like the first two victims." Beside Ava, August pulled on his chin. She knew he was thinking the same thing she was. "Three is a pattern, August. I think somebody is holding these people before killing them."

"We need more than patterns. We need to know how the three victims are connected." August shook his head. "The two kids seem to have been dating. But where does Brent Cutler come in?"

"Back to his old habits?" Rondeau offered. "He had a problem with women, younger ones at that."

Ava shook her head. "He never thought of them as friends though."

"What's that?" August asked.

"Just musing," Ava said.

"I'm going to have Dr. Tavers pull the first two victims from frozen storage and I'll scope their nasal cavities and lungs to check for the presence of the substance we found in Brent," Talia said. "That's all I have until more tests drop."

Manaia stood, gathering his things. "The toxicology and pathology reports are at the top of the list. You should have more information soon."

Ava flipped through her notebook. "Before you leave, I still haven't seen the missing person's report filed for Cindy Aquino."

"I put a call in to the Family Protection Task Force. They handle that. A Sergeant Rossi should be giving you a call soon."

"And the Deputy District Attorney who dropped her prostitution case?" Ava asked. "Jared Iverson."

"I'm running that down," August said. "I left a message yesterday afternoon at his office. Left your number and told him to call you ASAP."

Manaia gave them all a wave as he walked out. August turned to Ava when the door closed. "You said something about a consult?"

She filled them in on what Professor Katsaros had said about the symbols, the natural ingredients of the poultice, and what it might mean. She explained the culled-together ideas from different belief systems. A memory of an indigenous woman she'd once interviewed, her chin and cheeks adorned with tattooed symbols of identity, family, and honor, bubbled up, the woman's markings burning bright in her memory.

"A rite of passage," Ava said to herself, then turned to Rondeau. "I was thinking about symbols and ritual marking of bodies. Do your abilities include grabbing the shapes of the symbols the killer carved on the victims and creating a line drawing of them?"

"You wound me," Rondeau said, glancing up at the screen. "You want it all black?"

"As clear as you can make the shapes, however you can do it." When she saw his quizzical look, she said, "Just a hunch. Can you run them through the tattoo database?"

He said he could.

Ava continued. "I left a message for Dr. Masters, at the Behavioral Sciences Unit about the symbols to get a second source. He wrote a book on ritual killers, so I wanna pick his brain. I also sent a message to a consultant who knows a lot about covens, preppers, activists, exotic supplies vendors, and other communities in the area associated with fringe practices."

August narrowed his gaze at her. "Is this consultant Denny?"

An old hacker friend from her wild days, Denny had a tendency to dance along the razor's edge of legal way too often for August's taste.

She smiled. "I can't help it that he travels in those circles."

"What, is he a warlock or something?" Rondeau asked.

"He's been known to attend a solstice bonfire or two, maybe the occasional hoodoo ceremony, depending on the girl," Ava said with a smirk, ignoring August's annoyed look. "I just think that the CBI questioning these groups might not be as fruitful as what he could get with a friendly chat as a customer."

They tabled the issue and broke after a few more minutes of back and forth between Rondeau, who fully bought into all kinds of superstitious phenomena, and Talia, who lived and died by science. Ava was with Rondeau. She'd seen some things she didn't care to try to explain.

When Rondeau and Talia left to get to work, August and Ava sat alone in the war room. His gaze settled on her, a wisp of a frown on his lips. His pale blue button-up shirt, rolled at the sleeves again, navy chino pants, and bespoke lace-up boots gave him a tough, but refined vibe. She'd always liked his style.

"Spill it," she said with a smile.

"You need to get that looked at by an actual doctor," he said finally.

She waved the comment away. "I don't want the paperwork. Besides, the tape is working. It's not even bleeding anymore."

He leaned back into the chair, crossing his arms. "We need to find out who this young woman is. She threatened you and then attacked you. Do you think she followed you to the community college?"

"I don't see how. It was a last-minute decision." Ava's eyes blurred as she looked through August, remembering. "She acted, I don't know, shocked to see me there, honestly."

"I want you to work with a sketch artist or do an Identi-Kit on the tablet. Get your impressions down. We'll put out a likeness."

"I will. But first, I wanna talk to the Harbor Police. I know

Manaia said they already spoke, but something feels off about the whole thing. How did the bodies of local people end up on our beach if they were taken out to sea? Shouldn't they be further down?"

"I'm glad you said that." August pushed back from the table. "Because we're meeting with Captain Valencia of the Harbor Police in an hour."

"Really?" Ava grinned.

"The currents bothered me too."

"I don't care what people say, you're way more than just good looks."

"Who says that?"

"Can we get coffee on the way? The stuff I had this morning sucked."

FOURTEEN

If a Maine fishing town and a Southern California surf commune had a love child, it would be Oceanside Harbor Village. Along the north edge of Oceanside, the harbor with its bright seaport-style clapboard shops offered eateries, tour outfitters, kites and souvenirs, even candy stores. Ice cream stands and shaved ice huts sold frozen sugar to thirsty tourists already sunburned at ten thirty in the morning.

August took them along the curving main road past the shops, the small vessels bobbing in the crystalline water just off the boardwalk, and along the red metal gazebos over cement picnic table sets.

They drove along the shore, the village to their left and the sea on their right as they made their way toward the harbor and jetty. The red and white striped Oceanside lighthouse, though only ever an observation deck and not a functioning beacon, sat in the center of the village, surrounded by fluttering swags of red and blue triangular flags. Palm trees swayed in a cool breeze that brought with it the constant calls of seagulls. August drove around a huge brick rotunda and parked in a spot at the edge of the sand.

Ava could see the jetty from the car, and they hiked across the sand, skirting blankets and canopies, to the jagged rocks.

They climbed the jagged rocks, walking along the broken side-walk surface. Sailboats drifted lazily out of the harbor's mouth to the ocean, their sails rippling with the rising heat off the rocks. August stood next to her, one hand in his pants pocket, the other holding a bottle of organic green juice. Ava didn't even know juice could be green. The wind whipped at his hair, and a memory rose of the first time they'd gone out on his family's boat. The warmth of his hand at her waist, his breath on her cheek the moment before he kissed her. It had never entered her mind that they wouldn't last.

Clearing her throat, she forced herself to look out at the water. To focus on the task at hand. They waited in comfortable silence on the jetty for ten minutes until Captain Valencia jogged over. In uniform, he peeled his cap off when he walked up. Late forties, light brown hair, hazel eyes with weathered skin and a sun-kissed glow that spoke of a life spent on the water.

"Sorry for the wait, we have the flotilla for the fireworks setting up and that's causing some issues." He shook hands and then looked back at the harbor. "You had some questions about the currents and those blue drums that washed in?"

"The report said you were the first responder at the scene," August said.

"Yeah, that's right. We ramp up patrol during the summer months. The warmer weather brings homeless camps, party boats, and drunk tourists. I was on duty when the call about the barrels came in. Nasty business."

He explained that because Oceanside doesn't require a fishing license for angling off the pier or the jetty, they got a lot of regulars, but no names. One of the guys, a possibly unhoused man named Cliff, called 911 about the barrels on an old payphone near the parking lot.

"There are still payphones?" August asked.

"Yeah," Ava said. "Lots of people still use them."

"Mostly the homeless and street kids, but she's right," Valencia said. "Anyway, I showed up to check out the barrels, and they felt heavy, you know, and something was moving around when I jostled them. I rolled one a little and the smell nearly bowled me over. I called in forensics because we've seen drops like this by cartels, though that's usually further south. The field medics took readings or something and then just hauled everything back to their lab. I heard it was bodies inside the next day."

"Are there any security cameras out here?" Ava asked, glancing around.

"Nah, the kids would just spray them with black paint anyway. We have some covering the parking lot and the company that services the RV lot back there has some, but we don't have anything facing out at the ocean except for the ones in the marina area."

Ava nodded. "Those are the sea life webcams, right?"

"Yeah, live feeds, no recordings. It's for the schools, I think." Valencia crossed his arms. "The barrels didn't come from a car or truck in the parking lot, if that's what you're thinking. Whoever dumped them would have had to drag or wheel them across the beach. I looked. No ruts. And that early, with the tide just back out, I would've seen marks in the wet sand."

"So, a boat," August said.

Valencia nodded. "Best guess."

"Okay, where do you think the barrels came from?" Ava asked. "Can you explain why, if the victims were local and their bodies were dumped off a boat, they ended up back on Oceanside shores and not say, Long Beach or San Diego? How'd they stay here with the water currents?"

"The currents don't work that way."

"Do you mind expanding on that?"

Valencia nodded. "So, there's something called the Southern California Bight. It's an almost four-hundred-and-thirty-mile curve in the coastline that runs all the way down to San Diego. Now that swoop in the coastline is like a big, shallow bowl. It slows down currents, creates these circular eddies that trap floating objects, and it weakens incoming winds. All that creates a zone where things like those blue barrels can drift and loop in the same general area for a considerable amount of time."

"How close to the shore would the killer have had to dump the barrels for them to get caught up in this Bight bowl thing?"

Valencia looked out at a passing boat. "If the barrels were dumped say a mile to maybe three miles offshore, they could get caught up in the onshore current."

"You're saying whoever dumped the bodies might lack experience," August said.

"In terms of sailing, yes," Valencia said. "Unless, you know, they *wanted* the bodies to wash on shore."

"To cause panic?" Ava didn't buy it. "Maybe."

"All I know is the news last night about a serial killer prowling Oceanside sure upset a lot of people. Harbor Police are fielding calls from frightened parents asking if they should still send their kids to aquatic camp or not. They don't really get the bodies washed up a couple of months ago."

"Are there cameras at the mouth of the harbor to catch outgoing boats?" August asked. When Valencia nodded, he continued. "We'll need those."

"Listen, no pressure, but you know that Oceanside celebrates the Fourth of July early. The city was debating canceling the festivities but didn't want to make things worse."

"More like they didn't want to lose the money they'd spent," Ava said.

"That means hundreds of out-of-towners, locals, and every other drunk person will flood the streets making your jobs harder."

"We'll get them soon," Ava said, peeling the cardboard heat sleeve from her coffee cup. She folded it and shoved it into her purse. "They've been making huge mistakes all along."

August looked at her, but Valencia asked. "They?"

She nodded. "I think there's more than one killer."

———

A few minutes after they'd left Valencia, August halted her, his brows raised. "Okay, give."

"Let me gather my thoughts. Then I'll fill you in."

August put his hands up. "A curveball like that gets a few hours tops before I start bugging you to explain."

"That's fair."

They spent the next couple of hours wandering the RV lot and marina, talking to people, but none were local, and hadn't been in town when the barrels washed up. They walked through the grassy park and picnic area. Nothing. The fish and chips place nearby looked good, so they bought a value basket each. Ava made sure to grab extra lemon for the health nut, and they sat at the round plastic tables outside watching the surf camp kids fall off their boards. Ava checked her phone while chewing on a fry.

"Time's up," August said. "Multiple murderers. It's an interesting theory. You want to tell me how you got there?"

"It's not a theory. It's what's happening."

"Tell me why you're so sure it's more than one killer. And no, you aren't squirming out of this. I'm with you. Just walk me through it."

Ava thought while she chewed. Intuitive leaps often sounded crazy, but she tried to lay out her reasoning. "When I look at the crimes I see a weird dichotomy. There is a ton of control which suggests experience. But there are also multiple amateurish mistakes."

He nodded, squeezing lemon all over his fish. "I like it so far, keep going."

"Okay, first, there's the control. If it's one killer, he murdered two able bodied young adults, after holding them for days. That takes planning, a private place, and transportation. He had to bind them, kill them, and then break their bodies to get them into the barrels. But then we have amateur hour. The killer messed up *every single* body dump. Slipping bodies into the sea or burying them at a construction site usually makes people disappear. Yet we found the victims. In fact, the first two came to *us*. And then, the killer left all kinds of evidence behind. From ritualistic markings to whatever was in Brent's sinus cavities and eyes."

"Theres an argument that the consistency of the markings would indicate the control you're talking about."

"Okay, good point. But then the killer also left valuable luxury accessories yet stole an easily identifiable and traceable watch."

"And somehow abducted three people without being noticed," August said.

"*And* kept them for days. Again, without escape or death or detection?" She shook her head.

"Controlled."

"But then we swing to the manner of disposal. Not controlled. Not effective. In fact, of all the ways to get rid of a body, dumping your victims in the ocean so that they come right back to your kill zone is... I don't know, it just feels like you said, inexperienced. In every way."

"The ages of the victims are unusual. Two twenty-year-old kids and a middle-aged man? Runaways and a millionaire's son?" August tapped a french fry on the basket. "That bothers me. Sure, the killer's victimology might be based on opportunity. *Or* the killer might be older, choosier, patient."

"But shitty at disposing of bodies? There's no way this killer has been at this for long." Ava rubbed her face, grappling with the countless reports and crime scene images. Too many things clamoring for attention. "It's almost like the deaths were an afterthought. Just a quick bullet and gone. All the rest of the things done to the body were postmortem. And yet we weren't supposed to find them. We weren't supposed to see the markings, right?"

"Why do it then?"

Ava looked off toward the beach, at the mounded sand creating shadows in the craters of footprints. "The Egyptians didn't intend for us to find their dead. They were preparing them for the afterlife."

"What are you getting at?"

"I don't know." Ava finished her last fry and swiped salt off the table onto the sidewalk. "If that's what this killer is working from, a structured system, then that indicates organized thinking, planning, design. But their execution is chaotic, shoddy." At August's repressed grin, she shook her head. "No pun intended."

"So, two killers." August sat back, musing.

"I feel like it's leaning that way."

"What else?" He made a keep-going motion with his index finger. "You always have a dozen tendrils of thought on a given subject. I need more."

Ava grabbed some of his fries. "There's the glowing UV binding thing. It makes me think of music festivals or raves, like Dr. Tavers said. Bad decisions. Inexperience. If you line everything up, I think we're working with a younger demographic. The victims also bend that way. Two thirds are young, and on the fringes of society. Sure, Brent is an older man, but he has a history of dealing with very young women in an inappropriate way. They weren't teens, but just barely." Ava shrugged. "Also, why keep them so long? There were no signs of torture or assault. No pulled finger-nails or burns."

He nodded. "Interrogation signs."

"None. Just postmortem etching. So why keep them? And the autopsies showed no indication of any of the victim's mouths being covered or taped."

"How did they keep them quiet?" August crumpled his paper napkin. "That's more control."

"Exactly."

"They could have been drugged with something we don't normally test for."

Ava pointed at him. "Again, drugging speaks to sophistication. No one was hit in the head and dragged away. The skin on their wrists had no abrasions so the zip ties were not used the entire time they were in captivity or at least they didn't wriggle against the bindings, which might suggest continued drugging. That's even more complicated. Many killers lose control of their first victims.

There are often near misses before a killer perfects his technique. So, we have evolved capture and containment, but stupid disposal?"

"The duality again," August said. "Talia believes the location Brent was kept before he was killed was industrial. So not a house. Not a basement."

"No, it smacks of a found place. And that girl, the one who I keep seeing. She has a feral kind of look, you know. Given that Cindy and Jimmy were sort of street kids, an abandoned place is something they might know about, maybe have even slept there."

"Devil's advocate here," August said. "Many seasoned killers seek out and use abandoned places to conduct their crimes."

"Trust me, there are some places no one would know about unless they've lived on the streets." She looked out at the water, her thoughts starting to circle. "But why do that if you have a boat? You could go out to sea, and your victim could scream their head off and no one would be the wiser. Why risk a random stranger wandering close by while you're killing someone in a warehouse or open lot or whatever? It'd have to be pretty big though. The size you'd need to carry two people-filled barrels means it couldn't be something small, right?"

He shrugged. "Probably. The boat ownership definitely leans toward an older killer. A street kid wouldn't be able to swing it. So how does the girl or the two younger victims factor in?"

"That's what I mean. Something is wrong or missing. I can't see the whole killer, and I think maybe it's because these crimes, given the controlled and amateurish moves, *feel* like more than one person."

August sat back, his gaze on her for a moment. "It holds some water. Cindy and Jimmy were apparently together. It wouldn't be too big of a stretch to assume another couple took them out. It could explain why they seemed to have gone willingly."

"You're thinking something like a serial killer couple?" Ava chewed on the inside of her mouth, thinking. "No that would just make it two amateurs."

August tilted his head. "Not if there's an older half of the couple."

"It would explain the sophistication mixed with sloppiness. And statistically, it would be an older man, not an older woman. A female in a power position over a younger accomplice generally gets them to kill their husband or something like that."

August's gaze rested on her, his brows furrowed. "Either way, young couple or mixed, they could have rented a boat. California doesn't require boat renters to obtain a Boater Card. No lessons or anything." He finished off his green juice. "Most boating accidents happen because operators don't have the proper training or experience."

"That's good. That's something solid. We should check rental places while we're here." Ava fished her phone out of her bag. "I'll text Rondeau and get a list."

When she went to send a message, she saw Rondeau's name in her phone had been changed to *Coolest Computer Guru Ever*. She showed August.

He passed his basket of fries to Ava with a grin. "Makes you glad he's on our side, doesn't it?"

———

After lunch, they decided to drop off their CBI cards in Harbor Village while they waited for Rondeau to compile a list. Walking to shops and kiosks, they chatted people up. Often employees lunched on the beach and might've seen something. A white van, perhaps. Splitting up, August took one side of the harbor boardwalk and Ava the other. She hit a smoke shop, an army surplus store serving the marines from nearby Camp Pendleton, and a store that sold only baskets of seashells. She showed clerks and customers photos of Cindy, Jimmy, and Brent. No one recognized them.

On her way back, she was halfway through an ice-cream cone when she spotted a girl in a gauzy sundress walking ahead of her on the sidewalk. Ava tossed her cone and sped up, tracking the young woman through the crowd, through a covered breezeway that led to another set of storefronts. The ding-ding-ding of the boat bells, the lapping of the water at the side of the boardwalk, and seagull calls faded as she followed her.

The girl in the dress took a sharp turn at the other end of the breezeway, and Ava hurried to see where she went. Emerging from the tunnel, Ava looked left, then right, and saw the billow of material disappearing through a doorway.

Approaching with caution now, she peeked through the door. The girl had ducked into a yoga studio, and she stood speaking with the receptionist. Caucasian, tan, with a crown of light brown braids piled atop her head. They looked old. Like she'd slept in them. Ava walked past, glanced inside again, and caught the girl's profile. The one who'd hit her with a racket had delicate, almost Nordic features and full lips. And her hair had been nearly platinum, not brown like the young woman in the studio.

Ava glanced at the yoga studio's sign. The Ocean Within. She was taking a photo with her phone when it rang in her hand. She walked away, heading back toward the breezeway. Ava answered the unknown number.

"Uh, Agent Cortes?" A woman's voice asked.

"You got her. Who's this?" Ava scanned the walkway for August.

"It's Jimmy's, uh..." She sounded skittish, like she might hang up at any moment. "James Wright's mother, Carol. We met at my antique shop? You left a message asking how I was."

Ava stopped walking, softening her voice. "I remember. How can I help you?"

"Can we meet? Somewhere public?"

"What's going on? Are you in danger?"

Carol hesitated so long Ava thought she'd lost the call. "No, I'm afraid that we lied to you. I want to make that right."

"Lied how?"

"I just—" Her breathing sounded ragged. "Jimmy left more than one thing with us that last night and I think you should have them. For the investigation."

"Anywhere, anytime," Ava said, spotting August. He saw her, and she waved him over. "Name it, and I'll be there."

"Okay, there's a park." Carol set the meet and ended the call.

Ava dug in her purse, looking up as August approached.

"What's going on?"

"Remember when I said we might still get something from Jimmy's mom?"

"Yeah?"

Ava shook the cookie business card at him. "She wants to meet. She said she has something for us."

"Information?"

"Evidence." Ava was already walking toward the parking lot. "Of what might have happened to her son."

FIFTEEN

The City of Oceanside did summer well. Every year, Movies in the Park, a community-wide watch party, took place at John Landis Park. People came with their kids, blankets, picnic baskets, and coolers to watch a family-friendly film in the cool of the evening.

Now, at dusk, as the light waned, the crowd blended with one another in the low light. The surrounding park lights dimmed, and the white screen erected near the building flickered to life with the opening credits of a movie. The crowd hushed, and Ava wasn't sure if she'd be able to spot Carol. She opened and closed her jaw, adjusting the seal on her voice-activated earpiece.

August's voice sounded low and calm in her earpiece. "If you feel off, get out of there."

"You worry too much. It's Carol. She's a mom."

"How's that eyebrow feeling?" August murmured. "Still itchy?"

"Fine. I'll be careful." Ava moved to another part of the park, trying to make herself visible, aware that August and Manaia were tracking her every move from their vehicle in the lot. Speakers blared a laugh track, and music became as frantic as the cartoon chase on screen between a polar bear and a penguin. Two animals that lived at different poles.

The headache from the morning threatened to come back as she circled around the park. Remembering August's earlier comment about the killer using drugs they might not test for regularly, she texted Talia the gist of their conversation and asked her to expand the drug panel test to include synthetic drugs and other relevant substances on all three victims.

TALIA

Other relevant substances? Are you looking for anything in particular?

I'm just trying to cover our bases. Think outside the box.

You got it.

She heard her name whispered in the dark up ahead. A woman sat on a bench in the back of the crowd, hand raised. Ava walked that way and the woman came over to meet her.

Carol Ulbreck clutched her purse close to her body, her eyes wide in the dark.

"I'm sorry. I thought if there were a lot of people, there'd be no chance of being noticed."

"Do you feel like you're in danger, Carol?"

"No, I guess I'm just worried about Stan hearing that I met with you. This kind of gathering is way out of his comfort zone. His old golf buddies wouldn't be caught dead here with all these little kids running around."

"How about we walk a little?" Ava led Carol away from the speakers blasting the movie's soundtrack. They wandered toward the cement and metal fencing that separated the grass field from the play structures and stood in the shadows. "What's going on? You said there was a problem with your statement?"

Carol nodded, her hand gripping her purse strap like a lifeline. "My husband, he's from Iowa. He thinks a lot of things here in California are strange. He calls them Cali-weird."

"Yes, he said that about the little bottles of juice Jimmy's girlfriend left, right?" Ava prompted. "I think he called them gut shots?"

"He said he threw them away, and he did. Stan didn't lie. But I did. I didn't tell you that I rescued them." Carol reached into her purse and pulled out two small glass bottles the size of salt and pepper shakers. Filled with golden liquid, she handed them over to Ava. "These are the drink things Meadow... I mean, Cindy wanted me to encourage Jimmy to drink. I don't think they're good anymore. It's been a while and the color turned darker, but I thought you should have them."

Ava took them, sliding them into an evidence baggie she pulled from her purse. "Thank you, Carol."

"There's—" she reached into her purse but stopped. "There's more. Jimmy gave me something when he left. At first, I thought it was just that he knew his father would throw it away but now..." She pulled a bag of tea from her sweater pocket. "He didn't leave it on the table, he slipped it into my pocket when we hugged goodbye that night after the dinner. I felt it."

Ava took the bag of tea, tilting into the light. Inside a transparent, silky drawstring bag was what looked like potpourri. "Did he say anything?"

"No, but his eyes, Agent Cortes. He looked at me for a few moments after he let go, and it felt like a plea. A desperate, silent plea."

"What do you think he was trying to say?"

"He was afraid of the dark when he was little and would get this expression." Carol looked away, her lip quivering. "I don't know. I probably sound insane to you. Seeing things where there aren't any."

Ava shook her head. "You sound like a mother who knows her son."

Carol nodded quickly, wiping her face. "I knew you'd understand. You see inside people, don't you? What they're thinking or feeling."

"I understand loss," Ava said softly. She slipped the tea into another evidence bag. "Thank you, Mrs. Ulbreck."

"You'll find this monster?" Her tear-filled gaze held Ava's.

"That's what I do," Ava said, moving away. "Thank you, Carol, you did the right thing."

Back in the parking lot, she slipped into the back of the car behind August and Manaia and handed over the evidence baggies.

August held out his hand. "I wonder what Jimmy was trying to say."

Ava dropped her earpiece into his palm. "Did you read the tag on the tea bag?"

He flicked on the car light, reading through the evidence baggie. "Ascension Tea." He turned the bag over. "To quiet the ocean within."

"The Ocean Within. That's the name of a yoga place in Harbor Village. I saw it just a few hours ago when I followed a scraggly, gauzy dress-wearing hippie chick into the place while we were canvassing."

Blue light flooded August's face as he opened his phone. "I'll have Rondeau check it out."

"You're saying the girl you saw *wasn't* the one who attacked you though?" Manaia asked, his gaze on her via the rearview mirror.

"No, but it's an odd coincidence, right? Same hair braids, same slightly unkempt look, same style of dress," Ava said. "And you know what coincidences are."

"Briefly visible patterns," August said, quoting her. He turned in his seat. "When were you going to tell me about this encounter?"

"When it was relevant. Which it now is. Besides, it wasn't the racket-happy one." Ava leaned back in her seat. The cut over her eyebrow throbbed in time with the headache behind it. "Let's get that to Talia. I want to know what it is."

SIXTEEN

Talia liked to get to the lab at the crack of dawn, and Ava, a night owl, had to pry herself out of bed at five that morning in order to catch her. When she glanced in the bathroom mirror, she found that blood from her healing eyebrow had pooled underneath her skin overnight. Deep purple settled around her eye, making the existing bruise even bigger. She picked up her concealer and then put it back down. No hiding that. She took a couple of aspirins for the headache she'd woken up with and washed them down with reheated coffee from her fridge.

Ava threw on a fitted burgundy button-up shirt, black slacks, a waist holster, and her Doc Marten boots before heading out by half past the hour. On the way, she stopped at the Lit Lounge a few minutes from headquarters to pick up a box of breakfast pastries and a few regular coffees for the team. She had the cashier throw in a healthy-looking muffin.

August called while she was in line.

"Just a heads up, Talia worked all night on the evidence you gathered from Carol. I'm headed there now."

"All night?" Ava tapped her watch on the credit card reader, paying.

"Yes, at her request." She heard traffic noises in the background. "This is our chance to get ahead of things."

"I'll see you there." Ava left a cash tip in the fancy jar and thanked the cashier as she left, still thinking about the wretched hope in Carol Ulbreck's eyes.

Talia had set up in the OPD Field Evidence Lab, saving Ava a drive to the San Diego Medical Examiner's Office. Ava walked through the entrance amid the chaos of shift change and eventually found the autopsy suites and field evidence lab after a few wrong turns down eerily similar hallways. She found Talia at a lab table, peering into a microscope.

"Coffee break," Ava said from the door. When Talia looked over, Ava held up the box of pastries. "I heard you worked all night."

"I have to give it to you, Ava, you sure know how to make an entrance." Talia slipped off her nitrile gloves and dumped them in the biohazard trash. She walked over with a yawn, frowned when she saw Ava's eye, but asked instead, "Was it Manaia who told you I was here all night? He stayed late. All the Crimes of Violence detectives did."

"They're feeling the heat from this case."

She and Talia sat in the side office used by the forensic staff for recording notes and taking breaks. It had a small kitchenette with a fridge for lunches, a sink, and some table sets. Ava chose the table in the corner that sat angled so that both chairs could see the television mounted on the opposite wall. The morning news played, scrolling updates about the case, and Ava saw an old photo of herself taken during the Black Oak case four months earlier. She stood next to August under towering pines, deep in muted conversation while an anchor explained how the CBI's PIT investigation into the Blue Drum Killer seemed to be stalling out.

"We've been here like, five minutes," Ava complained.

"At least the glowing symbols carved on the victims haven't leaked." Talia opened the box and picked out a pain au chocolat. "That's a miracle in itself."

"Just a matter of time." Ava grabbed a cinnamon roll, unwinding it as she ate. Once again, she'd received no callback or voicemail message from DDA Jared Iverson. She wanted to ask him why he dropped Cindy Aquino's prostitution case. Likewise, with Sergeant Rossi and the missing person's report. Deciding her coffee needed both more cream and sugar, she went to the counter to stir them in.

"Either way," Talia said with a grin, "your text last night was more helpful than you think."

"What do you mean?"

"You'll see."

August arrived next and picked out the healthy muffin. He sat next to Ava to enjoy it, chatting with her and Talia while they waited for Detective Manaia.

"Traffic is a mess. They're putting up roadblocks in anticipation of the fireworks show," he said, taking a coffee and drinking it black like some kind of noir detective.

Manaia showed up minutes later looking refreshed in a dark suit and today's Hawaiian shirt sporting old cars and records. He grabbed a chocolate donut, ate half of it in one bite, and asked around a mouthful, "What'd I miss?"

They filed into the lab behind Talia who donned a pair of gloves as she led them to a table lined with evidence trays. One held the bottles of "gut shot". She held up the still-sealed bottle.

"I analyzed the contents. It's just ginger juice, orange juice, some spices, and turmeric. That's what gives it the bright yellow look."

"So it's like an immunity shot?" August asked.

Ava looked askance, then pointed at the bottle's vivid contents. "Please tell me your fridge isn't full of these," she cut him off. "Does the color explain the staining on Cindy Aquino's fingers?"

Talia pointed at Ava. "Yes. If she and James Wright regularly made this concoction, that would explain the stains on their fingers and the fingernails. I'm running a scrape test on the skin to be sure."

"You just drink them?" Ava eyed the dubious fluid.

"Some brands, especially those sold at gyms claim it enhances energy or immunity. If they're sold in organic markets, the concoction is marketed as good for the gut," Talia explained. "The ginger in it is known to help with stomach problems, but I don't know about immunity. Everything in the liquid is good for you. Turmeric helps with inflammation according to some studies, the orange juice gives a healthy sugar bump and vitamin C, so I can see why people use it like that."

"Anything special about the bottles?" August asked. He pointed with his smart pen. "Can we track down a manufacturer?"

"No, these bottles are available online. People who like to use a juicer at home, make a batch, store it in the bottles in the fridge, and use them throughout the week," Talia said. "No markings or label on the bottle either, but..." She picked up a dried flower with a pair of bulldog tweezers. "The tea is a *whole* different story. This stuff will make you talk to the moon and hear something back."

"What's in it, exactly?" Ava asked.

"Mostly edible plants like butterfly pea flowers, the kind that change the tea color from purple to fuchsia with lemon or some other acid. Also, chamomile, some powdered high potency THC, and something called *Amanita muscaria*. Also powdered."

"Amanita?" August asked, inspecting the flower.

"It's a mushroom." Talia leafed through a book on the table and held up a page with a photo of a red mushroom with white spots.

Ava raised a brow. "I thought those were deadly. What's it doing in the tea?"

"Maybe inadvertently?" Talia pointed at the book. "The genus Amanita has over six hundred different species, and you're right, it is one of the most toxic mushrooms known to man. The genus accounts for almost ninety-five percent of fatalities from mushroom ingestion."

"So, the purpose of the tea was to poison people?" Ava asked. The profile of the unsub kept getting more and more unclear. Killers who used poison were usually women.

"Not quite," Talia said. "I called a colleague this morning. He's a mycologist at the Jiangsu Agricultural University in China. He said that there is a subspecies of *Amanita muscaria* found in coastal regions that is *technically* edible. It grows near the shore or in wet caves and cliffs in Washington State, Oregon, and..."

"Let me guess, California."

"Ding ding ding."

"What do you mean, technically edible?" August asked.

"It's highly psychotropic."

"This is specialized knowledge," Ava said to August. He nodded.

"It makes you high?" Manaia asked.

"Sort of. The particular subspecies I'm talking about is often called Kava Flower or Blue Lotus. In microdoses, it can cause relaxation, mild dissociation, and heightened suggestibility. Also, mild audio and visual hallucinations."

"Is this similar to the hallucinogenic mushrooms used in some PTSD therapies?" August asked.

"This mushroom isn't like the magic mushrooms you're thinking about. Those are psychotropic mushrooms, backed with tons of studies. Their primary active ingredient is psilocybin or psilocin which are used in therapies for PTSD and depression, but also for recreational use. This is not that kind of mushroom. This will kill you if taken incorrectly."

August gestured at the book. "Psilocybin and psilocin are classified as Schedule 1 substances. They're illegal across California just like heroin and MDMA. But you're saying this has different compounds?"

"Yes, the active ingredients in the amanita mushroom are muscimol and ibotenic acid. Very different. And surprisingly, totally legal to have in California."

"You're kidding," Manaia said. "Why?"

Talia shrugged. "It's a gray area because amanita doesn't contain the same active ingredient to make you high that the other mushrooms do. Essentially, it's so rarely used that regulations are lagging. The ingredients in amanita are not specifically listed as a controlled substance."

"That is wild," Ava said with a grin. "So, it's not illegal to have it or grow it?"

"Don't get any ideas," August said.

"It is considered a dangerous poison," Talia said. "Improper preparation and dosing can lead to severe illness and even death. But no. Not illegal."

Manaia tapped something on his phone. "I'll run it by the Controlled Substance Program team and see if they've heard of its use on the street. You said Blue Lotus and what?"

"Kava Flower," Talia said. "This isn't a party drug. You'd be an emotional and mental mess while on it. And the extreme potency of the THC I also found in the powder would be sedating, and at that dose, maybe even cause paranoia, panic attacks, or other emotional responses. It would be the equivalent of taking peyote and going to a rave. Not a fun ride. This kind of tea should be purchased from a reputable dispensary, not collected and prepared by an amateur."

Ava remembered her own wilder days. "So, this isn't like making pot brownies."

"No. Whomever is making this has done their research. It would be dangerously easy to mess up the doses of all the ingredients and have it be lethal. This mix requires precision."

"There's your control," August whispered to Ava.

She nodded. "What about the tag we found with the tea?"

"That's interesting," Talia said, picking up the silky pouch.

She pointed to a blown-up photo of both the front and back of the tag on the computer monitor next to her. One side said, "Ascension Tea." The other, "To Quiet the Ocean Within."

The label looked homemade to Ava in the stark light of the lab. "Do you think Cindy or Jimmy made the tea with the amanita in it?"

"I would think so. I just have no idea where they'd get the ingredients," Talia said. "It wouldn't be easy to source, but it's not regulated like other approved psychedelic treatments. No one is tracking the purchase of spores or anything like that."

"I'll get Rondeau to check out online sources," August said.

"If he does find a source, they'd likely have extensive records due to its poisonous substance status," Talia said.

"What about inside a greenhouse, like weed?" Ava asked.

"I mean sure, but people do that because it's worth it monetarily. Marijuana sells well and the initial cost is minimal," Talia said. "If someone had a mushroom lab, it likely wouldn't be to sell it. They'd use it for something else."

August unwrapped a piece of gum and shoved it in his mouth, chewing with a vengeance. "And if they found it growing wild on some seaside cliff?"

"Then we would have no trail to trace," Talia said.

"So, no manufacturer to check, the tea is possibly homemade," Manaia said. "And Oceanside actively supports the cottage industry. Farm stands sell sourdough loaves, cookies, anything homemade on the streets around the area. All of that is on the honor system, self-reporting. There's almost no oversight."

"I don't think anyone is selling this," Ava said. "I think James Wright took it from somewhere and stuck the label in so that the tea would be associated with the Ocean Within studio."

"Then we need to go and take a look at that studio." August moved away to make a call.

Manaia looked at Ava. "This is good, right? This is movement."

"It fills in some holes we have in the murder case." Her gaze rested on the dried purple flowers in the tea. "But it also puts a whole lot of questions in my head about what's going on overall." Something about the THC and *Amanita muscaria* powder bothered Ava, and she walked over to stand next to Talia. "You drink a lot of tea, right?"

She smiled, nodding. "Not as much as you drink coffee, but a fair share. Why? What's brewing in that brain of yours? Or should I say, 'what's steeping in that brain of yours'?"

Ava drew back. "Did you just make a joke, Dr. Clay?"

"I have my moments." Talia chuckled. "What were you asking about the tea?"

"I read once that cheap tea has mostly powder, but good tea is actual twigs and stuff."

"That's true. Manufacturers actually have to use different tea bags based on how fine their tea is. Finer tea needs denser bags to keep the powder from escaping or blowing through the bag."

Ava stilled, chasing the thought. "Or maybe, into someone's face?"

Talia looked at her thoughtfully. "When I ran tests on the victims for the substance, all three of them had it in their systems, however Brent's level was much higher. Now, I attributed that to the fact that the advanced decomposition of the first two victims might have contributed to the breakdown of the substance. But given your theory of the powder entering the body by being blown on the face, I need to consider this." She jotted down a note in a nearby notebook before smiling at Ava. "It's an interesting theory. I'll run some more tests based on that supposition."

"Thanks. I hope I'm wrong." A chill moved down Ava's spine. If the killer could blow this substance in a victim's face, they'd be helpless until the drug compounds wore off. They'd be completely under the power of suggestion and likely wouldn't even think to scream as they were being killed. They wouldn't even think it was real.

August came back after his call. "Rondeau says he has something to show us." He nodded toward Manaia who passed them while speaking on the phone. "He's on his way to a meeting with the Chief of Police about their media strategy."

"Gross. Better him than me," Ava said. "There's no putting the whole Blue Drum Serial Killer thing back in the toothpaste tube though."

"I told him we're hitting the Ocean Within yoga place after we see Rondeau. He said he'd try and catch up."

August leaned on the table, catching Talia's attention as she scribbled furiously in her notebook. "You need to get some rest, Dr. Clay. Take a break."

"As a famous rogue agent says, 'I'll sleep when I'm dead,'" Talia said without looking up.

August's gaze snapped to Ava. "Do you hear that?"

Ava shook her head. "I think she's talking about you."

She grabbed Rondeau's mocha and followed August to the audio-visual lab. Rondeau sat at a workbench, laptop in front of him, while a display screen on the wall played four different black and white security camera feeds on fast forward. He stared at them, perfectly still.

Ava set the large double mocha at his elbow. Not a twitch. August cleared his throat, and Rondeau jumped to face them.

"Guys! I spoke with Detective Manaia about the results of the canvass by the drive-in site." He grabbed the coffee and tapped on his laptop, bringing up time-stamped screenshots from security feeds. "He found some people who said they saw a white or light-colored van around the time of the body dump. One guy at a gas station thought the driver was lost because the van kept circling."

"That's interesting," Ava said, sitting next to him and looking at the feeds. "August said you wanted to show us something?"

Rondeau pointed to the four screens. "I've been working through the security cameras from the businesses along Mission Avenue both south of the drive-in site and further north. Last night, I got a hit on the repeated appearance of a van in the vicinity of the body dump two nights before, like the construction site supervisor said." Rondeau stopped the recording and pointed to a small white blob at a stoplight.

"That's a van?" August leaned over Ava's shoulder, squinting.

Rondeau grinned. "The camera is actually focused on the parking lot of the liquor store, but don't worry. I have a buddy who works for LAPD in their Intelligence Unit. I asked him to clean it up and sharpen the image." Another clearer, closer view of the van appeared layered over the video feed. An industrial white panel van sat at the stoplight. "The camera doesn't catch the plates and the resolution still sucks, but this is the best angle. Look." Rondeau pointed to a purple shape on the paint near the back bumper.

Ava leaned in. "Is that a sticker?"

"Looks like one," Rondeau said. "I have something like it to get through my condo's gate."

"You think it's a parking decal?" Ava peered at the sticker.

"I do. I'm working on finding a better lit angle. To do that, I set up sections of surveillance video from along Mission Avenue at sequential times." He pointed to the video feeds on each of the four screens on the wall. "Every video in which that white van appears is up here. These are in the hours of the night between when Jones locked up after the day crew, and before the night crew showed up and dug up the body." He showed them the trail of the van until it went up Mission and away from view. "The white van circled the area for almost forty minutes."

"And it's the same one?" Ava asked.

"I see the sticker or whatever in each video. It's the same one. We got a partial plate from one of them. I'm running it through a predictive algorithm that inputs the missing possible digits of the license plate against the plates of white vans registered in the area. I included Carlsbad and Vista to see if we get a hit."

"This is an industrial area," August said. "People use vans to deliver furniture, hold paint supplies, delivery vans for flowers. We should cross check businesses who own similar vehicles."

"I'm on that," Rondeau said, tapping on his keys. "Also, we received security camera footage from a Captain Valencia. Harbor Police?"

"That's the cameras near the jetty monitoring traffic in and out of the harbor and marina," August said.

"We're digging into it now. Manaia has detectives helping sort through all the footage. It's nice to have some extra bodies on hand. Especially when they know what they're doing."

They filled Rondeau in on their meeting with Talia and everything she'd found with the tea containing amanita and a THC compound.

"Well, that's a new twist," he said.

"We want to double check the finances on all the victims," August said. "Just on the off chance one of them was involved in procuring amanita in powered form. I want to cover all the bases. We don't know how these people are connected."

"We already have the records for the first two victims. James Wright's bank account was zeroed out. Unused for months according to the bank. And Cindy didn't even have one that we could find," Rondeau said.

"Younger adults favor electronic pay apps, especially if they have housing insecurity," Ava said.

"We're running through their phone data. I'll take a look for apps or other online purchases." Rondeau crossed his sinewy arms and leaned casually on the edge of the table. "We might have to call in the big guns, boss. We're still waiting on financials for Brent Cutler. His father is causing delays. He says that their finances are so tangled that it would reveal proprietary information belonging to Dane Cutler's other businesses."

"We're getting them anyway. I just talked with Vincent. Tomorrow at the latest," August said.

Rondeau nodded. "Manaia has some guys from OPD's Property and Financial Crimes Unit checking the books over at his wine tasting room while we wait."

"Good," August looked around the empty room. "There's a ton of data coming your way. Do you want me to get more bodies in here to help?"

Rondeau shook his head. "OPD keeps throwing people at me. I'm good."

"We're hitting the yoga studio," Ava said.

"Wait!" Rondeau dug in the pile of papers, pulled out his secure tablet, and tapped on the screen. Ava and August's phones pinged a second later. "You asked for boat rental places around there, right? I sent you a list of about twenty of them, both large and small craft rentals based on the size of the barrels."

"You're a digital god," Ava said as they left.

"Let's remember that during Secret Santa, shall we?"

SEVENTEEN

The Ocean Within Wellness Center sat between a fancy stationery store and a boba place. Ava led August there through the breezeway where she'd first seen the young woman.

"For all I know, the gossamer thin linen dress could just be a trend," Ava said as they walked along the sidewalk. "Dress of the season, you know? And the braids. I don't know. I don't really do the fashion thing with this job. But it's something."

August opened the door for her. "Your gut isn't usually wrong."

Inside the studio, a wooden reception counter took up most of the floor space. Shelves filled with incense, candles, teas, and other spa goodies lined the walls. Natural driftwood photo frames displayed pastels of waterfalls and sunsets. Behind the reception counter, a doorway leading to the rest of the space sat closed, with an electronic keypad on the wall next to it. Soothing spa music drifted over them as they walked up to the young woman sitting behind the counter. She wore a black T-shirt with the studio name, nose in a math book, dark hair falling forward and hiding her face.

When they approached, she glanced up with a bored look, saw Ava's expression, and sat up a little. "Can I help you?"

They showed their badges. The young woman wore a name tag that read, Kinsley. She eyed their badges and then raised a single arched eyebrow. "What's the CBI?"

"We're like the FBI, but local." Ava nodded at the locked door. "Are the yoga classes back there?"

"No, they're on the beach. The class members meet at a specific spot at six in the morning." She rolled her eyes. "I think it's near a fire ring. At least during winter, it is."

"They meet during winter? That sounds needlessly torturous." Ava matched the young woman's dismissive energy. "As if yoga that early wasn't a bad enough idea."

Kinsley leaned in. "Right? They meet late at night too for like, moon bath yoga or whatever. It's a whole thing."

"I can imagine. Anyone stand out as particularly mental?"

"Not offhand. Just stay-at-home moms, college kids, locals on another health kick. You know, beach folk." She put her book down, her brows drawn. "Wait, you guys are in town to investigate the guy they found at the drive-in. I saw that on the news."

August held up his tablet. An array of photos showing Cindy Aquino, James Wright, and Brent Cutler appeared on the screen. "Do any of these people look familiar to you?"

Kinsley frowned at the screen, her lips pursed to the side as she thought. "I think I've seen the girl here before?"

"When?" August asked.

"She used to come in months ago, before summer, I think." Kinsley shook her head. "I'm not sure though, there's a lot of them."

Ava tilted her head. "A lot of who?"

"Sales force workers." Kinsley gestured around the shop. "This is the base of operation for the classes, but there are wellness seminars, too. And you can also sign up for delivery boxes filled with home-grown organic tea, local flavored honey, and immunity shots. Then there's the online store."

"Are you saying this young woman worked here?" Ava asked.

"I don't know for sure. The sales force is not the same as the yoga studio staff. They come in, sometimes, but they go straight to the back where we pack and keep the subscription boxes and other products."

Ava nodded. "Tell me more about this sales force."

Kinsley looked from Ava to August and then back. "I am not involved in whatever weird shit is going on with this place. I answered a job listing to sit here for four hours a day, which works with my class schedule, that's it."

"What weird shit?"

"They all have this wholesome, dreamy vibe. And they say weird stuff to each other, too," Kinsley finished.

"Like what?" August asked.

"Okay, so I liked this one guy my freshman year and went to a Christmas thing with him at his church. They were Catholics, so there was a lot of audience participation. The priest would say something and everyone else knew what to say back, and when to say it. I was lost." She shook her head, her gaze going fuzzy for a moment. "It feels like that."

"Can you give us an example?" Ava asked.

The young woman sat back on her stool and looked at the ceiling for a moment. "I don't know. They say, 'Peace,' a lot to each other. I make a point to avoid speaking with them at all costs."

"What makes them weird? Other than the greeting thing."

"They're all vegan."

Ava grinned. "What else?"

"They all wear this retro clothes style and braids with flowers. The dudes too. They remind me of hippies from the movies. Flower children, I guess."

"Do you carry something called, Ascension Tea?"

"We have samples. The boxes are sold out at the moment." Kinsley pulled an open box of tea packets off the shelf behind her and handed it to Ava. The packaging looked professional. Designed to feel homemade. A soft watercolor of a field of flowers took up most of the front, while italic script promised organic, sustainable gardens and superior bioavailability. The individual packet said Ascension

Tea, but when Ava read the ingredients, it only listed chamomile, lavender, passionflower, lemon verbena, West Indian lemongrass leaf, and valerian root. Nothing else. Ava lifted one of the single tea bag servings and held it up to the light. Resembling a packet of cut-up grass, twigs, and flowers, it didn't look remotely like the one James Wright slipped to his mother.

"You said there are a lot of these sales force employees?" August asked. "Do you know how many?"

"I mean, they come and go. I'll see them for a while and then I never see them again. And they always travel in pairs. Guy and girl or two of each, but always in pairs."

"Do you know why?"

"Don't know. Don't care." Kinsley put her hands up. "Look, I don't really want to get involved in whatever wonky shit is happening here. I've got one semester left, then I am gone."

Ava understood that. She'd have felt the same way. "Tell us about the wonky shit and then we'll be out of your hair."

"The past three days, they've been in and out of here moving more boxes than usual. Quiet, not smiling. Someone said something about the teacher and the other one told them to shut the hell up. That's not how they usually talk to each other. They're usually all polite and stuff."

"Is there just one teacher?" Ava asked.

"No, there are like five yoga instructors, all women. They aren't exclusive to Ocean Within. They hold classes at different studios too. I think they were talking about the owner, because the newer one referred to the teacher as 'he'."

"Why'd they call him teacher if he's not an instructor?"

"He only handles the private classes. I don't know where and I don't know anything about him."

They talked her around the subject for another few minutes, but she genuinely didn't seem to know much more. Ava slipped the Ascension Tea bag sample into her notebook while August left his card with Kinsley. As they walked back out of Harbor Village to the

SUV, they got another updated list from Rondeau. His text explained that he'd added some businesses but taken others off after the Crimes of Violence Unit eliminated several.

Ava and August hit one in the immediate area while they were there, the Municipal Marina. The late morning sun burned hot. It stung Ava's cheeks as they drove to the marina. She'd bought herself an iced coffee before they'd left the breezeway and swirled it in her hand.

"I think we should check for stolen boats, too. Do boats get stolen a lot? I know they are on land but are there actual pirates out there stealing people's little sparkly speed boats right off the water?"

"Pirates?" August grinned and shook his head. "No, less than fifteen percent of boat thefts are from a marina. There are usually a lot of cameras and roving guards. People live or sleep on their boats occasionally, so you never know which vessels are empty. If you're trying to steal a boat, casting off isn't quiet. Let's say you start banging and moving equipment on deck. If there's a fisherman sleeping it off in the boat next to you, they *will* hear. It would be a risk. Worse if you're firing up an engine."

"How would the marina know if it's getting stolen? What if someone is just taking out their boat?"

"Boat owners file a float plan, which is essentially a flight plan for boats. It gives a description of the vessel, passenger count, destination, things like that for safety reasons."

"Is it required?"

"No, but most people at least let someone know when they're going out." August pulled into the marina's parking lot. "But I did check. In the last few months, one boat was reported stolen from a private marina up the road. The guy later said it was actually a repossession due to non-payment of his loan. He was going through a divorce."

They decided to talk with the marina's manager first because August said if anything had happened to anyone's boat, they'd be the first to get complaints.

The marina manager's office sat on a swath of fake grass facing the rows of sailboats and engine craft. An angry-looking orange cat with brown eyes sat on the Formica counter, licking its extended leg. Ava and August introduced themselves to Sharon Warner, the marina's manager, who told them that no, they hadn't gotten any reports of stolen boats, and no, they didn't rent boats anymore either.

"It's an insurance thing," Sharon said in a gravelly voice. At least seventy, she stared at them with rheumy eyes nearly hidden by wrinkles. A scrunchie held a swath of gray and bright pink hair atop her head. "Those dum-dums think it's like driving a car. It's not worth loaning a decent craft to someone who doesn't know how scared they should be out there."

August nodded. "What about maintenance? Do you have a contractor who does repairs to the vessels?"

"Yeah, we subcontract to a guy. He does the grounds and slip maintenance for us too." Sharon leaned back, and grabbed a shiny, egg-shaped foam keychain from a hook, and handed it to Ava. "That's his information. You can keep that. I have a whole basket back here."

The floating keychain was aqua blue with black branding that read, *Jerra's Peak Ship*, across the surface. Ava took a photo with her phone of the business's phone number and scannable QR code on the back.

"And you say there have been no recent complaints about the boats?" August asked.

"Not really. We get some grumbling about the year-round fees. But people like having their boats ready whenever they want. That takes security. That takes maintenance." She nodded at the keychain in Ava's hand. "Jerra would know about damaged boats."

They left their cards, and Ava texted Rondeau with the maintenance guy's information while they stood outside the manager's office, strategizing. She stared at the boats, their hulls rising and dipping with the harbor's current. Sunlight flickered off the water, and she thought about the bioluminescent dye used on the victims.

Was Professor Katsaros right? Did all of this somehow have to do with the sea?

August tilted the map on his phone for Ava to see. "We should start up here, hitting the rental places with the photo array as we head inland."

Ava half-listened, running her fingers over the decorative shapes of sea creatures etched into the metal pillars of the marina's railing, thinking. Her phone rang, interrupting the process. She didn't recognize the number.

"This is Agent Cortes."

"Uh, yeah, this is Sergeant Rossi from Investigations Division, Family Protection task force. Detective Manaia asked me to call you about a missing person's report?"

She put him on speaker. "Yeah, thanks for calling me back. Agent Blake is also on the call."

"A pleasure," Rossi said, though his words came through chipped. "Listen, Manaia said you wanted to talk with me about the report on Cindy Aquino. Didn't you guys already find her? She was one of the ones by the jetty, right? The Blue Drum Killer Case?"

August pinched the bridge of his nose with his thumb and forefinger. He hated it when the press named the killers.

"She was one of the victims, yes."

"Because the report was completed with everything provided and duly filed as soon as it came in."

The defensiveness she'd picked up started to make more sense. Big cases sometimes had big fallouts.

"Oh gosh, no, we're not looking at the police on this. I actually just need the name of the person who filed the report *with* you. I'm told it was a friend, not family. We want to follow up on that."

"I sent over the report to Manaia already, but I'll give you the rundown." Papers shuffled on his end. "Okay, the woman who came in to file the missing person's report was young, college aged. She was really worried about the friend being trafficked. She seemed locked on that but couldn't really say why. Just that they both lived in a shelter which isn't the safest." More paper sounds came through. "Here it is. Her name is Heather Adams."

Ava took down the name and contact info. "Thanks for your time."

"Listen," Rossi said, clearing his throat. "We just thought this Cindy Aquino gal moved on. Like so many of them do."

"I understand. Not this time, I guess."

They walked to the car, and Ava called the number Heather Adams had left on the missing person's form, waiting out the rings. It kicked her to voicemail.

She cleared her throat and said, "Hello, this is Ava Cortes. I wanted to give you a call about a woman I'm trying to help, Cindy Aquino. I would love to get in touch at your convenience. No rush, I'd just like to talk with you. When you have a moment, please call me back at this number, okay?" After she hung up, Ava said, "I say we wait until I finish this iced mocha to see if she calls. Then we head to the first place on the rental list."

"Why didn't you say you were with the CBI?" August asked, starting the vehicle and turning on the air conditioner.

"Kids in the system trust precious few people. Adults aren't reliable and often aren't even safe. Social workers are trusted to a point, but police are definitely not. And we're like the most intense version of police."

"That's why you sounded like that."

"All social workers say the same things when they call. It's like they get the exact same script."

"Did you trust social workers?"

Ava held his gaze. "Some of them."

"The trafficking thing is a new twist," August said after a few moments. "Do you think there's something to what Cindy Aquino's friend suspected?"

"With this case, and with Brent involved, I wouldn't be surprised."

She didn't get to finish her drink. Five minutes after she left a message for Heather to call, she did.

"Hi, uh, this is Heather." She sounded young.

"Thanks so much for calling me back. I was wondering if I could chat with you about the missing person's report you filed for Cindy Aquino?"

"It would have been more helpful if someone wanted to chat with me when she was alive," Heather said. "I just heard she was found months ago. It was great learning about my dead friend on the news, by the way. Thanks for the call."

"I need to be honest with you before we continue, but please don't hang up," Ava said. "My name is Ava Cortes, and my partner and I are with the CBI. We're investigating Cindy's disappearance in relation to the Blue Drum Killer case. I heard that you thought she might be in danger of getting trafficked. That you lived in a shelter together and you were worried."

"Yeah, and no one believed me."

"I'd like to talk with you about how we missed that." Ava waited, but Heather didn't answer. She needed a push. "I'm going to tell you something the news doesn't know. Cindy was held somewhere, Heather. For days."

August shook his head, mouthing that they hadn't released that information.

Ava murmured softly. "I need your help stopping whoever did this before they do it again. I can come to you."

After a couple of moments of silence, Heather spoke. "Okay, look. I'm at work right now, but I've got a break coming up. I'll take it when you get here."

"Give me the address." Ava wrote it down. "We'll be there in twenty minutes."

EIGHTEEN

August handed off the boat rental list to Detective Manaia and his team, and they headed to the fast-food place where Heather worked. Halfway there, Heather called Ava back and told her that someone had called in sick and she'd have to push her break to after the lunch rush.

"We'll buy something and park. Are you serving?" Ava asked.

"Yes, I am. Pull into a spot with a car order screen."

Ava said they would and then told August what to do. While he drove, she checked her phone for messages and found none. Her head throbbed, and she rubbed her temples.

"Call me, you weasel," Ava muttered.

He watched her with furrowed brows. "What's wrong? Is it your head?"

"It's this DDA Iverson. I've left multiple messages at his office, so have you, and not a peep back. He's starting to hurt my feelings."

"He might have decided he lacked enough evidence against Cindy Aquino to press charges."

"That's fine. I just want to hear him confirm that, and I'll move on." Ava shook her head. "The more he acts dodgy, the more interested I get."

It took them closer to half an hour, given the noon traffic. They pulled into the fast-food parking lot amid a line of cars waiting at the drive thru. Atomic Dog was a fifties-style hot dog and hamburger place whose claim to fame was servers in roller skates like in the movies Ava used to watch with her grandmother. Male and female waitstaff zipped across the parking lot wearing aqua, atomic-age style uniforms and silver skates. On one side of the building, a row of parking spots with order kiosks lined the curb. You didn't even have to get out of your car to get the heart-stopper special delivered right to your lap.

August chose an order kiosk, pulled in, and shut the car off. He fiddled with the display screen, ordering a water, a cherry soda, and french fries. Ava rolled her window down, hoping for a nice cool breeze. She texted Heather and told her their kiosk number. Five minutes later a tall, thin young woman with a blonde ponytail and bright red lips sailed over to them on skates. She held a food tray and stopped gracefully right at August's door. Sweat slicked her nose, and her brown eyes settled on Ava as she handed them their drinks.

"Ava Cortes?"

"That's me." Ava looked over her sunglasses at her and took the soda. It came with a complimentary lollipop ring you were supposed to stir your drink with, for extra flavor. Ava threw the candy ring into her purse and sipped the ice-cold soda. Perfect. August set his water in the holder and handed her the fries.

"You guys just missed the rush so that's good," Heather said as she rolled back, looking over at the restaurant. "We can talk for now."

They showed her the tablet with the photo array of the three victims, but she only recognized her friend, Cindy Aquino. They met at the shelter.

"Cindy got kicked out of some residential drug program over pot and messing with some guy after curfew," Heather said, shaking her head. "So, she ended up at Bright Horizons over there off Oceanside Blvd. We were in the same dorm room."

"How was she? Hanging in there, spinning out, drifting?" Ava asked, slipping into old terms.

"She was hanging in there, trying to get her own place like I was. She did mostly gig work like deliveries, I think. She had one of those subscription cards for the city's electric bikes."

Ava had investigated buying one when they'd first come out, but the prices were astronomical. Definitely not something someone would spend money on for a delivery gig while living in a shelter.

"Do you know where she worked?" They knew from Kinsley that Cindy worked at Ocean Within, but Ava wanted to know how much Cindy had kept from Heather.

"She just said it was deliveries. I assumed it was like food orders or something." Heather rolled her skates back and forth like she was moonwalking. "Money was a real trigger for her. I mean, most of us are trying to make ends meet and that's hard, you know, totally soul crushing, but Cindy, she was angry. Like she was supposed to be somewhere else and the whole thing was a mistake."

"The whole thing?" Ava asked.

"Her life, I guess?" She flicked away a buzzing fly.

"Did she have anyone outside of the shelter? A boyfriend, family?" August asked.

"I think there was something going on with someone." She shrugged. "I don't know who. But she would go outside and call someone under this big tree in the yard. With the window to the dorms open, I could hear her yelling. She called the person on the phone a dick and a bastard. Which I feel are insults reserved for men. But I don't know."

"What did they argue about?" Ava asked. "Did you catch any words, or did she complain to you later about it?"

"She never talked about the calls, but she said something once about how he owed her."

"Tell me more," Ava asked. "The last call you overheard, what was going on at the time with Cindy? Was she stressed, acting weird?"

Heather thought about it, her gaze on some squirrels scouring the parking lot for crumbs. "I think it was her phone. It got stolen earlier in the week, and she spent days going around accusing everyone of taking it because it was expensive or she'd just gotten it. Something like that."

"Did it turn up?" August asked.

"No. I told her to drop it because she almost got her face beat in one night. You don't go around pointing the finger. Not with everyone afraid of losing their spot in the shelter." Heather shrugged. "Didn't matter anyway because the next week she somehow had another phone. Same kind. Expensive, not the kind you have to buy minutes for. Only she got weird with it."

"So, money was a trigger, but she somehow came to own not one, but two expensive phones and rented a city scooter?" August asked.

"Pretty much. I don't know how she got any of those things. It was strange, but nowhere near as strange as how she started acting."

"Strange how?"

Heather explained that several months before she went missing, Cindy started to act increasingly odd. She changed her hair from wearing it mostly down or in a ponytail to a crown of braids. Her style changed as well, going from jeans and T-shirts to retro dresses, skirts, and blouses she said she got from the thrift store. And she asked people to call her Meadow. Eventually ignoring attempts to speak with her unless they addressed her by the new name.

"She started complaining about the chemicals in the food there," Heather continued. "We ate normal food at the shelter. And it's not like she was opposed to drugs before. They really try there, you know. They want to help you if you let them. I got this job through the program, but Cindy still complained. But the weirdest thing was that she stopped being so mad all the time. By a lot. Like a faucet had just shut off."

August asked, "And the calls? Did she keep fighting with the mystery person?"

"She got sketchy about those too. Cindy would get a call, run off to talk in the bathroom, and then just leave. No matter what she was doing or who she was hanging out with, she'd just grab her stuff and walk out the front door. And she'd get quiet if you asked where she was going. I got worried. I thought with the fights and gifts and all the secrecy that she was being turned out by a boyfriend."

"Was she?" Ava asked.

"I'm not sure what was going on. I followed her once when she ran off suddenly and saw her getting into a creepy van. The kind you're specifically taught *not* to get into as a kid. That's all I know about whoever she was meeting."

"Come again?" Ava sat up. "What van?"

Heather shrugged. "She walked to the end of the block and a white panel van pulled up and she got in the back."

"Did you see anyone? Maybe the driver's face?" August asked.

"No. The door slid open, but slowly, like those automated ones, and I couldn't see more than a shape in the driver's seat. My glasses were broken then so I couldn't see anything besides that it was white."

"You said you thought it was a *man* arguing on the phone with her, not a guy. Why did you use that word? You said guy in other instances."

Heather blinked. "Okay, so I might have seen a text. Cindy was sitting on the couch in the common room one night, texting. I passed behind her on my way to the bookshelf, and I saw a message. It didn't sound like someone our age."

"What did it say?"

"Something like, 'When you reflect on our time, you'll feel more connected.' Like, who talks like that? No one my age."

"Did you say anything to her about it?" Ava asked.

"I shouldn't have, but yeah. She shut me down and said she didn't appreciate me invading her privacy. We didn't talk after that. She wouldn't even look at me when I walked in the room. A week or two later, she left the shelter and never came back." Heather turned away, dabbing at her mascara. "I hope her leaving wasn't—"

"It wasn't." Ava leaned across August, catching Heather's gaze. "You tried to help her. Just sometimes there's only so much you can do to save someone. You did the right thing talking to us."

She caught August's glance. He knew she'd lost a friend to violence when she was young.

"He stuffed her in a trash barrel, Ava." Heather's eyes filled with tears, but she blinked them away. "Stop this asshole."

Ava nodded, and Heather took off on her shiny skates.

"Maybe she'd been texting a psychiatrist or social worker?" August offered.

"Could be." But a cold stone dropped into the pit of her stomach.

"I'm calling Rondeau. The shelter is in the city center. There's bound to be security cameras near the corner where the van picked her up."

Ava listened to him talk, fiddling with the candy ring in her purse, crunching the cellophane wrapper, thinking about Carol's cookie business card—and her son, James. An older man whom Cindy believed owed her. That didn't sound like her boyfriend. Perhaps his parents had been wrong, and she was just a friend. But why take her home to meet them if they were just friends?

Maybe Brent Cutler hadn't learned from the whole Sea Siren Escorts debacle and went back to his old tricks. Then again, how did he end up dead exactly like the first two victims? Someone killed all of them, and she still had no idea who or why. She was missing something. Ava glanced at August, currently distracted by his conversation with Rondeau. Pulling out her burner phone, she sent a message.

> I need dirt on someone. Fast.

NINETEEN

The sun and heat pushed the headache into migraine territory. Ava and August decided to make their phone calls and file their interview reports from the Oceanside Police Department's air-conditioned station for the rest of the afternoon.

Manaia called with an update on the boat rental canvass just as they pulled around the rear of the police station. Nothing yet, but they were working on the list. A group of people stood near the pet supply shop a few stores over, where an adoption event was taking place on the sidewalk in front of the store. Portable fences hemmed in puppies and kittens for people to fall in love with and take home. Fans blasted the shaded animals with misty air.

As August drove toward the back gate, a tall, muscular young man with a scruffy dark haircut stood under the canopy watching them pass. He wore brown pants, a flowy pale green shirt, and beat-up sneakers. He wasn't looking down at the puppies. He stood stock-still, arms down at his sides, glaring at the passing SUV as if he'd been waiting there for them. August slowed, and Ava could make out a scar on his cheek. The young man turned and took off, sprinting across the parking lot and between the buildings. August looked at Ava and shook his head.

"That could've just been a random angry person," she said.

"That's the second hippie to find you and they're getting closer, Ava. You've been all over the news."

"So have you," she countered.

"You know that's not true. They love flashing your face on the screen as if it's not putting a target on your back. And you play into the chaos."

"I will use anything I can against these killers, including the press," Ava said, her voice raspy with frustration. "You think this was bad? You were at the Cutler mansion too. That cut throat gesture was as much for you as it was for me."

"You seem to have forgotten you were actually assaulted. If they're showing up at crime scenes and the station, then they might be following us. I'm asking Manaia to assign a patrol to your house."

Ava shook her head. "I'll be careful. I don't want a guy parked outside my house. I won't be able to sleep."

He let it go until they parked in the secure lot. "Taking a growing threat seriously isn't giving in to fear, Ava."

"Really?" Ava said, slipping out of the SUV. "That's what it looks like to me."

———

Ava settled back into the war room, while August left to ask building security to look at their outside camera feeds. Maybe they caught a good image of the young guy who'd been watching them before he took off running. Ava spent the next couple of hours working the information they gathered from Kinsley at the Ocean Within Wellness Center.

She put in a call to the city bike office and spoke with someone named Nick about their membership roster. He looked up Cindy

Aquino, Meadow, Meadow Aquino, and every permutation Ava could think of for both names. No one popped up.

"It could've been a gift membership," Nick said. "We get a lot of transitional housing centers and women's resource centers buying them to help their clients get to job interviews and doctor appointments."

Ava thanked him and thought she might run the problem past Rondeau. He might be able to use his techno wizardry on the issue. She called the information line for Bright Horizons and told them she was with the CBI and asked if they offered city bike cards to the people who stayed at the shelter. After a few transfers, she ended up talking to Norma from client services, who explained that some clients had a modified card via EBT and other low-income programs. But they had to be in a stable home, a halfway house, or similar situation. Not usually the shelters. Clients living in shelters were considered in transition, which made tracking the cards too hard. She checked several variations of Cindy Aquino's name and the name Meadow at Ava's request but found nothing. Cindy may have been using a membership card, but it wasn't hers.

After she'd hung up with Norma, Vincent called and pulled August into a videoconference with the chief of police.

"Make sure to tell the chief I say hi," Ava hollered as he walked out the door.

She took a break, wanting sugar. The candy machine down the hall from the war room offered decent choices, and the soft-looking cookies sounded perfect. She dug in her messenger bag for change, touched something pillowy, and pulled out the blue floating keychain with the maintenance guy's phone number on it. Back at the desk, she called Jerra's Peak Ship while eating cookies.

Jerra answered in a gruff voice. He spoke with a slightly broken Eastern European accent, maybe Russian, Ava thought. She explained why she'd called and that she'd received his name from Sharon at the marina.

"No complaints at the municipal marina. They know how much

private ones are and are usually happy. Also, I don't rent to strangers. Only to longstanding customers. If they need a boat while I am not yet done with repairs to theirs, I will lend them one of mine. But I know them. They can pilot well, are careful."

"Have you heard of any thefts from the municipal marina or private ones nearby?"

"No, no. And I work many places like the municipal marina."

"What about employees? Is there anyone that works for you that I can speak with?"

"No, I have no employees. I hire extra help for repairs if it is a big job. Day labor."

"What kind of repairs on the boats require extra help?"

"Sometimes I need help with storm damage to the slips and vessels. We do some minor hull repair if it is feasible. Also, for loyal customers, I will get a guy under your boat with scuba to scrape off barnacles and look at the rudders and propellers. That is extra."

"So, this extra help you hire occasionally, any of them young kids, like college aged?"

He hesitated for a moment, then said, "Yes. Sometimes."

"I'm not trying to trip you up with the tax man or whatever," Ava said. "I'm trying to catch a serial killer. I don't care how you pay them."

"No, it's not that. I am on the up and up as you say." Jerra explained that during the summer, plenty of kids were willing to work in the hot sun for decent money. He mainly hired them to help with the structural chores on the marina grounds, like repainting the railings, re-adhering slip guards on walkways, and light landscaping. "They come and go. Some are good workers. They know their stuff enough to help me with the boats."

That caught her attention. "Tell me about those. The ones interested in boats in particular. Are these kids boaters themselves?"

Jerra told her about several young men who worked for him, but only one had the mechanical chops to actually help him with engine repairs.

"He was good with tools, a fast learner."

"You worked with him. What did you guys talk about?"

"What do you mean?"

"Did he talk about family or how long he'd lived in Oceanside?"

Jerra made a humming noise like he was thinking. "He mostly asked questions, but not about engines. About sailing."

"So, he had experience with boats?" Ava scribbled down the information in her notebook.

"No. I would say he did not."

"What do you mean? He was good with boat engines and talked about sailing but wasn't a sailor?"

"He asked me basics. He didn't know anything about the other parts of a vessel, only the engine. It is like he only worked on boats but had no experience piloting or sailing them. But he was young so, I taught him what he didn't know."

Ava stilled. No experience and access to boats. "Would he know which vessels were maybe unoccupied or not going to be used by the owners soon?"

Jerra thought about that for a moment. "I suppose yes. We sometimes prepare boats for wet storage. That's long term. It's for when owners aren't coming out to use them for a few months and want them closed up against weather, like that."

"What is this guy's name?"

"Uh, let me check. This was months ago, maybe April. Huge kid. Scar on his cheek like a pirate. Very polite."

The kid who'd been out in front of the station. "Any information you have on him would be great."

Typing sounds came from Jerra's end, then, "Hunter. His name was Hunter. No last name. Young guy, around twenty or so."

"No last name?"

"No, and this is a little, how do you say, off? First, he told me this name. Hunter. But when I asked for information to pay after a week, he acted like he didn't want me to know and asked for cash instead. When I told him I don't pay under the table, that I just needed a name for the check, he asked me to use this app. Uh, PayNet. I send him money that way."

"What was the name on the account?"

"Only initials. H.M."

Ava thanked him and left him with her number in case he thought of something else. She tipped back in the office chair and stared at the holes in the ceiling tiles. Something scratched at the back of her mind. She was midway through a message to August when she sat upright, a thought catching tight in her mind. Did Hunter just happen to be at the right place at the right time, or did someone put him in contact with Jerra? She called him back, and he told her that the kid walked up to him and said that Sharon from the office had told him he was looking for help. Ava thanked him again, then dialed Sharon at the Municipal Marina.

"I have a name to run by you," Ava said. "Jerra said you sent a kid over to help him who went by the name of Hunter. Do you remember him?"

"Hunter? No. Let me check my files. Hold on." Ava heard the sound of scraping metal, and then Sharon came back. "Yeah, no I don't see a Hunter here."

"What about someone with the initials, H.M.?"

"I have a Henry Miller."

"Like the author?"

"I don't know about that," Sharon said. "He filled out an application, and I told him he didn't have enough experience to work for me, but that Jerra might need an extra pair of hands."

Ava's leg bounced under the table. "Do you have an address or a phone number for him?"

"No, he left that blank. Said he could come back on certain days to check for work if I wanted."

"Would he know or have access to information about the boat owners there?"

"Like what?"

"If they're going to use the boats soon or not?"

Sharon was quiet for a moment. "We have a three-ring binder that holds forms they can fill out if they are going to shut down for the season. They pay an extra fee to have one of our security guards check out their crafts at night. You mean like that?"

"Exactly like that."

August returned from his conference, and she motioned him over to her side of the table. She finished her call with Sharon and then turned to him, buzzing with the rush of the chase.

"I think I found something." She pushed her notebook toward him and relayed what she'd learned about Henry Miller. "Maybe the killer didn't own a boat or even steal one."

"He borrowed one." August straightened, a shrewd gleam in his eyes. "You think he's one half of the killer couple."

Ava nodded. "We need to go check out the boats at the marina again."

TWENTY

By three in the afternoon the Municipal Marina swarmed with officers from the Crimes of Violence Unit along with extras from other departments, called in by Detective Manaia. Word got out about movement on the case, and news vans arrived shortly after, kept back from the scene by police barriers and patrol officers. Detective Manaia, August, Ava, and Harbor Police Captain Valencia mustered in the marina office, taking up the back room. They set up maps and looked through the manager's binders for information on the marina's customers.

Ava and August consulted with CBI lawyers, then worked the phones, getting permission to board what Sharon called 'fallow boats.' Vessels for which the owners paid the year-round fee, long-term wet storage boats not yet opened up for the season or crafts whose owners did not intend to use them in the near future. August also had her check the guest boater log. They found that only small craft under twelve feet and sailboats had rented short-term slips during the time period, eliminating them. Problems with Harbor Police over jurisdiction slowed things down, as did the almost one thousand boats they needed to vet.

While Manaia and Valencia were working out logistic issues, Ava read the packet of information on Henry Miller sent to her by Rondeau. He had a juvie record, had issues with his high school resource officer, and a history of violence. She didn't see any association with a young woman in his files. At least, he hadn't been arrested with her. DMV information put him at six feet four inches. A big guy, a kid really, only nineteen years old. He'd never finished high school. A social worker's assessment mentioned a possible learning disability for which, it appeared, he was never tested. By high school, he had already had arrests for petty theft, fighting at the mall, and trying to pass a fake prescription for oxycodone.

The scar on his cheek had come from a fight at school when he was fourteen. According to the hospital case worker, his father had tried to superglue the wound closed, resulting in infection, surgery, and lasting nerve damage. He'd spent his teens in and out of rehab and group homes, and had no family to speak of, save for his father in prison somewhere in Utah. His mother had died when he was four years old.

After hours, August convinced her to take a break. They stood outside in a freshening breeze. A blue and white striped awning, extending over the door of the marina office, shielded them from the glaring sun.

August leaned on the clapboard siding next to her. "If you're right and this kid took a boat with no experience, it would explain why he didn't know to go further out to sea before dumping the bodies." He tilted his bag of baked chips at her. "I can't always see what you do when you're telling me." He smiled at her. "Then things like this happen."

She took a chip to be polite. "What do you mean?"

"A while ago you said that half of the killer duo felt like a fumbling idiot accomplice, and here we are. A troubled teen and a borrowed boat."

"I'm more worried about the smart half of the team." Ava glanced out at the mass of bobbing boats. At the far end of the marina, near the harbor beach parking lot, reporters and gawkers filmed the search. "The press is getting thick out there. I thought I heard a helicopter."

He took back the chip she was just holding in her fingers, crunching on it as he peered up at the sky. "It would be great if we found something then."

They picked a section of slip numbers and joined the boat-to-boat search, talking with people they ran into on the gangways, showing them photos of Henry Miller and the three victims. Manaia worked with the owners on the list to eliminate boats that were either too small to carry the blue oil barrels, didn't have a big enough deck, or were not power boats. August didn't believe an untrained amateur could pull off stealing a sailboat and bringing it back in one piece. Ava deferred to his expertise. The search lasted for a couple more hours before Rondeau called.

Ava and August stood on the swaying gangway, listening to him on speaker.

"We've been working with Detective Manaia on the fallow boats list you guys sent, calling and asking if anyone has had any trouble with their vessel," he said. "We told them it didn't have to be mechanical. Just an issue. One of the detectives here has a guy on the phone who's saying that a few months ago he went to get his boat ready for a family thing and found that someone had broken into it."

Ava bounced on the balls of her feet. "Can I talk to him?"

"Yeah, lemme work out how to transfer you via the network hub."

"Just give us his phone number," August said. "We'll call him."

They had Tom Ayes on the phone in less than a minute while they hurried to Aye's boat, *The Wandering Ayes.*

Ayes, an affable, currently bewildered man, told them he'd gone to check on his family's cabin cruiser at the end of March or early April and found damage to the hull and the deck.

"What specific damage?" August asked as they stopped in front of the blue hulled cruiser.

"It was a mess," he said. "There were deep scrapes on the aft deck from something heavy." August pointed to the rear deck of the boat in front of them as Ayes spoke. "There's a crack in the swim platform. I'll have to get the whole assembly replaced." August waved his hand at a hinged gate and ladder. "And I found significant damage to the hull near the finger of the slip. A big dent like whoever piloted the boat back into the harbor hit something." August raised his arm to point, but Ava swatted his hand away as Ayes continued. "Also, they burned through the gas I had just paid Jerra to fill it up with."

"Sounds like a kid stealing his dad's car. He parties in it, crashes it," Ava said.

"Could anyone in your family have done it? Did you file a report?" August asked.

"I hadn't gotten around to it yet. I filed with my insurance, and they wanted a police report, but you know, life got in the way. And no, no one else had access to the boat."

He granted the CBI and OPD permission to board the vessel and asked for copies of what they found to file with his insurance.

"This thing is huge," she said. "It's like an RV on water."

"Probably a forty-five-footer. This is a family boat. I think it seats eight to ten people." August pointed to the swim platform and hard canopy, noting the boat could accommodate the blue drums, then walked around the craft checking the hull. Ava called Sharon in the marina office to get information on the empty slip next to it on the right. According to her logbook, it was a sailboat, a small water cruiser that set sail in January for a long-distance voyage.

Ava relayed the info to August. "So they had privacy to leave and return without anyone noticing."

"This is a deep scrape. I'd bet it was from a pylon." August strode along the boat, nodding. He pointed to an orange streak in the damage. "See that? I think that's from the reflective paint."

The cruiser's swim platform did indeed look bent from great pressure. August took out his phone and called Talia, working out with her whether to call in a CBI forensic van or to go with the Oceanside Field Evidence Team to process the boat.

"I'm going aboard." Ava said, pulling nitrile gloves from a packet in her messenger bag. She climbed up the transom ladder to the deck and peered at the scrapes on the surface. The gouges led from just underneath the hard canopy to the edge of the swim platform. She imagined the blue oil drums tipping over and sinking into the deep, dark sea with Cindy and Jimmy's bodies inside. Two young lives ended for no apparent reason.

———

Almost an hour later, Talia arrived with a team from the OPD's field evidence lab to process the cabin cruiser. They shooed everyone back and put up a privacy screen to keep the growing number of looky-loos from filming. OPD set up barriers at the marina entrances, only letting in boaters with an escort to protect the scene. Then the people in paper suits moved in with their swabs and cameras, pushing Ava and August further back.

They stood in front of the marina office, watching the evidence techs work as dusk moved in. The temperature dropped, and the damp air gave Ava the chills. When she went to the SUV to grab her cardigan, her phone rang.

"Agent Cortes here." She pulled on the sweater, walking back.

"This is Harve from the Medical Examiner's Office here in Kearny Mesa. I had a request by Agent Rondeau about a series of images he wanted run through the tattoo database."

"The tattoo database? Oh! Yes, thanks for reaching out."

"Yeah, he sent in something like nine different symbols. We got a bunch back on almost all of them. Except for this flower-looking symbol. We only got one hit back for that one. I got a name if you want it."

Ava stopped walking. "Tell me."

He did, and she rushed back, waving her phone at August. He turned, lifting a dark brow.

"What's going on?"

She showed him the image Harve had texted her. A mugshot of a young, college-aged woman named Cara Bane. Arrested for DUI, she stood staring with a hooded, bored gaze at the camera. She wore a tank top and, tattooed on her shoulder, a stylized flower made of concentric, elongated ovals swirled across her skin in dark blue.

"What is this?"

"Remember Rondeau made tattoos out of the markings on the victim's bodies? We got a hit on one."

"Just one, really?"

"That's the thing, this is the *only* symbol where there was just one version in the database. It's also the only one my professor said she didn't recognize. She said it appeared to be designed."

His eyes searched hers. "I'm going to need a bit more, Ava."

"These connections I'm making are about as tenuous as spider webbing right now. But, yeah, according to Professor Katsaros, all the other symbols on the bodies exist in various belief systems or traditional practices except this one. This one is made up, basically."

"Like a signature." August took her phone, zooming in on the photo. "You said this is a flower?"

"I think it's based on a real flower," Ava muttered. Depictions of the flower she'd seen in photos flickered behind her vision. Snapshots of elongated petals in garden books, on her phone screen in an article, a history textbook came to mind, and then she saw it. A lapis-blue flower floating in a polished copper bowl. She blinked, her hand shooting out to grab his forearm. "I think it's a blue lotus."

August snapped his fingers. "The *Amanita muscaria* mushroom powder in James Wright's tea."

"Right." Ava pointed at the tattoo. "And like I said, this is not a recognized symbol. It's a design based off the flower of life, but it's unique. I think there's a good chance this Cara Bane might be connected somehow. I want to talk to her."

"Alright. Call her."

Cara's phone number from three years before no longer worked, and Ava could not find her on social media. At least not a Cara Bane that matched her photo. Ava looked up the address she'd given, and it turned out to be a tattoo studio in town. She called the business number and got the owner, Sullivan Bane, known as Sully. When she asked for Cara, he told her that she was his sister. Ava explained the situation, the tattoo, and the murders.

"I'll talk to you, but it has to be after my last client while I wrap things up. I've got clients stacked until closing, which is at eight, and then I'm hopping on a flight to Miami for a convention. I'll be gone for a week."

"Okay. We can make this fast. We're trying to get ahold of Cara. We believe she might have some information pertinent to a crime we're investigating."

"I wish you could, but she passed away two years ago."

"I'm sorry for your loss. May I ask how?"

"Car accident. The tattoo though, if it's the one I'm thinking, all loopy and mathematical, right?"

"Yes."

"I did that one. At the request of her creepy boyfriend."

"You met him?" Ava asked.

"Couple times, unfortunately."

Ava covered the phone's mouthpiece. "He can meet us, but we'd have to leave like, now."

August nodded, already walking to the SUV. "Let's go."

She let Sully know they were on their way. On the drive out of the marina parking lot, the sun sat low in the sky, burning crimson at the horizon. The crowd of onlookers standing on the jetty resembled rock statues in the dying light. As August drove them past, Ava wondered how Cara Bane might be connected to the whole mess and what she could tell them from beyond the grave.

TWENTY-ONE

Sky just wanted a place to sit and draw for one damn minute. A moment's peace from all the smiling and thank you's and having to fight the straight-up urge to slap people for the stupid things they said to her when she worked at the drive-thru or delivered their wholesome box of organic crap.

You should be in school, honey. No shit.

It's dangerous for you to go door-to-door. For you, maybe.

Sky sat on the end of the jetty, facing the open ocean before her, sketchpad and graphic pencil in hand. She drew the setting sun, using the negative space to make the rays of sunlight reach up from the depths of the sea. The oversized watch on her wrist shimmered in the light and she turned her wrist, watching the flash, and admiring it. Brent Cutler had taste, she'd give him that.

A couple on the jetty were walking back to shore, picking their way over the broken stones, when they stopped and one of them gasped. Sky looked over in time to see the man point at the harbor. She turned, lifted her sunglasses, then shot to her feet.

"What the hell?"

Cops crawled all over the marina like a bunch of cockroaches.

They walked up and down the little paths or gangways, whatever Hunter called them. She hadn't noticed any cop cars pulling up when she arrived, so something must have happened while her back was turned. What was that? Twenty minutes?

She closed her drawing pad, slipping her feet back into her sandals. Her pulse pounded in her head as she watched. A bunch of cops stood under the awning at the marina's office talking to a tall guy in a button-down shirt. Sky hurried back toward the shore for a better look. She passed other people standing and watching. Crossing the street, she jogged to the RV parking lot at the marina's edge.

Don't jump to conclusions, she told herself. The cops didn't seem excited. They weren't crowding around one boat. They walked up and down the gangways, definitely searching for something.

She forced herself to take a controlled breath. In and out. Cleansing the chaos. Centering her mind. Be still. Wait.

Nothing much happened, and she debated leaving. Calmed herself with facts. She and Hunter had been careful not only with Meadow and Jimmy but also with Brent. They'd been careful, worn gloves, and used bleach wipes on the surfaces. They'd done everything right. Well, almost.

A thrum moved through the crowd. Something was happening.

The group of cops broke apart, and she saw her. Agent Cortes. Long dark hair, small stature, the woman ran ahead of the tall man who accompanied her, like she knew where she was going. A buzzing sound blared in Sky's head as she watched a nightmare unfold.

No, no, no... She pushed an old lady aside to get a better look. *This can't be happening.*

Agent Cortes ran to the end of a row of boats and stopped. Right in front of the *Wandering Ayes*. Sky dropped her pencil and pad, hands flying to her mouth. She couldn't move. Couldn't breathe. Anger, and the unfairness of it seared through her. Could *nothing* work out right? She slipped her phone from the pocket of her dress. Hesitated. Hunter would panic. She had to think.

She'd done everything he'd taught her. What had they missed?

Flashes of the killings came back to her. She and Hunter had broken into the marina, assured the owner would not show up to the boat. It was so big, and Sky had wondered how they'd repark it or whatever, but that was Hunter's deal. He had been studying up on the boat since they'd chosen it. They worked quickly, hiding the cut-open trash bags and tape under the seats for quick use later. Setting up the UV dye poultice and the carving blade in the cabin. Sky had had a note delivered to Meadow in the work kitchen. She'd given one to Hunter to send to Jimmy in the packing warehouse.

The Teacher has called you. Meet at the van in the parking lot.

No one said no to his orders. The couple would arrive at the marina at the same time, and they'd be ready. Hunter had taken care of the camera he thought might be pointed toward the boat slip the day before. Sky chose that particular weekend because it was after the monthly fast. Neither Meadow nor Jimmy should have eaten that whole weekend, and she hoped that Jimmy would at least be weaker. The rest of their plan would go off like she'd imagined, she told herself. She would manifest it.

Hunter, who had regularly picked Meadow up when she'd lived at the shelter, was a familiar face to her. Both she and Jimmy got in without a fuss. Hunter texted her at a stoplight, telling her that they were whisper-fighting about something, but he couldn't make out what.

When Hunter got to the boat, Meadow looked so excited. She couldn't get over how nice the boat was and asked if it belonged to the Teacher. Sky told her something like it belonged to the whole community, and she seemed satisfied. Sky made sure to be nice to Meadow, despite how she despised her, and not to anger the Teacher.

Meadow just walked around gushing about the carpet and all the couch pillows. She tried to get Jimmy to smile, but he looked scared. Apparently, Jimmy had been much smarter than Meadow.

Hunter started up the cruiser and navigated out of the harbor so slowly, Sky thought anyone watching would know they'd stolen it. As they headed out to sea, Sky used the remote to ignite a faux fireplace, the wavering orange light and soothing music setting a calm scene. Meadow and Jimmy wandered the living and dining area while she worked on the next phase of the plan. The Blue Lotus.

This was the one lesson the Teacher hadn't taught her. He'd said she wasn't worthy to partake in it until she'd mastered her anger. He'd told her she might get lost on her inner journey without control of her heart. But as a reward for her devotion, he'd bestowed her true name upon her one night when they were alone. She knew he was right, and the family all assumed she had taken the tea with him, but the inner shame of not being as ready as Meadow had been made her stomach knot every time she thought about it.

What was so special about Meadow, anyway? Why did she get to jump ahead and not Sky? She'd seen the Blue Lotus in action, and it was potent. But Sky believed she was strong enough. No, she knew she was.

After she stole some from the Teacher's room, she used a little to practice how to prepare it without accidentally dosing herself. Sky first tried carefully sprinkling a spoonful on the bottom of the mug and filling it with water, but the powder swirled up with steam and she could smell it. Not good. Then, she emptied out a store-brand tea bag, carefully poured the Blue Lotus into the bag, and then re-sealed it with a hair straightener. It worked.

Now, in the boat's kitchen, Sky poured not quite boiling water into mugs from the cabinet. She unwrapped the doctored tea bags and lowered them carefully into the hot water. They sank. Out of the corner of her eye, she caught Meadow wandering around with her mouth open as she gawked at the setting sun. She walked over to where Sky stood cutting strawberries in half and putting them into a small bowl as a snack.

"This boat is so nice," Meadow said, leaning on the counter. "You know, before the Teacher, I would've been so jealous about people having a boat like this, but not anymore." She shrugged, her expression serene. "After his teachings, I just don't get mad about stuff like that anymore."

"That's growth," Sky muttered absently.

"The crazy thing is, as soon as I let go of all that jealousy, I end up on this beautiful boat." Her eyes opened wide in wonder and joy. Sky thought she looked idiotic. Well, that stupid look wouldn't last much longer.

Sky forced a smile and repeated something Orien had said to her numerous times. "The universe rewards our earnest desire to change."

Meadow watched her prepare the tea, then whispered, "Is this Jimmy's naming? That's what this is, right?"

"Maybe," Sky said with a conspiratorial grin. Meadow nodded, winking.

Sky had been present at Meadow's transition from Cindy Aquino. Had been the one to rub her lips with ice as her eyes rolled back and she babbled about how her mother didn't love her. Pathetic. Sky felt sure Cindy or Meadow didn't go anywhere at all that night. She didn't taste the echoes of the universe or explore the depths of time. The Teacher told Sky that sometimes people's minds aren't strong enough, not ready to understand, so they explore their inner ocean and make peace with that.

Sky thought Hunter might have done that when he took the Blue Lotus. He'd been with the family for longer than Sky, but wasn't trusted as much, which made her feel better about not having taken the tea yet. He wasn't sure enough, the Teacher had told her once. He hesitated and asked too many questions. Sky thought what Hunter lacked in depth and devotion, he made up in strength, which served her better anyway. But she would see what was really out there. She would learn the reason for her miserable existence. Why things happened to her and not to others. Why she was so smart and yet so lost. Why a dark coal of hatred constantly seethed in her chest and nothing she did helped her escape it.

"Is he coming soon?" Meadow asked. Her big doe eyes, all wet and trusting, were what had made her the Teacher's favorite. But the Teacher would understand. Meadow had turned. She had betrayed them. She was a threat. "Jimmy and I just finished our fast and we're starving."

She handed Meadow a mug of Blue Lotus, wondering if the fantastically larger dose would make her stop talking for once. "Go outside, relax, contemplate. He'll reveal everything to you in time."

Jimmy walked over and stood next to Meadow, his lips pressed into a thin line, eyes darting around. He looked like he wanted to run but took a mug when offered. Hunter killed the engine, and they drifted in the swells. He walked them out to the deck chairs. Sky sat in a chair facing them across a wicker coffee table. She held her own mug up in an air-toast and they followed suit.

"He wants your mind open," Sky said, taking a sip of her untainted tea. Hunter stood behind the couple, his size menacing. Jimmy, a surfer, would be no match for him.

Meadow rambled about the wellness center and the state of the food industry. So much for it shutting her up. Jimmy took sips, his lips pulling down in a frown at its bitter taste, but he drank. Sky tried not to look overboard at the vast, dark ocean. She hated large bodies of water and avoided them at all costs, but this was important. This was necessary.

Everything went well until it didn't. When the effects of the tea hit Meadow, she started to slur her words, her head lolling backward as she stared up at the night sky. She made a strangled, gurgling sound and drooled a little.

"What did you do?" Jimmy shouted. He shook his head as if to clear it and threw his mug down on the deck. "I knew something was up. He didn't call for us, did he?"

"He didn't, no." Sky smiled, a Cheshire cat grin that unnerved him.

Jimmy ran into the cabin, knocking things off the counter. Hunter got one part of the zip tie around Jimmy's wrist, but he twisted away. Flailing on the floor, Jimmy scrambled to his feet, grabbed the strawberry knife, and slashed at Hunter, cutting a meaty red swath across his palm. Hunter shouted with pain and tackled Jimmy. They fought, tangling and rolling across the floor until Jimmy ended up on top. Sky ran to her bag and grabbed the snub-nosed revolver from the front pocket. Jimmy growled like a caveman, fighting for his life, leveraging his whole body over the blade between them, driving it toward Hunter's neck. Sky watched for a moment, fascinated by the sheer will to survive on Jimmy's face. She'd clearly underestimated him.

"Sky!" Hunter shouted, his face red with strain, wounded hand shaking. "Please!"

She stepped forward, pushing the gun against Jimmy's skull just behind the ear. Just as the Teacher had taught her. She shot him, the sound like a firecracker pop in the cabin, and he slumped onto Hunter, gone.

"Why did you wait so long?" Hunter shouted, pushing Jimmy's body off him.

"I had faith in you, love," Sky murmured, her gaze fixed on the body.

Jimmy looked up at her with an unblinking gaze. She broke out of her trance at the sound of Hunter's pained moan and sprinted into action. She grabbed one of the trash bags they'd brought and placed it on the floor, rolling Jimmy on top of it to contain the blood. She glanced at Hunter's hand. It looked bad. Grabbing a towel from the kitchen, she tossed it to him.

"Stop the bleeding. You don't want to leave evidence."

He nodded, glancing at the gun in her hand. "What about Meadow?"

"I don't think she even knows what just happened." She pointed to the deck. "Get the poultice and carving blade from the cabin, then start the ceremony. There's a paper there by the poultice jar with the drawings if you need them."

"I know them." He looked a little insulted. "I helped with Lake."

Sky nodded, turning to deal with Meadow. They'd intended to interrogate them before killing them, but clearly that didn't work out.

Hunter, still angry from the cut on his hand, bandaged it with tape and gauze he found in a first-aid kit in the kitchen. He pulled a dish glove over his hurt hand before dragging Jimmy's body to the deck. What a baby.

Sky put the gun into her dress pocket and questioned the barely intelligible Meadow, smacking her cheek to get her to focus.

"Listen, Meadow. Hey. Cindy!"

"He's trying to be good." Meadow murmured, a doofy smile on her slack face. "He'll be better."

"Listen. We know that Jimmy is working with someone from the outside. That he's betrayed the Teacher and Ocean Within. He's feeding them information. Who is it?"

"How..." Meadow's gaze caught Sky as if she'd just noticed her presence. "You know?"

"Yes. We followed Jimmy. He met with someone and gave him an envelope. Who was it? What did he give them?"

"Shh." Meadow slurred after nearly a full minute, her eyes fluttering. "She'll never find him under the pizza."

Sky sat back, rubbing her face with both hands.

Inside, Hunter grunted and cursed as he uncovered the barrels hidden under the tarp on the deck. He got to work binding Jimmy's hands in front as if he were praying to Mother Night. Once laid out on the deck, Hunter carved the death runes, rubbing the poultice into them.

"Do you need help, hon?" Sky called.

"No."

"It has to be done right. They have to ascend or it would be murder."

"*I know.*"

"I'm just saying," Sky said as she stared at the barely conscious Meadow on the chair. "Under the pizza?"

Sky sat up straight, her head snapping to Meadow's backpack on the counter. She ran over, searched through the impossible amount of junk inside, and pulled out a brand-new looking phone. Sky hurried over to Meadow, slapped her awake enough for the phone's facial recognition to work, and got access. First, she toggled off the phone's lock then navigated to the text messages and found all of them deleted. A separate messaging app disguised as a calculator proved more useful. Under the creative listing of *Le Pizza*, Sky found a series of back-and-forth texts between Meadow and someone else. She skimmed them.

Her mouth went dry as the depth of Meadow and Jimmy's betrayal revealed itself. Meadow argued with someone about the Teacher and the family. The mystery man said that Jimmy had told him everything and listed off terrible lies and accusations, things taken out of context, embellished accounts of ceremonies and private conversations with the Teacher. All of it damning if misunderstood by outsiders. Meadow argued that Jimmy just didn't understand yet. That he was jealous of the Teacher.

Sky's jaw clenched, her breath coming out in short snorts. Meadow had known. She'd known that Jimmy was an infiltrator and that he was working with someone on the outside but had said nothing! Why? Was she having doubts? Why else keep the traitor a secret? Sky's chest filled with righteous hatred. She'd been right to act.

Sky watched as Meadow sank deeper into unconsciousness as the overdose hit her, thrashing and sweating. She threw up, and her breaths grew shallow, her face pale. The boat rose with a swell, and Sky's stomach lurched.

"We gotta head back soon," Hunter said at the door, his eyes wide, face ashen. "My hand won't stop bleeding, and I can't feel my thumb that good."

Sky took in his scarred face and puppy-dog eyes and nodded. "Okay, help me move her to the couch with the plastic on it."

They dragged Meadow inside and she flopped like a rag doll onto the sealed cushions, landing on her side. Using her phone, Sky took a photo of Meadow, then pulled the gun from her dress pocket and held it out to Hunter.

He stepped back. "I can't, Sky. I get nightmares."

"It's a rite of passage! Protecting the family, stepping up," Sky pushed. She needed proof he'd been involved so he couldn't turn on her later.

He grimaced. "I know, I just... I hate guns."

"Together, then. Like always," she said.

And they did. They shot her, prepared her body for the next level of ascension, and stuffed her in her own barrel. Once sealed, they pushed down the little swim gate at the back of the boat. Hunter dragged the barrels to the edge and tossed them over.

A sense of relief filled Sky. She took a cleansing breath. They had a lot to do. They had to clean the floor and make sure Hunter hadn't bled anywhere, but for now, she felt lighter. Powerful, even. The moonlight glinted off the dark water, and the cool air enveloped her. A gift from Mother Night.

———

Cop lights from the marina slashed across the water, ripping Sky back to the present. The cops were moving quickly, cordoning off the boat slips. Something was happening. A few of them stretched yellow crime scene tape around the *Wandering Ayes*.

We got all of it. What are they going to prove with a couple scratches on the deck?

The sun sank to an angry red disk, smoldering on the horizon. A white forensic van pulled into the parking lot. People with equipment and lights crawled out. Hunter wouldn't help. He'd freak out that they'd find his blood.

And he might be right. All the bleach wipes in the world wouldn't guarantee that they couldn't find something. He'd fought with Jimmy, and they'd rolled all over that carpet. She put her phone away, strode nonchalantly to the electric scooter she'd taken from Meadow, and headed home. She didn't need Hunter. She needed to speak to *him. He'd* know what to do.

———

Not far from the Cutler Mansion where she'd seen Agent Cortes, an equally large modern house of wood and glass sat a few streets over. Also with a beach view, but further from the coast. She pulled up to the six-foot iron bar gate and punched in the code. The gate opened, and she walked her scooter onto the smooth, curving driveway, careful not to make noise.

A large kid at the gate saw her, put a palm to his heart, and said, "Peace."

She returned the greeting. Further in, she passed the hand-carved sign nailed onto a palm tree that read Ascension House—Ocean Within Community.

Just seeing it loosened the band squeezing her chest. She passed more members of the community, nodding, greeting them with peace, smiling despite the growing dread in her gut. No one ever locked the front door, and she pushed in, passing macrame plant holders hanging from the ceiling. The long tendrils of dangling leaves shifted in the breeze as she entered. Someone once told her the décor reminded them of natural Swedish minimalism, whatever that meant. Wood and jute and a lot of cream-colored cushions, Sky guessed. Clean, bare, peaceful.

A group of people her age sat in a circle on a rug. Leaning on plush satin pillows, they shared a large hookah in the center. They took turns inhaling the smoky vapor, coughing and laughing. A girl sat in front of a guy drawing flowers on his face with body paint. Others in the group showed evidence of her artwork, with one girl's entire neck and chest decorated with green and blue butterflies. They called for her to join them, but Sky didn't need them. She needed *him*.

She headed for the courtyard at the rear of the house. Along the way, she passed a couple of brothers who'd grown their hair out like the Teacher. They smiled at her, but she didn't return their greeting.

Shrouded by massive eucalyptus trees, a solid wood fence, with candles flickering on the brickwork that lined the edges of the space, the cool, dark patio conveyed a secret, magical feel. Incense burned from hanging trays, making everything hazy. Soft, tinkling music played overhead from hidden speakers. A man in a white tunic and flowy pants, his long blond hair blowing in the soft breeze, walked around a group of women lying on mats in the center of the space. The candlelight illuminated his sculpted form through the thin fabric and Sky watched him move with rapt attention. His voice, low and smooth, encouraged the private yoga clients to relish the experience.

"The ascension ritual is communal for a reason," he murmured, padding barefoot around the prone women, hands clasped behind his back, his gaze on their slack faces. "The ascension tea is a doorway."

"Ascension is a doorway," the four women answered in unison.

"A glimpse into the truth," he said, circling them.

"Truth. Renewal. Ascension," they replied.

They didn't open their eyes, their words dreamy. Sky knew they were just play-acting or even kidding themselves. The "Ascension Tea" they drank before the guided meditation sessions was sold at the yoga studio and full of nothing but flowers. Readily available to the public. The actual Ascension Tea, the community's ceremonial elixir, that which *truly* opened doors of consciousness, was not.

"To partake together is to ground each other in trust and security." The last rays of the setting sun angled over the fence, framing him in light. Sky thought him so beautiful he was almost hard to look at. "You come here seeking peace. And peace, like the tide, asks only that you surrender to it."

He spotted her, and his smile pulled her close. She lifted her hand to her heart as she approached on light feet, careful not to disturb the ceremony. "Peace."

"You look like you've seen a ghost, Sky." He held out his hand, and she placed hers in his palm. He clasped his other hand over hers, drawing her nearer. Her stomach fluttered at his touch, his gaze penetrating. "What is wrong?"

"I need to talk with you, Teacher," Sky whispered, her gaze darting to the women on the floor. The outsiders. "It's urgent."

"Of course."

He turned as a young man walked out into the courtyard as if summoned. She hadn't met him but remembered someone calling him Sage.

"Teacher?"

"Continue to guide our friends for moment," he whispered. "I'll return shortly."

Placing his arm around her thin shoulders, the Teacher led her back into the house and out the side door to a vast garden. Members of the community assigned to tend it walked the rows of lavender, marigold, and other medicinal plants, picking flower buds and tea leaves for their subscription box items. They often worked late into the night by the glow of suspended string lights that crisscrossed overhead. The Teacher said that it was only by the light of the moon, of Mother Night, that the plants were at their most potent. Every one of the workers stopped and turned when he appeared. With a flick of his wrist, they silently dropped their harvest bags and exited the garden single file.

He walked to the memorial bench that sat under a tree that resembled a weeping willow and patted the space next to him.

"Unburden your mind," he said. "What troubles you?"

"I have to tell you something," Sky said. "But I want you to know, I was only doing what I thought was right."

"That energy comes from insecurity," he tilted his head, frowning. "I don't need reminding of your worth. Just tell me what happened."

She fought to control her breathing. To find that center, to calm the ocean raging within her, but fury bubbled just beneath the surface. This was Meadow's fault. She'd brought in the traitor.

Sky wiped the sweat beading on her lip with her forearm. "Okay, this guy, Jimmy, who *Meadow* brought into the family, was acting really sketchy. He asked questions about everything. Where the money the community made went, who really owned Ascension House. Raven even told me that he asked her if she could get him some of the Ascension Tea, but the 'real kind.' She didn't know what he was talking about, but I did. Hunter and I decided to follow him one day and we saw him meeting with an outsider. He wasn't a believer."

The Teacher didn't interrupt her or ask questions, just nodded as if she was just telling him about her day. Sky didn't understand why he didn't feel the same rage that burned beneath her skin.

"I understand you acted in the best interests of the community," he said, but tilted his head and caught her gaze. "But I sense more, Sky. What aren't you telling me?"

She hesitated for a moment, and then said, "I wanted to protect you. So, I did something about it. Just like you showed me to. I watched him for weeks, so I was sure before I did anything. I promise."

"And what did you do?"

She told him about the boat. How she took unsecured ceremonial tea with the Blue Lotus in it and tried to use it to get information. She told him how she did everything he taught her, how they made sure they were careful, yet this Agent Cortes still seemed to be sniffing around.

He nodded slowly, his piercing eyes never leaving Sky's. "I'm aware of her."

"She's talking to everyone. There was a news stream about how she's violent or like super smart or something. She's going to find out."

"Find out that Hunter was on the boat," he said softly. He swirled the pad of his thumb over her palm, sending streaks of awareness through her. "*You* were careful. And smart, were you not? You're good at this kind of thing, aren't you, Sky? Secrets and protecting yourself?"

Sky grew quiet, unsure of what he meant. "I'm not a bad person. I only wanted..."

"You don't need to hide who you are from me. Your lack of fear and guilt is natural. Evolved." His gaze held hers, and she found no judgement there. "I see you, my fierce and beautiful one."

Something moved in her. He knew her broken parts. Understood how she thought. And still accepted her. Admired the very things about her that made her feel different.

"They made me so angry," she whispered. "They betrayed us. They turned on *you*."

He nodded up at the stars. "You know at our truest core, we are all both predator and prey. A divine dichotomy that makes us unique in the universe. God and Monster. Victim and Vengeance." He turned to look at her, touched her cheek with the back of his fingers. "That rage is a poison. Breathe, Sky. Open to the moment."

She obeyed, closing her eyes and taking in a long, sharp, cold breath. Feeling him move next to her, he placed his warm palm on her thigh, holding her in place as his words washed over her. He led her in a breathing exercise, asking her about the killings.

"Jimmy didn't have a phone on him so we used Meadow's phone to arrange a meeting with the man Jimmy had been snitching on us with because I found out that Cindy had been talking to him too! She was arguing with him over money. So I sent him a message and made it seem like she wanted to clear things up with both of them."

"How did you keep him quiet?"

"We used that old warehouse. Hunter tied him up and we kept him, uh, sedated. And we questioned him. To find out what he wanted with the family."

"Did he reveal anything?"

"No. I think we used too much of the Blue Lotus. He got really hot and just babbled about traffic."

"Who else knows, my love?"

"Just Hunter. I promise!"

The Teacher rubbed her shoulder, his gaze serene. "Do you know if Meadow or Jimmy met with anyone else?"

Sky shook her head. "No, we made sure."

He sat back on the bench, his gaze drifting to the sky. "What could Agent Cortes find on that boat?"

"Nothing. Nothing. We were so careful. We did exactly as you would."

He smiled his approval. "The sacred speaks to us. It's the continual hum of the universe." His hand on her shoulder, he stroked her throat with his thumb. "Trust, Sky. If you breathe more deeply, you'll be more open to the truth."

She did. Feeling slightly lighter, better than before, distant from the panic. He told her a story about a wounded warrior who was lost, and those he loved were in danger. He and his friends were trapped by the enemy. No way out. All of them would die. But the wounded warrior knew what needed to be done. He had the honor of making a sacrifice.

"A sacrifice?" Sky asked.

"Only then, after serving his family and saving his friends, would the warrior know peace." The Teacher lifted her hand to his lips, brushing a kiss on the back of it, sending her heart racing. "This is a test, my fierce beauty. One that will decide if you are finally ready to face the Blue Lotus."

She nodded, eager. "I'm ready. I'm strong enough."

"*You* are, but Hunter is fading. Lost. That makes him dangerous to all of us."

"What do I do?" Sky asked, the answers to her soul's anguish just beyond her fingertips. "Whatever you want."

"Let him ferry our troubles with him to ascension where they will be meaningless." He leaned forward, his breath on her lips. "Give him to peace."

TWENTY-TWO

Ava and August left the crime scene at the marina a little after sunset and traveled a few minutes down the 101 North Coast Highway to the strip of antique shops, micro-hotels, and restaurants lining both sides of the street. The artist who'd done the tattoo on his sister, Cara, said he could only wait until eight thirty, no later. On the way there, August received a text. He clenched his jaw after checking it but said nothing. He'd never withheld information regarding a case, so it must be something unrelated.

While it bothered her to know he was upset, she didn't push. That never turned out well. He'd say something if he needed to.

The Ink Slinger Tattoo Parlor sat at the end of the street next to a smoke shop. After parking at the curb, August slid the CBI placard on the dash, and they walked together to the door. Sullivan Bane flipped the lock and let them in.

He told them to call him Sully. Pitch-black, spiky hair, sinister goatee, and neck tattoos belied the slight baby fat still in his cheeks. Early thirties, but in a cool way. He smiled, and his two sharpened canine teeth sparkled with silver. They followed him in, and Ava spotted a flyer on the front counter offering a discount on glow-in-the-dark tattoos during the upcoming Friday the Thirteenth special. She grabbed one and slid it into her leather notebook as he led them to his station.

Sully held up his hands, encased in nitrile gloves. "Do you mind if I clean up while we talk? I'm on a tight schedule. My plane leaves in a few hours, and I still have to pack my gear."

August nodded. "Of course. We appreciate you speaking with us."

The small, three-chair parlor went with a biker vibe. License plates on the walls, glass cases showing jewelry for piercings, books thick with designs beneath plastic covers. Sully picked up a spray bottle and a cleaning wipe.

August watched him work. "We think there's a connection between your sister Cara's tattoo and a series of recent crimes."

"Well, I wouldn't rule it out," Sully said with a rueful smile. "Cara had a way of attracting trouble even when she was minding her own business."

He explained that he was Cara's guardian after their parents died in a small plane crash. He was five years older than Cara, and their dad, a successful medical equipment vendor, left them enough money to be comfortable. Sullivan managed it for them both, giving Cara an allowance from her portion, the rest of which she'd get when she turned twenty-five. She was a year away from receiving her money when she died.

"The teenage years with her were a dream. I thought, *what is everybody always complaining about?*" Sully shook his head, spraying and then wiping the tattoo chair. "Then, a few months after her eighteenth birthday, Cara had a mental breakdown. The doctors said she had bipolar disorder and that she'd been self-medicating with alcohol. She didn't tell me, but she'd been kicked out of school a couple months before. I tried to get her help, but she refused to see the psychiatrist. Wouldn't stay on her meds. Said they made her feel like she wasn't inside her own mind. Then, Cara got arrested for fighting in a grocery store. She said the woman was staring at her."

"That was around the time of her DUI arrest?" Ava asked.

"Yes. I was still cleaning up her assault and battery mess when she got pulled over and arrested for driving drunk. She almost ended up in prison. If it weren't for the inheritance money and a good lawyer, she would have. Instead, we got probation with completion of a treatment program." Sully looked down at the rag in his hand and his shoulders slumped. "She was an A student with a bright future a year before."

"I hadn't had any luck getting Cara to speak with counselors, so I wasn't hopeful, but she found one that met at the beach. She seemed open to the more casual approach, and I supported it because, like something had to work, you know?"

Ava nodded. "Did it?"

"For a while. She did the whole six months required by the plea deal and I hoped that she would stay with it, but she didn't. Her last court ordered meeting was her last with the group. I was bummed. They seemed to have been helping, but during the meetings and even after, she'd talk about this guy named Orien. How connected to the vibrations of the universe he was. Which was classic Cara. She believed all that astrology, horoscope, New Age stuff."

"Were they just friends?" Ava asked.

"I don't think so." He arranged some packs of sterile wipes in the bag. "In fact, I suspected she started seeing him while she was still attending the sessions, and I knew that was against the rules. There's not supposed to be any relationships in the program, right?"

"Not usually," August said.

"So, I told her I wanted to meet the guy. She'd agree, but then it wouldn't work out for one reason or another. She was sick or he 'got called away.' I asked what he did for a living, and she said he worked with people. Whatever that meant."

"Did you ever meet him?" August asked.

"I had to." Sully ran his hand over his spikey hair. "She started acting different. Changing things about herself."

"What kind of things?" Ava sked.

"For one, we had a standing lunch date every Thursday at a burger joint that she picked. Suddenly, she was a vegan and didn't want to go there." Sully threw up his hands. "I know that doesn't sound like a big thing, but then when we did meet up at some plant-based cafe for avocado toast, she still wasn't happy. She went off the entire time about ocean pollution and GMO food. It was bizarre. Cara didn't give two shits about what was in her burger unless they forgot to add the extra bacon. It was wild, a total one-eighty."

"You said other things changed," Ava said. "Can you tell me what, specifically? Her hair, manner of dress, speech patterns."

"All of that," Sully jabbed the roll of cellophane in his hand at Ava. "Literally what you just said. Cara used to work at a makeup store at the mall, and she loved the stuff. Had tons of it. One day, she just up and dumped it all. I went to her apartment to pick her up and saw bottles of hair styling lotions and makeup and all her curling iron things in trash bags and boxes. She said they were a mask. She used to style her hair. Like we'd be late for things because she was so particular. Not anymore. A simple braid down her back. I asked why, and she told me that if she meant to find her true self, she shouldn't hide from the world anymore." Sully shrugged. "I didn't know what to do. And then I saw her with this guy at her new job, and it all made sense."

"What do you mean?" Ava asked.

"She landed a job at a local café. I dropped by to say hello. Found her not working but eating at a table in the corner with a dude." He scrubbed the chairs down with angry swipes.

"When she saw me, she freaked. Got all pale and stammered like I'd caught her cheating. And the guy, I didn't even recognize him at the time, he looked totally different from where I first saw him."

"I thought you'd never met him?" Ava asked.

"I dropped her off on her first day of beach counseling but stayed in the parking lot because I saw all these homeless-looking dudes in the group."

"Makes sense," Ava said. "Something looked off and you trusted your gut. That's good. Go on."

"While I waited, I looked up the program's website. It was legit. An addiction counselor named Owen Meeks ran it. The website had his photo up and that's how I knew what he looked like." Sully's brows knitted. "I didn't realize until much later that the guy I saw her with at the sandwich shop, the one she'd called Orien, was him."

"He was the counselor?" August frowned. "Dating a patient?"

"I know," Sully said. "I had a hard time believing it myself. I mean, other than his photo on the counseling program website, I'd only ever seen him at a distance, but close up, this guy gave me the creeps."

"Why?" Ava asked.

He zipped his satchel, thinking. "Everything, really. Like, at the counseling meetings on the beach, he'd wear jeans and a hoodie. But when I ran into them at the sandwich place, it was like he was putting on a bit, like a New Age holy dude or something. He had on this flowy shirt and pants like he was on a visit to the Sahara. And he spoke in this hushed, soothing tone when he greeted me like we were in church and not the middle of downtown Oceanside. And his eyes never left me. He looked at me like I was a bug he might squash, but Cara acted like he was a rockstar."

August caught Ava's eye, nodding subtly.

"Tell me about the tattoo." Ava brought up an enlarged photo of the one found on Brent's body. "You don't sound like you liked him, but you gave her a tattoo that you said was this guy's idea. How'd that happen?"

"She drew it a lot after that beach counseling program. She said it was Orien's design." Sully rolled his eyes. "It's not original artwork. I do original pieces for clients. The symbol she said was Orien's, isn't. It's a rip off of the Lotus of Life or Flower of Life which is a metaphysical symbol. Cara's tattoo had some changes, lines connecting the concentric ovals, an almost blade type of look. It's aesthetically pleasing, but utter nonsense, like taking a Yin Yang symbol and changing the circles into stars with lines. Just wrong."

"Why'd you do it then?" Ava asked.

"She started talking about doing it herself with a needle and India ink." Sully threw up his hands. "I didn't want her to get an infection. I told her I'd do it for her if she agreed to do it right, at the shop, with all the sterile precautions. She agreed, thank God." He hesitated. "When I inked her, Orien was there. He looked way too into it, almost smug as he watched his design become a part of her skin. I almost punched his face in."

"What do you mean?"

"He had this eerie, faint smile when she'd flinch or hiss at the pain. Like he got off on watching her get branded with his ideas."

Sully told Ava and August that after the tattoo incident, he'd paid for a private investigator to check Owen out. It turned out he came from a good family. He had attended several private boarding schools but kept getting kicked out for bad behavior. There were allegations of sexual assault, battery, etc.

"I think his family made the complaints go away," Sulley said, walking to his desk. He opened the bottom drawer, dug in the back, and pulled out a manila envelope, handing it to Ava. "The PI did a great job. It just didn't really change things all that much. Maybe you can do something with it."

"Did Cara confirm their relationship?" August asked,

"No, but I could tell. The way he was with her that day. Caressing her face, kissing her neck when she hugged him. They were clearly together, but whenever I asked about it, she just said that dating wasn't even a thing anymore."

"Come again?" Ava asked. "What do you think she meant?"

"I don't know. She kept talking about the nature of love and how it's fluid and unselfish. Hippie shit." Sully hesitated, playing with an ink cup in his hands.

"Did you ever bring up the name change? Did you ask Cara why Owen now went by Orien?"

"I tried but she said Orien wasn't who I thought he was. She wouldn't elaborate." Sully shook his head. "I did hear Orien call my sister Lark a couple of times. Quietly, like it was a secret. A lover's name. I put a call in to the program after I'd hired the PI. I told them about everything, including letting them know I thought a counselor dating one of his patients to be unprofessional bordering on abuse of power. They said they'd look into it."

"Did they?" August asked. "Do you have the name of who you spoke with?"

"I never heard back." He rubbed his face and sighed. "But three days after the call, I found her on the kitchen floor, tripping out of her mind on God knows what, screaming about the Sacred and that Orien knew things he shouldn't. She went nuts. I couldn't calm her down, so I called an ambulance."

After getting out of the hospital, he threatened Cara that he'd get the court to withhold the trust money if she didn't go to one of those rehabilitation retreats. She did, in Sedona, for almost four months. He visited her every weekend.

"She didn't want to see me at first. When she did talk, it was only about him. She said that Orien accused her of betraying him and that she would never see him again."

"It turned out Orien wasn't lying. Cara and I never heard from him again. He just disappeared off the face of the earth," Sully said. "She'd look for him, too. When we were out, in a crowd, I'd catch her scanning for him. But she never mentioned him again. Something changed. She got better with the meds and the counseling. They helped, and Cara finished school. She was working as a physical therapist when she was killed."

Ava frowned. "You said it was an accident?"

Sully smiled sadly. "A drunk driver hit her one night when she was on her way back from an AA meeting. Isn't that a screwed-up twist of fate?"

After they worked Sully for a few more minutes, he got antsy and said he had to head out. They thanked him and left. On the way back to the marina crime scene, Ava stared out the window at the sky gone dark with nightfall. This Orien character, he fit. An exploiter of young and lost kids. Smart, manipulative, and without remorse. A predator. Her favorite kind of prey.

"What do you think?" August asked.

"I think we're getting close. And I think he probably knows it."

"Meaning?" August looked over, his face cast in orange light from the sodium streetlamp.

"Guys like Owen don't cower when cornered. They attack."

TWENTY-THREE

August drove them back to the marina and the boat crime scene in silence. Ava didn't try to engage. Leaving him to his thoughts, she dug into the manila folder Sully had given them. Cara Bane hadn't deserved her fate. She'd done the work, got her life on track. Was her death just an accident?

She also thought about Owen Meeks. Orien. That a mind like his, the mind of a predator, could be behind all of this added up to her. His plans, using young adults, made sense with all the amateurish moves.

Back at the marina, they found Rondeau in the office working with the manager, Sharon, on the security camera feeds. They sat together at her desk, staring at his laptop. A bag of popcorn sat between them.

"Hey guys! We found something!" she said.

Rondeau smiled. "Sharon and I have been going over the outgoing and incoming recordings of the harbor traffic." He nodded at the black and white video playing on his laptop. "I talked with Captain Valencia at Harbor Police. He's at the boat now with Detective Manaia. Told us to check at least three nights before the bodies washed up by the jetty. Sharon is aces at identifying crafts and their owners. Couldn't have done it without her."

She beamed, shoving a handful of popcorn in her mouth. He explained that, according to the marina's records, the *Wandering Ayes* left the harbor with no sailing plan filed, a month before the blue barrels washed up at the jetty.

"From what we can tell, the vessel went straight out, was gone for almost four hours, then returned after dark. Then this happened." He started the security feed, and the video showed the vessel ramming a pylon entering the harbor before turning toward the slip. "The camera covering that area of the marina had black paint on the lens."

August clapped Rondeau on the back. "Good job."

He left to meet Talia at the boat, and Rondeau and Sharon went back to work examining more camera footage for a glimpse of the killers with other cameras in the marina. Cold and hungry, Ava took the file Sully gave her to a corner of the manager's office and read through it while eating a granola bar she found in her purse.

The file provided new details and some photos of Owen and Cara on the beach walking together, hand in hand. Images of him handing out sandwiches to what appeared to be unhoused people near the pier. The DMV reported a lapsed driver's license, expired five years before and never renewed. His home address belonged to a building that no longer existed.

The PI, Dana Dashiell, wrote a detailed report, but Ava had written enough of those herself to sense a disdain underneath the professional language. She called the number on a card stapled to the file folder.

"Yeah, I thought you'd call," the woman said. "Sully just left me a message saying he talked to you guys at the CBI. He gave me permission to speak with you all about the case."

"Your report is top notch, but I get the sense there might be more?"

"Oh yeah, there's a ton more. That guy is a bad time waiting to happen. I guarantee it," Dana said. "He had this blog called, Inner

Ocean where he spouted all kinds of nonsense. I talked to a reporter I know, she covers the occult and things like that for the LA Times, so she really knows her stuff. She confirmed the things this guy spouted were nonsense. 'Unrecognizable feel-good hooey,' was the term she used."

"None of this is in the packet you gave Sully."

"No. I found out about the blog after the report. I kept an alert on my browser for a few key words, mostly his names, Owen and Orien. I told Sully, but by then, Cara had already been in some trouble, and he'd had her committed or something. Sad stuff."

"Is there anything I should know about this guy? He might be involved in a case I'm working on. Three homicides."

"That tracks. The guy is a time bomb in my opinion." Dana told her she'd spoken to his former work colleagues. "Owen used to work for a call center that sold vitamin supplements to old people. Super shady MLM type of stuff. One of the guys he worked for said that he and Owen went out to a bar in town, and he used this fake guru persona on college freshmen girls from out of state to get tail."

"Sounds like a charmer," Ava said. "Did you come across social media or anything like that?"

"No, he's been systematically erasing his digital footprint for years."

"Is it possible he changed his name?"

"If he did, I couldn't find a record of it. He just lives off the grid, I think. From what I heard about him, he got whatever he wanted from people. No reason to believe he's stopped doing that."

"Does he have family?"

"He did. Not anymore. His parents had him late in life, late forties for the mom, mid-fifties for the dad. By the time Owen or Orien, whatever you wanna call him, graduated from a private college, they were in their sixties and seventies. Both are decades gone now. From what I could cobble together, he was in his early thirties when he was dating Cara. She was twenty-two, if I remember correctly."

"Impressionable." Ava nodded, staring at his photo. "Controllable."

"I called the beach counseling program where Owen met Cara. They said he quit one day via text. No explanation, no warning, just a message saying he needed to move on. I think he got wind Sully had reached out to them."

"I got the impression from Sully that Owen was smart, ahead of the game."

"You're not wrong. He majored in psychology and it shows. I'm telling you, read this guy's blog. He tried to delete it, but the internet is forever. I found it on the Wayback Machine site." She gave Ava the blog URL. "He is a predator, Agent Cortes, through and through. I followed him one time to the farmers market. He's good looking. Women of all ages noticed. He left with a few numbers. All from *very* young women."

After the call, Ava tried doing her own search for Owen Meeks. Dana didn't lie. Owen seemed to fall off the face of the earth right after the incident with Cara. She'd ask Rondeau to try to dig up more with his digital magic. After sending him a text, she packed up her messenger bag and headed outside to find August. He stood on the gangway next to the *Wandering Ayes*, his arms crossed.

She briefed him on her conversation with Dana.

"I have to download the blog, apparently, so I can't read the archive at the moment, but Dana seemed to think there's something there."

August nodded, chewing mercilessly on a piece of gum. Ava tried to catch his eye, even stepped in front of him. "What's going on? Is it the case? Because we're moving, it'll break open soon. The facts are lining up."

She counted the facts off on her fingers. "Brent Cutler, the third victim, told his father that the emergency credit card was maxed out for a 'friend in need.' And Cindy Aquino's friend at the shelter thought she might be seeing a rich guy. An older one because of how he worded his message."

August just grunted, so she continued. "At first, I thought the older guy was Brent, but now, I'm thinking it must be this Owen character. According to Dana, he likes them young and eager to please like Cara and that hippie chick."

"When?"

Ava blinked. "What?"

"When did you make the connection between an older man and Cindy Aquino?"

"I don't know." His accusatory tone put her back up. "Why?"

"Did you have your hacker friend Denny looking into Brent's financials? Is that how you came up with the older man theory?" Suspicion, and maybe anger, smoldered in his eyes. "Because you didn't say anything to me about it."

"No, I didn't ask Denny to do that. I asked him to check out fringe groups in the immediate area, which I did tell you about." Ava crossed her arms and returned his cold stare. "What's your problem this evening?"

August shrugged. She didn't buy his nonchalance. "I just want to know when you got there, and how."

"I just don't think the Brent and Cindy relationship skews toward client and sex worker."

He leaned in, his gaze holding hers. "Why?"

"What's wrong with you?"

He shoved his hands in his pockets and looked away.

Ava regarded him for a beat before it dawned on her. "Someone told you I put in a request to speak with the Sea Siren Madam, didn't they?"

"Eliza Cartwrtight's lawyer just called me about it. He said you made the appointment days ago."

"That's right." Ava shrugged. "So what?"

"So what?" August's brow furrowed. "Why, Ava?"

"It was just in case—"

He shook his head. "Don't. You *always* have a reason for the things you do. You don't flail in the dark. You leave me to do that."

Talia leaned out of the boat, her brow raised above the sterile mask. "Everything okay out there?"

"Yes," they answered in unison.

With a gesture of surrender, she went back to work, leaving them staring at each other.

"I don't need this," Ava said, rubbing at the aching cut over her brow. She turned to go, but he got ahead of her.

"We can't do this again." He stood in her way. "We can't work this way. I need you to stop keeping things from me. I can't run this team when I'm playing catch up with you."

She looked up at him and sighed. "I went to an AA meeting."

He looked at her, a little more horrified than Ava thought necessary. "You what?"

"Wait." She put her hand up, thought for a second. "I actually went to three."

August froze, blinked. "That was such a violation of privacy. You infiltrated a safe—" He turned away. Ran a hand through his hair and muttered under his breath. He paced away, then back. "Is that why you smelled like cloves that morning? Because you snuck into a meeting? Did you pretend to be an addict? Maybe give a convincing story you stole from, I don't know, me?"

She gasped, her mouth agape. "I would *never* do that."

He let out a rueful laugh. "I've yet to see something you wouldn't do."

"Just tell me how you really feel, August," Ava said. "I'll explain my thought process, since you asked so *nicely*. Brent's dad said he was trying to help someone. Cindy's friend at the shelter said that the man Cindy yelled at all the time on her phone owed her. The guy at the meeting mentioned Brent talked about saving someone and wanting to make things right. It all added up to *not* a client and a sex worker, but a friend or even more."

"I don't care." He rubbed his face with both hands. "There's a limit, Ava. Why don't you have one?"

Heat burned through her chest as she jabbed her finger at the boat. "Because *they* don't."

"And you think that makes it okay? For you to cross lines? That's your reason for invading the sanctity of a meeting like that?"

"We were all outside, talking freely. I repeated nothing anyone said in the room."

"You can't split hairs—"

"Yes, I can. I can split hairs, mislead, and do whatever is in my power to stop these guys. That's why you wanted me on your team, right?"

"The problem is, you don't stop with suspects or witnesses! You didn't tell *me* about a vital piece of information. I'm your partner—"

"No, you're not! You're not my partner, August. You're my boss."

He stopped cold, staring at her.

She softened her tone. "As partners, we played off each other. It worked back then. If we made a mistake, we had Vincent covering our asses. But now the shit I pull falls on you. I wanted to be sure before I said anything. I hadn't made the connection *until* I told you."

"You didn't want me to know you'd gone against my wishes."

"No, I didn't. Because you were wrong." Ava shrugged. "I did the same thing to the chief of police earlier. I'm not picking on you or defying you. I'm hunting a killer. Exactly how I always do. By any means at my disposal."

He looked away, his jaw working. "And Eliza Cartwright? What do you think she can tell you?"

"I had a hunch after the AA meeting. I thought she could clear it up. It's nothing solid."

"So you can't tell me yet," August said.

"Right. They denied my request anyway."

He shook his head. "She changed her mind. She wants to speak with you."

Ava tried not to smile. "Really?"

Talia shouted from the deck. "Guys, we have prints!"

They boarded the *Wandering Ayes*, and donned shoe booties and gloves and joined Talia.

"Whoever stole the boat, wiped it down with bleach of some kind. We're finding faded spots on the carpet, the couches, and wallpaper in the bathroom near the faucet. A thorough job, but not professional by any means. They left prints in multiple places." They followed her and a field tech named Jimbo to the vessel's helm. "Tell them, Jimbo."

Short, curly brown hair, cleft in his chin, intelligent eyes. Ava had seen him before, during her time working the task force with OPD and Manaia. He hooked his thumb over his shoulder as they walked to the front of the boat.

"There are several smeared prints on the outside of the swim platform gate, but I'm not sure they'll yield much. The other prints? They're a different story." He told them that they'd dusted for prints in the other rooms and found a thumbprint dead center on the cover of a ceiling light in the little food pantry off the kitchen. "It's almost like someone left it deliberately."

"We're running all the prints through the system, but there's one more you guys need to see," Talia said and nodded at Jimbo.

He pointed his flashlight at the helm's dashboard. A single bloody print sat just below the ignition.

Ava leaned in and smiled. *Gotcha.*

———

They waited inside the marina manager's office for the print results. August walked off for a while and came back with hot drinks. His standard peace offering. He stood next to her, sipping his black coffee. She drank the fully loaded mocha he'd brought her.

After a while, Rondeau turned his laptop so they could see the screen. "We got names back on the fingerprints. The one on the pantry light cover returned the name, James Wright, one of our victims."

Ava shook her head, swallowing against the lump in her throat. "First, he tried to tell his mom he was in trouble and now this."

"The other prints belong to the second victim, Cindy Aquino. And the one on the ignition belongs to a Henry Miller."

"That's Hunter," Ava said, looking at his mugshot. "You just keep popping up everywhere, don't you?"

Rondeau looked at her, confused. "If Jimmy left that print on the light, then he was alive when he got on the boat. He'd have to be, to reach the ceiling."

"What happened from the time they boarded to Hunter dropping them in the ocean in barrels?" August's gaze spanned the harbor. "Did Henry Miller take them sailing and it went wrong?"

Ava scrolled through his arrest record and found his last known address. On parole, his last check-in occurred two weeks prior. "Let's go ask him."

TWENTY-FOUR

Ocean Hills Sober Living was a million-dollar home a handful of blocks from the beach. Built in the fifties, the house had been chopped up into individual dorms like a frat house. The owner rented the house to the city for its sober living program through the Department of Health Care Services.

Given that it was nearly eleven at night and knowing that CBI channels would be faster, August worked on the arrest warrant for Henry Miller based on the bloody print in the stolen boat and for damage to the property. He also arranged for a search warrant to give them access to Henry Miller's living space and personal locker. The electronic warrants came back approved within twenty minutes thanks to Vincent pulling strings.

Deciding to muster at the marina since everyone was already there, Manaia pulled some patrol officers from crowd control near the marina's gate to act as backup. Ava, August, and the four extra officers all stood around the open trunk of Manaia's unmarked SUV, using the lamplight overhead to check their equipment while they worked out the approach. As Ava dug her vest out of the equipment trunk in the back of the CBI vehicle, August and Manaia's discussion turned heated.

Manaia wanted to act fast before someone tipped Miller off. He maintained that the news continued to have every scrap of information the police did, the second they had it, so they needed to move quickly. August disagreed. He reasoned that since they suspected Henry Miller of killing at least two people, possibly three, stealing a boat, and stalking the CBI at the station, they needed to exercise extreme caution., Wait until morning, and use the time to surveil the place and verify he still even lived there.

Ava saw both sides. When Manaia wouldn't back down and threatened to make entry, without the CBI if necessary, they worked out a compromise.

They went over the property map and discussed the facility's ingress and egress points. Rondeau would stay behind at the sober living house with the OPD group to secure the scene after they took Henry Miller into custody. He'd start going through electronics, etc. Manaia, Ava, and August would bring Hunter back to OPD for processing and questioning.

"He's a runner," Ava said, describing the scene at the police station where he'd watched them. "And he's a big guy. Over six feet for sure, built like a lumberjack."

"You heard Agent Cortes." August adjusted his bulletproof vest. "This guy has a history of violence and drug use. You call for backup if you spot him."

Climbing into two separate SUVs, August, Ava, and Manaia in the lead vehicle, they made their way to the house. An unmarked SUV behind them carried the four patrol officers. Ava donned her equipment in the dark vehicle, slapping down the straps to her bulletproof vest, August's voice in her earpiece. *Testing... testing.*

Late night hadn't slowed the summer traffic around the beach. Street barricades and signs put up by the city in anticipation of the coming fireworks show directed pedestrians and cars into detours, making it hard to navigate. The energy-efficient LED streetlamps cast an eerie, pale blue light on the people on the sidewalks. Music thrummed in the distance, a heavy bass beat that tickled Ava's nose. A truck soared past them, then another, the wind buffeting their SUV. Several more cars sped past on either side, horns honking.

"What the hell?" Ava looked at August as the portable police radio squawked on the seat between them.

All units be advised, we have a street takeover reported just off the I-5 at the Mission Avenue exit near the high school. Use caution. On-site units report a 10-34, disorderly crowd and road blockage. Witnesses report multiple vehicles drag racing and doing one-eighties in the street. Possible 10-94, there may be fireworks in the area.

"Isn't that ..." August asked.

She nodded. "Exactly where we're headed."

"Do you think its connected?"

"No," Manaia answered. "It's the end of June, kids are out late, we get these every year. Especially around the Fourth of July holiday." He sat in full gear behind her. Tilting his head, he spoke into the radio at his shoulder, directing the patrol officers behind them to take a side road and drive parallel. "It'd be bad if we were coming from OPD, but from the marina we have alternate routes. We can stay off the freeway, use side streets."

Ava pointed out the windshield. "There, take Surfrider Way."

"And the barricades near the offramp?" August asked, peering over his left shoulder and changing lanes.

"They're saying the crowd knocked them down." Manaia held onto the SUV's grip handle as August made a wide turn on the shoulder, veering around stopped traffic in front of them.

A wad of tricked-out cars and trucks clogged the road. Crowds of people lined the street, circling the cars doing donuts at high speeds in the center. Countless teens and young adults jumped around, screaming and laughing, as smoke from the burning car tires billowed through the scene, cutting visibility. Music pounded from huge speakers in the beds of trucks. A few guys waved their shirts like matadors in front of the charging cars, jumping out of the way. Fireworks shot over the scene, the acrid smell of sulfur filling the air as the fiery tails of bottle rockets streaked across the dark sky. Patrol cars pulled up, their lights slashing the shadows, bullhorns warning the crowd to disperse.

"Well, that was chaotic," Ava said, twisting to watch the melee as they took a turn and drove away from the scene down a side street. "I wish they'd had those when I was a kid."

"I'm legitimately surprised you didn't spearhead one," August said.

"Get more patrol out here," Manaia shouted into his shoulder radio at dispatch.

They pulled onto Harron Drive, where the sober living house sat at the end of the street. A couple of blocks from the takeover scene, the scent of fireworks and tire rubber drifted to them along with the low beat of the blasting music. Cheers from the crowd and the bleeps of the squad cars sounded through the trees. Coming to a stop just outside their destination, they hit the ground quickly. Manaia and two officers from the OPD entry team went in first with Ava and August behind them. The other two officers ran around to the back.

The house manager answered the front door, read the paperwork, and let them in. The TV blasted some kind of video game, flashing the living room in light and dark. They spread out, looking for Henry, asking kids standing around gawking where he was. None of them knew. Some of them cussed them out. A few took off running out the front door. August tapped Ava's shoulder, and she followed him to the rear of the house toward the bedrooms.

They cleared one room, then another. In the third, a young man cowered with a cat in the closet. Manaia, who'd come up behind them, moved him back out toward the living room with the rest of the occupants. Down the hall, a door slammed shut.

"Last one," August breathed into her earpiece as they moved toward it. "Check. Check."

"Go," Ava said.

He kicked the door open, raising his gun, and stopping its swing back with his boot. Ava slipped in, swept the room with her weapon. A sullen-looking kid stood with a bag in his arms like he held on for dear life. Tall, skinny and black. Not Miller.

"Where's Henry Miller?" Ava asked him.

He didn't answer but glanced at the open window. The lacy curtain billowed inward. Ava ran to it, leaned out, and spotted him getting up off the grass and sprinting across the side yard.

"He's running!"

"Wait—" August shouted, but Ava had already jumped.

She dropped onto the porch roof, ran to the edge, then leaped down onto the grass. Weapon held against her thigh, she took off after him. As a kid, Ava's big mouth and sharp tongue meant she'd learned to run fast. It worked in her favor now, too.

She tracked her quarry across the yard, gaining with the uneven terrain as he skirted yard furniture and a wooden cornhole board.

"Henry Miller," Ava shouted as she ran. "Hunter! Stop!"

He glanced over his shoulder, his eyes full of fear.

"Backup approaching from the south, next house over," August said in her ear. He didn't even have the decency to sound winded as he caught up to her. "The kid in the room said he shoved something in his pants. Possibly a gun."

Henry scaled the far fence, slipping under shadows from the older trees, and dropping into the next house's yard. Ava landed on the dirt a second after, then August. Where was this kid going? Motion floodlights flicked on as he crossed the yard, and he stumbled before leaping another fence.

August hopped the higher fence like it was nothing, Ava a step behind. They followed Henry as he veered left, slipping between two houses. Police lights and the sound of screeching tires hit them, and she realized what he was doing.

"He's heading for the next street over. The takeover," Ava said, pulling out her flashlight. She scanned for movement ahead. Overgrown hedges and towering bunches of oleander bushes grabbed at them as they ran.

August shouted into his radio, directing Manaia and his officers. A garbled message from Manaia came as they pushed through an open gate. Location of their backup. Their flanking positions.

We see you. We're to your left, closing in.

Furtive movement in the distance near a garage door caught Ava's eye.

Ava stopped, raising her weapon. "Freeze, CBI!"

Henry's head whipped toward her, and then he ran in the opposite direction, screaming into the phone at his ear as he sprinted down an alley. Ava, gaining, heard him shouting.

"They found me!" he screamed. He leaped over a hedge. Crossed the wet grass toward the headlights and screeching tires. "Help me!"

"If he makes it to the takeover, we'll lose him," Ava shouted, breath coming hard.

"Breaking right," August yelled through Ava's earpiece.

August shot out in an arc to intercept, his legs pumping, hands cutting the air as he closed in on Henry's position.

Gunfire cut through the music and noise. The takeover erupted into a frenzied mass of cars and bodies going in all directions. People screamed, running in fear. Horns drowned the voices in Ava's earpiece.

She crouched as she ran, unable to discern fireworks from gunfire. Twenty feet away, a crowd of kids running from the sounds hit August like a wave, taking him down with them.

"August!"

"I'm good. Don't lose him!"

"I see him. Target's running along the trees on the south side of the street," Ava shouted.

"Where is the gunfire coming from?" Manaia yelled from the radio, the sound of the panicked crowd in the background. "Do you have him in sight?"

"I'm on him!" She spotted Henry heading into a group of running kids. An engine roared and a dirt bike zoomed in front of her. She went down.

Lights flashed behind her eyes, but she scrambled to her feet. Shaking her head, she scanned the dark, panning her flashlight. "I think... I think I lost him."

Another shot rang out, and Ava caught the muzzle flash. She raced toward it, weapon out, gaze locked on the light-haired young woman peeking out from behind the trees.

The woman had a weapon. The source of the gunfire. Henry raced toward her, his arms windmilling. Stumbling. The hippie chick glared out at Ava from the shadows.

"It's her," Ava said. The headlights of escaping cars framed them in blinding light. Something in the girl's hand glinted in the flash.

The girl screamed at Ava. "You did this!"

"Drop the gun!"

Henry's head whipped around.

Another muzzle flash. A loud pop. Henry crumpled to the grass.

Ava fired, diving behind a tree. A quick peek showed her the girl leaning over Henry's body.

Rising, Ava shouted, "Get away from him!"

A shot whizzed over her head. Ava ducked. When she looked again, the girl was gone. Lost to the night.

"I need a bus to my location," Ava yelled, running for Henry. She skidded on her knees in the grass, her flashlight beam picking up his seizing body. His eyes rolled back as his body bucked on the ground. Fine powder dusted his face.

He'd been dosed.

Ava hollered into her mic again. "Gunshot wound, send a bus to my location!"

She reached for her earpiece and realized it was missing. She'd been shouting for help at no one.

"Ava!" August ran up to her, weapon out, lip bloody, his gaze traveling her face and body as he looked at her on the ground. "Are you hit?"

"No, but he is."

August stood guard, giving directions to the paramedics.

"Henry, stay with me," Ava shouted over the noise and the panic. "Henry!"

The young man's body went still, eyes wide and unblinking.

"No, no, no!" Ava started compressions. He had to live. "Don't let that bastard win, kid!"

A minute later paramedics arrived, pushing her out of the way. She warned them about the powder and then slumped back on her heels in the grass, hands at her cheeks, watching as the heart monitor ran a flatline across the screen.

A wave of dizziness washed over her, the adrenaline pushing everything to a frenzied throb in her head.

"This wasn't supposed to happen."

"You're bleeding." August crouched next to her, his light aimed at her forehead. "Looks like you're going to get those stitches after all."

"They're killing each other for him," she said.

"Who?"

"Orien." Ava's hands trembled as she held up one of Henry's limp wrists. Fresh markings marred his skin, still bleeding. "He's cleaning house."

TWENTY-FIVE

Despite Henry Miller's EKG readings, the paramedics pumped him full of epinephrine, scooped him up, and took him to the hospital where an ER doctor declared him DOA. August went with the body, making sure the ME bagged the hands. Talia met him there to take custody of Henry Miller's remains for autopsy. Manaia stayed at the scene and led a search for the female shooter Ava described but found nothing. He and the other officers rounded up witnesses. The ones he found had seen nothing in the fray. At least that's what they said. They didn't find a gun on the body or the phone he'd been talking on.

After the shooting, Ava met with a scene supervisor from the OPD at the sober living house. As a matter of procedure, he took her weapon and statement, then released her. She caught a ride to the ER with a patrol car, where an intern, who looked like he'd barely started shaving, cleaned, stitched, and bandaged the reopened cut over her eyebrow. He cleared her of a concussion, gave her extra-strength ibuprofen, and told her to go home and sleep. Afterward, she took a ride back to OPD with the patrol guy who'd waited outside the hospital for her. She grabbed her SUV and went home.

Ava pushed through her front door, dropped her messenger bag on the floor, and sank into the couch. She lay back, staring at her ceiling, trying to get the sight of Henry Miller's spasming body out of her head. Her boss called a moment later. Ava checked her watch. Midnight. The woman never slept.

"How did you know I was still awake?" Ava asked when she answered the call.

"I didn't. That's what ringers are for," Vincent said with humor in her voice. "Listen, I talked with OPD. You're good on the shooting. You can pick up your weapon in the morning. I'm told this girl shot up a takeover causing panic. Then took aim at my agents."

"She wouldn't have hit me with that pea shooter," Ava said. "She didn't even try. I believe she was there to kill Henry Miller. He was on the phone, begging for help, and I think she pulled him in and killed him because we were onto him."

"You're on the right track, then." An announcement over a speaker in Vincent's background sounded. Flight boarding. "The mayor seems to have me on speed dial, while the Chief of Police won't take my calls."

"Tell them they'll get all the credit. I think August will blow a gasket if my face ends up on the news again."

"Is he twitching yet?"

"Whenever I walk in the room."

Vincent chuckled. "August keeps me up to speed, but you always have a few working theories. Which direction are you headed?"

Ava stood, pacing next to her couch. "This Orien is the mastermind behind all of this. Cindy Aquino, James Wright, Brent Cutler, and now Henry Miller are all connected to each other. They all wound up dead with those symbols carved on their bodies. They're all connected to Orien, I know it. I just have to find out how. If I can find a nexus, the point in the constellation where they all come together, the whole pattern will reveal itself. I know it."

"I'm getting interest from national news and the attorney general.

Wrap this up, Ava. Stop this guy before someone tries to send in the Feds."

"You're threatening me with the FBI?"

"You know the assistant director still blames you for his pool blowing up."

"First of all, I warned him that might happen."

After the call, Ava showered, threw on a T-shirt and yoga pants, and tried to sleep, but her mind kept reeling from the chase. Drifting off, she thought about mathematical symbols and the patterns of life and death. Flashes from her teens of moving from home to home that weren't hers. Her luck in having the funds to save herself. People in that world she'd walked away from, without looking back. And when she did, years later... well, not everyone gets out.

———

Ava tossed and turned all night. A headache behind her injured eye wouldn't let up, and by five that morning, she gave up. She shuffled into the living room, microwaved a mug of water, and then flicked on the light over her breakfast table. She sat down and looked through the relics she'd taken during the investigation. Earlier, Ava had spread each item out on the surface, grouping them in piles, as she tried to work out the tangles in the case.

She pushed the arcade token from the drive-in, and the mosaic tile from Cutler's lawn to the side. They didn't seem relevant. Opening the plastic-wrapped cookie from Carol's Collectibles, she took a bite, thinking about James Wright, surfing, and dreams of championships. He'd desperately tried to reach out to his mother by planting the tea. Why hadn't he *said* anything? What was the nature of his relationship with Cindy Aquino? How did he end up in Owen Meek's orbit?

She worked while she ate, picking up the bookmark from the Lit Lounge where they spoke with Horatio Jones, the construction site supervisor. He'd told them about the white panel van loitering near the body dump. Was it the same van that picked up Cindy Aquino from the shelter for her mystery dates? She made a note to check in on Rondeau's search for the vehicle, then slid the bookmark aside.

Then there was the puzzle of Henry Miller. Hunter. His blood and prints were on the boat. He was connected to the marina through the maintenance guy, Jerra. He'd had the muscle to overpower the victims and stuff them in a barrel. Yet that young woman killed him before he could be captured. He'd run right to her. Like she was in charge.

Ava grabbed the sandwich baggie with the crushed dandelion crown, and she held it up to the light. The young woman who attacked her at the junior college was the constellation point connecting them all. She was sure of it. She needed to find out who she was. And what relationship she had with Owen.

The Anchor Point coffee sleeve crinkled in Ava's grasp. How much did Owen know about what Henry and the young woman did? Did he order them to kill, or had she gone rogue? Did he help them cover it up? Was the boat his idea?

The Ascension tea bag next to her elbow smelled like lavender, and she ripped open the envelope and dunked the mesh bag into the microwaved water. It smelled lovely but tasted like garden scraps. Where was the tea coming from? Where did they source the potent hallucinogenic mushroom powder? So far Rondeau and the Crimes of Violence Unit hadn't found any trace of its purchase.

She unwrapped the lollipop ring from Atomic Dog and used it to sweeten her tea, swirling it around while she thought about Heather Adams and Cindy Aquino's phone drama. The shelter and the phone calls with the older man. Did he pay for the phone and the electric scooter? And if so, why? Who was he to her?

Manipulating the objects, Ava tested her theories about the sequence of events. She flipped through her notes, remembering the interviews and jotting down new questions. She hashed out hunches, clustering her ideas into a free-form bubble map.

The flyer from the tattoo parlor sat underneath her elbow, and she picked it up, staring at the advertisement for glow-in-the-dark ink. She remembered the symbols carved on the victims. The swirls of light against death. All of it, Owen's design. No, *Orien's* design. Henry Miller's murder served Owen especially well. He couldn't be a witness, couldn't turn on the group and save himself. Orien sacrificed him to save the whole.

Anger coiled in her chest, squeezing out her breath, and she swept her hand across the piles, scattering the relics across the floor. She had to find this hippie asshole fast. Before he decided that someone else needed to die for him.

The sun rose in a soft peach sky. Ava grabbed a bottled coffee drink from her fridge, poured it over a glass of ice, and took four of the ER ibuprofens with her first sip. Halfway through her frozen waffles, an alert pinged on her burner phone from Denny. A report on the fringe groups she'd asked him to look into. She texted him that she had more questions. Ten seconds later, the burner rang.

"Hey Denny," she said with a yawn. "Thanks for the report."

"Lady Justice." His deep Tennessee drawl made her smile. "Doesn't the CBI issue you a bedtime?"

"There was a chase. I ended up running around in the dark and somehow, into a dirt bike." She realized her voice sounded scratchy.

A silent beat. "You alright?"

"Yeah," she said, rubbing her temple. "There was a thing going on at the same time, and I was shouting over the noise."

"You sound like you're squinting."

"You can't hear that," she said, un-squinting her eyes and listening to him chuckle. "Are you just getting in?"

"That, I am. I shot off the report for you to read later but I can give you the gist right now if you want."

She put him on speaker and finished her waffles while he told her about the covens and LARPER clans and alien abduction support groups he'd checked out. The surf punk crime ring currently brewing near Carlsbad and the palm readers in Oceanside had heard some things about the Blue Drum Killer and the bodies in the barrels, but not much more than Denny could gather himself from the news.

"I put out some feelers on local unsecured servers. They run shadow chat boards out of them."

"Who does?"

"Doesn't matter. The accounts are anonymous so sometimes I get good regional intel in exchange for cryptocurrency. I keep seeing posts and comments about this new group on nodes for this area. I've seen a ton of warnings about a bunch of kids that hit people up for money, try to sell you things in baskets, that kind of thing. Not dangerous according to the boards, but annoying. I'm seeing descriptions like flower children, communes, that kind of thing. I reached out to a buddy of mine at the chamber of commerce and he says they're actually a big problem."

"These kids wear retro clothes and the one who attacked me had flowers in her hair."

"Sounds like we're talking about the same group. There's mention of a guy, I think he's their leader. He's some kind of guru or teacher. I get mixed descriptions. Either way, he's having them do more than sell herbal tea. I heard you can get some pretty interesting deliveries."

"Drugs?"

"Young girls."

Ava pushed her plate away. "Dammit. Why do they always go after the girls?"

"From what I hear these young women are runaways or former sex workers, but they have the look, you know? Packaged innocence."

"And you know this is true?"

Denny hesitated, then said, "Yeah. I talked to a nun out here who helps girls at the church shelter. She gave me the name of one who used to be involved. I talked to her. It's true."

"Do you think she'll come forward?"

"Not easily. She has warrants, but she also has a lot of details.

Might be worth some sort of deal. Her street name is Jade. I'll let her decide if she'll give you her real one."

"Give her my number." Ava scratched at the bandage on her brow. "Also, I was at this yoga studio, Ocean Within, I know it's connected. Did you hear anything in the ether about that place?"

"I have." She could hear the sound of large motorcycles revving in the background. "I traced the deliveries back to the yoga wellness place you mentioned. It turns out the Ocean Within property is managed by a rental company, but it looks like the owner and beneficiary are shrouded with a shadow LLC so I can't get to who runs it or where the funds initially came from. Unless you remove your restrictions on how I acquire things for you."

Ava sighed, rubbing her eyes. "Tempting, but I can't risk it. Or you. Let me see if I can get Rondeau to do the rest."

He gasped. "Are you cheating on me with another tech guy?"

"Hey, I need what I need," Ava said with a smile. "Thanks for doing all that, Denny. I owe you."

"You will never owe me, Ava." He paused. "There's a rumor that these kids and the guru live in some kind of communal house near the coast. A large, gated property. I'm working on who owns it, but there's something you should know."

Ava finished off her coffee drink. "What is it?"

"Chatter popped up this morning that there's going to be some kind of event coming in the next day or two. A memorial for one of their own who just died. You know anything about that?"

"That was where I was last night. At the scene of his shooting. We were trying to pick him up for questioning and things went sideways. I believe his accomplice shot him."

"That's cold." Denny hummed like he usually did when he was skimming his notes. "Do you know what the red tide is?"

"Yeah," Ava said, taking her plate to the sink. "It's the annual glowing algae phenomenon that happens to the surf, right?"

"Yeah, during the day the algae bloom is red which is where the name comes from. But at night, the water turns electric blue when the waves irritate the organisms."

"Okay, that's around this time of year?"

"The posts are saying the conditions are right for the next few days, and I hear the glowing is part of the memorial this hippie group has planned."

"Bioluminescence and the ocean," Ava muttered as flashes of the glowing symbols on Brent's skin came to mind. "I guess it *does* all go back to the sea."

"They'll meet late, close to midnight according to the chat boards, but Ava..." Denny hesitated, then. "You know I've met all kinds of psychopaths in my travels. These guys, these charming personalities are dangerous."

"Don't worry, Denny," Ava said. "So am I."

TWENTY-SIX

After the call with Denny, Ava printed off the document he'd sent in her home office, then packed the file in her messenger bag to read later. She showered and fussed with the dressing over her eye before changing it to a large band-aid. She donned black work slacks, lace-up boots, and a dark blue cotton blouse. Sunglasses would deal with both the headache and the worsening bruise around her eye.

Arriving at the OPD by eight, she retrieved her firearm and headed straight to the war room. Rondeau was already set up there.

"Where's our illustrious leader?"

"He got pulled into a meeting with Detective Manaia and the Chief of Police. Our suspect getting murdered during apprehension makes us look like a bunch of yokels."

"Yeah. Glad I don't have to deal with the brass." Pulling off her shades, she caught his gasp.

"What?"

"You look like you wrestled with a rockslide and came in second."

"There go the Secret Santa points you earned last night." Ava grinned. "What're you working on?"

"We're still searching for the white panel van Cindy's friend said picked her up from the shelter. We're making headway. An ATM across from the shelter caught something. We're running two more possible images through a sharpening algorithm."

"But it was there?"

"I think so. We just need to sharpen the image. I *will* get what that sticker on the back says. Why?"

"I need help with a few things."

He rubbed his hands together. "Hit me with it."

She told him a property management business rented the Ocean Within business and that it was somehow mixed up with LLC's but that was as much as she knew. She handed him the printout of the document Denny sent her.

"This is highly detailed data. How did you get it?" Rondeau asked, his gaze on the paper.

She shrugged. "I know a guy. What I need is a name or a bank account, a chink in the armor. For now, I want to know if there are ties connecting the wellness studio and the teas with a man named Owen or Orien Meeks."

"Okay, I'll look into it. We're supposed to get the final batch of Brent's financials today, so I'll keep you posted on that as well. What else? You said a few things."

"My source mentioned something else. A possible call girl angle. He's heard rumors about special deliveries to go with the organic subscription box Ocean Within offers." Ava told Rondeau about the trafficking victim Denny told her about. "She's a possible victim. I'm waiting to hear from her, but the information gave me an idea. We should check other shelters like the one Cindy Aquino stayed at for similar issues. Maybe something will pop."

"Jade." Rondeau raised a light brow. "Was this victim another young woman?"

Ava nodded. "She's a little skittish, but she has details from what I'm told. Damning ones."

"This case just keeps getting worse, doesn't it?" Rondeau ran a hand through his hair, shaking his head. "I'll get this to Manaia and the Crimes of Violence squad."

"Thanks. Lastly, the tattoo parlor guy, Sully, told me his sister, Cara, dated this Orien guy."

"The one you think is connected to the yoga studio?"

"Yeah. He had a blog according to the private investigator the brother hired. It's deactivated now, but she said it's archived here." Ava gave him a slip of paper with the details she'd copied from the file. "I downloaded it to my laptop, but it won't open."

He got it open on her secure tablet, and she settled at a desk in the corner to go through it. Going back to a year before Cara, Owen had already started using the name Orien on his blog. Ava looked up the name. Derived from Latin origins meaning dawn or rising sun, an Indo-European root suggested new beginnings. She jotted in her notebook that he aligned himself with ideas like salvation and renewal.

Through long, daily posts, he created an alternate persona. At first, he shared his thoughts on different concepts of renewal, night, the ocean, expanding your mind, and other beliefs. His comment engagement on those posts started low but gradually climbed. Photos and three-second videos of him smiling while drinking coffee or raising a flower to the audience's view didn't hurt. He moved in a deeply magnetic way she didn't quite understand. Several women in his comments called him Son of Dawn, another said he rose with morning in his eyes. He 'hearted' every comment.

He also responded to every comment, often addressing 'conversations' in the following blog post. It drew people in. Their opinion mattered, and the handsome man with all the answers heard them. Intrigued, Ava kept reading, witnessing his evolution. Orien went from a college guy shouting pop-psychology into the endless black hole of the internet to a benevolent, sexy, non-threatening man who really 'saw' people. Women, especially.

He started talking about harmony with the world and nature around them. He preached health, wellness, centeredness, and generosity. People in the comments ate it up. One post announced that he wanted to share his knowledge of meditation and yoga with the community and said he would offer classes soon. A few weeks later, he introduced a waiting list for his sessions. Then he offered private lessons with exclusive, undivided attention from 'the teacher' along with a guided meditation. Business must've been booming because Ava found mention of creating a 'space of peace' of his own soon.

He saw something these girls needed, and he became it. A friend in a sea of unsafe adults. A home that accepts. A family that stays.

Ava studied what he wrote, writing down phrases, stories, or symbols he alluded to in his blogs. Orien took ideas from a mixture of Asian, Middle Eastern, South Asian, and other religions. Repackaging what he must've thought seemed cool. Women wanted strong female energy. Powerful, feminine, mysterious, and yet... understood by him.

His beach yoga and meditation sessions took off. Orien offered them the power to control their inner oceans. Unfair treatment, betrayal, loneliness, all of it could be banished by drinking his tea, taking care of your body with his immunity shots, and time with him on the beach.

He contorted religious, cultural and philosophical ideas to fit his message. She noticed his language change. Words like peace took on multiple meanings. He used it like a greeting or to speak about death. He started to refer to his online followers as acolytes of the Collective Energy. Shortly before he abandoned the blog, he made more changes. The collective became the commune, then the community, then family. He also leaned heavily into the lunar worship of Mother Night and the divine female energy. Renewal and inner light. Ava realized he was shaping his message, refining it for a specific audience. A younger, female one.

Ava took a break, grabbed a coffee and a bag of chips, and sat back down with her tablet. She looked up arrests in the area, concentrating on female Caucasian suspects under twenty-five with blue eyes. Not sure if the blonde was natural, she left it blank. But those eyes. The anger and fury in them when she swung the tennis racket at Ava's head were seared into her mind. Ava added fighting to the search parameters. After forty minutes of slogging through complaints and arrest reports, she recognized a face and sat up in her chair.

She stared at the mug shot, unsure. The teenager in the picture had mousey brown hair and a little more weight on her. Sadie Schneider. The young woman in the photo had been arrested for fighting at a bus station. After an argument over money, the ticket agent said the suspect reached through the kiosk window and pummeled her with her own stapler. She did not stop until the security guard, a sixty-eight-year-old retiree, pulled her off. She bit him for his trouble.

Ava smiled ruefully. "Oh, yeah. That's her."

According to the CPS file, Sadie entered the foster care system at five years old when her parents left her in a drug house when the local police raided it. No one knew who her parents were or where they'd fled. No one ever filed a missing person's report. Sadie did not last long at any placement. Often the foster family requested removal for violence against other children. At fifteen years old, while living in a group home, Sadie lodged a sexual abuse complaint with her social worker against one of the counselors. By the look of the file, no investigation occurred, and Sadie was removed from the home. Sometime later she appeared in a juvenile detention unit. Ava leaned back, her stomach knotting. No one had protected her, so she'd learned to do it herself.

Ava found the social worker's phone number and called her. Lonnie Lee, an easy-going woman with a Wisconsin accent who told her she'd grab the file and be back in a moment.

"Oh yeah, I see what you mean. That young girl was full of spit and vinegar, let me tell you. During the investigation into her allegations, we moved Sadie to another home, an emergency placement with a senior couple who specialized in troubled teens. She didn't stay there for more than a week before she took off. Without her statement, they closed the investigation."

"Where did she go?"

"Beats me. We never heard from her again, and then she aged out of the system. In fact, this is the first time I've heard about her since then. I hope she's doing better."

Ava wasn't sure a murderous rampage was better, so she asked instead, "Do you think the accusations were true?"

Lee stayed silent for a moment, then, "I've never seen a kid with so much hurt and rage. Something caused that."

Ava thanked Lee and rang off, going through the rest of the file on Sadie, before stopping on a photo taped to a medical report. A little girl in a baby-blue dress sat in front of a fake forest backdrop. The school picture cast her pretty clothes and perfect ponytails in soft light. Bows adorned the front of her dress, and she gripped the end of one ribbon with pink-painted fingertips. Despite the cheerful scene, the little girl's gaze held incredible sadness.

Ava leaned forward, burying her face in her palms, squeezing her eyes shut as she pushed away her own memories of lashing out at help, of hurting people before they could hurt her. Of feeling so incredibly alone, twisting in the winds of life. All of them, Cindy, Jimmy, Henry, even Brent to a degree, were vulnerable in some capacity.

She thought about family, and the similar clothes the young women wore, the name changes, the eating habit changes, the exploitative use of free labor, and most of all, the ritualized markings on the victims' bodies. All of it painted an increasingly troubling picture of what was going on.

After taking a short break, she got Talia on the phone in the autopsy theater. She'd just finished Henry's autopsy and told Ava to meet her in the lab. Ava walked down the hall and found her hunched over a microscope.

Ava slipped onto the stool next to her. "Have you been here all night?"

"I have." Talia's gaze landed on her face. "You re-injured your eye."

"Don't worry, a teenager stitched it up." Ava nodded at the microscope. "Did you find anything surprising during Henry's autopsy?"

"Yes and no." Talia slid a file folder with notes toward Ava. "The gun that killed him was the same one used on the other three victims. A twenty-two at close range behind the ear. He had powder residue in his nose and eyes, just like Brent. The same mixture of potent THC and amanita powder."

"When I ran up to him, he was seizing." Ava rubbed her eyes. "How was he not dead already? He took a shot to the head."

Talia nodded, walked over to the light box, pulled an x-ray off the surface, and turned it toward Ava. Holding the film up against the ceiling light, she pointed to a section of the skull.

"You see that bullet track through the edge of the tissue? The round entered his head and sort of skimmed along the inside of the skull instead of bouncing around in the brain. He would have died anyway, given the massive hemorrhage that resulted, but it wasn't instantaneous. The caliber was too small, and the angle was off. That gave his mucous membranes the time to absorb the enormous dose of amanita powder blown in his face. I believe that caused the seizing."

Ava nodded, flipping through Talia's notes. "Could that mixture, that powder be used to control someone? You know, if they lived?"

"I mean, yeah, the mixture at the doses I'm seeing would allow for a sort of mild scopolamine situation. Plus, these victims were not necessarily mentally stable in the first place. They're runaways, statistically they're doing drugs or suffer from a mood disorder. That would make them highly suggestible to begin with. Throw in mind-altering drugs and that could open the door for undue influence. Like following a CBI agent."

Ava chewed on her inner cheek, thinking, *flower children, commune, family, community.*

Talia watched. "You look troubled."

Ava hated that her face registered her worry. Or maybe that her colleagues were starting to know her that well. "I think that this thing is worse than we thought." She flashed on the angry, lost gaze of a little girl lost. "I think there might be more bodies in barrels out there. These kids learned how to do this somewhere. My bet is their leader."

Heading out to find August, Ava dug through her bag for a snack when her phone pinged. She glanced at the message and stopped walking.

Tolman Green, Eliza's lawyer.

> She'll meet with you, and only you, in one hour. Take it or leave it.

Ava veered toward the police parking lot in back, answering as she strode to her SUV.

> I'll be there.

TWENTY-SEVEN

On the way to the Vista Detention Center, Ava tried to reach August without success. Probably still stuck in the meeting with the Chief. While waiting at a stoplight by the tracks, she got stuck by a train. She checked her watch. The faster commuter train had passed earlier. This was the slow one. She sighed as the rumble and clatter of the freight train grew close. Thankfully, the SUV's insulation reduced most of the signal's volume. Resigned to waiting, Ava dialed an old number on impulse.

Dr. Seth Masters, head of the CBI's Behavioral Sciences Unit, answered with his Oxford-refined voice. "I wondered when I was going to hear from you about this case."

"Oh, so you're psychic now?" Ava asked as the boxcars passed with aching slowness.

"I just know my patients and my colleagues," Seth said easily. "Given the time you spent in foster care yourself, I thought you might reach out. The loss of a young woman, also in the system, by a possible john would surely bring up memories for you."

After the Ghost Town Killer case, the CBI mandated that Ava see a counselor. When she balked, Seth stepped in, having worked with her on the Ghost Town Killer's profile and being privy to the investigation. He had a clinical license and was one of the few people who could understand the kind of monsters Ava dealt with. Vincent approved. His influence allowed Ava to move laterally to White Collar Crimes during the investigation into her part in the suspect's death. Because of this, he knew about her past in the foster care system.

He also knew about her friend, Venus Novokov, who had been her sister in that chaos. Older than Ava by a year, she aged out of the system. She'd tried to find a nine to five, but no one would give her the time of day. She eventually took a job at a gentlemen's club and started hanging out with a dangerous crowd. They lost touch once Ava aged out and started community college. Venus died five months later. Strangled in the parking lot of her apartment by a repeat customer, who delusionally believed she was his girlfriend and had cheated on him by dancing for another man.

Ava listened to the dull clanging of the railroad warning lights. "I see you've been following the case."

"August keeps me in the loop on PIT cases," Seth said. "This one in particular must bring up conflict."

"Not really. I haven't killed anyone yet." After the boxcars came the tank cars, then the hoppers filled with loose rubble.

"You often spoke to me about gaps in the system. Cracks that older teens and young adults fall through. The lack of a safety net once they turn eighteen. You told me once that it was as if they expected you to suddenly know how to be an adult at the stroke of midnight with no connections or family."

"Seth..." Ava sighed, her gaze fixed the last of the train cars trundling past the crossing. "I'm aware of the problems with the system. Right now, I'm just trying to catch this guy. He's wrong in so many ways. A true predator. I can see what he's doing and to be honest, the logic tracks, if that makes sense."

"It does for you. Your adaptive intelligence, your ability to see multiple perspectives, understand different ways of looking at things can be both an asset and a source of doubt. Just because you know your way around the minds of killers doesn't make you like them."

Ava thought it did a little. "Our deal was that you wouldn't treat me like a patient once I wasn't one anymore. You gave me a clean bill of mental health, remember?"

He chuckled, "Of course. What did you want to talk about?"

"I wanted to ask you about the language of cults. I think I'm seeing that here but want to run it by you. Would that include name changes?"

She told him about Cindy, Henry, Cara, and Owen changing their names. As well as the fact that neither James Wright nor Brent Cutler seemed to go by another name, causing a break in the pattern.

"I believe your instincts are right. Name changes can be a shedding of the old identity and boundaries. It's actually quite common. Nuns, monks, royalty, even western marriages normally have a name change. It's a line that one crosses to create a new self. It's also a way of being special, known, and seen."

"If James Wright didn't have a new name, that could mean, what? He wasn't accepted? Was he new or not up to that level?"

"Here is where we enter supposition. As most groups like this make up their own rules, anything is possible."

"All these kids have nature-centric names. Is that relevant?"

"It can be, yes. Often the leader of a family or group will pick the new name. Like a rite of passage."

She told him about Orien's relationship with Cara Bane and her mental breakdown after he thought she betrayed him.

"This Orien figure exhibits controlling and manipulative behavior toward younger partners. At risk youth would most certainly fall under his spell, regardless of their life experiences. They are still emotionally immature and that makes them alarmingly ripe for someone like him. Even if there is no evidence of a bona fide cult, this man is dangerous."

"He's manipulative, smart." Ava told Seth about the blog. "The story of his journey to become 'the teacher' in his posts read more like editing a book than exploring faith. His changes felt practical, deliberate, like... like a con man working a mark."

"I agree. And Ava, if you do meet him, take extreme caution. This kind of personality will be mesmerizing, alluring, and built for the female gaze, but if you push him, that mask will peel away. If he feels cornered, he will likely respond with controlled aggression."

"What do you mean by controlled aggression?"

Seth paused, then. "You won't expect it when he strikes."

———

Ava arrived at the Vista Detention Facility on time despite the train. The beige stucco monolith loomed over the sprawling county complex, which contained the jail, the North Division Courts, and a satellite Sheriff's Station office. The facility's brutalist style reflected function, durability, and security.

She parked in the law enforcement and attorney lot and checked in. The acrid smell of industrial disinfectant assaulted her as she entered the visitation area. The heavy clank of the metal doors reverberated through the sparse room.

While waiting in the lobby outside the visitation booths, Ava outlined ideas in her leather notebook. She squinted against the caged fluorescent lights overhead, jotting down names, thoughts, and hunches. Troubled, she traced over her initial sketches of the Sacred Geometry symbols until the lines made deep grooves in the thick paper. Her thoughts returned to Sadie Schneider and her young, furious face.

The guard announced Eliza Cartwright's name, and Ava stood, made her way to the phone cubicle, and sat on the metal stool bolted to the cement floor. A former beauty queen, Eliza had been flirting with her mid-fifties by the time Ava took her down, though she didn't look a day over forty. At the time, she had an excellent plastic surgeon, enough money for all the skin serums in the world, and a personal chef. The foundation of her beauty must be genetic because as she sat perched elegantly on her stool, her graying hair swirled into a chic bun atop her head, she still looked like a beauty queen in her orange jumpsuit. She picked up the phone receiver and held it delicately to her ear.

"Ms. Cartwright, thank you for meeting with me."

Sparkling hazel eyes met Ava's, and she smirked. "You've been making a name for yourself, haven't you? It seems your stint in the Siberia of White-Collar Crimes served you well. I'm surprised you had time to visit little old Eliza."

"Nothing surprises you." Ava narrowed her gaze at her. "Why did you agree to meet?"

Eliza shrugged. "There's so little news of the outside world these days. I was bored."

"Tell me the real reason. I don't feel like walking into a trap."

"But you'll set them, yes?"

"Yes. It's part of my job." Ava shrugged. "I'm not apologizing."

Eliza sighed dramatically, then, "I'm up for a parole hearing. My lawyer tells me things are looking great with my good behavior. I'm a trustee in the library. A model inmate. I'm feeling hopeful. Then, all of a sudden, I start getting messages that the infamous Agent Ava Cortes is asking to speak with me. The timing felt suspicious. Naturally, I was alarmed. I agreed to meet with you because I wanted to make sure you weren't trying to ambush me at my hearing with another attempt to get me to reveal my black book. I will not. It is the only thing keeping me alive in here."

"I don't care about your list of names. I hunt killers not philanderers." Ava put her hands up. "You won't see me at your hearing. No one has even reached out to me."

Eliza considered her for a moment, then smiled. "Fine. What did you want to talk to me about then?"

"I'm here about Brent Cutler's murder," Ava said. "I assume, given his instrumental role in your current incarceration that you've been following the case?"

"I follow all your cases, Ava. Especially ones that loom out of the shadows to haunt you again. How *is* Brent's cantankerous father doing these days? Does Dane still want your head on a platter?"

"Ms. Cartwright, let me get down to business, as you were so fond of saying. I believe that Brent somehow ran afoul of a cult."

Eliza's tinkling laugh filled the echoing space. "I'd expect nothing less of Brent. He always did have a taste for the outliers."

"Anyone in particular?"

"You know, angry girls with dark hearts are so deliciously rebellious. It makes the men who want them feel young." Eliza looked aside, considering. "The other victims are interesting. I hear the young woman was a pro. Brent tended toward the more exotic, if you will. He especially liked Asian women."

Ava kept the disgust from her face. "I don't think that's what this is."

"No?" Eliza sat back, a whisper of a smile on her lips, like she knew something. "What else could it possibly be, Agent Cortes?"

"Stop playing games, Eliza. You and I both know Brent wasn't Cindy Aquino's client. I think they were more than that. I think he was trying to help her get away from this group and died because of it."

"Brava, Ava. I always admired the way you could sift through the hidden, tangled threads of people's lives and find the dark knot. You're right, by the way."

Ava leaned forward. "Tell me what you know about her."

Eliza mimicked her posture, the receiver still at her ear as she glanced around. "There was a dinner prior to your whole nasty sting operation in which you entrapped me. Brent was there. He had been drinking heavily and was hopelessly intoxicated, really in his feelings by the end of the night. That's when he brought up a young woman. He said he'd started seeing her a few weeks before."

"Did he give a name?"

Eliza shook her head. "It was strange. He wasn't talking about her like a future conquest as was his habit. This was... different."

"Different how?"

"Brent was distracted, preoccupied. Of course, I didn't know at the time he was working out a deal to turn on me. How *did* you pull that off?"

"You said he was feeling bad about a girl?" Ava redirected. "You found it odd?"

"Yes. Brent had trouble remembering the names of his dates, let alone worrying about one." Eliza lifted a dainty shoulder in a half shrug. "Not his normal mindset. He seemed almost regretful about his interactions with this person. Like he'd done something wrong."

"Did you know who he was talking about?"

"I don't know every lady of the evening, Ava. We don't have union meetings." Eliza chuckled. "But I don't think she was a working girl."

"Why is that?"

"When Brent spoke about his paid dates, he called them sessions. But when we spoke at the party, he said he'd just met up with her or started seeing her. It felt... personal."

Ava leaned forward on the table. "Did he say those words? 'Started seeing?'"

"Something to that effect. No idea where they met, though I got the impression she was a college student. He made a comment about dorms." She lifted a graceful finger. "Oh, and I'm almost certain she was of Chinese descent because he asked me during that dinner for my advice on a gift he wanted to get her for Chinese New Year. What was appropriate. He also asked a friend of mine for money advice on setting up a trust. It was all so wholesome, to be honest."

Her words hung in the air, and Ava felt a puzzle piece lock into place. The money he'd taken from his father finally made sense. "What was he trying to do, exactly? How was she in trouble?"

"I don't know what he was trying to do, my dear," Eliza said with an uninterested shrug. "Probably trying to ride to the rescue. That seems to be the hobgoblin of middle-aged men. The need to feel important in someone's life again."

Eliza could offer nothing more. She'd given Brent the number of an accountant but had no idea if he'd followed through.

When Ava asked for his contact information, she said, "You have it. Milton Frederick. He was one of the twenty people you and Detective Manaia arrested that night. I heard he died awaiting trial for a Ponzi scheme a year later. Fragile man. He really didn't have the constitution for crime."

The guard standing behind Eliza yelled that her time was up. Ava didn't think the madam had much more to offer anyway, and she'd already gotten what she came for.

On her way out of the detention center's parking lot, Ava called the Cutler residence to see if Dane Cutler was home. His housekeeper said he was working. Cutler was a councilman because he had the time. His work involved managing his family's wealth. If he was 'at work' like the housekeeper said, he was at Brent's work. Probably fixing the books. August called Ava back while she was deciding what to do.

"Hey, the meeting just broke for a few minutes. Where'd you go?"

"I just spoke with the Sea Siren Madam." Ava gave him the gist of her conversation with Eliza while she slid into traffic. "I need to talk with Dane Cutler again. I'm heading to the wine tasting room right now."

"Why?"

"That asshole has been lying to us from the beginning."

"Wait for me, Ava."

"I'm going. You can meet me there or hear about it after."

TWENTY-EIGHT

It took Ava thirty minutes to get to the Bramble Wood Cellars tasting room. August arrived before she did. He was leaning against his SUV, arms crossed, shades on, hair rustling in the wind like he was in some kind of car ad. She parked, walked over, and he told her that the Chief of Police wanted to call in the FBI to take over.

"Let him." Ava shrugged. "I get paid either way. But if another body drops while the Feds are playing catch up that's on him. I'll make sure the press knows that, too. I'm sure Ricki Rogers would have no issue frying him up for public consumption."

"Vincent said the same thing but, you know, diplomatically." He followed her to the entrance. "Why are we here? What'd you learn?"

"He's been covering his own ass this whole time."

Brent Cutler's tasting room and restaurant leaned heavily into the coastal Italian aesthetic. Light, breezy colors from the shore made up the palette. Pale blue chairs, lemon tree artwork on the walls, and crisp white linens. The menu offered artisan pizza with goat cheese and fig, served on hand-carved paddleboards, sourdough baguettes with pesto butter, handmade pasta, sea bass fillets with pistachios, and locally grown cherry tomatoes. A foodie's dream.

The scent of basil and oregano and deep, rich sauce floated to Ava as they entered the tasting room. A full house, at half-past six. Ava glanced at the patrons sitting at round tables underneath driftwood and hand-blown glass chandeliers, while music lilted softly overhead. Ava and August flashed their badges at the hostess near the front door, and she called over a manager.

He wore black pants, a formal white button-down, and a concerned look. His slicked-back hair gleamed in the sun coming through the lace curtains.

"Is there a problem, detectives?"

"It's *Agents* Cortes and Blake," Ava said with a smile. "And no problem at all. I just need to follow up with Mr. Cutler on a few things."

"I'm sorry, he's not available," he said, his pencil mustache quirking. "Would you like to leave a message?"

"Are you his lawyer?" Ava asked.

"No—"

"Then we don't need to talk to you." Ava pushed past him, ignoring his objections.

August came up behind her, telling the manager to back off. He murmured in Ava's ear. "What are we doing, Ava?"

"Getting to the truth."

They found Cutler in a back room standing at a high table with several bottles of Syrah opened in front of him. He swirled a glass of wine under his nose. Deep purple and opaque, she caught just a hint of currants. She knocked on the door jamb. Cutler looked over and frowned.

"Sir," the frazzled manager said from behind Ava and August. "I told them you were busy."

Waving his manager away, he said to Ava, "You didn't call."

"I didn't want to warn you." Ava moved closer, standing across the table from him, she looked over the bottles, catching his gaze. "Your granddaughter died in one of those blue barrels and you said nothing. Why?"

August stilled, his eyes on Cutler.

The older man's face paled. He set his wineglass down. "I don't know what you're talking about."

"I just spoke with Eliza Cartwright. She gave your son the name of her personal accountant. Milton Frederick."

Cutler crossed his arms over his chest. "Am I supposed to know who that is?"

"He specializes in creating trusts. Particularly, family trusts. He manages inherited wealth, to be exact. Is that why you kept blocking us from getting to Brent's financial accounts?" Ava reached over and took his wine. She took a sip, and the warm berry and chocolate flavors coated her tongue. "When all this started, you said that Brent took money. Cash from the emergency credit card you gave him 'for a friend'."

"Yeah, so?"

"He didn't say friend, did he?" Ava asked. "He said *daughter*."

Cutler's gaze flitted to the door, like he wanted to run. "You don't know what you're talking about."

"You can cut the crap. I had the medical examiner run Cindy's DNA against Brent's." The swabs she asked Dr. Tavers for hadn't come back yet, but she was ninety-eight percent sure. August watched the exchange, his fingers pulling at his chin. She'd deal with that later. "There's no denying her now, Dane. She's your flesh and blood, and you hid it from the agents investigating her murder. I want to know why. I personally think it's because you had something to do with her death."

Cutler's eyes went wide. "You're insane!"

"Really? Because it fits. I mean she would have been an heir. A threat to Brent's financial future. A usurper from the wrong side of the tracks. Not to mention your career. A councilman's granddaughter isn't supposed to be a working girl." Ava shrugged. "Why not just bump her off, right? She was street scum. Not a *real* Cutler. No one would care—"

"Stop it!" Cutler glared at her, his lips pressed into a thin line. Then he sagged, his palm going to his forehead. "He told me about her the night we argued about the missing money from the emergency credit card."

"She was another problem amid the existing storm," Ava prompted. A cork sat on the table next to her, and she took it. Squeezing it in her palm. "You were angry."

His head snapped up. "I was furious! Was her death beneficial? Yes. But I didn't do anything to her. And I didn't ask anyone to do anything to her, either." He turned away, his hands on his hips as his gaze traveled the myriad vintage bottles on the racks. She gave him a moment, after which he turned back. "I mean... We were in the middle of a trial, dammit. And he told me some teenager showed up here at the tasting room, saying he was her father. Of all the times to have an illegitimate kid pop up. What was I supposed to do?"

In the middle of a trial, with Brent's marriage ending, and with the threat of more federal indictments rolling in, Brent revealed he'd had an affair with a woman he had met during one of his stints in rehab fifteen years before. A fellow addict. He never told his wife, and he had no idea the union had resulted in a child.

"Drugs and sex," Cutler said with a sneer. "That's all it was. Not a relationship. They snorted coke together, nothing more."

"Well, a little bit more happened, obviously. Do you know what happened to the mother?"

"No, I don't. Why should I? She's off doing drugs I imagine." Cutler paced behind the table.

"You told him to keep her existence quiet?" August asked. "Because of the case?"

Cutler nodded. "Could you imagine what the press would have said about her? She was a whore. A druggie like her mother. I couldn't have that coming out on top of the shit show the Sea Siren trial was turning out to be."

"And then? After the trial?" Ava asked. "Did you ever meet her?"

"I had no reason to. Besides, by the time the trial ended Brent had stopped talking about her. I assumed she went away."

"Why did you think that?" August asked.

"I imagined he'd paid her off or something. I don't know. Not my problem."

"Then why did you interfere with her arrest?" Ava asked.

Cutler glared at her, his jaw tilting up, defiant. "I'm done talking to you two. Lawyer."

"You're not under arrest, sir," August said.

"Lawyer." Cutler took back his wine and downed it in one gulp. "Arrest me or get out of here."

"She was your granddaughter," Ava said. "You were going to consign her to a pauper's grave?"

"She was just another one of Brent's many mistakes," Cutler said. "I have no grandchildren."

Ava leaned across the table and jabbed her finger in his face. "I will find every single scrap of evidence about Cindy Aquino that you either hid or destroyed, you understand me? You will *not* make her disappear!"

Cutler looked at her, the pain of the past two years filling his eyes. "Lawyer."

———

August strode silently, and between the angry gum chewing and the hard look in his eyes, Ava knew his state of mind. She'd kept him in the dark. Again.

"Everything happened so fast," Ava began, but he put his palm up, shaking his head.

"When did you know?"

She took in a deep breath. "Remember when I mentioned Eliza knew everyone's dark secret? This was Brent's. I think the hesitation I sensed during his deal negotiations was this. I think he was worried we'd find out about Cindy."

"You still could have told me before we walked in."

"I wanted to hit him fast—"

He shook his head. "I'm tired, Ava, and I don't..." He sighed, his gaze slipping from hers. "I've been going since six this morning. I'm heading back to the hotel. Calling it a night."

Without another word, he climbed into his SUV and drove away.

———

Ava pulled into her driveway a little before seven. Still ramped up from the confrontation with both Cutler and August, she decided to go for a swim while it was still light out. After a quick change, she took her favorite path toward her alcove beach spot, running toward the craggy silhouette in the evening light. Taking the steel steps two at a time, she walked across the warm, rocky ground and leaned against the rock wall, catching her breath.

People running after work and couples on their evening walks passed by on the sidewalk overhead. She stripped off her clothes and shoes, leaving them by the stone wall. As she walked out to the ocean, the cold water rushed up to meet her feet.

Ava spotted an A-frame sign sitting near the surf with a red tide warning. She'd forgotten about Denny's call that morning. According to the chat boards, the Ocean Within community planned to gather soon with the arrival of the glowing waves.

Unwilling to swim in the algae bloom, Ava walked back to the rocky outcropping, slipped back into her clothes, and found a smooth boulder to sit on. Tilting her head to the low sun, she slowed her thoughts as the orange rays warmed her face. The sound of the waves soothed her, and she closed her eyes and let her mind wander among all the images, evidence, and statements. Every scrap of information she'd seen whirled lazily around a central figure.

The sound of footsteps on the steel steps brought her out of her reverie.

They stopped, and she opened her eyes to see why.

Orien—Owen Meeks—stood near the bottom of the stairs, staring down at her. His loose clothing fluttered in the wind.

He held her in his gaze as he took a step closer. "Hello Ava."

"Well, if it isn't the Son of Dawn," she said, rising from the rocks to face him. He'd ambushed her, and it sent her pulse racing that she hadn't seen it coming.

Surprise showed in his eyes before he smiled. "You've been reading my musings."

"And you've been stalking me. Or is it the universe bringing us together?"

"I think we simply share a love for the sea."

She understood why people were drawn to him. It all made sense. She couldn't take her eyes off him. His crystalline blue eyes, rimmed with soft understanding, full lips parting in a smile, the setting sun peeking out from behind his light hair. His low, smooth voice soothed her racing pulse, despite him being the one who had caused it.

"I don't think that's why you're here." Ava's gaze flitted to the sidewalk above and the various people on the sand behind her. He wouldn't try anything. "You want me to see that you've been watching. That you can get to me."

"You truly see life through the lens of violence, don't you? Not everyone wants to do you harm, Agent Cortes."

"Ya know, I don't have this job because I suck at it." She joined him at the foot of the stairs, but he didn't move. He looked down at her, his gaze direct. Unflinching. Knowing. "This may be an epic meeting in your mind, but you're just another Tuesday for me."

A scowl pulled at his brows for a split second before a placid expression slammed back down. When he spoke, it was with the calm patience of a weary teacher. "You have no idea what you're getting yourself into. Not by any stretch of imagination. You're in over your head, Ava."

"Much like the girls you target. Preying on the impressionable?

Kids without families? What, women your own age aren't interested in the façade?"

"From what I understand, you would have greatly benefited from my classes during your impressionable years."

"Maybe." She shrugged, tired of his antics. "But I'll tell you something you clearly don't understand yet."

"And what's that?"

She stepped up, pushing past him, forcing him to step aside. When she was four steps above him, at eye level, she turned and held his gaze. "It's only a matter of time until I tear down your whole world."

He looked away, closing his eyes as the wind tousled his hair. Then continued down the stairs and out onto the shore without another word.

Ava watched him for several moments, wishing she had enough to bring him in for questioning. His silhouette showed through the thin material of his tunic as he moved deliberately, even elegantly. He was right. He'd have been a vision to someone like her back in the day, and that pissed her off. Even as an adult, she found it hard not to feel something in his presence. Those kids didn't stand a chance. Ava turned and bounded back up the steps, wondering why death often looked so beautiful.

————

Heart still ramming in her chest, she walked back to her street in the dark, the warm night air drying the sweat from her running clothes as she went. A light in her home shone through the trees, and she paused, not remembering if she'd left any on. As she drew closer, she slowed, her hand going instinctively to her waist and the gun that wasn't there before she saw it. A black Harley-Davidson motorcycle with a silver laughing skull graphic on the tank parked at the curb.

She climbed her steps and peered in through the window at the large figure standing at her stove. Chin-length dark hair, heavy metal T-shirt, motorcycle boots with chains.

"Hey," she said, pushing her door open. The stubble on his lantern jaw, deep brown eyes and a wicked smile held the promise of dark things. She noticed a new tattoo on his arm since she'd seen him last.

He effortlessly flipped an omelet before turning to her. "Hello, Lady Justice."

TWENTY-NINE

While Denny finished cooking, Ava showered and changed into sweats and a T-shirt. Deciding to deal with her hair later, she put it in a ponytail. She winced as she applied alcohol and then another bandage to the stitches on her healing brow, thinking about past wounds. Which then had her thinking of Denny.

Ava met Denny when she turned eighteen. After inheriting the trust and her grandmother's cottage, she moved back in and rented out the rooms to her college friends. She and her roommates threw a housewarming party which spread into a block party during which Denny showed up. He rolled into the drive on a dirt bike, wearing a leather jacket, jeans, and that killer smile. He was nineteen. Smart and wild, he'd been exciting and mysterious and not at all bothered by her personal hurricane.

They'd gotten close. And then he was gone. He'd drifted in and out of her life ever since. She'd get a letter from Singapore, or a book wrapped in brown paper from a street bazaar in Spain. Her mantel and bookshelves held trinkets from his travels. As uncontainable as the wind, Denny always managed to show up right when it counted.

Back in her kitchen, she took in the hearty breakfast spread out on the small table and smiled. She did love bacon.

"What's the occasion?" she asked, slipping into a chair near the window. His leather jacket and saddlebag sat in the corner on the floor. "Are you back in town or passing through?"

He walked over with a mug of coffee for her and a beer for him. He also carried a bottle of ghost pepper sauce, which Ava was sure hadn't come from her cupboards.

He slipped into the seat opposite her. "I'm not sure yet. I'm chasing down something over by the Oceanside Transportation Center. It's probably nothing."

"The train station?"

He nodded. "Over by Tremont."

Ava took a bite of her omelet. Bacon and cheddar. Her favorite. "If you're involved, it probably isn't nothing."

He smiled. "That's a little like the pot calling the kettle black, isn't it? You're a state agent that will only use burners for your personal phone."

"Rondeau gets everything that comes to my work phone. Besides that's called compartmentalization, and it's a time-honored tradition within the government in case you weren't aware."

"Oh, I'm aware of the government's shady dealings." He chuckled, sipping his beer thoughtfully. "How are you doing with this case, really? And don't give me some cookie cutter answer. Tell me the truth. I can't be the only one who thought of Venus when you told me the details."

She took a sip of coffee, collecting her thoughts. "What I'm feeling skews more toward survivor's guilt and anger that the shit that was going on back then is still happening to a new generation of kids." Ava pointed to her injured eye. "The young woman who gave me this has been in the system since she was five. Five."

Ava told him about Sadie Schneider and what she'd done. She mentioned the photo of the sad girl in the blue dress in the CPS file. The one no one ever looked for.

Denny nodded. "Cases with kids, even teens, are always hard."

"I don't know. I feel like my judgment is clouded." Ava rubbed her temples with her fingertips. "Maybe I'm too close to all of this."

"You feel a kinship with this kid. That's understandable." Denny tipped his bottle and took a drink. "It's not a bad thing. Not if you use it right."

"I spoke with a woman who knows the streets. She said something about wild girls with dark hearts. My picture would have been next to that definition in the dictionary when I was a teen, Denny. Angry—" A noise at her window pulled Ava's attention, and she looked over, catching a flutter of wings. "Knowing what I do of Sadie Schneider's past, what she's been through, she's a powder keg. And that fake guru bastard lit the fuse. After meeting the creep that's doing this, I see it. I felt it. What they're drawn to about him."

Denny's brows furrowed. "Did he come for you?"

"No, he's just... making it known he's aware of me." Ava shrugged. "It was nothing."

"Yeah, well, what you call nothing most people call danger."

"Speaking of the pot calling the kettle black." Ava raised her coffee cup in a salute. They talked more about the fringe commune group he'd mentioned before. Other than Jade, Denny couldn't find any other ex-members, which they both found a little alarming.

"I *was* able to track down that communal house I was telling you about." He gave her the address. It wasn't far from the Cutler Mansion, more north by Oceanside Boulevard, on Tate. The expensive part of town.

"Does this Orien guy own it?"

"No. The owner's name and number are on the paper. He rents out multiple properties and might not know how that house is being used."

"Thanks, Denny."

"I also have that other thing you asked for." Danny slid a portable hard drive across the table to her, on top of a manila envelope.

"After the Ghost Town Killer case, you had me check into a

rumor about a drifter who'd been staying at the local church around the time your family was attacked."

"The police blotter during that time frame mentioned a drifter causing problems in the area, but when I asked the local shelters for information, I came up empty."

Denny nodded. "I took that and worked with a pattern recognition program. I fed in all the information we have on your family's case. And cases we felt might be connected either via proximity or the killer's MO." Those brown eyes held sadness now, not danger. "I even spliced in some of the stuff we got, you know, creatively. I got back a lot of crap. But there was this one name that popped up a couple times."

"Okay..." A tremor moved through her chest. "And?"

"It belonged to a priest who had been serving there during those years but transferred shortly before your family was attacked. I talked to him. He ran a charity that reached out to homeless veterans. I asked about this drifter you mentioned, but he had a bit of trouble remembering. He's old. As in his Bible was made of stone tablets old. But he said he would look back in his journals. His name is Father Padua. But guess what his charity was called? St. Sebastian's House."

"St. Sebastian?"

Denny nodded. "The patron saint of soldiers."

Ava couldn't let herself hope. "There were rumors the drifter was a veteran."

"I think you should talk with him. It might be nothing, but it might not be, you know?"

Ava stared at Denny, her mouth going dry, pulse pounding at her temples. "Father Padua. I-I can't believe you found something solid."

He reached out, taking her hand in his. "Listen, Ava, we don't know what he knows. I want you to keep that in mind—" Denny cocked his head, going still.

A moment later, August rushed through the front door. Hand at his hip, he scanned the room, his gaze falling on the two of them eating at the table.

"Patrol said they clocked movement in your side yard," August said, relaxing a little. "And then you weren't answering your phone."

Ava looked at him, a little impressed. "You assigned a protection detail to me anyway?"

August shrugged. "You would have."

"Little intense, no?" Denny asked with a grin.

"You see her eye, right?" August held up his phone. Their eyes met. Locked. "We've been calling you. Rondeau found something."

"Isn't she off duty? That's usually when people *relax*. You should try it sometime." Denny's grin widened.

August ignored him. "Can I speak to you outside, Agent Cortes?"

"Why so formal, man?" Denny leaned back in his chair. "We both know you used to have a drawer here."

Ava stood, wiping her mouth with a napkin, and kicked Denny's chair so that he almost fell backwards.

"Shut up and finish your breakfast," she said with a smile.

He chuckled as she walked out onto the porch with August.

Outside, she met his eyes again. Saw something dark in them. "What's wrong?"

"Rondeau said he couldn't reach you either."

"I think my phone died." Ava hadn't put it to charge when she returned home. "What happened—"

Denny pushed through the door wearing his leather jacket, walking between Ava and August on the porch, his saddlebag forcing them apart. He strode down to his motorcycle and strapped on the saddlebag.

Slipping on his helmet, he said. "A pleasure meeting you, Agent Blake. Enjoy your play."

August's brows rose. "My what?"

"Leave him alone, Denny." Ava walked down the few steps leading to the grass. She shook her head and gave him a hug. "He's one of the good ones."

Denny wrapped his arms around her, his breath at her ear as she felt him slip something into her back pocket. Pulling away, he planted a kiss on her temple near the bandage and then winked. "I like him. He's not as stuffy as I thought he'd be."

He nodded to August and then mounted his bike and drove off, rumbling up the road.

August shook his head. "What kind of start-up employs a motor-cycle gang member?" he muttered.

"They make spreadsheets or something." Ava unfolded the paper Denny slipped her and smiled when she realized it was the personal calendar and itinerary for DDA Jared Iverson. "It's not like Denny meets with clients anyway. He does their network security. What did Rondeau find?"

"Two things. First, he said you mentioned a call girl angle? Let me guess, Denny?"

"We had a call this morning. Remember I asked him to look into the local outlier groups? He's been on the boards and hearing some things. I asked Manaia to run the idea past Crimes of Violence. Did they get something?"

"They have an undercover asset working the area on another case. She said she's heard some rumbling about new girls working out of the industrial area. Manaia thinks one of the warehouse offices looks good for the point of contact. These escorts are working a farmer's daughter gimmick. That's the asset's words, not mine." He shrugged. "There might be something there."

"And the other thing?"

"Rondeau figured out what the sticker on the panel van belonged to. We used the video from the ATM across from the shelter. We got an image of a young woman matching Cindy Aquino's approximate description getting into it at the corner. It matches the videos we have of the van from the liquor store camera just down the street from the body dump at the drive-in. We also ran the photos past the construc-tion site manager, Horatio Jones, and he said it looked like the one he saw that night, right down to the purple sticker."

"That's great!"

"The sticker is part of a gated community. Manaia called after I left our meeting with Cutler and I went with him to speak with the security outfit servicing the area. The manager confirmed the van belonged to a house in the neighborhood but wanted a subpoena to give out specific customer information. It took a few hours, but we served them and we got the address."

She smiled. "Let me guess. It's on Tate Street."

"How did you..." August pointed down the road Denny took. "He's not cleared to know details of the case."

"He found it on his own."

"And felt the need to hand deliver it this late?"

"Yeah, what kind of stalker visits a colleague's home at night?" Ava walked back up the steps, leaned on the railing, and crossed her arms. Shaken by Denny's news, she pushed it down, choosing to tease August to distract him. "What play?"

August shoved his hands in his pockets, his jaw working, then said, "I just bought tickets to a show at the Old Globe in San Diego."

"Really?" Ava narrowed her gaze. "It's Shakespeare Summer. You hate Shakespeare."

"Do you want to hear about the raid we have planned or not?"

Ava brushed past him and went back into her house. "Come tell me about it. I think I can scrounge up something with vegetables in it."

August followed her into her kitchen, stopping at the counter with Denny's other bottles of beer. "He drives that bike drunk?"

"They're non-alcoholic beer," Ava said, leaning into the fridge.

"I thought you didn't like the taste of beer."

"I don't keep them in the fridge for myself." She stood and held one out to him. "I don't keep them in there for him either."

"Oh." August walked over, taking it. He cracked it open and took a swig. "Listen. I know you have a right to your private life. One I'm not a part of anymore. I know he's been a good source of intel for you in the past but falling back into old habits might be asking for trouble."

"Do you think we see each other romantically?"

He tried and failed to look aloof. "Do you?"

"Not since I was eighteen."

"I'm not trying to pry, Ava. I'm merely concerned about the case. Chain of command, record of evidence, you know."

"Totally. This conversation is definitely only about justice and evidentiary procedures," Ava agreed. "Did it ever occur to you that Denny and I are too similar? I mean, we're so alike, it would be like dating myself and from what I've seen, that's a nightmare."

August's grim look broke. "It wasn't so bad."

"Tell me about the rental house," Ava said, taking the last strip of bacon from the cutting board.

August pulled out his phone. "After the security company gave us the information on the van's owner, Manaia put an unmarked car on the street to watch. It's only been a few hours, but he says the place has constant traffic."

Ava cleared the table. "What do you mean?"

"Teens or young adults coming and going all day. We think some of them live there. Boxes being loaded into a blue van. He didn't see the white one. Lots of luxury cars on the property. Manaia sat out there with binoculars for a while himself and noted at least half a dozen women in yoga pants and sports bras entering some kind of outside courtyard from a side gate."

"When do we hit it?"

"Not so fast." He took another swig. "The van was easy. The construction supervisor, Horatio Jones, and Cindy Aquino's friend at the shelter, Heather Adams, both saw it in person. That bolstered the videos of it simply driving by. The house though. The judge didn't bite the whole apple. She granted us a separate, narrow scope surveillance warrant that allowed Rondeau to fly a drone overhead to take a peek. We spotted what we believe to be the white van in question tucked behind a workshop near the rear of the property. We see a lot of young people, possibly underage teens there and they're working out in some garden area. With the way things went sideways at the sober living house with Hunter, Vincent wants a different approach."

"How different?"

"Measured and well planned. Without any minors getting hurt in the fray—and that place is crawling with them. Vincent has the DA working on getting us a warrant for the house and vehicles now that we have compelling drone footage of the white van. I contacted the owner and he's cooperating. He says the rental contract is with a property rental company of some kind."

"I gave Rondeau information on that this morning."

"He told me. We ran it against the rental agreement. They match."

The hum of the chase gave Ava a charge. "And we have enough?"

"Vincent says the lawyers think the judge could grant us a warrant based on what Rondeau found in Brent Cutler's finances and his phone records."

Ava perked up. "We finally got those?"

"Yes, Brent wrote himself checks from his father's credit card and then submitted them to his bank for cash."

"That tracks. Cindy told her friend Heather that the guy she was speaking to on the phone owed her. I think Cindy was talking about her father, Brent Cutler. I believe he was giving her cash, I just don't know what for. She left the shelter, so maybe it was for living expenses?"

"We noticed something strange. Brent was writing the check to himself to cash. So, he'd be the only one to see it, yet he made notes in the memo section. They looked coded." August pulled up a photo on his phone.

Block letters scrawled across the line at the bottom of the check read *For Cindy,* followed by a string of numbers and letters.

"What does it mean?"

"CBI Intelligence Unit worked out that it was a business license number. They connected it to an anonymous LLC in New Mexico that led to a blind trust held by Cara Bane, with the beneficiary of that trust being Owen Meeks."

"We have proof he rents that house, then. No doubt," Ava said.

"With the check, the tea from Jimmy pointing to Orien's yoga studio, the fact that Cindy Aquino worked at the yoga studio, it's a pretty good case. And remember the cash app? The one Henry Miller had Jerra the boat mechanic send him money through?"

"Yeah, the one listing H.M."

"We've been going over Henry's phone records since we didn't recover the phone. Not only did Henry send money from that app on his phone to a subsidiary of that same LLC right before he died, he sent a text directly to Brent's cell from that number."

August swiped his phone screen, showing Ava a screenshot of a text conversation. From Henry Miller to Brent Cutler.

> Back off. She belongs to the teacher.

> She's my daughter. I'm getting her away from that monster.

> We know who you're working with. They'll both die if you try to tear the family apart.

Brent responded with a photo of Cindy entering a wooden gate.

> I know what goes on in Ascension House. I know who Orien really is. What he's done. I'll expose everything if he doesn't let her go.

August rubbed tired eyes. Ava wondered when he'd last slept well. He hated hotels. "Activity stops for almost a month. Then Brent gets a photo of Cindy lying unconscious on a couch. But it was sent from *Cindy's* phone. We have a record of its purchase in Brent's financial records."

The photo appeared under Brent's last text conversation with Cindy about Orien and the Ocean Within cult, as he called it.

Whoever sent Brent the photo of his dead daughter also sent a two-word text.

You're next.

"I think this led to some kind of confrontation and Brent was killed," August said. "Vincent thinks we have enough circumstantial evidence for a warrant to search the communal house."

"At least one of Orien's followers is violent. I think her name is Sadie Schneider. She's the young woman who attacked me and killed Henry Miller. One or all of them at the house might be armed. They might be guarding Orien. Which brings up something I have to talk to you about." Ava took in a slow breath. "Don't freak out, but when I went out for a swim earlier this evening, I had a visitor show up at Alcove Beach."

August's hands balled into fists.

"He kept his distance, but he was letting me know he's been paying attention."

His jaw clenched. "No. He was letting you know he could get to you."

"That kind of thing goes both ways. It's his mistake if he tries something."

Crossing his arms, August said, "That's all well and good, Calamity Jane, but I'm doubling your protection."

Ava put her hands up in surrender. "Whatever gets us off the subject and moving on this case. He probably only decided to harass me because he feels us closing in."

August's gaze rested on her for a beat too long. She caught a glimpse of something like vulnerability. Like worry. Then the veil came down, and he was "Uber-Agent" again. He nodded, pulling out a stick of gum, and folded it into his mouth. "The raid. We need to act quickly, but safely. Things which tend to contradict each other." He leaned against the counter. "Any ideas?"

Ava stared at the image of Cindy Aquino as she'd been before being stuffed into a barrel and tossed into the roiling sea. Before the ravages of decay destroyed her. "He truly is a monster."

"We'll get him, Ava. Tomorrow at the latest. We have him up against a wall."

She remembered Seth's words about cornered predators. "Which makes him more dangerous than ever."

THIRTY

Corsair Beach. Midnight. Low tide.

A strip of surf crashed in the distance, waves glowing bright blue as they churned against the sand. Rumbling as they raced for her feet only to dissolve into a foamy hiss. The deep night of a waning moon offered almost no light. The small beach was so dark, puddles of trapped phytoplankton sparkled with the receding waves like bowls full of stars. Salt air and the scent of seaweed wafted to Ava as she stood in the tide pools. At her feet, stranded crabs the size of quarters left glowing trails of light with their movements. Pinprick stars and a mist moving off the water gave the shore an isolated, liminal feel. As if she stood at the doorway to another world. The bioluminescent spectacle of red tide truly delivered.

To avoid bothering others during a red tide viewing, locals often brought battery powered tea lights, the kind used for Christmas décor, instead of flashlights. They sat lined up along the top of a rock retaining wall at the edge of the sand. Free to use it and then leave it for the next person. Ava didn't take a spot. She wanted to remain hidden.

Wearing dark sweats and running shoes, she stood with her arms crossed, her gaze on the silhouettes moving on the exposed, wet sand half a dozen yards away. She could make out their flowing dresses and shirts. They sang softly. A low, melancholy tune that sounded old. Holding hands and whirling in lazy rings around flickering candles, they looked like ghostly passengers haunting a shipwrecked shore. She felt voyeuristic. Watching their death ritual as they sent rings of flowers carrying tea candles into the receding waves. Hunter's name came to Ava on the wind, and she listened to the soft cries of those who knew him, her throat tight.

A figure appeared between the group and where she stood several yards away, headed her way. A man in a white tunic that glowed a pale lavender as if touched by moonlight. Waves scuttled across the sand between them. When the water receded, his feet left ethereal blue footprints on the wet sand.

He opened his hand, revealing a tea light in his palm. Locks of his long blond hair glowed like filaments of gold. Ice-blue eyes held ironic warmth. He truly did look like a movie version of a holy man.

Orien stopped a few feet from her. "Is this *you* making a point, Agent Cortes?"

Not bothering to look at him, she said, "Your little visit was cute, but I wasn't the one trying to hide. You, on the other hand have been scurrying around in the dark and I still managed to track down your creepy ass." She held his pale, empty gaze with hers. "There's nowhere in this city that will keep you safe from me."

"Safe from you? What would I have to fear?" He smirked. "You have nothing."

She didn't react, just jerked toward the others. "What is your group doing?"

"Our family is mourning. One of our own was struck down yesterday."

"Yes. I witnessed one of your followers murder him in cold blood. Did you tell her to?"

He smiled. An unsettling expression that didn't reach his eyes. She saw cold calculation there before he turned and surveyed the group at the tide pools. "They are taking part in our Ascension Ceremony. As I said, we lost a member tragically. His family is honoring and releasing the life energy of their loved one."

"Does this lost loved one have a name?"

Orien shook his head. "His family deserves privacy."

"Henry Miller didn't have family," Ava said. Orien didn't answer, his gaze boring into her, almost through her. She took a step toward the group. "What are they doing?"

"Drift offerings." He angled his shoulder, not quite blocking her, but almost. "To Mother Night so that he's welcomed by the open arms of the sea."

He had a strange cadence. Hypnotic and slightly slower than typical speech, Ava thought. Controlled.

"Does the sea know Hunter shot and dumped his fellow followers in it?"

The candle cast his face in angled shadows. "As far as I know, the Blue Drum Killer disposed of those unfortunate victims."

"What about his little girlfriend?" Ava touched her bandaged eyebrow. "She has a hell of a backhand. Is she here tonight?"

Orien glanced behind him again at the group, and Ava noticed some of the candles had gone out. "Why are you here, Agent?"

"It's a public beach. A natural wonder." Ava smiled. "I just want to ask her a few questions."

He didn't move out of her way. "Like I said. A family is in mourning."

"Are you sleeping with one of your young followers over there? One of your *family*?" Ava turned to face him over the flickering flame. "I thought a couple of them resembled Cara Bane."

He didn't react to her mention of his ex. Instead, he tilted his head and said, "You've been digging up my past as if that will discredit all I've been and all I will be."

"You can't help it, can you? Marcus Aurelias? Do you tell them that time is a river, too, or do you change it to a wave? I mean it still fits, and it caters to your audience. Tell me, is this ritual different than

Renewal? I have to say, I'm doubtful the powerful and mysterious Mother Night would choose a man to speak for her. Kind of goes against female empowerment, no?" Ava nodded to the group casting flowers in the sea. "*They* wouldn't know that. Many of them barely finished high school. But I read the real thinkers. You're just a weak facsimile conning these kids."

He didn't answer at first, his gaze off toward the ocean. "Ask any of them. I'm helping them help themselves, and they know it."

"Is that what you call your indoctrination?"

"That would suggest control, which I do not seek. In fact, I rebuke it. My heart is for those that struggle. Who are lost."

"Your heart, if you still have one, is dark as pitch and you know it. No control? They just all eat and dress and talk the same as you for no reason?"

"They do what they like. Wear what they like. I try to help them shed the damage done by their parents or the foster care system that many come from. You know something about that, don't you, Agent Cortes?"

"Wow, you figured out how to use a search engine." She started walking toward the group. Slow but deliberate, watching his reaction. He tensed but didn't stop her. "You made a mistake with Brent Cutler, didn't you? That's what started all of this."

He strolled beside her, the candle flickering in the night. "I don't know what you mean."

"I couldn't figure out what the money was for. He wasn't paying for her services because he was her father. But you already knew that didn't you?" Ava raised her voice as they drew near the group. "You know, Cara said something when you destroyed her mind. Over what you thought was a betrayal."

"And what was that?"

"She said you knew things you weren't supposed to. At first, I thought that meant supernaturally, because her brother said she believed in that kind of thing. But then I realized what she meant when we uncovered your special deliveries."

The muscles around his mouth tensed. "I have no idea what you're talking about."

"No? The subscription boxes come with perks from what I hear. Nice, innocent looking ones." Ava glanced at the nearby followers and realized the singing had stopped. Good. They should hear this. "You know what your followers have done, because you sent them to do it. And then you recorded them somehow. Brent was paying you blackmail, wasn't he?"

The dancing stopped, the conversation pulling them closer. They emerged from the dark as they neared the group.

"Don't disturb them," Orien said with an edge.

"Cindy told you who her father was, didn't she? She thought you'd be impressed." His gaze flicked away. Returned. She was right. "And you were, weren't you? At least by his bank account."

"I don't know what you're talking about."

"I can see why Brent would be a good mark. The guy was used to paying to keep his dirty secrets from coming to light. Why not one more? Did you ask her to do it or did she volunteer?"

His gaze flitted to the group, but he couldn't hide the momentary smirk that pulled at his lip. "I would never condone or request such a thing."

She'd turned on her own father for him.

"Mmhm," Ava nodded. "Her grandfather, Dane Cutler, is a close friend of the mayor. Imagine his influence on how the case is handled. How much more staff and attention will get thrown at the hunt for her killer."

"I doubt he wants that."

"I don't give a shit what he wants," Ava snapped. "I found Henry Miller. I found Cara Bane. I'll find Sadie Schneider. I'll track down every one of your little Mansonettes and one of them will talk."

"I do hope the Blue Drum Killer will be brought to justice." Orien blocked her way again. "You speak of lost children, yet you're more adrift than they are."

Her body shook as she fought the urge to throttle him. "Are you going to help me find myself too?"

"That's not what you need." He stepped into her space, towering over her, blocking out the rest of the group with the breadth of his shoulders.

Ava smiled sweetly, not stepping back. "Do I need what you gave to Cara… or was it, Lark?"

"She was a troubled woman."

"You would know. You were her counselor." Ava pitched her voice louder. "The name changes are a pattern of behavior, Owen. You should've changed the symbols. You left your handprints all over these kids. Personally, I think it's the magic tea that's gonna get you. Amanita, potent THC, all of it mixed in with flowers from a garden I can DNA test. You're cooked."

The charm disappeared, replaced by a cold, blank look. "We sell it to the public. Anyone has access."

"Weird that you didn't ask me what amanita was," Ava said. She looked at the pale faces gathered in the dark behind him. "Your Blue Lotus tea is in the blood or was blown into the faces, of Cindy, Jimmy, Brent, and Hunter. Did you know that? And your follower, Sadie, blew Hunter's brains out right in front of me. She isn't ashamed of what she's done, Orien. That's the problem with true believers, isn't it? There is no way you'll be able to keep her quiet once I have her. She'll brag about everything, and I mean everything, you taught her."

"I have no idea who this Sadie is."

She saw no signs of confusion on his face, so Ava pushed. "What happened? Did Sadie get jealous? She seems the type. You must have been paying a lot of attention to Cindy. She was your golden goose, with all the money her dad was giving you. That had to breed resentment." Ava waved a hand at the group. "If I pull ID's out here from your little harem, am I going to find a high schooler?"

He shrugged. "As you pointed out. It's a public beach. I have no control over who comes to view nature's spectacle. And you're grasping at straws. Twisting facts to make your case. You almost lost your job for that before, didn't you? The pressure to find someone so evil must be enormous."

"Look in my eyes. Do I look like I'm afraid I won't get you?" Ava took a few more steps toward the group. There were more than she realized. "Loyalty is nothing compared to life in prison."

Orien angling her away. "I'm surprised at you, Ava. Surely you understand loyalty. After all, you covered up a murder with your lover, did you not? Must be awkward working with an ex?" He leaned in, the fake flame fluttering between them. "I know your deep dark secret."

"Oh yeah, which one?" Ava noticed a young woman standing away from the group on the tide pools nearest the waves. Delicate, almost fragile, her pale face inscrutable in the dark. "If Sadie Schneider goes missing or turns up dead, I'm coming for you."

Orien raised his hand and flicked his wrist. The young woman turned and ran into the center of the group, blending with the clustered silhouettes. A whispered name on the lips of the dark figures came to Ava before he silenced them with a glare... *Sky.*

"Oh, that's beautiful. You picked it, didn't you? You've been so creative thus far."

"You're so broken." She tensed when he tucked a strand of hair behind her ear. "Finding the man who killed your family won't calm your ocean within. It won't do anything but pull you further into his monstrous world."

Ava reared back, creeped out by his touch. "You don't know what you're talking about."

"What would your brother, Tomás, think about your life? You're alone. Can't maintain a relationship. In a job where you risk your life and I think... chase death. Would he think his sacrifice for you was worth it?"

All the candles had gone out. The crowd of silhouettes moved closer, surrounding her and Orien. A mass of shadows moving in.

"Keep my brother's name out of your filthy mouth," Ava snarled.

"There it is," Orien said with a grin. "The rage, the fury that wreaks havoc on everyone and everything around you. You *are* destruction, Ava. You hurt those you love. You don't know what that darkness in you is, but I do. And it may destroy you in the end. But I can help you."

She heard the ting of a switchblade. He lunged, and his hand slashed downward.

She blocked his swing and rammed the heel of her hand against his nose. His head rocked back, and he stumbled. His candle fell to the sand, going out. The crowd surged toward her.

"Stop!" Orien shouted. They froze at his word.

He stood panting in front of her, his nose bleeding black in the moonlight. "That was reckless even for you. Why are you *really* here, Agent Cortes?"

She looked down at her wrist, pulling back the sleeve to check her watch "Distracting you."

He froze, glaring at her with venomous eyes. "What?"

"We raided your commune tonight. I have everyone you left behind."

Orien jerked as if slapped. With an incoherent scream, he charged her, reaching for her throat. They tumbled onto the wet sand. The surrounding horde of mourners shouted too, attempting to pull her off him. Ava grabbed Orien by his tunic collar, twisting and yanking it around his neck, strangling him with the material, her legs a vice around his chest. She grabbed wet sand and rubbed it into his face.

"Go, go, go!" August's voice in her earpiece came to life as Rondeau, Manaia, and a dozen OPD officers broke cover from behind rock clusters and parked cars on the street, their weapons trained on the group.

Orien clawed an exposed rock from the sand and swung it at her head. Ava twisted away, losing her grip on his shirt.

"Run!" Orien gasped, coughing. His followers broke apart, scattering to the sea, down the unlit beach, onto the street and into the park area. They stampeded past Ava, yanking Orien from her grasp. She tried to get up, but someone's fist connected with her chin and she went down again.

Wet and slimy with seaweed, she staggered to her feet and triggered her earpiece, "They took him. Orien is on the move. A big group. They're running with him like he's the president."

"We're on them!" Manaia came back.

She scanned for August. Flashlights slashed the night, and she slipped and slid in the tide pools trying to get to dry sand. August came back with two young men in cuffs. He handed them off to a waiting officer and crossed to her.

"We got most of them," he panted. "Almost a dozen. That's in addition to the followers we detained during the raid."

"How the hell was Sadie here?" Ava shouted, pacing. Adrenaline made her hands tremble, and she opened and closed them. "I thought she was at the house."

"So did they. Manaia is figuring that out."

"I can't believe—"

"What happened?" August took in her shaking hands. "You didn't give the distress signal."

"That asshole tried to cut me. There was no time." Ava put her hand to her forehead, and it came back streaked with blood. "Where is he, anyway?"

August hesitated, "OPD said they didn't see him."

A wave of dizziness washed over Ava, and she slumped to her knees in the sand, the edges of her vision tunneling. "He can't win."

THIRTY-ONE

Sky knew that Orien owned a fifties bungalow home in South Oceanside. It was there she'd fled. A former follower whom they'd killed together had owned it before, and Orien had made her sign some kind of document before she died. Sky wasn't sure how that worked, just that Orien called it his place. Since a couple of years had passed and no one else had ever shown up at the house, she guessed he was right. Located in a senior community, no one knew about it but Sky.

And Cindy.

She'd first come here with Orien back when *she* was his most beloved. Hot tears streaked her cheeks as she sat on a folding chair on the backyard patio next to the small, kidney-shaped pool. The lights underneath the water made rippling shapes dance beneath the branches of the massive magnolia tree that shaded most of the yard. The heated water created whorls of steam that rose from the sparkling surface.

Sky sniffed, chewing on her fingernails. He was angry she'd come to the beach. And then that agent came and made things worse. Rage roiled through Sky. Images of Ava hitting Orien made her clutch her stomach. This was all that woman's fault. The agent told the others on the beach what she'd done to Hunter. What she'd done for Orien. It didn't matter now, Sky told herself. She couldn't go back to Ascension House, anyway. When the agents and cops invaded, she'd been in the garden, lying on the bench, gazing at the stars. Banned from the ceremony honoring Hunter, Orien told her it was penance for taking his life. That she couldn't mourn him among the others.

She understood, sort of. He'd been a threat, and Sky felt she should be rewarded, but she didn't argue. Orien promised they'd speak afterward, and so she waited. Humming softly, she'd relished the cool night breeze. Then the harsh voices, smoke, and screams had started, and she'd run. Hiding in the gazebo, she spotted the cars and vans, the men and women in armor, guns out. The smell of pepper spray drifted on the wind. They spread out, checking down the shoulder-height rows of plants, grabbing people with harvest bags and putting them in cuffs while their radios squawked.

Sky skirted along the far fence and hopped the gate to the next yard, fearful. But also thinking. If the cops were at the house, were they also going after Orien and the mourners? She'd taken the electric scooter to the beach to check on them. It was the right thing to do. What you did for family. You ran to the rescue.

So why had he been so upset then?

Sky closed her eyes, gripping the armrests with shaking hands. Moist air clung to her skin, her hair, bringing with it the smell of pool chlorine and grass. If Orien still loved her, he'd find her here. He'd come to her.

Sky waited. Counting silently like she had as a child in the closet. Listening for the right kind of quiet. A safe stillness. Letting herself breathe again. After what seemed like an eternity, she heard the crunch of gravel. The glass door slid open, and the porch light flicked on automatically casting a soft orange light on the lawn. Sky squeezed her eyes shut, willing it to be real. A desperate hope swelled in her chest. A warm hand caressed her shoulder, and she froze, her breath caught, body rigid.

"I've been searching the night for you, Sky." Orien's voice washed over her, and she opened her eyes.

Heart soaring, she fought back sobs of relief. "You came for me."

"I would never forsake my dangerous beauty." He knelt before her, his face bruised, blood and mud staining his tunic, eyes full of serene kindness. "I thought you'd been taken."

Shaking her head, she sat up straight. Covering his hand with hers, she turned and kissed his fingers. "I will kill her for what she did to you."

He smiled, then stood, holding out his hand to her. "Come here, my love."

As she did so, she realized that two of his security lieutenants stood at the sliding door. Orien waved them away.

"What are we doing?"

"Renewal." He took her hand and led her to the pool, walking in front of her, coaxing her into the warm water. Mud bled from his tunic, washing away the violence of the night. The pool lights lit up his gaze with a fiery intensity as he pulled her close. Movement to her right caught her eye, and she saw a third lieutenant lay something at the edge of the pool. A tray with two silver goblets and a beautiful, bejeweled dagger. The one he used for death ceremonies.

Sky's mouth went dry. "I'm sorry."

"You have nothing to apologize for. You were protecting the family." They floated to the edge of the pool, and he handed Sky a cup.

Eyes on the blade, she asked, "You're not angry?"

He shook his head. "All you've done is prove your worth and your devotion to us."

"That's all I was doing... I promise."

"I know." He raised his own goblet. "I believe you've mastered your anger. You've forged it into protection. That's why I believe you're ready to face the Blue Lotus now with me."

She nodded, both afraid and excited. "Together?"

"As always," he said softly, and they drank.

It didn't take long. When the potent mix hit, Sky watched the beautiful colors of the trees and furniture drip and puddle on the ground. Her mind reeling, she listened to the wind whispering to her. She was loved. She was worthy. She was invincible. Full of joy, she leaned back in his arms, her hair dragging in the water as she stared up at the swirling stars.

"Sky," Orien murmured, holding her close. "Dance with me."

The pool and fence spun lazily around them as they floated, clutching each other, Orien's whisper at her ear. He asked her about Brent, and Sky told him how she'd taken his information from Cindy's phone.

"The night you and Hunter killed Cindy and Jimmy on the boat?" Orien asked, his breath brushing her cheek.

Sky nodded slowly, giggling when she told him how she'd walked right into the shelter Cindy used to live at and called Brent from the communal phone. She pretended to be a friend of his daughter's and lied that Cindy had given her a hard drive with information on Orien and the Ocean Within. He agreed to meet her at a safe place, which she said was the bungalow. Then Hunter held him down while Sky dosed him with the Blue Lotus powder she'd taken from Orien's bedroom. The one he'd shared with her. They kept him there for a couple of days before moving him.

He asked her other questions, but the tea and the floating made her dizzy. His face burned bright as if lit from within by a giant fire, and flames flickered in his eyes. Her mouth wouldn't work as she tried to explain what they'd done and why.

"We tried to find out what Brent knew and who he told—" Flashes of that night came to Sky, and she flinched. "But I think he was already dying…"

"What did he tell you?" Orien's voice echoed in her head like thunder, and her heart sped up.

Brent told them that Jimmy was Cindy's ex-boyfriend. She'd broken up with him when they started fighting over her involvement with the family.

"Jimmy went to Cindy's dad and told him about the family," Sky slurred. "Brent said they were building a case."

"A case for what?" Orien asked, taking them to the deep end of the pool. The water was up to her shoulders.

A hint of fear crept in, but he was so beautiful. Like Zeus, lit with lightning. "Brent said trafficking. He said you send girls out to have sex with clients. That's where the real money from the subscription boxes came from. That you blackmailed your own followers. And I hated him for saying that. I knew he was lying. You would *never* do that, so I hit him with a pipe, and he fell."

"You shouldn't have interfered, my little one." Orien said, taking her in dizzying circles faster and faster. "What evidence might Ava have against us?"

She giggled again, the light feeling making her thoughts fuzzy. "Nothing. We told no one. I knew not to tell you anything to protect you."

Orien remained quiet, the look on his face worrying Sky. Had she upset him with her silence? She couldn't think of how to make it right because the stars kept spinning like pinwheels and she felt herself falling.

"The tea you used. It can be traced back to us. To our gardens," he said, as they bobbed slowly in the water. "I hear that they've found evidence."

"I..." Each time they bobbed low in the water, Sky went further and further underneath, sometimes forgetting to hold her breath. She gasped, choking on the water. Coughing, she tried to walk to the stairs, to get out of the pool, but Orien held her hands in his. The water moved as if it was alive. Like it was hungry. She shook her head, trying to clear it. "I did it for you."

"Yes, I know. And I'm so grateful." His hand slipped to the tray, closing around the dagger's handle. "These agents are mortal enemies to our family, and I need my warrior, Sky. My stone goddess."

"You know I'll do whatever you want."

"I need you to do what is right." Orien tilted her chin up with his fingers, making her look up at him. His gaze felt like forever. "You are truly my equal. The light to my darkness. Cold and hard and beautiful."

He kissed her. Like he used to. Like he had before Cindy and Jimmy and all that came after. Weakness moved through her, and she leaned into him only to freeze when the cold steel of the dagger's blade pressed against her skin.

A sliver of fear moved through the haze of drugs, and she asked, "Are you going to kill me?"

He smiled then, a shining, warm glow that made her almost cry. Holding the blade to her throat, he hugged her close and whispered, "What is death, but another journey?"

A prick of pain, not much, really, and everything faded away.

THIRTY-TWO

Power Moves Gym. Ava found early morning gym people fundamentally flawed. There was something wrong with someone whose first thoughts of the day involved sweaty equipment and gritty protein shakes. A sunset run along the shore, yes. A spin class at the crack of dawn with throbbing house music and a shouting trainer? No thanks.

The only upside to a twenty-four-hour gym was that they sat relatively empty for vast swaths of time, save for the reception staff. Five in the morning proved to be quite desolate as Ava sat on the wooden bench that ran down the middle of the locker aisle, listening to the sound of the lone shower splashing on the tile floor. Steam billowed from the stalls, filling the room and drifting along the lockers like a storm front.

She leaned against the support column bisecting the floor, her eyes closed. After the fiasco at the beach, she'd regrouped with the team at the station, and they set out to find Orien and Sadie. They were gone. Orien liked name changes. Maybe she should have CBI Intelligence look for any passports with the name Sky. Orien could have one under an additional false identity. Frustration coiled in her chest. She'd had him in her grasp, and now Sadie might be in his crosshairs because Ava had decided to press his buttons.

The faucet squeaked, and the water shut off. Slapping footfalls on damp tile came closer, and a man turned down her aisle. He froze with the towel around his waist and a shocked look on his pudgy face. Young, a ginger, and way too pale to live in California. She'd looked him up. He was a rising star with some dangerous tastes. Perfect.

"Mr. Iverson?" Ava asked, flashing her badge. "I need to talk with you, sir."

"Now?" Surprise became anger, and he shouted. "This is outrageous!"

"So is hiding from a state agent, Mr. Iverson."

"That's *Deputy District Attorney* Iverson," he snapped. "You'd do well to remember that!"

"So should you, sir." Ava rose, walking toward him, holding up the piece of paper Denny had slipped into her pocket. "This is your personal itinerary. A friend of mine gave it to me and boy, do you have a lot going on, *Jared*." She tapped her nose. "I can see why you're such a fan of the Devil's Snow."

"Are you out of your mind?" His gaze flitted to the door. "How dare you accuse a member of the law—"

"There are no cameras in here. You don't appear to be wired." Ava shrugged. "No one here but us. Tell me why Cindy Aquino's arrest was the only one you dropped."

Shaking his head, he adjusted his towel. "What are you trying to prove here? That I squashed a prostitution arrest? It's my prerogative to choose who and what I prosecute. I don't owe you an explanation."

"That could have been said on the phone the first time I called you. Yet you hid for almost a week."

"I wasn't hiding. I was busy." He shook his finger at her like a scolding teacher. "And you're as insane as they say you are. I promise you. I'll have your badge for this stunt."

"I've heard that before. But you should know I have images of you snorting a line longer than my hand while partying in a nightclub

VIP room." She showed him a photo she'd printed from the portable hard drive Denny had given her. A woman had taken a selfie, her peace sign framing a figure hunched over a table in the background. Jared, with a rolled hundred up his nose. "Cocaine is still illegal in California, is it not, counselor?"

He stared at the photo in horror. "Did you have me followed?"

"What kind of budget do you think I have?" Ava chuckled. "No, this was posted by," she tapped the woman in the photo. "Let's call her... Mimi. She tagged the club in the photo. I doubt she even noticed you or your career ending move behind her."

"This is blackmail." He grabbed the photo and ripped it. "And images can be doctored."

"Did you know that Mimi's father served time when she was little for having two joints on him? Yeah, five years. Of course, pot was still illegal then but, whatever." Ava shrugged. "How much you want to bet she hates the DA's office? Let alone one who does drugs at night and prosecutes others for the same thing by day?"

He looked down his nose at her. "Proving that's me is nearly impossible."

"I don't need to prove anything, Jared. The first person to post is who the public believes. You know that. Besides, one whiff of impropriety at a district attorney's office and you're gone. And rightly so. The date your pal Mimi posted this puts your party the night before a big case. Didn't you lose that one?" She arched a brow. "I think you can get sued for that."

"Look, that's not why I lost..." He stopped himself, resignation hardening his face. "What do you want?"

"I want to know who told you to drop the case. Was it Cutler directly—" his gaze slid from hers and she smiled. "Ah. It was the mayor himself, then."

"I didn't say that."

"Then say it. I want the truth," Ava snapped. "Cindy Aquino. She was murdered and stuffed in a barrel, and I want to know what you had to do with it."

"Nothing!" Iverson took a deep breath. "I ran into my boss at court, and he said that maybe the Aquino case wasn't as strong as I needed and that all the other arrests were better bets. He said the girl was not with them and he knew from a 'good source.' And that always means... higher up."

"And you took that to mean the mayor?"

"Everyone knows it means the mayor. He's famous for pushing his agenda onto the Chief of Police. They aren't friends."

"I gathered," Ava said. "So, you vacated it all?"

He nodded. "Cindy Aquino was just scooped up in the raid. She wasn't a professional. I checked. But then *the day* you guys showed up to work the Blue Drum Killer case with Detective Manaia, I get a note on my car that says I should keep out of your reach."

"Mine specifically?"

"The CBI as a whole, but you specifically, yes."

Ava narrowed her gaze at him. "That's your entire involvement in this case?"

"Yes, I swear." He shifted on his feet. "Are we done? I'm getting cold here."

She reached into her pocket, pulled out the portable hard drive, and tossed it to him. "That's everything."

He caught it, holding it close like it was precious. "That's it?"

"I mean, other than stop doing self-destructive shit in front of cameras," Ava said as she headed for the exit. "You're supposed to be the law."

THIRTY-THREE

Details of the communal house and beach raids hit the newsrooms, as well as an anonymous leak detailing the ritualistic carvings on the murder victims broke overnight. They interviewed experts on ritualistic murders, calling the Blue Drum Killer a psychopathic monster, which only made things worse. August sent a text blast to the team calling for a PIT meeting at OPD later that day. Heavy coverage for the morning shows hit. First one news network, then all of them ran the video footage of the bizarre markings on Brent's hand. Ava watched it. The recording of Brent's body looked like it was taken in situ with someone's phone, which pointed to anyone at the crime scene that night. Ava had her money on one of the construction workers.

After harassing DDA Iverson, Ava stopped at her favorite bakery for a chocolate croissant and a mocha. She hoped the caffeine might quell the headache threatening to bloom behind her forehead. Already hot, the day had a party atmosphere as the crowds heading to the beach for fireworks ramped up. Everyone wore red, white, and blue despite the Fourth of July being days away. Soldiers from Camp Pendelton, teens on vacation, tourists, and families flooded the streets, ready to spend their paychecks at the bars and stores up and down Mission Avenue and the shore. She listened to reporters rehashing old serial killer cases in California on the morning radio news shows on her drive back to the station. Detours and traffic cones clogged the roads on her route. People stopped mid-street stalking parking spots. Work commuters and tourist traffic piled up.

The sun blazed obnoxiously bright as Ava arrived at the station around eight thirty. She went straight to the war room to look at evidence, wanting to see if she could pinpoint where Sadie might have gone the night before. She wouldn't have gone back to Ascension House. They'd been raided. Not the yoga studio, since Manaia served a warrant for the front and back rooms last night as well.

Orien disappeared from the beach without a trace. Seth warned her during their call about personalities like Orien. That he struck without warning. Her fingertips went to her bandaged eye. Last night's aggression had been anything but controlled. It had been raw fury. Did she miscalculate Orien's reaction? Maybe. Maybe not yet.

She logged into the OPD network, pulled up the report logs, and spent the next hour and a half going over every piece of new information that came in. She read through case notes from Manaia, the Medical Examiner's Office, Crimes of Violence, fellow PIT members, and CBI Intelligence.

CBI's Intelligence Unit located the Ascension House's owner, who had listed the home through a luxury rental company. He was told that the renters were a retired couple, not an entire commune of hippies. Last she'd heard, he was already on a plane back to raise hell. Ava was happy to leave that to OPD to sort out.

Detective Manaia's report about the pawn shop sweep came back empty. No one had tried to pawn an expensive, vintage timepiece that matched the description and photo from the insurance company. After studying Sadie's file, Ava guessed she kept it.

Talia posted a forensic report on the communal home. Still going through the home and work kitchen on the property, she had yet to find any evidence of *Amanita muscaria* or the high-dose THC in the residence. They were still inspecting the outbuildings and attic.

Rondeau spoke with Henry Miller's uncle, who was coming into the station later that day. Apparently, the uncle had looked for his nephew for over a year after Henry ran away.

Rondeau had also uploaded financial reports on Brent Cutler, highlighting the purchase of an electric bike subscription and several phones. He mentioned an odd lease expense, and she flipped to the statement summary he'd included.

She ran a finger down the screen, looking at every purchase over the last six months. Several pages in, she spotted what Rondeau was talking about. Brent had paid a year-long lease up front for a safety deposit box at a bank Ava didn't recognize. She went back through his file and couldn't find any other instance of the bank's name in his financials.

A place to hide something? Maybe, with his finances so entangled with his father's, Brent needed a bank far removed from the Cutler name. Someplace his father wouldn't know about or have access to.

She called August but had to leave a message. Then she called Manaia and told him about the safety deposit box.

"What if Brent's version of helping his daughter involved gathering evidence against Orien and the wellness center?" Ava asked Manaia.

"Like take them down, not grab his daughter and run?"

"What if Cindy was a true believer? What if Brent tried to prove to her what Orien was, and that's what got him killed?"

"You think Brent stashed the evidence in a safety deposit box?" The sounds of the bullpen came through from Manaia's end. The Crimes of Violence squad were working overtime interviewing suspects from the night before.

"I'd like to find out. Wouldn't you?"

"I want to make sure our current warrant for Brent's financials covers it. Let me get back to you." Manaia rang off.

At almost nine, Ava noted several arrest reports already coming into the system, and she dove in. Twenty-four followers had been detained at the house. Twelve more at the beach. She cast the files onto the wall display screen, flipping through the faces, looking for anyone familiar. They all looked so young. When they'd run them through the system, they'd identified underage runaways, missing persons, and other vulnerable kids. Social Services had already entered the picture to deal with the minors. Some of the young adults also had priors. Orien knew who he could control and manipulate. People with no support system or family watching out for them. That's what had made Jimmy such a threat. He wasn't alone.

"I don't understand how he holds so much power over them," August said from the door. He nodded at the photo on the wall screen. "The guy looks so obviously slimy to me."

Ava forced a smile. "That's because you grew up in one home, surrounded by family. Cults traffic in hard truths that speak to people like these kids. To them, the world *is* a dangerous place. People *can't* be trusted. And they feel the system *is* aligned against them. Most kids have learned those lessons in spades by the time Orien gets his talons into them. They're the perfect targets."

He sat next to her, taking in the new bandage on her forehead. "Are you alright?"

After the beach mob nearly trampled her, he insisted on her getting checked out again. She was fine. Not even a ripped stitch. Her pride, on the other hand, had taken a beating.

"He brought a switchblade like some kind of old school thug." She studied the expired driver's license photo of Owen Meeks on the wall. "Can you believe that guy was a counselor?"

"Having met a few, yes." She knew he'd been forced to see one during his parents' contentious divorce.

"Okay, child psychologists don't count. You were eight." She glanced at the door. "When's the meeting?"

"Been delayed a little. Talia is stuck in Kearny Mesa at the

Medical Examiner's office. Did you ask her about DNA testing on the tea?"

"I might have asked if it was possible. Is she saying it is?"

"Didn't you threaten Orien that you could?"

"Ruffling feathers is my favorite pastime."

Both exasperation and a begrudging fondness crossed his face. "I guess we'll see at the meeting. It's at noon now. I'm conducting interviews all this morning with the Crimes of Violence Unit. Some of the older followers, mid-twenties, they're starting to crack."

"They're smart enough to see that the tide is turning."

"Vincent said there are rumblings about raiding the memorial service, but the lawyers said it was on public land so, we'll see." August fished a piece of gum from his pocket and shoved it in his mouth. "Manaia told me they figured out how Schneider ended up at the beach. Apparently, several of the young women taken into custody at the communal house gave the name Sadie Schneider. They were all blonde."

Ava traced the name Sky on the paper in front of her. She'd looked it up. It meant wanderlust or free spirit. "She's in danger."

August nodded, swiveled his chair to face hers. "I have to tell you something."

"By the look on your face, it's not good."

"There is a video with you in it that someone posted on a social media. Whoever did it also alerted the news stations. They're running with it."

"Running with what?"

August held up his phone. "EmberSpirit8 recorded your altercation with Orien last night. Rondeau said they're a follower, a young woman."

"Do we know who it is?"

"No. The account is brand new."

August played the video for her. It was terrible. Dark, shaky, almost no light save for the fake candles. The person recording caught Ava's face lit up with the orange glow, Orien's back to the camera. It appeared as if he advanced slightly and then Ava lashed out, striking him in the face, sending him stumbling backwards. Then the camera went black.

"Well, that's edited."

August nodded. "Rondeau is on it. This EmberSpirit8 is saying you attacked Orien unprovoked."

"He drew a weapon."

"We've got audio of the conversation, but—"

"He tried to slice me open out there on the sand."

August closed the video. "Unfortunately, you can't see that."

"I both heard and saw the blade. I wasn't mistaken."

"The person who posted the video wrote in the caption that you lost your footing and Orien tried to help you. In response, and possibly out of embarrassment, you lashed out."

"I don't see the issue. We have video. He lunged at me with a knife. I responded appropriately, if not a little more restrained than I should have."

"You'd be surprised how bad night video of a crowd on a dark beach can be. We have audio, but it could go both ways. Vincent wants you to stay well out of the range of news cameras. She says they're fielding queries about the hot-tempered Agent Cortes. Again."

"If I truly had a bad temper, he'd have a broken nose and not just a bloody one." She slipped out of the chair, pacing. "What about his weapon?"

"We didn't find the knife," August said. "He probably took it with him when they escaped."

Ava waved his comment away. "Look, I don't care about that right now. Orien is out there, he knows we're coming for him, and I don't think he'll just slink away quietly. He'll want to save face."

"How?"

"I don't know. But if someone slapped me around in front of my followers while calling me a pimp, I'd want to get even."

Leaning back in his chair, August said, "I'm asking Manaia for patrol to sit on your house. They're running your face on the news."

Ava wandered over to the table in the back of the room that held a coffee carafe and a basket of granola bars. She picked out the last chocolate chip one while memories of Orien's followers played in her head. He commanded them with one word. They obeyed, even as he used them as a shield. They'd flanked her, circling around like a force field.

She turned, shaking the granola bar at August. "This guy sees himself as a revered leader. He used those kids to protect himself. Everything about him is calculated and cowardly."

August nodded. "A showman."

"Exactly." Ava returned to her seat. Flashes of lectures she'd attended about fringe societies, pages she'd read about secret toxic enclaves and their patterns, their behavior, came back to her. They went after the girls and the gold. And they always, without fail, tried to insulate themselves from harm. She unwrapped the granola bar, thinking. "He uses smoke and mirrors and a cast of dozens, but it's a show. He guards himself. His identity. His space."

"Okay?" August leaned on his elbows. "Where are you going with this?"

"He used the studio as a sell point but met with clients off site. That's a layer of protection. Distance," Ava mused. "Who's to say he didn't do that with the communal house?"

"What do you mean?"

"He used the studio as a front. We could've staked it out all month and never seen him. That's the point of contact, but not physically. The clients had to find him on the beach for their class, remember? Then Manaia said that classes were going on at the mansion too, right? You said he saw women wearing yoga pants and sports bras going into the courtyard."

"You're saying that the communal house is just another front. That he doesn't live there?"

"It might appear as if he does. What I'm saying is, if his pattern of protecting himself holds true, he has another place to fall back to if the communal house is infiltrated. One that doesn't have a connection to his Orien identity or Ocean Within."

"A safe house." August pulled out his phone. "Clean papers."

"Yes. Like that." Ava sank back into her chair, picking the chocolate chips out of the snack bar and popping them into her mouth. "He used a front to rent the communal home. What if he's doing that again to hide his access to a secondary residence? A hideaway?"

August tapped his pen on the table. "I talked with Behavioral Science this morning. Seth said that he'd classify this whole group as exhibiting cult-like behaviors. If that's true, then maybe their finances work the same."

"How do you mean?"

"Remember that New Age group out of Sonoma? They tried to do a mass suicide type of thing, but one of them called 911?"

"The alien cult?"

He nodded. "There were rumors that members of that group handed over their cars, boats, and homes to the leader. This was before the death pact. Apparently, their leader viewed the shedding of worldly things to him personally as a sign of devotion. The survivors confirmed it was expected."

"Okay, but these kids have nothing."

"Sure, but their parents might have more. What if Cindy Aquino wasn't the only victim who had family trying to help her?"

Ava finished her granola bar. "It makes sense to me, I'm just not sure how to go about digging into this. Finance is your purview."

"I have an idea." August rose from his seat, heading for the door. "I'll be back."

For the next couple of hours, Ava immersed herself in the incoming reports, specifically Detective Manaia's file on the communal house raid. Recording from the body camera he'd worn showed an efficient, casualty-free entry. Caught off guard, the members in the house surrendered peacefully save for a few runners. Manaia had been ready and brought K-9 units to help. They separated the suspects by age, speaking first with those over eighteen. The problem was, their answers seemed rehearsed. The video of a quick conversation between Manaia and a suspect sounded almost verbatim to the next three people he spoke with.

Each one gave only a single, nature-based first name. Forest, Phoenix, Hazel, River. If most had not had fingerprints already in the system, they might never have known who Orien's followers really were. When questioned, they all claimed to have no idea where Orien lived other than the communal house. They also insisted they did not work for him but merely volunteered to help with the wellness center's charitable endeavors out of personal conviction. Everyone denied ever meeting followers named Sky or Meadow or Jimmy, or Hunter. They tried the victims' real names as well. Nothing. When Manaia showed the victims' photos in arrays, they claimed not to recognize anyone. And none of them had ever heard of the Blue Lotus, nor had they been offered it. The savvier ones didn't say anything at all and asked for lawyers.

They weren't talking. At least not yet. Ava rubbed her temples, a headache now in full swing. She needed a break. Getting up to leave, she ran into Rondeau and Talia on their way in for the meeting. Checking her watch, she realized it was nearly eleven.

"You guys are early."

"I've got some equipment to set up," Rondeau said. "How's the eye?"

"I can see out of it, so good," Ava said.

"Where're you off to?" Talia held a stack of files in her arms. "I wanted to hear all about your showdown with the cult guy last night."

"I'll be back. Caffeine calls."

She ran into August in the hallway near the interview rooms, his phone to his ear. He put his hand over the mouthpiece, brows furrowed.

"Something happen?" he asked.

"No, I'm just hungry. I'll be back in time for the meeting. You want something?"

He shook his head. "Hold on. I'll go with you."

"I can just grab you something."

"No, I'll go. I've got some good news." He finished his call, and they exited the rear of the station and climbed into his SUV.

"Who was that?"

"I've been talking to the city recorder's office about deed transfers. I think I have a solid list to check."

"For Orien's secret hideaway?"

"I hope. Where are we going?"

"A family from my neighborhood has a food truck over at The Strand that's amazing. Their social media said they were setting up between the kiddie-park and Pier View Beach Club."

The thirteen-minute drive took them twenty with traffic. Lunch hour commuters backed up the stoplights and intersections heading out toward the coast. The Beach Club sat at the corner of Seagaze Drive and The Strand. Surrounded by a pizza shop, a couple of craft beer pubs, and a small arcade, the popular spot tended to be busy. They drove along the shore, past groups of safety-orange-shirted kids stretching on the sand for surf camp lessons. A few women jogged with their sporty baby strollers. Ava let her window down, taking in the sea breeze. They passed a tinned-fish shop, which was new, and she thought she might grab a few tins for Talia.

They found a spot in the parking lot across the street from Pier Beach Park. A small, grassy picnic area across the street from the beach with a bathroom structure and cement picnic tables. The pier, only a couple of blocks down, looked congested with swarming bodies. The amphitheater right next to it, on the other side of the parking lot from Ava, held hundreds of people staking out their seats for the fireworks show. Sailboats slid across the glistening sea as a salty wind blew onshore.

The scent of grilled meat floated to them as they approached her friend's food truck. A decent crowd of people waited around the bright green and orange vehicle. The sign read, the Nimble Nacho, and Ava explained to August that the food truck had all kinds of nacho toppings. Carne asada, fajita-style chicken strips, ground taco meat, several kinds of melted cheeses, as well as garnishes like green onions, olives, tomatoes, and sour cream.

"It's amazing." She pointed to the racks of chips behind the cooks in the food truck's kitchen. "You pick a bag of chips or in your case, the one bag of mixed baby greens salad over there, and they slit it up the side to make a pocket. Then you just choose what you want in it. The best part is that you can walk around and eat without fussing with a bowl. They give you a fork and voilà! Lunch."

To Ava's shock, August said, "That doesn't sound half bad."

They waited their turn, and when they got to the window, August's phone rang. He glanced at it. Frowned.

"Get me the chicken," he said, stepping away. "*Minimal* cheese."

"Double cheese, got it," Ava called after him. As he walked around the food truck to the picnic area. Ava greeted her friend, Stella, and placed their order.

A former nurse, Stella thrived on activity and smiled with happy exasperation. "It's a good turnout, no?"

"I see that."

Ava stepped aside to wait, glancing over her shoulder at August. He stood at the edge of the kiddie park a few yards away, his back turned, shoulders tense. She wondered what was going on. Hand to his ear, he leaned into the phone, shaking his head.

Not good. When she started toward him, his head snapped up, and he waved her over.

"What is it?"

He rested one hand on the back of a bench, listening to the caller. The stressed syllables of a frantic voice came through, but Ava couldn't make out the words. She tugged on his sleeve, leaning in.

August ended the call. "That was Rondeau. Someone attacked Manaia. He was getting gas and somebody went at him with a bat and ran off."

"What?" Ava's heart rate sped up, her senses now on high alert, scoping the area around them for threats. "Is he okay?"

"Details are sketchy. I don't know if he's—I think they got him to a hospital." He nodded, doing the same. "We need to get you out of here."

"Where did they take—"

She saw the vehicle before she heard the screech of tires. Behind August, just up the road, a white van whipped around the corner from a side road. The engine revved as it barreled down the street. People on the sidewalk turned to stare as it roared past. Ava froze when she saw the driver. Pale hair, mouth in a murderous grimace, the woman jerked the wheel, speeding toward Ava and August.

Sky. The van careened over the curb. Smashed through bushes and a newspaper kiosk. It veered sideways as it bore down on them.

"August!" Ava shouted, but he was already reaching for her.

They dove for the cement benches. The squeal of tires and groan of twisted metal filled her ears as the van crashed into the canopy. August's arms wrapped around her as they toppled together, spinning through the air, the hot roar of the engine behind them. The van hit the picnic shelter with a shudder, debris blowing out from the wreckage as Ava and August slammed against something hard.

THIRTY-FOUR

Ava writhed on the cement, the breath knocked out of her, ears ringing. Her shoulder and hip hurt as she moved, but they weren't dislocated. She looked for August but couldn't see him through the dirt kicked up by the crash.

Pulling her weapon from her waist holster, she staggered to her feet, trying to walk off the pain, peering up at the van. It sat crumpled atop cement picnic tables, hot engine ticking, wedged and broken beneath its spinning front tires. Sky slumped over the steering wheel behind the hissing engine. Smoke and dust hovered in the air. The metal canopy listed overhead, bent and unstable.

She coughed from the dust. "August?"

He groaned. "Still here."

Scanning the debris, she saw the toe of his boot peeking out from the other side of a chunk of cement. She tasted blood at her lip and wiped it with her shirt collar as she rounded a sheared-off bench and knelt in front of him. Bloody scrapes marred his cheek, but he was conscious. "Hey. You okay?"

"Oh, that sucked," he wheezed, clutching his side as he tried to sit up, his face pale. "Are we clear?"

"I need to call it in. Don't move." Reaching for her phone, she found it cracked in her pocket.

"Here." August winced as he pulled a portable police radio off his belt and handed it to her.

A flare of worry dogged her as she called it in, her attention on his short, labored breaths. She raised the radio to her lips, forcing calm into her voice.

Dispatch, this is Agent Ava Cortes with the CBI requesting immediate backup and medical assistance to my location. Officer down. I repeat, officer down. Attempted vehicular assault. Suspect incapacitated in the driver's seat. Send EMS immediately.

The crowd from the food truck made its way across the grass, led by her neighbor, Stella, who had her phone out, calling for help.

"Ava!" She hurried over, a bag of chips still in her hand. "I called 911!"

"Good, be careful. The whole canopy here looks unstable." Ava turned back to August. "Hold on, I'm going to check on Sky. Make sure she's not armed."

"It was her?" He leaned back, sweat at his brow.

Stella's dark eyes were wide with worry. "What can I do?"

Ava pointed at August, still on the ground. "Fix him."

The approaching crowd surged around a lone figure who stood like a statue in the grass. Arms at his sides. Blond hair, linen shirt, brown pants. The young man caught Ava's gaze as she moved toward the van's driver's side.

She glanced back at August, "Pull your weapon."

He did, but he held it with only one arm. "What is it?"

"I don't know yet." Ava waved Stella and the others aside, shielding August. The young man looked familiar. She'd seen him at the beach, on the sand behind Orien. "He's one of them."

The young man zeroed in on her, his arm stiff at his side, a weapon in his hand.

"Drop the gun!" At Ava's shout, the crowd erupted in panic. She leveled her weapon at his chest as people ran past her over the debris and behind the van to the road. "Drop it!

"Ascension!" he shouted as he raised the weapon.

She shot him. Three in a cluster mid-torso. He went down. The crowd screamed, running for cover. Out of the corner of her eye, Sky leaned out the driver's side window, revolver in her hand. Nose bloody, hair awry, hate in her eyes. She grimaced, aiming as Ava turned a millisecond too late.

Gunfire shattered the van's window. Sky screamed and ducked back into the driver's seat. She scrambled out the other side, bounding over debris like it was nothing.

Ava's gaze snapped to August. At the smoke curling from his gun. "You saved—"

"Go!" His breath came in gasps. "I'll secure... his weapon... Go!"

"Stella?" Ava looked at her friend.

"I've got him," Stella said, helping him lie down.

Ava took off after Sky, barking into her radio as she navigated the panicked crowd.

Dispatch be advised. Active shooter in the area—all units use extreme caution. Secondary shooter is down. Civilians present. Large crowd. I am 10-31 in active pursuit of primary suspect heading south toward the pier and shops. I need perimeter and crowd control immediately. Request all available units ASAP. My partner is 10-99, extreme distress. Send multiple buses now!

Ava scanned the people running away. She spotted the dress, pale blue this time, splattered with blood and whipping in the wind as she crossed over to the parking lot. Sky lost a flip-flop but kept going, half-hopping across the hot asphalt.

Ava pushed herself, picking up ground, ignoring the pain shooting down her arm from her shoulder. She scanned the approaching area, scoping out potential ambush spots. Souvenir shops, fast-food places, stores, all sat near the pier entrance. Sky could go into any one of those places and take someone hostage. Ava saw her running between vans in the parking lot, glancing backward and then ducking out of sight.

The radio in Ava's hand buzzed. Jogging to a stop at the edge of the parking lot, her gaze flitting from person to person, she listened.

"This is Rondeau. Ava, are you there?"

"Yeah. I'm here." She panted, leaning down to peer through the car windows, looking for Sky.

"I'm on scene. Where are you?"

She told him, rasping out what had just happened as she picked her way forward. "I see her. She's making her way to the pier a block from here. I need backup. She's armed."

Out of breath, Rondeau said, "I'm right behind you."

"August?"

"Paramedics are almost here."

Spotting Sky, Ava popped up, weapon aimed, "Sky, stop!"

Long blonde hair fluttered as Sky whirled around. The girl fired, the rounds slamming into the car next to Ava as she ducked. When she popped back up, Sky was gone.

"I think she's headed for the shops near the pier. We need to flank her," Ava shouted, crouch-running forward.

"Units are on their way, but I'm it for now."

"You've got those long-ass legs. Book it down the sand. Head her off at the shopping center entrance."

"Copy that."

Ava called it in, scampering between the cars, working her way forward. To her left, the massive wooden pier jutted out into the sea. Festive flags fluttered from the pylons, and tourists stood on the sand watching the surfers and kites. Beachgoers sprawled under canopies and umbrellas, their kids playing with sand toys, oblivious to a killer on the loose. Just like the foot traffic. Milling families and groups gawking into shop windows and meandering along the boardwalk. Waves crashed in the distance and seagulls screeched, muffling the sound.

Sky cleared the cars, running out of the parking lot, across the top of the amphitheater steps, heading for the stores and cafés opposite the pier.

Ava yelled her location into her radio as she darted toward the pier.

Suspect heading to shopping area near the pier entrance. Be advised, officers in plain clothes on scene. Use extreme caution.

Ava sprinted across the remaining distance, following Sky under a breezeway to the courtyard with shops. She held up her badge, shouting for everyone to clear out, but they stared at her, confused. Losing track of Sky, she stopped in the middle of the center, surrounded by options, listening. A boba drink place, an ice cream shop, a little taco spot.

Then she saw it. A surge of people, spilling out of the arcade, young adults shouting and glancing back inside with fear. Ava bumped through the escaping bodies and through the arcade's glass doors onto the dark floor.

Techno music blasted overhead, mixing with the game noises blaring out of dozens of individual speakers. She motioned for a few stragglers to get out and kept going. Flashing lights flared from screens. It was dark, lit only by black lights. Squiggly designs on the arcade's carpet threw her off. She blinked, getting her bearings. Everything glowed.

There. Movement near the Skee-Ball games. Sky's pale dress lit up like a safety vest as she ran full bore along the air hockey tables.

Ava pursued, rounding the corner, catching up. "Sky, stop!"

Sky whipped around, her face and arms glowing with swirling symbols. She held up her flattened palm and blew. A cloud of powder blasted at Ava, the bits and pieces glimmering purple in the black light.

Ava spun away, squeezing her eyes shut. *Don't breathe! Don't breathe!*

She leaned against a shooting game, wiping her face with her shirt. Spotting a half-full bottle of water on the floor, she splashed that in her eyes for good measure. Blinking, she chanced a peek around the game cabinet. A ray of sunlight shone through an exit door slowly swinging closed and Ava ran for it. Crashing through the exit, Ava's head snapped left, then right, then toward the pier in the distance. Sky hopped over the chain dangling between a divider, her hair flying.

Ava veered after her, hurdling over bushes and potted succulents, sprinting down the pathway toward the pier's opening. Eyes itching, she pulled August's radio from her belt.

"I need back up at the pier!"

"This is Rondeau. I'm at the fish restaurant on the other side of the amphitheater steps. Where is she?"

"Up, go up," Ava shouted.

Sky was fast, already past the entrance. She ran up the middle of the pier, shoving past people, gun in her hand. "She's on the pier. Be careful, she just blew that drug powder in my face."

"What?!"

"Get to the pier!"

Ava crossed The Strand, stopping to let a four-bicycle family group go by. Her throat burned. She ran up the amphitheater steps to the sidewalk level, then across the pedestrian bridge connected to the pier's boardwalk. "I'm almost there."

"I'm coming up!"

"Clear the pier. Get people away from it."

"Copy that."

Twenty yards down, Ava shot out from between a bunch of people wearing foam Lady Liberty crowns. She ran past the fishing rod rental kiosk and the bait shop, her eyes on Sky up ahead. Pelicans flapped their wings, startled as she raced by. Men fishing, kids with pinwheels, old ladies walking arm in arm, all flashed past her.

The pier was one of the longest wooden piers on the West Coast, six football fields long, Ava thought, gritting her teeth against the shards of pain in her hip. She had to close the gap. Legs pumped as she sped up, gasping against the stitch in her side. Behind her, she heard Rondeau, and she glanced over her shoulder. He waved his badge, shouting for people to get off the pier. Confused, they gaped at him with startled faces. Up ahead, Sky slowed, her limp more pronounced. Blood trailed on the wooden beams of the boardwalk at Ava's feet.

A weird buzz filled Ava's mind, her face flushing hot. She rubbed her eyes, focusing on Sky, who pushed past people, throwing them like obstacles in Ava's path. They got angry, shouting, turning on her as they realized what she was doing.

"No, no, no," Ava murmured.

Sky stopped fighting them, raised her gun and fired into the air. Everyone scattered, fleeing back down the pier toward Ava. A wave of frightened families trampled over one another. Ava threw herself against the railing, bracing herself, trying to stay on her feet. Sky turned, moving away toward the end of the pier. Ava dragged herself off the railing, pushing through the crowd, swimming through the bodies as she fought to get to Sky. Then, through the throng, she saw Sky grab a little girl, hooking her around the neck with her arm and pulling her close. Ava's gun came up, trained on Sky's chest. The kid looked eight, maybe nine, and terrified.

"Let her go!"

"I'll kill her!" Sky yelled, pressing the revolver against the little girl's head, rabid fury on her face. "You know I'll do it!"

The air around Sky contracted and then expanded like a ripple of water around a stone.

Oh, shit.

Ava blinked, telling herself it was the sun. The buzzing in her head grew, drowning out whatever words came out of Sky's mouth. Ava glanced over her shoulder. Rondeau ran up, blocking the distraught parents, urging them back. Behind him, patrol officers ran up the boardwalk, controlling the crowd.

Her mouth dry, Ava turned back to Sky, speaking slowly, fighting the effects of the powder. "She's innocent—"

"*Nobody* is innocent!" Sky screeched, her voice breaking. She swayed, blood oozing from a gash on her forehead. It dribbled down her nose and lips, soaking the front of her pale blue dress. "Nobody is anymore..."

"I don't want to shoot you, Sadie, but I will." *Hopefully*, Ava mused and almost giggled. *What the hell?* She shook her head, trying to clear it.

"Don't call me that! My name is Sky!"

"Okay, Sky, let the little girl go. This is between you and me, right? I hit Orien. I made him mad." Ava wiped the sweat from her brow, her heart ramming into her ribs. The path to Sky stretched out impossibly far. "You want me, right?"

"Ava," Rondeau said behind her. "What are you doing?"

The symbols on Sky bled, and Ava realized her skin wasn't just painted with the death markings, it was carved. Her face and neck, her arms and hands, her legs and feet, they all bled. Mixed with the poultice, her skin appeared bumpy and swollen, the blue dye running down her skin. What Ava hadn't seen in the dark, she now saw in the light of day. Orien's brutality beneath the symbols.

Sky backed up with the child, noticing the police cars pulling up at the entrance to the pier. Lights flashing, a helicopter flew toward them from the shore, the rotor thrumming the air.

"You ruined everything!" Sky yelled, her eyes frantically searching the crowd.

"I did. I'm sorry. Let the girl go and deal with me."

Brilliant blue fire burned behind Sky's eyes, throwing Ava off, but she kept going. "He told you he'd be here, right?"

Sky froze. "What?"

"You keep looking for Orien." Ava took a step forward, pulling in deep breaths, willing herself to stay focused. "This is your fallback point."

"Shut up!" Sky backed up, dragging the whimpering girl. Her gaze flitted along the pier, toward the beach.

"Did he tell you he'd be here? That you're not alone?" Ava angled herself to the left, looking for an opening. Rondeau crossed to her right. She saw him in her periphery, raising his firearm. "Orien promised you would disappear together. He'd finally be yours completely."

Sky looked confused. "Did you... did you talk to him?"

"He's not coming." Ava kept her eyes on Sky's weapon. The young woman had her finger on the trigger guard, hand shaking.

"You're lying. He said he'd be here." She took a few more steps backward, almost to the bait shop at the dead center of the pier. The helicopter bore down on them, the rotor wash throwing around paper napkins and sand. The news logo emblazoned on the side made Ava's blood boil.

She raised the radio to her lips, but it melted in her hand. She shouted into it anyway, wondering absently if she was on the floor somewhere drooling and not really on the pier. "Get that bird out of here!"

Sky screamed something at it, aiming her gun into the air. Seeing the opening, Ava fired wide, grazing her shoulder, spinning her to the left. The little girl ran towards them, screaming as Rondeau caught her. He pulled her away, shielding her with his body as Sky stumbled away, shooting wildly behind her.

Ava didn't bother to take cover. The bullets moved so slowly, leaving streaks of light as they whizzed past her like some kind of video game. She sprinted straight for Sky, chasing her the rest of the way down the pier. Past the newly built restaurant with terrified people streaming out of it, all the way to the edge.

High above the water, facing the endless sea, the undulating waves made Ava dizzy. Backed up against the far railing, Sky climbed onto the top ledge, dress whipping in the wind, gun aimed at Ava. Her other arm dangled at her side, bleeding at the shoulder.

"Leave me alone!" Her hand shook, and then she shoved the barrel of the gun under her jawline, finger on the trigger.

Ava skidded to a stop, her weapon still trained on Sky. She put her free hand up. She ran her gaze along the girl's scarred skin. "You're hurt, let me help you."

"Just—leave us alone! He'll be here." Tears streamed down her wounded face, the dye and blood from the cuts on her cheeks bled together. "He'll be here!"

"Listen to me!" Ava waited a beat, then lowered her weapon slowly. Holstering it, she moved closer. She smoothed the edge out of her voice, softening her expression. "He's not coming, honey. I'm so sorry."

"But I did everything he asked." Her face crumpled into sobs, her voice going shrill. "Cindy's dad came back for her! He threw her away and came back. Why doesn't anybody ever come for *me*? Why am I always so alone?"

"You're not alone. I'm here." Ava put her hands up, inching forward. Her radio bleeped with Rondeau's voice, and she muted it. "Let me help you. You need medical attention."

Sky touched her skin, looking at the blood on her hand with surprise, her breath turning ragged. "I let him do this to me. I let him, and he's n-not here."

"They'll heal. You'll heal." An echo of laughter floated up from the sea, and Ava froze. Venus.

"Is what you said on the beach true? Did he send girls out to turn tricks for him?"

"There's an ongoing investigation—"

"Tell me the truth!"

Ava licked her lips, debating, then said, "Yes. We made contact with a victim."

A strangled moan escaped Sky's lips. She teetered on the ledge of the railing, bleeding, dress flapping around her legs. A strange look crossed her face. An almost serene blankness.

"There are more bodies," she said, her voice now hollow. "In the junkyard behind a blue and white VW van. We killed them together. Orien and I did. He taught me how. That's where me and Hunter got the barrels."

Alarm spiked through Ava. Confessing while holding a gun to your head was bad. "You have information to trade then. For a deal. Hold onto it."

Ava wasn't sure she'd even heard her. "He has this bungalow. And so much money. Stacks of it in the bathroom wall, behind the mirror. Passports too. He said he had one for me." She shook her head. "He gets in your head, you know? He makes us tell him our darkest secrets and our biggest fears and then he uses them." Her lip quivered.

"You're young. You were under his influence. He drugged you. The DA will take all that into consideration." The helicopter flew overhead again, its thumping moving through Ava, making her want to jump out of her skin. "Please come down, Sky. Walk out of this nightmare with me."

"He said he loved me," she whispered, and Ava saw the sad little girl, the one in the picture. "I don't think anyone else ever has."

"Don't die for him. He doesn't deserve it."

"I heard you talking to that man in your kitchen. The tall one with the leather jacket. You told him you had a dark heart." Sky shook her head, lifting her face up, eyes closed. "I think you're wrong. You're here with me when no one else is."

"Come down, huh, Sky?" Ava reached out, her hands shaking in time to the pulse pounding in her head. "Take my hand."

Sky shook her head slowly, the gun drifting from her jaw. "There's no way back. Only forward."

Ava inched closer, the material of Sky's dress a foot away, keeping her eyes on the weapon under Sky's chin. The muzzle still too close to Sky's head.

Sky looked down at Ava, her eyes full of pain. "What is death, but another journey?"

"Wait, listen to me—" A flash of Venus's face superimposed over Sky's. Ava jerked at the sight of her dead friend. Then, the swirling, coiling symbols on Sky's body glowed impossibly bright, hurting Ava's eyes as they slithered around her limbs like snakes. Her blonde hair rose, the ringlets splaying out like a halo, her eyes glowing the eerie blue of the red tide. Medusa, beautiful and power-ful, like Venus, had often drawn Ava. She bit her tongue—hard—

and the pain broke through the drug haze. The hallucination fell away.

"Ascension," Sky whispered.

"Don't!"

Ava reached for Sky, scrambling onto the railing as she grabbed her dress. Sky leaned back, and they both fell, the gun roaring over Ava's head. The ocean sped toward them, black and deep and roiling. They tumbled two stories down, Ava fighting to get her feet under her, a scream in her ear that might've been hers.

Ava lost her grip on the dress as she knifed into the water. The cold of the ocean enveloped her. The pain of impact shocked her. Sharpened her thoughts. She treaded beneath the surface, twisting, searching for Sky.

Finally she spotted her, clawing at the water as a plume of bubbles erupted from her mouth. Her dress tangled around her flailing legs. No matter how much her limbs thrashed, she didn't move any closer to the surface. A realization sliced through the drugs.

She can't swim.

Ava lunged for her, kicking with all her might. The markings on her face moved as her mouth opened in a silent scream. Sky's terrified gaze locked on hers as her limbs stopped moving. Her expression relaxed as she gave Ava a tired smile.

Ava continued to slice through the water, her shoulder weak and painful as she dove for her, but the current threw her back. Lungs burning, Ava tried again as Sky sank further and further into the depths until all she could see was blonde hair and trailing bubbles. Ava's vision grayed, but she shook her head, trying again.

Something splashed down from above, then another, and another. Multiple people jumped in. She saw Rondeau, his hair floating around his head. He snagged her wrist, but she yanked away, trying to turn back. He held fast, his powerful strokes propelling them to the surface.

They surfaced, Ava coughing, her head filled with light and sound and pain. Rondeau shoved a lifeguard rescue buoy underneath her arms as he treaded next to her. Red swimsuits and trunks flashed in her peripheral vision as the rescue team dove in. They found Sky, pulling her up onto a rescue boat. Blood poured down her neck from her head, but Ava couldn't tell if she was dead. They started CPR and oxygen. A lifeguard shouted, and the boat took off.

"Are you okay?" Rondeau asked, looking at her with wet eyelashes and horror. A harbor police boat came up behind him.

"That depends," Ava said, looking over his shoulder. "Do you see a dragon right now?"

THIRTY-FIVE

The Harbor Police and lifeguards took Sky to shore, where a medevac helicopter whisked her away to Oceanside Regional Hospital. Ava thought she heard something about a bullet wound. She told Rondeau what Sky had said about a bungalow and other bodies, trying to keep her thoughts straight. OPD flooded the scene, and a sergeant named Roz took Ava's weapon into evidence. A very tan, very blonde woman, Roz had gentle eyes that called to mind the serenity of manatees. Which Ava told her.

Rondeau herded Ava into another ambulance, and they drove her to the hospital with lights and sirens, while a paramedic tried to get an obscenely long needle into her arm. Ava didn't believe all the fuss was entirely necessary. Then again, she also heard cartoon boing-boing noises every time the ambulance hit a bump. She decided they might be right.

When she got to the hospital, Ava kept asking about Sky, but no one had any information. A grizzled ER doctor checked her out and took X-rays of Ava's shoulder, hip, and hand. They confirmed the absence of a break or separation to her shoulder, but they'd found something called micro-tears to the tendons surrounding her hip joint. The grizzled ER doctor told Ava she might limp for a week or so, but she'd heal. They put her in an observation room with an IV in her arm to flush out the drugs. She didn't know what they used, but her head ached like she'd overclocked her brain. Nausea and fatigue hit her. She had a fever for no apparent reason, and her tongue swelled where she bit it, making it hard to talk. The nurse told her to try to sleep, and Ava did.

Hours later, with the low sun angling through her window, Ava awoke to whispering in her room. She groaned, cracked an eyelid open, and spotted her boss, Agent Vincent, speaking on her phone.

With her trademark silver bob and intelligent hazel eyes, Vincent regarded Ava with a bit of wry amusement. "Well, hello there, Rip Van Winkle."

"I'm convinced you are a vampire."

"Ah, so that answers the question about the drugs being out of your system."

"No, they are." Ava sat up in the hospital bed. "Don't you ever sleep?" A tray of food sat on a rolling table in front of her. It held a plastic cup of apple juice, a cellophane-wrapped turkey sandwich cut into triangles, and a foil-covered cup of applesauce. "It's already lunch?"

She shook her head. "Dinner. How're you holding up?"

"I'm not seeing mythical creatures anymore, so I've got that going for me." She took a sip of apple juice. It stung her tongue, but her throat was parched, so she drank it anyway. "What's going on? No one could tell me anything earlier."

"That's on me. I put a lid on things until we got the situation under control."

"I get that, but August looked bad, and I need—"

"He's out of surgery." She put her hand up at Ava's startled look. "The crash broke a rib, which caused his left lung to collapse. His shoulder also dislocated with the hit. They took him to surgery as soon as he arrived and repaired both injuries. His surgeon said he'll be out of commission for a few weeks, but he'll be fine. He's still waking up in recovery."

Ava sat back, letting out a breath. "And Detective Manaia?"

"He's banged up a bit, but he'll heal," Vincent said, texting someone. "He was lucky. A coach and his son were in the next car over and stopped the attack. We have video of the assailant's face from the pump's camera. It wasn't this Sky woman, but we'll figure out who she is."

"But he's okay?"

"More than okay. I'm hearing talk of Detective Manaia and the Crimes of Violence squad getting a commendation." Vincent looked down at Ava. "The Blue Drum Killer *and* a sex trafficking ring. I guess this cult should've stayed off your home turf, huh?"

"Let that be a lesson." Ava hesitated. "Sky?"

Vincent shook her head. "She missed her head with the bullet when you guys went off the pier, but only just. She took off some scalp near her temple, which is where all the blood you saw probably came from, but she took in too much water. She drowned, Ava. I know you tried to save her."

Ava nodded, pushing down the emotions she'd learned years ago to bury. She fiddled with the straw in her drink. "Can't save them all."

Vincent looked at her for a beat. "Are you sure you're okay? Rondeau said you were, and I quote, 'tripping balls,' when he jumped in after you. Something we might consider downplaying if asked."

"No worries there," Ava said, scratching at the new bandage over her eyebrow stitches. One thing she'd always liked about Vincent was that she didn't pry. "Please tell me you found this animal."

"He never came back to the communal house. We've been scouring the area. With no address, bank account, or valid identification, he might be in the wind."

"Sky told me that Orien had a bungalow. I think I said something to Rondeau."

"You did. He's back at OPD working that angle right now. Talia too, so we're covered."

"And the gun?"

"We sent divers down for it. It's in evidence. Listen, now that you're medically cleared, we need your official statement. You have a meeting tomorrow morning at OPD. I'll text you the details." Vincent pointed to the IV in Ava's arm. "After that, concentrate on getting better. I need you back."

"This case isn't closed."

"You took out a serial killer and saved street kids from being trafficked. Call it a day, Agent."

Ava shook her head. "I stopped the weapon. Not the killer. Orien is still out there."

"We'll get him." Vincent reached into her leather satchel, pulled out a binder, and set it on Ava's lap. "Matter of time, is all."

"What's this?"

"Why you do it," Vincent said and then left without another word.

Ava opened the binder, pulled out the piece of sketch paper that was inside, and held it up. A lone baby bird in a nest, the sun kissing its downy feathers with light, its weak, outstretched wings extended. The artist had drawn it mid-cry, the tiny beak open to the sky. Forever waiting. A single, sinewy letter adorned the lower corner. S. Ava swallowed against the lump in her throat while she tucked the drawing away, thinking about lost futures and stolen lives until a nurse came in.

She checked the empty IV bag and pronounced Ava good to go. She let her grab some scrubs to wear because her clothes were wet and shoved in a personal effects bag. The doctor discharged her with orders to go home and rest her bruised hip and strained shoulder. Ava gathered her things, went to the gift shop for some magazines, and headed up to the surgical floor.

The aftercare nurse at the front counter gave her August's room number, and she made her way down the hallway. His door stood open, privacy curtain drawn, and she raised her hand to knock on the door frame but paused at the sound of a woman's voice. English accent, tinkling laugh, and Ava hesitated, wondering if a nurse was in there with him. They murmured softly to each other. Through a slit in the curtain, she saw a delicate hand intertwined with his.

Not a nurse. She couldn't help but wonder if the Shakespeare tickets were for her. Backing up, she took the magazines to the reception counter with a note and left.

Despite the tray of food, Ava's stomach growled. Nearly eight at night, the silver crescent moon shone when she made it out to the parking lot. Ava looked around for a moment before realizing she didn't have a car. She debated between calling a friend or ordering a rideshare when Manaia pulled up in a patrol car.

He leaned out his window, his face red and swollen. "They let you leave already?"

"Yeah, I'm good as new. I think I'm stranded though. Are *you* good?"

"A little sore. Are you up for something right now?"

"Up for what?"

"We found Orien's bungalow. I'm on my way there now."

She slid into the passenger seat of Manaia's personal vehicle. On closer inspection Ava realized he had bruises on his cheek and neck as well. Half his lip was an alarming size. Angry red scabs marred the skin of his knuckles, and his ear had a bandage wrapped around it. He looked at her with as much of a grin as his injuries would allow.

"You look like someone's personal pinata," Ava said.

He chuckled. "I knew bringing you in would stir things up but, damn, Ava."

"I try my best." He'd look fine in a few weeks. "Your mom is going to freak out when she sees you."

"Nah, it makes me look badass. For a runt, anyway." He looked over and a flash of tension crossed his features. "Can I ask you something?"

Ava nodded.

"He accused you of covering up a murder for your lover. Is that why you were at White Collar Crimes?"

"Yes."

"Was he referring to August?"

"Yes and no." Ava looked out the window, her stomach tumbling. "Orien had it twisted. He's spouting what the news said at the time not what the investigation found. I was cleared. I didn't cover up anything. I was investigated for a suspect dying in my custody. August was in the building and was accused of being involved in the death. He wasn't and I made sure they knew that."

Manaia looked at her with furrowed brows. "Okay, what happened then?"

"You know how I can be tenacious?"

"Most would say obsessed, but yes." Manaia said.

"The Ghost Town Killer murdered people in horrific ways, at least a dozen victims. We'd been after him for weeks and he eluded us. When we started getting close, he abducted our witness, killed her, and displayed her to taunt us. No evidence. No way to take him down. I knew that we had to catch him in the act. Plain and simple. I used a reporter, Ricki Rogers, to leak that I had damning evidence. I believe I even hinted I might not be opposed to manufacturing it, a fact to which she alluded." Ava hugged herself, the screech of metal streaking through her mind. "He called me directly and asked to meet at a park."

"Let me guess. You went alone."

"I didn't have a chance. He ambushed me in the sheriff's station parking garage."

Manaia looked over at her, horror on his face. "He took you?"

Ava nodded. "I knew the risk."

It had taken August hours to find her. Hours during which she was tortured.

"We were up on this catwalk thing connected to a platform when August came barreling in. It was the only time he'd ever not waited for backup." Ava looked out the window but saw the rusted walls, felt the bolts snapping from the wall. "Oster was a former special forces soldier. He'd planned for that. He'd *hoped* for that." Her voice cracked, and she cleared her throat. "Let's just say that he planned to use August as my next form of torture. Ava shrugged. "I never gave him the chance."

They drove in silence.

"I saw a photo of you coming out of the building with handcuff's on."

Ava nodded. "The whole scene was chaotic. I was not in my right mind. He'd hurt me pretty bad."

They took a turn down a neighborhood lined with old houses. "I don't understand why you were investigated."

Ava chewed her inner cheek. "Let's just say, I could have done a lot of things differently."

"So back when we worked the Sea Siren Madam case, the heartbreak I mentioned seeing on your face. That wasn't for your job." Manaia nodded. "Explains a lot of things."

"Come on. Working with me wasn't all bad." Ava forced a smile.

Manaia nodded. After a few minutes, he said, "My sister is throwing a luau for her kid's second birthday next week. She told me to tell you. They're roasting a pig."

"Say no more. You know I never pass up free food." Ava stared out at the passing city for a few moments. "What's going on with Orien's bungalow?"

Manaia nodded, his smile fading. "You gotta see it."

———

The bungalow sat on a street in South Oceanside. An older neighborhood with single-story, fifties-style bungalows and big lawns. Firetrucks and patrol cars clogged the street. Ava and Manaia parked and walked together up to the remains of a smoldering house. Halogen lights lit up parts of the ruined façade and cast sharp shadows on the grass. The fire chief hemmed and hawed when they tried to go in and have a look. The fire was out, and the damage was contained to the kitchen, so he let them take a peek with an escort.

Following Manaia and a firefighter with a huge flashlight, she walked through water and black sludge to the back of the house. The stench of burnt flesh hit her, and she put her hand over her mouth and nose. In the center of the small kitchen, a blackened corpse, likely male from the size, lay in a circle of deep fire damage. Sitting in a crater of destroyed floor, the charred limbs contorted under the remnants of a white tunic. A frizzled mass of hair clung to the burned scalp, and fire damage to the facial features unidentifiable.

She caught sight of Talia outside the sliding doors, gathering a sample of pool water. "What's she doing?"

"Dr. Clay doesn't believe we'll get usable DNA off this guy. Manaia pointed to the floor. It rippled and bubbled underfoot. "The fire chief said the blaze burned unusually hot. They sent a sample to the lab to see what it was, but yeah, the guy is just a hunk of charcoal now."

"Did you guys find anything that ties this place to the cult?"

"There are bloody rags in the bathroom and evidence of the UV ink poultice. We think Orien carved up Sky out there. Dr. Clay believes there's blood in the pool." Manaia pointed through the sliding glass door to the pool and patio. "If he brought her here, then there might be evidence of other victims here too. Talia's scouring the entire property. She hasn't stopped moving since she arrived."

More victims. Ava shook her head, her stomach turning. "I don't get it. Orien sent Sky out to kill us only to kill himself?"

"Some of my guys at the station said a few of Orien's followers admitted he intended to self-immolate in protest of a corrupt system. He told them the authorities would never take him alive. They said he spoke of it often." Manaia held up an evidence baggie with a handwritten card. "He left a suicide note claiming you planted evidence after assaulting him at the beach. Seems like he wanted to take you down with him. We're running it for prints, but it looks legit."

They went back outside to get away from the smell, and he told her about the cash they'd found. Ava's earlier statements to Rondeau about Sky's confession helped Manaia uncover the stash hidden behind the bathroom mirror. Almost half a million dollars in bundles stacked between the studs.

"We found a burner phone we believe was used to blackmail Brent. Talia pulled a print from it and ran it through the Crossmatch scanner. They were Cindy's." Manaia shook his head, bewildered. "She blackmailed her own father."

Ava nodded. "I saw it in Orien's face when I asked."

They'd also found several forged passports with various names. All with Orien's photo. None for Sky.

"Talia found a container with what she thinks is the amanita and THC powder in a heating vent an hour ago. We're taking the house apart. He obviously didn't expect the fire to be put out so quickly. He left a lot of evidence here."

"Yeah, and a lot of death in his wake."

Walking back to the car, a burst of fireworks flared overhead, lighting up the sky. Blue and white explosions thundered across the night, raining scintillating sparks as the city celebrated.

Ava turned, taking one last look at the smoldering ruins. "What a waste."

THIRTY-SIX

A week later, Ava stood on the deck of the *Fair Thee Well*, an older white motorboat that belonged to the city's Indigent Disposition Program, a service that scattered the ashes of unclaimed victims at sea. Out on the water, with the mist burning away, she thought about past sins and future hopes and wondered whether she still believed in either.

Early July brought with it chilly mornings, and Ava relished the crisp air as they sailed out to deliver the ashes of the lost and forgotten. A retired funeral director named Morton welcomed her aboard with pleasure, happy to have another mourner to honor his clients, as he called them. Though he almost always sent them off alone, he wore a formal black suit. He piloted the boat himself, and left Ava to her thoughts as he took them out to sea.

Based on Sky's confession to Ava, the OPD Field Evidence Team recovered three other bodies buried in the junkyard. They were in blue barrels like she'd said, hidden behind a blue and white van. The victims appeared to be three more runaways. Young men shot in the same way as the others. All of them with death markings. No one reported them missing, and if not for the case, they might never have been found.

Henry Miller's uncle took his body home. Jimmy Wright's parents flew his remains to Hawaii, where he'd always wanted to go. Dane Cutler arranged a loving memorial and grand funeral for his only son. He would have continued to pretend he had no grandchildren if it weren't for someone leaking that information to the press, forcing him to include her in the memorial.

RickiLeaks came in handy occasionally.

But not everyone had someone. So Ava stood on the deck of a ship designated for those with no one. Those who might not be remembered. Who'd slipped from the earth unnoticed and unclaimed.

They sailed out to the required three nautical miles, where Morton dropped anchor. He busied himself, pulling out a silver champagne bucket from a deck cabinet and setting it on a prepared table. Seabirds dove and swooped over crystalline blue water. Gentle ocean swells beneath the boat felt lulling, peaceful. A sweet man, Morton carefully poured Sadie Schneider's ashes into the bucket and covered them with rose petals and the crown of daisies Ava brought. He read a poem about sorrow and forever. A hymn played softly from a portable speaker. He respected her life and regretted her departure.

With the service finished, he solemnly lowered the bucket over the side of the boat on a chain and gently tipped the container until the ashes tumbled onto the surface of the ocean with the flowers. A cloud of pure white billowed out into the rippling waters. Some wind picked up a puff of ash and a little flurry rose into the morning sky and disappeared.

Ava dropped a handful of rose petals into the ocean. Then, her face to the sun, she whispered, "Ascension."

THIRTY-SEVEN

Late August brought an unusual heatwave. The weatherman promised a scorcher and predicted temperatures to hit a hundred degrees by the end of the week. Vincent told Ava to take some time to work on the hip injury, which she did. Physical therapy and then jogging daily to build up strength. The doctor had cleared Ava for duty earlier that week, and Vincent already wanted to loan Ava out to a task force working a drug mule case near the Oregon border. She was due to leave in a few days.

Ava finished an early morning jog at her favorite spot, Alcove Beach. Her hip felt strong, but her shoulder still ached in the mornings. A daily swim seemed to help. She picked her way across the rocky shore to a retaining wall that sat at the foot of the stairs. The wind carried with it the scent of saltwater, and she relished having the sea to herself.

Peeling off her small runner's pack, and T-shirt, she set them on the rocks for later. She knelt to take off her sneakers. Then pushed off the rock wall as she stood, she headed for the water. She met the cold waves with a hiss and then dove in, slicing through the water, her strokes powerful as she pushed her bruised shoulder. The cold of the ocean soothed her aching muscles. Morning sun warmed her face, and she drifted for a while in the swells, thinking about the case and what had come to light in the past weeks.

Manaia had secured a warrant for Brent Cutler's safety deposit box. It contained video surveillance of several young women and men arriving at a modest house far from the sunny shores, delivered by a white van. The license plate appeared clear as day on the video. Brent had recorded footage of the van delivering the girls to customers' homes, and the videos Orien had in the house left no question what the young followers of Orien were there to do for paying clients. Crimes of Violence was working with a sex trafficking task force to identify customers and contact victims. Brent had also acquired bank records and other private information about multiple identities with Orien's photo attached. But it was the personal video Brent recorded and left in the safety deposit box that hit home.

Ava had watched it with the team. Brent, sitting in his wine tasting room, wearing a dark blue sweater, eyes clear, told the camera that he and Jimmy had been working together to gather enough evidence of Orien's wrong doings to convince Cindy to leave the commune.

"I messed up," he said, his voice cracking, gaze earnestly beseeching the lens. "I didn't step up when she first came to me and I think... I think maybe this wouldn't have happened if I'd been a better man. But I'm going to make it right." He nodded. "I'm going to make it right."

It turned out that Jimmy, Cindy's ex-boyfriend, had gone to Brent to tell him about Orien and his cult. How Cindy had gotten mixed up in something bad and that he was going undercover to persuade her to walk away. Brent agreed to help, providing a phone so that they could keep in contact with her. The electric scooter for her deliveries. And other things she promptly gave to Orien and the family. They were trying to rescue her.

Cindy tried to blackmail him with compromising videos of herself with Orien, threatening to release them to the public and ruin the Cutler name. Brent had paid to keep the charade going. The shamed father paying for silence, and all the while Jimmy secretly recording Orien's guided meditations with underage girls featuring illicit drugs. He also recorded conversations about bank accounts from outside closed doors. Brent had left so much damning evidence. The prosecutor grinned like the Cheshire cat when she saw the contents. Denny's contact with a former victim, Jade, resulted in a deal for her and with her cooperation, everything he did would come to light.

Starting to chill, Ava adjusted the bun atop her head and swam back to shore. Her running shirt now lay on the rocky sand. Grumbling a bit, she snatched it from the ground and sat on a warm boulder. Saltwater dripped from her hairline into her eyes, stinging them. Shaking off the shirt, she used it to dab the water from her eyes, then buried her face in the soft material, her mind on a phone call the night before from Denny. Father Padua had found his journals.

The crunch of rocks close by made her look up. She sensed movement, her forearm coming up defensively before a blur of steel slammed against the side of her head. Pain blared through her face as she rolled with the blow, twisting away. Another hit landed on her back, sending more pain through her side. A haze of long hair, spittle on grimaced lips, and searing fury in crystalline blue eyes.

Orien.

Ava spun, leading with her elbow, landing a blow to his jaw. His head whipped sideways. He staggered, flailing on the uneven rocks. She advanced, twisting on her front leg. Landed a roundhouse kick to his chest. He flew back, crashing onto the stones, gasping for the breath knocked out of him.

She advanced, froze when she saw the gun. She reached for her sidearm and found only wet skin.

"Feel lost without your gun, Agent Cortes?" He climbed to his feet, sneering despite the nosebleed. Arms up, she backed up until her bottom hit the retaining wall of rocks. He wiped his face with his surfer T-shirt, and the long, ill-fitting shorts he wore sagged. He had on ratty slip-on sneakers and those golden tresses hung limp and stringy. He looked like a surf bum.

He glared at her, wheezing a little. "I knew you wouldn't have it. Because you run this time *every day*. Stop here, *every day*. You really should change your routine. But then again, why would you? You thought this was over." He shook his head. "Why are you sheeple always so stupid?"

"You're s-supposed to be dead." Ava's gaze snapped to the sidewalk at the top of the stairs. Too early for foot traffic. No one would hear her scream. "I saw your body."

He spat blood, moving closer, weapon extended with a steady hand. "An acolyte's final act of service to his teacher. I take it the accelerant and fire destroyed the DNA. Otherwise, you wouldn't have that stunned look on your face."

"Your followers told us—"

"What they were supposed to tell you." He picked his way across the rocks carefully, his other hand rubbing his chest. "Turn around. I'm going to frisk you."

Ava stilled. "You're not putting your hands on me."

He leveled the gun at her face. "Do it or I blow your brains out right now."

She saw no sign of the calm teacher from their previous interaction. She turned around and placed her hands on the wall, her jaw grinding at his touch. He ran his palm over her shoulders, down her back and ribs. He took extra time going over her buttocks and thighs. It took everything not to slug him.

"I watched you. For days." He leaned in, hot breath at her ear. "You relaxed, Ava. That was a mistake."

A distant horn sounded, and a ship in the distance slid across the dawn horizon. The crashing waves muffled the traffic noise from above. He was too close. Feeling in control.

"Why didn't you leave?" she asked.

"Turn around." He ordered. She did, placing her hands on her head, and he ran his palm down her chest, along her stomach.

"We have you dead to rights on three more murders. You should have left."

"As far as anyone knows, I did." He stopped. Placed the muzzle of the weapon between her breasts and caught her gaze. "Don't move."

Ava nodded, her fingers closing around the hard edge in her palm. "You know, it was the hair on the corpse," she said as his fingers traced up her inner thigh. "It would've burned. You're way too in love with that hair, Orien. With how you look in general. You would never destroy your looks like that."

A cold grin split his face. "Don't try to save face now, Agent. You had no idea I was alive."

His hand reached the band around her upper thigh, and the small holster for a three-inch self-defense knife tucked under her swim shorts that most women keep when jogging alone. She knew the exact moment he realized the sheath was empty. He reared back, and Ava knocked his gun to the side with one hand, releasing the blade in the other before slamming it into his chest. One, two, before he flinched with a shout of pain.

She pivoted in his grasp, her shoulder against his chest as her blade sliced down again, shredding a path down his thigh. He screamed, staggering backward. Ava moved in, aiming for the wrist of his gun hand.

It clattered onto the rocks.

He gaped at his chest, stumbling as he pressed his palm against the wounds. Blood flowed between his fingers before he dropped.

He lay on the rocks, his arms and legs jerking. She kicked his weapon further away. Running back to the retaining wall, she grabbed her runner's pack from the rocks, fished out a phone, and dialed 911.

Hurrying over to him, she knelt, using her balled-up shirt to keep pressure on the wound as she gave police her ID and location. Then she dropped the phone on the rocks and kept trying to stop the bleeding. It pooled up through her swim shirt and seeped over her fingers.

"You should have run," she said. "You should have stayed away."

"H-How did y-you..." he gasped for breath, bubbles forming at his lips as his eyes swam. "How did you know I would come after you?"

Ava shook her head, the scent of blood in the air. "Because I would."

He groaned, writhing. A wild panic twisted his features. He clawed at her hands putting pressure on his wound.

Sunlight slashed across his face. All that suffering. Cindy and Jimmy. Brent, a father just trying to save his kid. Hunter, desperate for a family who loved him. And Sky, a girl Orien twisted into a killer. Too many lives stolen.

"You were wrong, Owen. I do know what I am," Ava whispered, her eyes going to the flash of blue and red as an ambulance stopped on the street above. Paramedics with their bags hurried down the stairs.

She watched the light fading from Owen's eyes. He searched her face, fear and anger contorting his handsome features. Struggling to talk, he gurgled desperately.

She leaned in, holding his gaze. "It's not your fault. I'm just a better monster."

His last words, rising with a crimson bubble at his lips, erupted silently and were gone.

———

The paramedics took over and Orien or Owen Meeks or the Teacher, whoever he really was, died en route to the hospital. The police came, and Ava asked to speak with Detective Manaia. He took her statement and her knife, then called Agent Vincent, who sent August who'd stayed in town to work through all the tangled money, properties, and other financial knots Orien left behind. He arrived wearing an arm sling. Slightly thinner than before. A little tanner. She wondered what he'd been doing during his mandatory rest. The patrol officer had her sitting in the back of his car with the door open. The paramedics gave her a chemical ice pack, and she held it to the cheek Orien had pistol-whipped.

August walked past her without a word, took the steps down to the alcove beach, and spent a half hour down on the rocky shore talking with Manaia and the OPD Field Evidence Team. She wandered over to the railing, looking down at the crime scene. One of the forensic techs bagged her backpack, jogging shoes, and bloody swim shirt. A field evidence tech came over and took photos of her injuries. Her face, bruised knuckles, the cuts and scrapes from the fight. She went back to the patrol car and sat inside, her head throbbing.

August returned, a little winded from the walk back up the steps, a piece of gum taking the brunt of his emotions. He looked her over. "Are you okay."

"Yes."

"You told Manaia you jogged down to swim, put your runner's pack, shirt, and shoes and what not on the sand, and when you came back, Orien surprised you and you fought. You pulled your safety knife during the attack and defended yourself."

"Sounds right. The knife was under three inches. Perfectly legal." Ava watched his face. His chomping didn't let up.

"You don't run with a knife."

"We haven't been together for years, August. You don't know what I do now."

"Since when do you run with a pack?" She didn't answer, and he sighed, looking over the hood of the patrol car. "Did you know he was coming after you?"

Ava schooled her expression. "What makes you say that?"

"Your track record."

"How could I have known this would happen? Everyone thought he was dead."

"Ava, I could've arranged protection. Surveillance. I know you were especially close to this one, but if you let your emotions take over like this. If you set this up—"

"He broke children, August. He broke *her*. He destroyed their minds and bodies to feed his own narcissistic ego."

"You *were* looking for a fight, then?"

"No, but he brought one."

He hesitated before asking, "When did you grab the knife?"

"When he frisked me."

"How did you know he'd do that?"

She crossed her arms. "I didn't."

"Ava..." He took a step back, his eyes wide. "This could have gone so wrong."

"It didn't."

"You can't keep—

"Look, I was just living my life and he came after me. You may not like how things ended." Ava rose from the car, dropped the ice pack on the seat, and moved past him. "But it was him or me, and I won't apologize for it not being me."

His jaw flexing. "You run at night, Ava. You hate early mornings."

"Like I said, August. We really don't know each other that well anymore."

She walked away. Met with the scene supervisor, who cleared her to leave. August offered to drive her home, and she would have refused, but he mentioned stopping for takeout, his idea of a peace offering. She couldn't say no to that.

They ate in silence on her front porch, listening to the soft tinkling of the seashell chimes dangling from her roof. The sun rose bright and hot over The Strand, and the jogging stroller moms were already out and about.

He looked at her for a moment longer, then said, "I didn't see you at the hospital."

Ava fished a fry out of her breakfast burrito, not looking at him. "I left magazines and a note."

August turned, wincing as he adjusted his shoulder. A second surgery had been needed to correct the damage from the crash, and whether he'd admit it or not, he still hurt from it. He hesitated, a strange look on his face, then, "About that. I think we need to talk."

Ava froze, her gut knotting. "Why does that sound ominous?"

"It's not. It's—"

Her phone rang. Relief flooded through her as she went inside to answer, but it wasn't her burner. The work phone on her kitchen counter rang again, and she picked up.

"I need you in Los Angeles as soon as possible," Agent Vincent said without preamble.

"I thought I was heading to Oregon?"

"Change of plans. Your team has a case."

"*My* team?"

"For this one, yes," Vincent said. "August is still on light duty. He'll consult from a desk, but he's not cleared to go out into the field."

Ava glanced over her shoulder at him on the porch. "And he's okay with that?"

"It's ride second to you on this, or I give the case to another team. He won't want that. He knows LA." Vincent sighed. "Plus, I think he's getting antsy being at home. This is the only way I'll let him back in until he's fully recovered."

"LA, huh?"

"Yeah," Vincent said. "Something weird is happening in Hollywood."

"You're just now realizing that?"

"I told you this might be coming. I just got off the phone with the LAPD Chief. He's screaming about those multiple strange accidents that somehow aren't. It's a chaotic mess."

"Don't threaten me with a good time," Ava said, her mood lightening a little as she watched August stretch his legs out and close his eyes in the sun. Was this what he had wanted to speak to her about? "When do we leave?"

———

The story continues in *Fade to Dark*, click here to order your copy now!
https://a.co/d/oiGZMeJO

Did you enjoy *Dark as Pitch*? Leave a review to let us know your thoughts!
https://a.co/d/o3dsMJnM

AVA CORTES: CRIME THRILLER SERIES

Deep Dark Lies

Dark as Pitch

Fade to Dark

Gilt Edge

A Willow Grace FBI Thriller by C.C. West

Shadow of Grace

Condition of Grace

Hunt for Grace

Time for Grace

Piece of Grace

Flight of Grace

Rite of Grace

Ava Cortes CBI Thrillers

Deep Dark Lies

Dark as Pitch

———

Join Without Warrant's private reader group on Facebook!

https://www.facebook.com/withoutwarrant

ABOUT THE AUTHOR

Raquel was a military brat who grew up on Marine bases throughout the United States. An avid stargazer, she often travels into the desert near her home to view the meteor showers or throws launch parties for major NASA events. When she's not writing she can be seen geeking out over movies, reading anything she can get her hands on, and having arguments about the television series Firefly in coffee shops. She lives in Southern California with her husband, six kids, and her beloved Huskies, Zena and Keanu. Raquel is known for pulse-pounding fiction with a breathtaking pace, and she continues to bring riveting characters and epic worlds to life in exciting new thriller series.

www.ingramcontent.com/pod-product-compliance
Lightning Source LLC
Chambersburg PA
CBHW051755050726
47598CB00006B/2294